Marita Co..essful authors. Her previous novels include *The Hat Shop on the Corner*, *The Stone House* and the number one bestseller *T.....Magdalen*. She is the winner of the prestigious international Reading Association award and is a regular contributor on radio and TV. A romantic by nature, Marita wa.swept off her own feet and got married aged twenty to her tall dark handsome husband. They live with their family in ...ublin.

www.booksattransworldireland.ie

www.rbooks.co.uk

THE MATCHMAKER

MARITA CONLON-McKENNA

TRANSWORLD IRELAND

TRANSWORLD IRELAND
an imprint of The Random House Group Limited
20 Vauxhall Bridge Road, London SW1V 2SA
www.rbooks.co.uk

THE MATCHMAKER
A TRANSWORLD IRELAND BOOK: 9781848270138

First published in Great Britain
in 2008 by Bantam Press
a division of Transworld Publishers
Transworld Ireland edition published 2008

Addresses for Random House Group Ltd companies outside the UK
can be found at: www.randomhouse.co.uk
The Random House Group Ltd Reg. No. 954009

Penguin Random House is committed to a sustainable future for
our business, our readers and our planet. This book is made from
Forest Stewardship Council® certified paper.

Typeset in 11.5/15pt Ehrhardt by
Falcon Oast Graphic Art Ltd.

2 4 6 8 10 9 7 5 3 1

Printed and bound in Great Britain by Clays Ltd, St Ives plc

For mothers and daughters everywhere

Acknowledgements

To Francesca Liversidge, my wonderful editor, for her constant encouragement and for making writing and working together such a pleasure.

Special thanks to Lucie Jordan, Rebecca Jones and Richenda Todd for all their assistance with *The Matchmaker*, and continued gratitude to the rest of the brilliant Transworld team.

To Caroline Sheldon, my agent, for all her hard work and support. For all at Gill Hess, Dublin with enormous gratitude to Gill and Simon Hess, Declan Heaney, Geoff Bryan and Helen Gleed O'Connor for looking after me and my books so well.

For my own perfect match, James; thanks for always being there.

For my family: Mandy, Laura, Fiona and James, my son-in-law Michael Hearty and my little granddaughter Holly. Thank you for making my life so happy and for giving me plenty to write about!

Thanks to my sister Gerardine, her husband Blaine and

children Rachel and Graham.

For three very special aunts: Angela Conlon, Una Doyle and Genevieve McKenna, who have been so supportive and helpful since I started writing.

For *'les girls'*: Ann, Grace, Karen, Yvonne, Helen and Mary for all the fun and friendship we've shared over the years. *Vive la France!*

Thanks to Anne Frances Doorly for making me smile and laugh for the most part of my life.

Thanks to Sarah Webb for her kindness, insight and the gift of her friendship.

Thanks to Catherine Harvey for being such a wise and wonderful best friend.

Thanks to Anne O'Connell for reading the first chapter of my first book, and encouraging me to write the rest.

For all my writer friends in Irish PEN – a great club to be in.

For my fellow 'Irish Girls' writers; thanks for all the great book launches, dinners and regular get-togethers.

Thanks to all the bookshops and booksellers who bring writers and readers together and have given me such great support.

Thank you to all my lovely readers, especially those who have been there from the beginning.

For everyone involved in the publication and sale of this book, a heartfelt thank you from a grateful author.

The most beautiful thing in the world is a
match well made.

Jane Austen, *Emma*

The Matchmaker's Tips for a perfect Match . . .

1. Opposites do definitely attract.

2. Best friends can make the 'best' husbands.

3. Interfering in the lives of daughters, sisters and friends usually helps . . .

4. Distance can make the heart grow fonder; but usually of someone else!

5. Remember bad boyfriends make equally bad husbands.

6. Men who are still living at home with their 'Mammies' at thirty will (no matter what a girl does) always be Mammies' boys!

7. Good Men are not like the 46A bus . . . they do not come along that often!

8. Seeing a man when he is sick, in his pyjamas and is at his absolute worst, and still managing to find him somewhat attractive, is very encouraging.

9. Always accept lunch, dinner and party and concert invitations as given time they may lead to a diamond ring.

10. Remember falling in love can happen at any age.

Chapter One

It seemed to Maggie Ryan that she had been matching things all her life, from simple socks and underwear in drawers and linen baskets to table mats and table settings and menus, furniture, curtains and clothes, to the more complex choice of the perfect gift for the people she cared about, or the talents of her children with school subjects and hobbies. Matching people was another matter as it always tended to get a bit more complicated. Bringing people together, however, was what she was good at, and something that she actively enjoyed. She smiled thinking about today's big Sunday lunch with family and friends gathered around her rather ancient dining table.

As she looked out over the square of elegant red-brick Georgian houses that formed a neat rim around the lush hedges and greenery of Pleasant Square, she smiled again. 'Pleasant' was the perfect word for it, she thought, this historic square with its old family houses tucked between Leeson Street and Ranelagh where she had lived for thirty-two years. She and Leo had raised their family here, opposite the east gate of the park with its tantalizing view of the herbaceous borders and flower beds.

The square itself, though not very big or imposing, was still considered one of Dublin's most desirable places to live, and the houses that surrounded it architectural gems. Verdant oak, ash, beech and chestnut formed leafy pathways through the small park, enjoyed by generations of the square's inhabitants. Pleasant Square's appearance had barely changed over a century and a half and Maggie couldn't imagine living anywhere else.

She glanced at the 'Sold' sign outside number 29, on the corner opposite. She had to admit she was curious to know who had bought the O'Connors' house. It had gone to auction about two weeks ago. Over the past month streams of visitors, would-be purchasers and inquisitive locals had viewed the three-storey home. Property prices in the city had literally gone through the roof and an old house with character so near town coming on the market was bound to attract interest. Despite being rather ramshackle and a bit run-down the house had sold for a fortune and rumour had it that the purchaser was a man of property, a wealthy investor. Whoever the mysterious buyer was, he had made a wise decision!

She remembered moving into this house, number 23, when she was a bride, Leo Ryan sweeping her up into his broad arms and insisting on carrying her up the steps and across the threshold, the two of them racing up the stairs and along the landing to the huge bedroom and the big bed, where they had stayed for hours, scarcely believing that they were man and wife and were now legally able to sleep together.

The house had been let as flats for years and was much the worse for wear when they first saw it, but Leo, with his eye for investment, had seen the potential. Over time they had both worked to restore the old house to its original condition, junking flimsy partition walls, sinks and two-ringed gas hobs, replacing multicoloured carpet and lino with polished floors, restoring original plasterwork and revealing the magnificent boarded-up fireplaces in the drawing room and dining room. Year by year they had turned a house full of tatty bed-sits into a comfortable family home as they worked and raised their three daughters.

The girls were grown up now. Grace, Anna and Sarah were independent young women, bright, beautiful, kind and good-hearted, just as daughters should be. She was proud of them, all so different. Grace, an architect, wrapped up in her career; Anna lost in the world of literature and academic life; and Sarah, who was still struggling to find a niche of her own but was devoted to her small five-year-old daughter Evie, who was the apple of her grandmother's eye. She loved them dearly but she had to admit their single state perplexed her.

Sometimes she wished that she could stop the clock, turn back time, have Leo alive again, back beside her, the children still young. But it seemed nothing could stay the same: Detta and Tom O'Connor deciding to move to England to be near their son Cormac and his family and selling up was just another example of it. Soon a new neighbour would be moving into the old Georgian house on the square. It was stupid for her to get sad and emotional about it. Pull yourself together, she told herself. You've a busy day ahead. She'd invited everyone for lunch to say a fond farewell to Detta and Tom before their big move to Bath next week. Lord knows they deserved a nice meal and a proper celebratory send-off from the square.

Grabbing the Sunday newspapers off her doorstep she retreated to the warmth of the kitchen and the promise of a quick read, a mug of fresh roast coffee and two slices of wholemeal toast with honey before ten o'clock mass. Then she would come home and pop that enormous leg of lamb she'd got from John Flanagan the butcher into the oven with a few sprigs of rosemary from the garden and begin the preparations for lunch.

Chapter Two

Pulling the duvet up over her face and ears, Anna Ryan tried to keep herself warm and block out the nasty world that was waiting for her to emerge from her cocoon of sleep, drink and daydreaming. Her mouth, tongue and throat felt as if they were growing some kind of obscure turgid bacteria; how she wished she had had the foresight to bring a glass of water to bed with her last night. She contemplated the clock and the skinny strip of daylight that teased through her heavy chocolate-brown curtains. It was midday already.

Why did she do it? Waste her time going to one of those awful student-type parties in an overcrowded apartment in Temple Bar where you had to shout over the Killers to be heard and where everyone was dressed in black and drinking cheap red wine, talking about scripts and trying to be sophisticated? Why did her drama students always have to be so predictable! She should have had more sense and left early like she had planned – made a polite appearance and then got a taxi home instead of staying there till four a.m. arguing about the state of the Abbey Theatre and whether plays should aim for Broadway or broke. She must be mad talking to a load of twenty-year-olds about the complicated influences on the structure of Irish drama on a Saturday night. She was pathetic. She had hoped Philip would turn up, only discovering at midnight when she texted him that he had gone to Kilkenny to run a workshop with a theatre group over the weekend, a fact that he had forgotten to mention to her. Philip Flynn worked with her in the college's English department and as neither of them was involved with anyone, a somewhat unusual relationship had developed between them. With a mutual passion for theatre and literature, they often attended events together, sharing a bottle of wine or supper afterwards. There had been one or two late-night boozy romantic skirmishes between them but somehow good sense had prevailed and they had managed to avoid spoiling it. He was an interesting man and although others considered him self-centred – self-absorbed – and somewhat aloof, she under-stood the passion for drama and poetry that drove his personality. Still, a phone call from him would have been nice and saved her making an absolute eejit of herself!

She groaned, staring at the wall, wishing the day was over before it had even begun. She would have dearly loved to give in to her hangover and loll in bed for the rest of the day but she remembered that she had promised to go for Sunday lunch at her mother's. If she didn't show up Maggie Ryan would have a search party out hunting for her, which meant that one of her sisters would turn up, give her a lecture and see the calamitous mess and state of her house – a fate she intended to avoid at all costs.

18

Stretching gradually, she braved getting out of bed. She looked and felt absolutely mind-blowingly awful. Clutching at walls like an invalid, she gingerly made it to the bathroom. Her brown wavy hair was in a frizz that even the bravest hair-dresser wouldn't touch and her freckles stood out like paint spatters on her pale face; her eyes were smudged and smeared with that stupid natural plant dye mascara that she had been trying out. Throwing cold water on her face and neck to revive herself she realized carbs and coffee were urgently needed and, wrapping herself in the duvet, struggled to the kitchen for a mug of coffee and a slice of toasted brown bread. She had only instant and a half a carton of milk, but the brown bread she found was in no fit state to be handled, let alone toasted. Desperate, she searched her kitchen presses and the fridge for something to eat, torn between a half-packet of water crackers and a pecan-nut cluster bar. She opted for the water crackers, which she smeared with butter and a slice of Edam cheese topped with a smidgen of peanut butter that was rather ancient-looking but still in date.

A good hot shower and she might even begin to feel human in about an hour, she thought. Scrambling among the clutter of newspapers and books strewn on the kitchen table she searched for the copy of the new volume of poems by an incredible woman Russian poet who had moved to Ireland. It was here somewhere . . . Ah! Finding it, she gave a sigh of contentment as the caffeine began to work its magic. Curling up in the chair, she began to read.

Chapter Three

The Sunday streets were quiet as Grace stared out the window of her apartment overlooking Spencer Docks. Barefoot in her oyster-coloured silk wrap, she listened to a church bell ringing, calling the faithful of the city to mass and watched as below a rowing boat skimmed its way across the water, the crew perfectly in time, the oars lifting and dipping in unison. A perfect Sunday morning, dry and clear with only a hint of cloud in the sky.

The coffee-maker was on and the smell of toast filled the apartment. She opened the fridge: eggs, yes, bacon, none; she'd cook scrambled eggs for breakfast. She grabbed three eggs from the shelf, whisking them quickly with butter in the small saucepan. The creamy yellow eggs were almost cooked when Shane walked in.

She blinked, surprised to see that he was dressed already for she had intended they should share breakfast in bed. He had obviously showered for his fair hair was still clinging damply to his forehead and neck as he reached and kissed her.

'Mmm, that smells good,' he said, lowering himself on to the kitchen chair.

She piled some eggs and toast on to his plate, passing him the coffee and some butter.

'I'm starving,' he admitted, tucking in as she sat down beside him.

The eggs were just perfect. Nothing worse than over- or underdone scrambled eggs. There was definitely a knack to it, she thought as she began to eat.

'Why did you get dressed so soon?' she asked.

'Things to do,' he said, buttering more toast. 'Johnny phoned me last night. There's a sale on golf clubs over in Howth. We thought we might run over and have a look and then maybe play a few holes. The weather looks as if it might hold so we may as well.'

'There's lunch at my mother's at two thirty,' she reminded him.

'Sorry, Grace, but I just can't make it.'

He didn't sound the least bit apologetic and as she studied his handsome face she realized that spending the day together had never been part of his plan.

'She'll be disappointed,' she said, trying to conceal her anger, 'but she's invited quite a crowd.'

'There you go.' He laughed, reaching for the coffee. 'No harm done.'

She wanted to say to him: Forget Johnny, forget golf. Forget lunch at my mother's. Why can't we just stay here for the day looking out at the water, being with each other. But she didn't.

21

'It was a great night,' he said dipping his toast in the egg. He had butter on his lip; his beige cords were brushing against the tanned and toned skin of her bare leg.

Grace said nothing, thinking about the expensive meal they'd shared in Peploe's on St Stephen's Green the night before. The busy restaurant had been packed and they had been so lucky to get a table. They'd talked for hours, telling silly stories, taking it in turns to impress each other by being outlandish.

'I'm not sure if those Irish coffees were such a good idea, though.'

'They were,' he insisted.

She laughed, remembering how they'd fallen into a taxi and gone straight home, Shane holding her close all the way, racing upstairs and dancing to Sade on the stereo as he made her take off her shoes and stockings and sit out on the balcony with him watching the moon. It had been such a perfect romantic night and Shane had been tender and funny and held her until she had fallen asleep in his arms.

'Will I see you later?' she asked, turning away from him as she got up to make more coffee.

'I'll text you. Depends on Johnny and what time we finish. We might just get a quick steak in the clubhouse. So don't worry about me, OK?'

It wasn't OK but she wasn't prepared to admit it and nag and fight like some needy woman.

'Listen, Gracey, I'll let you know if I can call by later. If not I'll see you tomorrow.'

'Fine.' She smiled brightly, layering some marmalade on a slice of golden toast.

He smoothed her tumble of shoulder-length blond hair and then bent and kissed her lips. He tasted of coffee and sugar and his skin and hair smelled of her expensive Jo Malone orange and lime shower gel.

'Thanks for breakfast and everything,' he said, kissing her one last time as he grabbed his jacket and wallet and keys.

Resisting the urge to argue with him, she walked him to the door and watched him get the lift.

Afterwards she stayed sitting for ages, her coffee going cold as she contemplated her relationship with him. Seagulls screeched along the river; a bold cormorant dived up and down as if it was looking for treasure, watching the waves below as it moved across the water. Shane was probably off swinging a golf club somewhere, totally oblivious to the fact that he had upset her. It was stupid, she knew. He hadn't done or said anything deliberately hurtful. It was more what he hadn't done, had left unsaid.

They had been going out for nine months. She knew that didn't mean she owned him but she hoped that he enjoyed being with her as much she did with him. They saw a lot of each other at work, and that was the way their relationship had started. But outside of work it was different: they needed to make time for each other, no matter how busy their schedules were or how many projects they were working on. She was prepared to make the effort, to give their relation-ship the time, but she wasn't sure that Shane O'Sullivan was.

She glanced at her watch, suddenly realizing it was past

midday as the sunshine streamed in the window. She could sit here for the rest of the day moping around or get dressed and go for a brisk walk along Sandymount Strand before heading home for a meal at her mother's. The comfort of Sunday lunch beckoned.

Chapter Four

Standing at the bedroom door, Sarah studied her sleeping child: Evie's long dark eyelashes fanning across her cheek, her black hair in a tangle across the pillow, a smile on her lips. Sometimes it took her breath away just to look at her. Her daughter was utterly, totally beautiful.

'Mummy, are you watching me?' a sleepy voice asked.

'Of course,' she replied, clambering into bed with her and pulling the pink gingham quilt up around them.

'Why?'

'Because I love you, and when you're asleep and dreaming you make all kinds of funny faces.'

'What are they like?'

Curled up beside her daughter, she demonstrated and Evie giggled aloud.

'I was dreaming up a dog,' Evie said slowly, her blue eyes shining. 'A big white dog, with soft hair and a black nose . . .'

'That was a nice dream then,' Sarah agreed. Evie was going through a doggy phase. Sarah had searched the mothering manuals, but there was no mention of what to do about a child who was so obsessed about getting a dog that she even dreamed about them.

'His name is Snowy.'

Sarah just could not afford to take on a dog at the moment with all the costs involved: food and injections and vet's bills. Evie didn't understand how tight their finances were and how a hungry dog could be the last straw that would upset the delicate balance of their budget.

'Some day, pet, we'll get a dog,' she promised, 'but not just yet.'

'When?'

Sometimes she wished that Evie wasn't so clever. 'Well, we can't get a dog while Granny still has Podge. He's a very old and slow cat and it wouldn't be fair to him to have a new young dog running around the place and in the garden. It would scare him, wouldn't it? The dog would probably bark at him and chase him and I think poor old Podge might not even be quick enough at running to make it up a tree. It would be cruel. Do you see?'

'I see, Mummy.' Evie nodded, giving a big disappointed shrug of her shoulders.

'What's that for?' Sarah joked. 'Your granny's cooking us a lovely dinner today and Grace and Anna and Oscar from next door are coming over too.'

'Can I wear my pink dress and my new pink tights then?' pleaded Evie, bouncing up and down with excitement in the bed.

'Of course, but you have to have a bath after breakfast and

wash your hair,' Sarah bargained as her daughter covered her in kisses before jumping out of bed.

Sarah watched her bounce out of the room and smiled to herself. It was funny how the worst thing that could have happened to her had ended up being the best. Finding out at nineteen, in the middle of college, that she was pregnant had seemed a disaster. A baby had been the last thing she wanted, but now – well, she couldn't imagine life without Evie.

She had been madly in love with Maurizio, an Italian exchange student in the year above her. He was over from Milan for six months studying media technology. Small and dark and very handsome, he had asked her to show him how the contrary college photocopying machine worked and she'd ended up helping him copy his project. He had repaid her with coffee and a sandwich in the student café afterwards. Maurizio told her that Irish girls were the most wonderful creatures in the world. Sarah had, of course, believed him. She was so crazy about him that she could barely breathe. When she told him that they were going to have a child he had asked her to move back to Italy with him – live in a student house in Milan, transfer from her Art and Design course in Dun Laoghaire to college there.

'Wait till the baby is born,' her mother and father had advised. Sarah, overwhelmed by their support and love and insistence that they would help cover all the costs of having a baby, had agreed.

Maurizio had returned to Milan and his studies, coming to Dublin for three days when baby Evie was born. Evie had his dark, almost black hair and long eyelashes and, Sarah suspected, a little of his Italian temperament, but her blue eyes, heart-shaped face and fair Irish skin were a carbon copy of her own looks. At first Maurizio had sent some money and she had made the effort to visit his parents in Italy for a week. It had been a disaster. His father wasn't well, the Carlucci family's apartment in central Milan was on the tenth floor and smaller than she expected; Evie's waking for night feeds woke the whole family and probably half of their neighbours too.

She had returned home exhausted. Maurizio only made it to Dublin for five days that summer to see his daughter. He was doing a masters degree, transferring to Rome; he was excitedly looking forward to the future. Sarah realized that Evie and herself were not part of it. There had been no big fight or angry words, they had simply drifted apart. Over the years his contact with his child had lessened, his financial support dwindled, leaving Sarah disappointed but not really surprised.

Motherhood had totally changed her. When Evie was born she had insisted on being with her all the time, refusing to hand her baby over to a crèche or someone else to mind. The maelstrom of emotions she felt for this small being who was so dependent on her made her decide to quit her course, stay home and be a full-time mother.

'Are you sure that's what you want?' her father had asked.
'I'm sure.'

She was still sure, and didn't regret an hour or a day that she had spent devoted to her small daughter. Her parents had been more than generous, turning the basement of their house into an apartment for herself and Evie, refusing to accept any rent for it.

'Sure, all we were doing was storing stuff there, and who in God's name needed a table-tennis room,' Leo Ryan had pointed out as two bedrooms, a small sitting room and a bright kitchen had been created and painted up with new heating and new fittings installed. When Evie was two and a half Sarah had gone back and finished her course at night, her mother encouraging her to get her qualification and babysitting on Tuesdays and Thursdays for her as she wrote her thesis and took on her final year project.

She lived on the small income she got for working part-time in the local national school, which meant she was broke most of the time. She helped out with their library and gave art classes to the older children. The odd design job came her way through old college contacts and if she needed extra money her friend Cora, who ran a successful catering company, was always glad of an extra pair of hands either in the kitchen or serving at some of the fancy Dublin parties she catered for in people's homes. Still Sarah had no regrets. She watched as her friends' careers began to take off, and knew she wouldn't change places with them for the world, for she had Evie.

Chapter Five

Sunday lunch. Maggie Ryan was a great believer in the tradition of Sunday lunch. Some considered it old-fashioned, but she clung firmly to the tenet that gathering around the table for a good meal at the end of a busy week was the best way to keep a family together. It ensured time with her children, kept her in touch with relations and was a relaxed way to entertain friends. Leo had always enjoyed it, carving up beef or lamb or turkey or pork loin into slices as he sipped a glass of red wine and put the cares of the week behind him. When he'd died she had abandoned the whole idea of entertaining, hating Sundays with a vengeance because they highlighted his absence, making it an awful day. Gradually, however, over the past few years, as her anger and grief had subsided, she realized that she hated being on her own Sunday after Sunday and had reinstigated the tradition.

Today the smell of roasting lamb and potatoes pervaded the kitchen and she had just added a tray full of peeled onions to the dish at the bottom of the oven. She had a large rhubarb crumble ready to pop in the oven later for dessert and some sticky toffee ice-cream in the freezer that she knew her little granddaughter adored.

The big mahogany dining table was set and she had lit the fire in the drawing room as there was still a nip in the air. Satisfied with progress in the kitchen, she decided to have a read of the papers, putting her feet up for a few minutes before the onslaught of visitors. Podge, her aged marmalade tabby cat, snoozed beside her in the chair.

Sarah and Evie were naturally the first to arrive, having only to make the short trip from the basement apartment up the stairs to the main part of the house. Sarah was wearing her usual jeans and T-shirt, topped by a pretty pink tapestry waistcoat.

'Imagine! I found it in the Oxfam shop,' she beamed as Maggie hugged them both, Sarah's long straight fair hair such a total contrast to her granddaughter's cascade of dark locks. Evie made a beeline for Podge who was lost in some cat reverie.

'How old is he, Granny?' she asked.

'About twelve, I think.'

'Will he die soon?'

Maggie cast a look of alarm over at Sarah, not wanting to upset her granddaughter. Maybe they'd been talking about death in school?

'Don't worry, Evie,' she reassured her. 'I hope that Podge will live for another few years.'

Sarah shot her a grateful glance, offering to help with the food as Evie's attention strayed from the family cat. She

31

certainly was a live wire and full of chat as she bounced around studying the table.

'Granny, why are you using the special plates?' she quizzed, scrutinizing them.

'That's because I've extra visitors coming,' she replied, 'and I thought they might like these plates with their pretty pattern.'

'She's full of questions about everything at the moment.' Sarah laughed. 'It's non-stop.'

'There's nothing worse than a quiet child,' teased Maggie. 'Parents are always worrying about them. At least you don't have that problem!'

The doorbell went and Maggie watched as Sarah ran to open it. Her neighbours Gerry and Helen Byrne and their son Barry, who was home on a visit from London, had just arrived, Gerry carrying a bottle of expensive-looking red wine and Helen a bunch of purple and yellow freesias, to give her hostess.

Barry almost lifted Sarah off the floor in a bear hug. The two of them laughed and chatted as Sarah took their coats and offered to put the flowers in water; Barry followed her down to the kitchen in search of a vase. Sarah had known the Byrnes all her life: they had been good friends to Maggie over the years and a tower of strength when Leo had died.

'This is just like old times,' Gerry exclaimed, warming himself in front of the fire.

'Can I get you a drink?' Maggie offered.

'A glass of wine for me, and Helen will have her usual gin and tonic.'

Maggie hoped that there was lemon in the fruit bowl in the kitchen as Helen was fussy about adding a slice of lemon to her drink.

Grace arrived next. She looked amazing in a pair of slim-fitting cream cords and a beige cord jacket, smelling of that expensive American perfume she always wore.

'I've just had a lovely walk along Sandymount Strand.' She smiled and hugged her mother.

'Where's that boyfriend of yours?' Maggie asked. 'I thought you said he was coming too.'

'I'm sorry, Mum,' she apologized, 'but Shane couldn't make it. It was a last-minute thing.'

Maggie said nothing. She could read the disappointment in her eldest daughter's eyes.

Why Grace had got herself tangled up with someone so self-centred was beyond her. Shane O'Sullivan worked in the same architectural firm as Grace. She wasn't sure it was at all wise for her daughter to get romantically involved with a colleague, especially one who seemed so unreliable. They'd been going out for almost a year but she had to admit she just couldn't take to him. Grace on the outside might seem composed and direct but underneath she was sensitive and caring. She deserved a boyfriend who was a lot better than a handsome heartbreaker like Shane. Maggie had to bite her tongue on her opinion of him but to her mind he seemed to be constantly letting Grace down; today was only another example of it.

'Who else is coming?' Grace asked.

'I've asked Detta and Tom. You know, I'm going to really

miss them. They've been such good neighbours over the years, and when I think how kind they were when your father died and I couldn't even think straight . . .'

'I heard their house was sold,' Grace said, all interested. 'Who bought it?'

'I'm sure they'll tell us. Oscar of course is coming. He loves a good Sunday roast. Anna should be here soon.'

Grace smiled; her mother loved having people around, cooking and entertaining and chatting. Her parents had always been a social couple but now her mother had to work hard to fill the void left by her father's death.

'Can I do anything?' she offered.

'No, you relax,' urged Maggie. Her eldest daughter worked far too hard. At the top of her profession, her job in one of the city's busy architects' firms consumed her. She went from one project to another, constantly putting in long hours and overtime, with scarcely any time for a personal life. Maggie's motherly worries were interrupted by the arrival of Detta and Tom O'Connor bearing two rather ancient bottles of champagne.

'We found them in that old wine cellar under the stairs. We felt we must celebrate, Maggie. Can you believe it, the house sold and us upping sticks and starting over at our age,' declared Tom, beaming like an overweight schoolboy in his usual navy blazer, his round face flushed with excitement.

'When are you moving?' asked Gerry, congratulating him.

'The removal people are coming on Thursday,' answered Detta, full of emotion, her double chin wobbling. 'All the boxes are already there and we've so much to pack and label correctly but they'll help us, and then on Thursday evening we're getting the car ferry over to Holyhead. We'll stay the night there and the next morning drive down to Bath.'

'Next Sunday, God willing, we'll be with Cormac and Lynn and their three boys. We've bought a small cottage only about a half-mile from their house.'

The bottles of Moët were well chilled and Gerry helped Maggie to open one. Maggie was just passing a glass to Detta when Oscar from next door appeared. He moved slowly, his arthritis obviously troubling him again, his long thin frame cushioned by a heavy tweed jacket. Anna arrived just a minute after him.

Maggie welcomed them both but asked no questions, taking in the black T-shirt and unironed olive-green skirt and boots, and the dark circles under her middle daughter's eyes and her pale skin as she hugged her.

'You OK, Anna? Do you want some champagne?' offered Sarah, not surprised when her sister demurred.

The enormous leg of lamb was done to perfection, the potatoes nicely roasted when Maggie called everyone to sit down. Sarah and Grace helped her to carve and serve the food.

'A toast to Detta and Tom,' she called. 'It's sad saying goodbye to the best of neighbours but we all wish them good fortune in their new home in England.'

Gerry and Helen nodded in agreement and seventy-five-year-old Oscar made a small speech of his own.

'May the road rise to meet you,' he said softly. 'The square won't be the same without such dear friends. How I'll manage in O'Brien's on a Wednesday night without Tom along for our regular pint of Guinness beats me.'

'Gerry will have to buy you one instead,' said Helen, squeezing his arm.

Talk around the table flowed full of stories about the antics of the neighbours and their various offspring over the years.

'I used to be so embarrassed by our five boys,' admitted Helen. 'They must have broken more panes of glass around the square than anyone else. They destroyed flower beds and planters and window boxes and Lord knows how many times the park people were on to us about the goalposts they set up in the square. Not to mention the bike races . . . and do you remember that big tree house they made?'

'We weren't that bad,' protested Barry, 'we just had a bit of a wild streak and you and Dad were softies!'

Sarah laughed. She had always been great pals with Barry. She'd had a crush on him for a while when she was a teenager but then realized that she'd much rather have him as a friend. He lived in London with a beautiful girl called Melinda and their baby boy Daniel. He was only home for a few days this time so it was lovely to get together and catch up.

Maggie noticed that Evie was being very good at the other end of the table and eating her lamb which Sarah had disguised with gravy as Barry and she chatted away.

'I heard it was a heated auction,' Oscar said, 'and that there were four or five bidders for the house?'

'We couldn't face going to it ourselves,' admitted Tom.

'Detta was worried it would drive her blood pressure through the roof.'

'The house went for far more that we'd hoped,' she confided excitedly. 'Who'd have believed it with our clunky heating and the bathroom that needs tiling and our rattling windows and the leak in the laundry room, but we've got a nice little nest egg for going away.'

'Did a family buy it?' asked Sarah hopefully. 'Maybe they might have a little girl around Evie's age. It would be great for her to have someone so near to play with.'

'We would have liked a family to buy it too,' admitted Detta, 'but it was some wealthy businessman. As far as I know he's not even married. It's a pity.'

'An eligible bachelor moving to the square, how interesting!' said Maggie, suddenly curious about this new male neighbour.

'Maggie!' teased Helen.

'He's not married, has just bought an expensive piece of property and will be living literally a few doors away from us. You and Gerry would be the same if you had daughters!'

'Mum!' remonstrated Grace. 'You know nothing about him!'

'Are all girls' mothers like that?' Barry asked Sarah at the far end of the table.

Sarah, who was putting a few more peas on Evie's plate, cast an embarrassed glance at her mother.

'Bachelor or not, apparently he has great plans for the place,' Tom added. 'Great plans.'

'Who is this fellow?' asked Oscar. 'Did they tell you?'

'Mark McGuinness. That's the name Billy King mentioned, apparently he's a big noise in the property world.'

Grace most certainly had heard of him. He'd recently out-bid one of their clients on a valuable site over in Malahide. They'd hoped to develop rather expensive apartments on it while he had gone for planning permission for town houses and a small retail scheme. 'Mr McGuinness has a reputation for buying up old properties and derelict sites, knocking down and stripping houses and buildings and refitting them and selling them on at a large profit,' she warned.

'Well, hopefully whatever his plans he will do the necessary repair work to restore number twenty-nine to its true glory.' Gerry smiled. 'These are such beautiful old houses.'

'Oh, I hope he doesn't knock too much of the old house down,' said Detta, worried.

'No, he'll have to keep within the planning restrictions for a Georgian house,' Grace added firmly, feeling slightly alarmed at the thought of an investor like him buying a house on the square.

Maggie smiled to herself, as she watched Grace talk about houses. Ever since she'd been a little girl she'd found structures, walls, roofs and windows fascinating. Leo and herself had always shared a love of old buildings and there'd been plenty of family outings to see Big Houses across the country.

Anna Ryan sighed, ignoring the conversation going on around her. She could do no more than play with the food on her plate: she felt so awful. She should have stayed home in bed. She wasn't hungry and had no interest in what some property type did to the O'Connors' house, which, truth to tell, had been falling down around them – or so she'd thought, the last time she'd gone to a drinks party there. Shabby chic, Dublin auctioneers called it. Whoever had bought the place was going to have to sink a load of hard-earned cash into it to bring it up to scratch.

'Anyone for coffee or tea?' asked Maggie as she passed around servings of the piping-hot rhubarb crumble – not forgetting to give Oscar an extra big helping.

'Nothing like home-cooked food,' her elderly neighbour thanked her. He seemed to exist on a diet of microwaveable meals and fry-ups ever since his wife Elizabeth had died.

He was one of the sweetest men she knew and Leo and he had been firm friends. Elizabeth and Oscar had been like benevolent godparents, always ready to help out in a crisis as their three girls were growing up, and had always been part of Ryan family occasions. Now that Oscar was on his own Maggie made even more of an effort to keep an eye on him and ensure he regularly ate at their table.

When the meal was over and emotional farewells had been said, the girls had helped Maggie load their old dishwasher. Maggie had promised Detta a hand in the morning with packing up her good china and selecting what could go to St Vincent de Paul. Gerry and Helen had promised a return lunch in their place in two weeks' time, something she would look forward to.

Once everything was washed up, Maggie could finally

relax. She cradled a mug of coffee in her hand, looking around her with satisfaction. She loved this kitchen, not just because it was the warmest place in this big, rather draughty house, but because it was the centre, the hub, the heart of the family. Leo had loved the drawing room, with the sun slanting in on his armchair where he could read the newspapers or listen to the radio in peace, but for her it was this kitchen every time. Across the table from her, Sarah, Evie, Grace and Anna were playing Snakes and Ladders. Evie had persuaded her aunties to join in and shrieked with excitement when anyone had to slide down the big green snakes. She was mad on board games at the moment and loved this old-fashioned one which Maggie had rescued from the bottom of a shelf in Grace's old bedroom. Watching them play, heads bent down, laughing and joking, reminded Maggie of when they were children.

A woman couldn't have better daughters, she thought, and yet here they were on a Sunday evening on their own. Single and unmarried with not even a decent man between them! Where had she gone wrong? They'd grown up in a house full of love and yet for some bizarre reason love evaded them . . .

'That new neighbour sounds kind of interesting,' she ventured. 'Detta said he's single.'

Anna groaned. She was in no mood for her mother's matchmaking or encouraging little talks about single men.

'Mum, we don't know that he is single,' admonished Grace. 'He's well known and wealthy and for all we know has been married and divorced three times over or has a list of girlfriends as long as my arm.'

'Anyway, he could be one of those awful guys who thinks that they're God's gift,' added Sarah, shaking the dice. 'Men are different now!'

'There are no knights in shining armour riding around Dublin, believe us,' said Anna vehemently. 'And there's absolutely no point looking!'

Maggie sighed, wondering where all the decent men had gone to. Everything was changing these days, not just property and business but love and marriage and romance. Call her old-fashioned, but was it too much to ask in this day and age that her daughters be swept off their feet by some lovely man, fall madly in love and marry him? Maybe Anna was right and suitable men were few and far between. If that was the case then perhaps it was time for a little motherly interference on her part, as Maggie was determined to find Grace, Anna and Sarah the perfect match.

Chapter Six

Sarah stood on the doorstep of the O'Connors' house. She had 101 things to do this morning but somehow her mother had persuaded her to help Detta and Tom pack up for their big move.

'Moving house and packing is a daunting task at the best of times,' her mother reminded her, 'but can you imagine how hard it must be for them leaving their family home at their age and starting over?'

Sarah had always had a soft spot for Mrs O'Connor, who had slipped her a cheque for fifty euros when Evie was born and who without fail, Christmas after Christmas, arrived with a gift for Evie and a big Cadbury's chocolate selection box for her.

The doorbell sounded through the house as Detta eventually appeared to open the door.

'I've been awake since crack of dawn,' she admitted. 'I couldn't sleep with all the excitement and emotion of saying goodbye to the place! Poor Tom had barely a wink of sleep either and his arthritis is at him. I could hear him downstairs wandering around at six o'clock this morning.'

'Sarah was free today so I asked her to give us a hand,' her mother explained as they stepped inside. 'How's the packing going?'

'It's taking a bit longer than we expected,' Detta admitted hesitantly.

What an understatement! Everything was piled up in a heap: furniture and clothes, old toys and books and games and the bric-a-brac of many years. Sarah had always known Detta was bit of a hoarder, but now, seeing it all spread out before them, a look of dismay passed between her mother and herself. Where would they even begin, she thought as she surveyed the rubbish that spilled over the floor and couches and chairs and tables.

'Well, that's why we're here to help,' said Maggie, nonplussed. 'Maybe we should have a quick run through every room and see where you need us.'

Embarrassed, Detta led them around the house and the full – and awful – extent of the task ahead was revealed. Tom had organized for their larger furniture to be collected as it was going to auction next week: the mahogany dining table and chairs and sideboard along with the old piano and couches.

'God, Detta, you have far too much!' Maggie blurted out. 'Your new house will explode if you take all these things with you. Half this stuff has got to go.'

Sarah Ryan grimaced to herself. Grace, Anna and herself had regularly faced similar calls to arms over the years as Maggie attacked their messy teenage bedrooms, but to see her mother in action in someone else's house was a bit embarrassing. However, looking at poor Mrs O'Connor's face, she could see she was relieved that she had some help. Sarah squeezed her hand reassuringly.

'Where do we start?' Detta asked forlornly, looking around her, as Tom O'Connor tried to escape to the kitchen with a mug of coffee and the *Irish Times*.

'Why don't we start up here in the main bedroom; Tom and you can decide what clothes you both need,' said Maggie, taking charge.

If there was one thing her mother was good at, it was organizing people and making sure things got done, which was exactly what was needed, Sarah thought.

'Detta, we'll need plenty of black bags and some of those boxes the movers left you.'

Sarah ran downstairs to fetch them and returned to find her mother helping Detta go through the wardrobes. They were full to bursting, mostly with clothes that no one would wear again.

'Are you and Tom really going to bring all these clothes to England with you?'

Detta shook her head firmly.

Maggie lifted out suit after suit, and numerous sports jackets, two old tuxedos and a fishing jacket which Tom had forgotten about and insisted he would definitely make use of now.

'Perfect for fishing in the river . . .'

Detta cast her eyes to heaven.

Her own side of the wardrobe was next. Even a quick

glance revealed that at least half of her clothes were fit only for the bin. Her good dresses, two suits, some trousers and skirts were set aside to go in the portable wardrobes the movers would supply. The rest would go to the charity shop or be thrown away. Sarah rooted through her chest of drawers: old make-up, congealed bottles of nail varnish, dried-up mascaras and gone-off perfumes were all consigned to the bin. They discovered three hats in their fancy hat boxes, still wrapped in tissue. Detta opted to keep the Philip Somerville one for fun and send the rest to St Vincent de Paul. Sarah suggested that Tom's tuxes could go to a vintage shop along with the expensive double-breasted suit he'd bought thirty years ago, which was far too small for him; she added three or four expensive jackets of Detta's along with two evening dresses that she'd worn to balls years ago.

'These are vintage Chanel and Sybil Connolly. The shop will snap them up.' Sarah grinned and put them carefully away.

By midmorning Maggie and Sarah insisted they take a break. They'd been through the other bedrooms, which were even worse than the master bedroom, being cluttered with clothes their children had abandoned on wire hangers. Sarah even spotted two old school uniforms in the back of the closet in the fourth bedroom.

'I remember when Cormac wore that the first time he went to Gonzaga College.'

'It'll have to go,' said Maggie firmly as they trawled through shirts, trousers and sweaters, filling two boxes with clothes they wanted, the rest all to be given away to charity.

Sarah went through the stuff from their bathroom, finding old soaps and talcum powders and bath products. 'Most of this stuff is out of date and would probably give you a rash!' she told Detta as she binned them in giant black plastic bags.

In the end upstairs began to look a little clearer, as if it was ready for the move. Downstairs was another matter.

By lunchtime they had boxes of books allocated to the charity shops along with old LPs and a load of ornaments and wicker baskets. The side of the living room containing stuff that was to be given away was rapidly filling up.

Exhausted, Detta sat down on a pouffe, flicking through a pile of old gardening magazines, talking about all the good times they had shared under this roof as Tom carefully wrapped their crystal wine and brandy glasses in old newspaper. They were definitely making progress.

Sarah disappeared to the kitchen and made lunch for everyone with cans of soup that she found in the larder, some of the French bread sticks that her mother had brought along and a big pot of tea.

'We've got to keep our strength up,' she said, smiling as they all sat down to eat.

Detta stared out at the garden from the kitchen table, watching a blackbird. 'Who will feed the birds when I'm gone?' she mused. 'You know, I first moved into this house when we were expecting Cormac. It was only meant to be a temporary arrangement as Joan O'Connor, my mother-in-law, was a difficult woman. It wasn't easy living under the same roof as such a scourge! Still, in the end it all worked

46

out, and Joan doted on our two, she was mad about them. Then when Joan herself got ill and frail we minded her, took care of her in her old age. It all only seems like yesterday.'

Tom blinked with emotion as he sipped his tea. He showed them the pair of gold cufflinks of his father's that had turned up at the back of one of the bookshelves and the medal he'd won for playing football when he was sixteen.

'Absolute treasures!' He beamed, putting them safely away in his blazer pocket.

'It must be sad, leaving,' Sarah probed gently.

'Naturally,' sighed Detta, looking around the old kitchen, 'but another part of me is excited. This house is much too big for us now that the family's gone and Tom and I have found a lovely place that we can manage. It's perfect: two bedrooms, a bright sunny kitchen and a small bit of a garden with a view of the woods. The best thing is we're close to Cormac and his children. We're only around the corner from the boys' school.'

'We've been rattling round this old place for far too many years,' added Tom brusquely as he buttered a slice of bread. 'It's grand when Cormac and the kids or Niamh and her family are home on a visit but the rest of the time you can see what it was like. We were just using the one bedroom, and the sitting room and the kitchen. The rest of the place was going to rack and ruin.'

'What an old house like this needs,' said Detta firmly, 'is a new family.'

After lunch, Sarah was sorting out a pile of books in the sitting room with her mother when they noticed a car draw up outside. Maybe it was someone else volunteering to help?

They watched as a man parked an expensive black Range Rover at the kerb. He climbed out, considered the house from the outside and then walked up to the front door. Tom went to answer the doorbell.

'Come in,' they heard him saying, 'you're very welcome.'

'I know I'm not getting the keys till Thursday afternoon but I just wanted to introduce myself,' said the new owner. 'See if there's anything that I can do to help with your move. Make the transition a bit easier and also swap our contact details.'

'It's the new owner,' her mother said, all excited. Detta scrambled to fix her hair in the mirror over the fireplace before Tom led him into the room.

Tom introduced them all to Mark McGuinness. 'This is my wife, Detta, and our neighbours Maggie Ryan and Sarah her daughter. They live across in number twenty-three. As you can see we're hard at it trying to pack everything and they are giving us a hand.'

Mark McGuinness nodded politely.

Sarah studied the tall, dark, rather handsome man in his expensive suit who was going to move into the house. He was good-looking with the kind of over-confidence that money buys. She hated guys like him who thought big bank accounts and cars and contacts were worth more than a sense of humour and the ability just to be down to earth.

'Packing up is an awful job,' he commented, looking at the piles of black bags and boxes. 'We all hate it.'

'Are you hoping to move in soon?' asked her mother.

'No! Not straight away,' he said, glancing about him. 'The house needs quite a bit of work so I have a team ready to start in a few weeks.'

'You'll probably put in one of those wonderful new fitted kitchens, it's what most women want these days,' continued Maggie. 'I suppose your wife has all kinds of plans?'

'Actually I'm not married,' he said firmly, 'but you're right, I do plan on a good kitchen.'

'Anyway, welcome to Pleasant Square,' said Maggie, barely able to disguise her relief at discovering he was definitely not married.

Mark McGuinness followed Tom upstairs as he offered to show him around the house and point out the eccentricities of their ancient heating and plumbing systems.

'Detta, I'm sorry but I'm going to have to go,' Sarah apologized. 'I've to collect Evie from school.'

'Thank you so much, pet,' the older woman said, hugging her close. 'I don't know what Tom and I would have done without you.'

'What about the vintage stuff?' she asked. 'Will I bring it to the shop in Temple Bar for you? The Chanel jacket might fetch quite a bit.'

'You do whatever you want with it, Sarah love.' Detta smiled. 'All the proceeds are yours.'

The new owner had just come back downstairs. He was, she supposed, rather dishy in a mature way but far too serious and definitely not her type.

'I'd better be getting back to the office,' he said. 'Are you sure there's nothing I can do to help?'

Maggie Ryan hesitated for a second but, seeing all the boxes of books and bags of stuff they had gathered up and that enormous car parked outside the window, decided to throw caution to the wind and ask him.

'Well, actually, if you're driving through Ranelagh maybe you could help us and take a few of these bags that are going to the charity shop there? Tom's car hasn't a lot of space, while yours is huge.'

Mark McGuinness looked momentarily surprised, but they'd put him on the spot and he didn't want to appear ungenerous and renege on his offer.

'Sarah can show you where it is as she is going in that direction anyway!' her mother continued.

Honestly, Sarah could have killed her for putting her in such an awkward situation with an utter stranger. He must think she was mad!

It took only a few minutes for them all to load up the Range Rover.

'Here's my business card and mobile number,' Mark said to Tom. 'I'm away in Prague on business for the rest of the week, so I won't see you. My solicitor will look after things. Good luck with the move and I'll forward on any post and messages.'

'Take care of the place,' Tom said hoarsely as he shook his hand.

Sarah clambered in beside him in her dusty jeans and sweatshirt, suppressing a giggle at the sight of his beautiful car full of black plastic bags and boxes and household junk.

'Where are we heading?' he asked politely.

'If you take a left and then a right it will bring us back up towards the village. The other road is a one way. The Vincent de Paul shop is only a few yards from my daughter's school,' she said. 'I can give you a hand with the bags and boxes before I collect her.'

'You have a child?' he said and she could see him glance at her ring finger.

'I have a little girl, Evie, she's nearly six,' she explained watching his expression. 'I had her when I was in college. Her dad lives in Rome.'

'It's tough raising a kid on your own,' he said softly, 'very tough, but I bet you're a great mum and that she is a great kid.'

'The best!' said Sarah, surprised by his change in attitude.

His car phone suddenly went and he spoke quickly to the caller on the speaker phone arranging a meeting in town.

At the charity shop, despite the dust, he insisted on lifting in most of the boxes and bags. Sarah thanked him profusely for helping, then stood on the pavement and watched him ease the car back into the traffic. He mightn't be her type but she had to admit Mark McGuinness was certainly a perfect gentleman.

Chapter Seven

Maggie Ryan watched from the bedroom window as the huge removal van pulled up outside the O'Connors' house. The removal men were busy up and down the granite steps, lifting the remainder of Tom and Detta's possessions into the back of the container truck. Upset, Maggie was half tempted to crawl back into bed and stay there for the rest of the day. She would miss them terribly and it felt like another piece of her old life with Leo was slipping away. They had been far more than neighbours, they had been such good friends. But immediately she felt guilty. You should be up and dressed and helping, she chastised herself, instead of standing here in your dressing gown feeling sorry for yourself.

She had a quick shower and slipped on her beige trousers and a cream sweater, pulling the hairbrush quickly through her short fair hair with its highlights disguising the grey at her temples. A flick of mascara on her fair eyelashes, a slick of her usual coral lipstick and spray of Rive Gauche and she grabbed her purse and house keys. She had a lovely carrot cake she had bought in the deli yesterday and she would go over and make sure that things were going smoothly for the older couple.

Maggie looked on as room after room was emptied. She kept the kettle on and made endless mugs of tea. Rory, the younger mover, insisting he took five heaped spoons of sugar. It was like syrup and she watched open-mouthed as he drank it. The cake went down a treat too.

She could see Tom was trying to maintain his composure as he directed the removal men. They had some kind of system going with numbers and names on boxes. Oscar Lynch had appeared over to wish them a safe journey and had finished off the last slice of the cake. Over the past two days many of the neighbours had called in to say goodbye and wish them well.

'There'll always be a bed for you in Pleasant Square if you fancy a visit,' Oscar insisted, tears in his eyes as he said good-bye to his old friends.

Detta and Tom thanked him warmly for his kindness but both Maggie and Oscar knew in their hearts that as far as Detta and Tom were concerned there was no coming back, it would be too painful.

Once all the O'Connors' books and furniture and personal possessions were removed the house looked so empty, shabby and forlorn. Maggie instinctively knew Detta and Tom needed time to say farewell to the house on their own so she said her own goodbyes and left. Her last glimpse was of Detta clutching her husband's hand as they walked through the hall and stairs. How hard it must be for them to leave their house with its lifetime of memories!

Back at home Maggie gave in to her emotions. She cried as the removal van left the square and Tom and Detta drove away to their solicitors in Fitzwilliam Street to hand over the keys of the house before they set off for England. The only consolation to losing such good neighbours was that they were being replaced by such an eligible bachelor. To her mind Mark McGuinness was perfect husband material. Sarah had refused to be drawn about her car trip to the St Vincent de Paul shop with him but had admitted he was actually 'quite nice'.

Maggie was just making herself a reviving cup of coffee when the phone rang; she was delighted to hear her older sister Kitty's voice on the other end of the line. Kitty was all excited, talking ninety to the dozen as she had done when they were kids.

'I've got some good news for you.'

'I could do with some of that,' admitted Maggie.

'Orla's got engaged!' Kitty announced. 'They've just been to Venice for three days – it was so romantic, Liam proposed while they were in one of those gondola things and Orla's over the moon with excitement.'

Maggie stifled a pang of jealousy. Kitty's only daughter Orla was a lovely girl, a primary-school teacher; she was almost thirty-three years old and had been dating Liam O'Connell for years. It was high time they got married.

'Harry and I are so pleased for them and he's insisting on us having an engagement party here at home on Saturday,' Kitty went on. 'He says it will give both families the chance to meet up before the wedding itself.'

'That sounds like a great idea.'

'Promise you and the girls and Evie will try and make it? It's from eight p.m. onwards.'

'We wouldn't miss it for the world,' said Maggie. It was thrilling to hear that *someone* in the family was getting married!

Chapter Eight

Orla Hennessy's eyes were shining as brightly as the dainty diamond ring on her finger as she and Liam O'Connell greeted the guests at their engagement party. There were balloons and candles and a massive bouquet of flowers in the hall of her parents' Rathfarnham home and all the guests were caught up in the excitement. Grace, Sarah and Anna all admired the engagement ring while Uncle Harry plied them with glasses of champagne.

'It's one of the most beautiful rings I've seen,' exclaimed Maggie, admiring the sparkling solitaire diamond then hugging Orla. Among all her nieces and nephews she had always had a soft spot for Orla, who was the apple of Kitty and Harry's eye, the only girl after two older brothers.

'Your three will be the next,' joked her brother-in-law Harry as he kissed her.

Maggie smiled, wondering yet again which of her girls would be first to get engaged and thinking longingly about all the lovely things an engagement brings.

'God, we'll never hear the end of it,' muttered Grace

under her breath to her sisters. 'Mum and Kitty will have us demented.'

'Mum's obsessed with one of us getting married.' Sarah laughed ruefully. 'I think half the mothers in Ireland must be the same!'

'All they want is an engagement announcement in the *Irish Times*, a ring on your finger and a man on your arm!' complained Anna. 'Comes from reading too many romances and watching too many Hugh Grant films!'

'Anna!' protested Sarah. 'I love Hugh Grant films too, and I think it's wonderful that Orla and Liam are getting married. They've been in love for years!'

Uncle Harry, in an extraordinary pink-and-white-striped shirt, was in flying form, constantly topping up everyone's champagne flutes while Kitty was already in full mother-of-the-bride mode, talking about churches and venues and florists and dresses.

Maggie Ryan smiled indulgently at her sister. She truly was happy to see Orla finally settling down with the man she loved. It had been a bit of a rollercoaster romance for the young teacher because Liam was a busy hotelier who had moved job every few years. He'd worked in a hotel in Cork and then Killarney and now was managing a fancy golf hotel in Kildare.

'Of course we're having the wedding in Mountrath Manor,' Liam said. 'They have to look after us well!'

Grace, Anna and Sarah were thrilled for their cousin too and looking forward to a big family bash.

'I've been to so many weddings in the past three years I've

nearly lost count,' admitted Grace. 'Rome and Marbella last summer, Brooklodge, Adare, the Four Seasons . . . Nearly all my friends are married but Orla and Liam's will be great craic as it's a family occasion!'

Sarah couldn't believe it when Orla took her aside and asked if she would let Evie be her flower girl at their wedding in September.

'Conor's little girl Amy will be one too and it would be so sweet to have the two of them walking up the aisle together.'

'Evie will be over the moon,' said Sarah. 'Orla, you are so good to think of her but you should ask her yourself. She's playing out in the kitchen with a few of the kids.'

A few minutes later Evie raced into the living room, bursting with the news. 'Mummy, I'm going to be a flower girl for Orla's wedding and I have to wear a special dress and carry flowers and have flowers in my hair!' she cried, jigging up and down with excitement.

'You will be a beautiful flower girl,' said Sarah, scooping her up in her arms for a big kiss.

Maggie was having a quiet moment sipping her glass of wine when she noticed Alan Ferguson, a friend of Harry's, heading in her direction. He had separated from his wife Julia two years before and his face lit up when he saw her. She shuddered. Why did men like Alan assume that just because she was a widow she might be interested in them? All he wanted to talk about was sport and the latest GAA match he'd attended in Croke Park. Was it any wonder poor Julia had left him! Making her excuses she went and sat down on the couch to chat with Liam's parents who were lovely Westmeath people and delighted to see their son finally taking the plunge.

'We thought the day would never come!' joked his mother Mary. 'Honestly, what he was waiting for is beyond us!'

'They don't believe in rushing into things these days — they think they have all the time in the world,' added his father Paul, a tall thin bespectacled man who was the image of Liam. 'And houses cost a fortune so it's hard to get on the property ladder.'

Maggie watched as Kitty passed a tray of fancy canapés around the crowded room, her face aglow. She was wearing a lovely silver-grey outfit that she'd bought in Brown Thomas. Her sister looked well, filled with happiness for her daughter and future son-in-law. Her sons Conor and Gavin were both already married, one living in Malahide and the other down in Cork, and she had three grandchildren. Six years ago she had had an awful time when she had developed breast cancer and had a breast removed. Harry and the boys and Orla had struggled to cope with her illness. Thank God, after her surgery and treatment she had made a great recovery and this wedding news was particularly special as Maggie knew one of her sister's biggest fears had been that she wouldn't live to see her daughter walk up the aisle.

Maggie raised her glass of wine as Harry congratulated the happy couple and Orla and Liam thanked everyone for coming to the party. A good man is hard to find, she thought, yet somehow Orla had. She and Liam had found each other and were now going to make a future together.

She looked at her own lovely daughters chatting with their cousins and smiled to herself. One of these days, if she had any say in it, there would be sparkling rings on their fingers too.

Chapter Nine

Recuperating from the previous night's engagement party, which had ended in a mass rendition of 'The Fields of Athenry', Maggie decided to check her phone and email messages. She was relieved to see that there had been a good response to her discreet advertisement in the *Irish Times* seeking a new tenant to rent the small three-bedroom mews at the bottom of her garden, which had access to Pleasant Lane. Her previous tenants, three nurses, had been lovely girls but a bit of a headache, given to late-night parties on their monthly pay day and unfortunately flooding the upstairs bathroom. One had broken the microwave oven, blowing two of the kitchen sockets at the same time. The damages had been sorted out at the end of their rental period and the girls were now moving to an apartment nearer to St James's Hospital where they worked.

It was Grace who had first suggested converting the run-down former coach house at the end of the garden, where they stored bicycles and old garden furniture and junk, into a modern mews which could be let out to provide an additional income to supplement the benefit from Leo's insurance policy and her widow's pension. How she hated that word 'widow'. She'd never imagined herself having to face life alone. At times she cursed Leo for leaving her so unprepared for life without him, and turning their plans for his retirement into silly dreams. Her husband's death had been totally unexpected. Leo had suffered a minor heart attack following a round of golf and had been admitted to hospital for tests. There he had undergone emergency heart surgery; a triple bypass which he had actually managed to come through, only to die a few days later from a simple blood clot in his lungs. How she had survived those initial awful black dark days, she didn't know. She had wanted to hide away and stay in bed, refuse to face what had happened, but Grace and Anna and Sarah and her young grand-daughter had needed her. Somehow they had got through the funeral, supported by family and good friends. The days had turned to weeks, the weeks to months and now years – and she found it hard to believe that it was just over four years and ten months since Leo had left her.

The building renovation project had taken almost a year. When the small three-bedroomed mews with its modern kitchen, large windows, French doors and paved terrace overlooking part of the garden was finally completed she had sat down and cried, knowing that it was a job well done and that Leo would be proud of her. At first it would be let out to provide extra income and in the future she could either sell it or move into it herself. So the mews had been rented and apart from a few small hitches had provided a nice additional bit of money.

Once the nurses had left, her Polish home help Irina had helped Maggie to clean and polish the mews from top to bottom. She had bought some bright new cushions from Habitat and complete sets of white cotton bed linen, which freshened the place, and a fancy new microwave. Jotting down the names and numbers and email addresses she began to return calls to set up appointments for potential new tenants to see the mews.

This afternoon she was showing the place to the first people. Fingers crossed that one of them would be suitable.

There was a couple who seemed good on paper; three single girls, which rang a kind of alarm bell; two single guys who only wanted a six-month let as they were waiting on an apartment they'd bought; a young Scottish businessman who had recently moved to Dublin; and a single girl. Grabbing the keys and her phone she walked down the garden path. She found this very hard. Leo had been a good judge of character but she knew she was a sucker for hard-luck stories. She determined that after showing each of them around she would take her time and check their references before making her mind up who should be her new tenant.

The couple arrived bang on time and Maggie was surprised by their age difference.

'I'm not sure that I like that old stonework,' complained the young blond woman as Maggie showed her around the ground floor. 'And the fridge is rather small.'

The good-looking older man with her said little, but jotted

things down on a notepad as Maggie led them upstairs. She noticed that he wore a wedding ring, while his much younger partner with her pouting lips and narrow hips didn't, and he reddened with embarrassment as his girlfriend bounced on the double bed and cajoled him to join her.

'I want a plasma TV in here too, Michael. For the nights when you're not here.'

Maggie tried not to be judgemental but in the end could not help deciding there and then that over her dead body was she going to provide a hideaway love nest for the couple, which his wife would have no clue about.

The three young girls were up from Cork and were in first year in UCD. Nurses were one thing but students without accommodation a few months into the term another. God knows what they had done in their previous apartment!

The two guys were polite and easygoing and were very taken with the place, remarking on the stonework and lovely decor but after chatting to them for a few minutes Maggie realized she could rule out any possibility of them being potential husband material, as these two were most definitely not in the market for eligible females. They were nice guys but would only commit to a six-month lease as they were just killing time till their own new apartment in Stepaside was ready. The serious young single female lawyer with impeccable references who was entranced with the place seemed a very good prospect. The last applicant hadn't appeared and she was fast coming to the conclusion that the young woman was her best bet as a suitable tenant. She was just about to phone her when the Scotsman finally made an appearance.

'My flight was delayed,' he apologized, 'and then I got stuck in that awful traffic from the airport. I hope I'm not too late to see the place, it sounds exactly what I'm looking for.'

He was so enthusiastic that despite his being nearly two hours late she decided to show him round. She could see he was taken with the mews and asked her all about the restoration. He was small and thin and rather intense-looking with spiky black hair; he was wearing black jeans, a leather jacket and a T-shirt with the Red Hot Chili Peppers on it. Sarah had a poster of them in her bedroom. He looked more like a musician than a businessman but was definitely the arty type that appealed to her youngest daughter.

'You should see the concrete box I'm staying in for the minute!' he laughed. 'I don't know why anyone would build them like that. Give me a lovely old building like this any day of the week.'

'I'm glad that you like it.' Maggie smiled. 'It was a labour of love restoring and modernizing it.'

'I know I'll be back and forwards to the office in Edinburgh regularly, but what I really would like is somewhere a little different to live during my time here in Dublin.'

'The sockets in the kitchen will be replaced before anyone moves in,' she promised.

'Don't bother on my behalf,' Angus Hamilton said, his thin face serious. 'I can do it myself. I'd probably like to connect up to broadband or wireless if that's OK, and hook myself up to digital TV.'

She must have looked slightly baffled because he reassured

her, saying that he had studied engineering before specializing in computers and designing software.

'What do you do?' she asked, curious.

'I design programmes for computer games,' he told her. 'It's a huge business. We work with animators and designers and come up with concepts and games that people want to play. We're working on a game with leprechauns!'

'Really?'

'No, I'm joking, but it's not a bad idea. Our company has offices here and in Edinburgh and I'll be going back and forth between them.'

'So it would be just you living in the mews.'

'Yes.' He grinned. 'I'm on my own.'

That night as she sat watching the television Maggie weighed up the candidates. The thirty-year-old female lawyer Celine Heaney worked in one of the city's smaller law firms and was busy studying at night for the Law Society exams in Blackhall Place; she certainly didn't look the type to give wild parties. The charming young Scotsman seemed open and friendly and determined to enjoy his time in Dublin. Without a qualm Maggie decided on Angus Hamilton. The house was already far too full of single females. Having a man around the place again would make a very pleasant change and the fact that he was an eligible bachelor was a definite bonus . . .

Chapter Ten

Grace had endured a hell of a day. She'd discovered during a pitching session with a possible new client that projection figures prepared by a new junior colleague were almost two hundred thousand euros out. She was snowed under with work and her enthusiasm was getting her into trouble as she found it almost impossible to say no to any of the innovative and exciting projects that were coming her way: converting a derelict warehouse in the heart of the city into a contemporary restaurant and gallery space; designing a house for one of Ireland's young rock gods; and coming up with an appropriate scheme for elderly tenants who were being rehoused in the Liberties. Her boss Derek Thornton had called her into his office only twelve days ago and told her that she was being considered as a junior partner: there was a solid block of support for her and the work she was now attracting to the company. She could hardly believe it but was determined to prove his faith in her ability.

It was good to get some recognition for her hard work, but since her chat with Derek she noticed that Shane had been a little bit distant in the office. It was crazy but at the moment they were both so busy with various projects that they scarcely had time to see each other. Shane had already cancelled going to the cinema tonight citing a deadline tomorrow.

After work Grace planned to go home, get into her pyjamas and veg out on back-to-back episodes of *CSI*, when her mother phoned asking her over for dinner.

'I'm making mushroom risotto with parmesan,' she coaxed, knowing well that it was Grace's favourite meal in the entire world.

'OK, OK,' she gave in. She guessed it must get lonely for her mum at times with them all caught up in their own lives and careers. Since her dad had died it seemed as if her mother had only half a life. Her parents had been so close, a great couple, always together, talking and laughing and arguing and making up, mad about each other. Her mother didn't complain but they all knew how much she missed him and how lonesome and sad she got at times. To lose the man you love must be the hardest thing.

'I can't stay too late though, Mum,' she warned her, 'as I've some work to do when I get home.'

'That's fine, Grace; I'm going to my book club meeting with Kitty later, at about nine.'

Pulling up on the square Grace couldn't believe the amount of equipment around the place. There was a huge builders' skip blocking the footpath outside the O'Connors' old place. The workmen were gone, finished for the day, and she stopped outside the house, curious, trying to read the application notice attached to the gate. She hoped that they were not damaging the original door and architrave or the skirting boards. The planning application was for quite a lot of work and she wondered if some of it had already begun, which was technically illegal. Since the house was obviously empty she decided to take a look. She walked along the gravel path and up the granite steps. Leaning across the wrought-iron railing she stared into the front living-room window, noticing straight away that the magnificent Adam fireplace was missing. What kind of savage would take out one of the finest design features in the house and get rid of it! she fumed. God knows what else this new owner was doing to the place, she thought as she tried to look at the ceiling plasterwork.

'Can I help you?' asked a male voice.

Embarrassed, she turned around to face a man in a navy business suit carrying a laptop. Tall and heavy-set, his dark hair in need of a cut, he didn't appear particularly friendly.

'I was just having a look at the house,' she said in her best professional manner, pulling herself up to her full height, aware that technically she was trespassing.

'Everything is in order, I can assure you.'

'I would hardly say that,' she said frostily. 'The magnificent Adam fireplace that was one of the house's main features has been removed. It's a disgrace.'

'And you are?'

'I'm Grace Ryan. My family live in number twenty-three.'

'I'm Mark McGuinness, the owner,' he said slowly looking her up and down as if she were the local nosy parker out snooping. He seemed to be mentally pricing her black work suit, expensive taupe-coloured shirt and Italian black soft leather shoes.

Grace cursed silently to herself. She was standing on his property and had most definitely crossed the boundary line of professional behaviour.

'I'm actually an architect and I work in Thornton's,' she explained, seeing he was not the least impressed by her professional opinion.

'I always use Linden O'Donnell,' he replied. 'They've worked on most of my projects.'

Nothing he could have said would have annoyed Grace more. Everyone in Dublin knew that Graham O'Donnell had worked for Thornton's ten years ago, and had left saying he wanted to set up a more innovative practice, taking two or three major clients with him. His firm was now their biggest rival.

'I'm curious as to why you would take out the fireplace and destroy one of the house's best architectural features!' she continued defiantly.

'This is my house now,' he reminded her, 'and I can do with it what I want.'

'But that doesn't mean you can flout standard planning regulations,' she argued, her temper rising.

'Miss Ryan, I can assure you that no laws have been broken,' he said. 'While the house is listed, it doesn't have a total preservation order on it.'

'Are you telling me that you have dumped that Georgian fireplace?'

'Relax, the fireplace is in good hands,' he assured her. 'There was a crack in it which I'm having repaired by an expert and then it's going to be stored safely so no further damage can occur to it during the renovation.'

'I see,' said Grace, suddenly feeling very foolish. 'I'm sorry, it's just that I can't stand watching these type of old houses being destroyed.'

'It is not my intention to destroy anything,' he replied angrily.

'All I meant was that a beautiful old house like this is in need of a little TLC,' she said, becoming ever more aware of his expensive suit, gold cufflinks and watch — and the amazing flecks of green in his brown eyes.

'The house is a wreck!' Mark McGuinness said flatly. 'It needs a great deal of work — new heating, plumbing, wiring, part roofing and a kitchen, decent bathrooms and a proper master bedroom. And I'm putting a large extension on to the back.'

Why would someone like him buy a wreck of a place unless he intended making a fat profit on it!

'I believe the investment will be worth it and should add substantial value to the property,' he said, almost reading her mind.

'Excuse me,' Grace said politely. 'I have to go. My mother is expecting me for dinner.' She cringed, it sounded pathetic, as if she were some old maid going home to her elderly mother. What must he think! She could see the laughter in his eyes. Embarrassed, she tried to manoeuvre past him and escape.

'Are you Sarah Ryan's sister, by any chance?' he asked, stepping out of the way.

'Yes,' she mumbled, wondering how on earth he knew Sarah. Her sister had never mentioned meeting him.

'You would never guess that you two were sisters,' he said casually. 'You're completely different.'

Grace reddened as it was clear which one he preferred.

'Enjoy your meal,' he said sarcastically as he turned away from her and began to open his front door.

Grace had worked herself into a fury by the time she found her mother busy listening to the news on the radio as she cooked.

'That McGuinness man is so bloody arrogant and full of himself!' she said. 'He thinks he's better than everyone else. He's just storming ahead gung-ho stripping the O'Connors' house and putting in everything new!'

'It's his house,' her mother reminded her. 'Detta and Tom had let it go to rack and ruin. You should have seen the damp patch on the back bedroom wall and the basement is full of an awful mould! God knows how Detta ever put a foot in it.'

'I was talking to him outside and he's so rude and unfriendly!'

'Well, you two certainly got off on the wrong foot.' Her mother was clearly puzzled. 'I think he's rather attractive and Sarah likes him too. He drove her to the Vincent de Paul shop in Ranelagh to get rid of the O'Connors' old boxes and bags of clothes and stuff.'

Grace set the table for two as her mother talked.

'He's very eligible – by all accounts wealthy, and he's single,' continued Maggie.

'Mum!' she protested.

'I'm just saying that Mark McGuinness is the kind of man a girl should be interested in,' she said, passing her a plate of creamy risotto. 'Maybe I should invite him to lunch or dinner here.'

'Don't you dare,' warned Grace, knowing full well her mother was likely to ignore her.

'He's our new neighbour, after all, and we should make an effort to be friendly. Besides, he might enjoy a bit of company and it would be a chance for you and Sarah and Anna to meet him properly.'

'Mum, we don't even know if he's going to move into the house yet. He could be planning to resell it in a year's time.'

'I doubt it, I see him in and out of the place most days and if you ask me he's here to stay.'

Grace sighed. Her mother had turned into some kind of crazy Irish mammy obsessed with marriage and weddings and assessing men's potential 'husbandability' as Sarah called it. All she wanted was for one of them to get married. She only hoped she wouldn't set her sights on that awful McGuinness man for one of them.

The risotto was perfect, and Grace found herself having second helpings as her mother regaled her with the search for a new tenant, her worries about Oscar Lynch's worsening arthritis, and the bloody awful book that they were reading at her book club.

'We all hate it, it's dire and depressing but very literary!'

73

she explained. 'Still, we'll argue about it, have a few glasses of wine and a bit of a chat after. Maybe you should think of joining a book club, Grace. It's fun!'

'Mum, I don't have the time,' she protested. 'I never get the chance to read unless I'm on holiday.'

'Then maybe you should make the time, Grace. Seriously, there's more to life than work. If you wanted to join our book club I could ask the girls if they'd mind.'

The thought of sitting around with her mother and Aunt Kitty and their middle-aged friends discussing the kind of books they read filled her with horror.

'Mum, I am *not* joining a book club!'

'It was only a suggestion,' Maggie said, starting to clear away the plates. 'I worry about you being on your own and working so hard. You're in Thornton's all day and then you go home to that empty apartment. It must get lonely. I know you have a busy life and a wonderful career, but I do know what it is like to be lonely, Grace.'

'Honest, Mum, I don't know what you're talking about. I don't get time to be lonely. And besides, you're forgetting I've got a boyfriend.'

'Of course you have,' said her mother, raising her eyebrows slightly and barely able to mask the disapproval in her voice as she went to put on the kettle and make two mugs of tea.

Grace decided there was no point getting into an argument with her. Her mother had had it in for Shane ever since he'd missed that stupid Sunday lunch and Orla and Liam's party. She had no idea of the pressure on a relationship when you both worked long hours and had so many commitments and project deadlines to meet.

By the time she returned to her empty flat an hour later, Grace had decided that her mother had in fact gone mad. Imagine wanting to invite Mark McGuinness to eat in their home! She was such a schemer. She'd phone Anna and Sarah and warn them what Maggie was up to. She checked her messages first, disappointed that there was no word from Shane.

And as for her mother's suggestion that she was lonely and should join a book club . . . it was just daft. At almost thirty years of age she certainly didn't need her mother meddling in her affairs.

Chapter Eleven

Irina Romanowska started off the morning with a three-hour early shift in the Spar shop, near the estate where she lived, unpacking newspapers and milk cartons and bread deliveries as the first customers trooped in. Mr Delaney, the owner, was in bad form as he'd had a row with his wife. Irina made him a mug of tea and put an extra spoonful of sugar in it, hoping that it would sweeten him up so he wouldn't growl at his customers or for that matter at her.

Afterwards, having taken off her blue and white uniform and fixed her short blond hair, she got the bus into the centre of town and then took the Luas tram to the stop near where Mrs Ryan lived. She had worked for Maggie Ryan since she had first come to Dublin, doing ironing and a bit of cleaning on Wednesday mornings. In the afternoon she worked in the Dunnes' big house in Rathgar. She hoped that Caroline Dunne was out today as the thirty-two-year-old tended to follow her around checking everything and inspected her work every day before letting her go.

Mrs Ryan was in the kitchen and made her sit down and join her for a cup of tea before she started.

'Did you have a nice weekend?' asked the Irish woman as she passed Irina the jug of milk and a packet of chocolate chip cookies.

'I worked on Saturday in Spar shop but on Sunday I was free.'

'We all need our day of rest, Irina.'

'I had a rest, because on Saturday night I went dancing and to the pub with my friends.'

'Did you meet any nice Irish boys?' quizzed Maggie Ryan, curious.

Irina shook her head and laughed. All mothers asked the same question. 'My friend Marta said that there are no nice Irish boys, or maybe we just have not met them.'

'I think sometimes my daughters might agree with you.'

Irina liked Mrs Ryan's daughters. Sarah, the youngest, had a little girl called Evie, who sometimes came to play when she was working. She found Irish people were for the most part friendly and welcoming to strangers like her.

'On Sunday, I went to mass in the big church with Father Peter who says the Polish mass. All the Polish people go,' she explained

'Well, it's good to hear someone is using the churches!' replied Maggie Ryan, thinking of all the young Irish people that had abandoned mass-going. Even her own daughters were not half as religious as they should be.

'Then we go for lunch, a big lunch in the restaurant near the hotel at the airport. Two of my friends work in the restaurant and they organize with the owner to have a special lunch for Polish friends. I like to meet so many of my own people and afterwards we go to listen to music in a big pub in Temple Bar.'

'It's good that you are enjoying yourself, Irina, and not feeling too homesick for your own country.'

'I do miss my father and mother and my two brothers,' she admitted, thinking of her family at home, 'and some of my friends, but Ireland is a good country – good for Polish people, I think.'

'Well, I'm glad to hear that.' Maggie smiled as she got up from the table. 'I'm going into town to meet my sister Kitty for lunch, her daughter's getting married in a few months' time and we're going to have a look around the shops for some clothes for the wedding.'

'In my country weddings are a big party.'

'It's the same here, we all get dressed up for the day and spend a fortune,' laughed Maggie. 'Some day it will be your turn, Irina, and you will be such a beautiful bride.'

'But I don't even have a boyfriend,' Irina confessed.

'Give it time and that will change,' teased Maggie.

'Do you think so?' she asked, suddenly serious.

'Of course,' said her employer. 'There's a man out there who is the perfect match for you, it's just a question of meeting him!'

Irina smiled. Maggie Ryan with her romantic notions was nearly as bad as her mother!

'Irina, I have a new tenant moving in on Friday evening,' she explained a few minutes later as she pulled on her jacket and searched for her car keys, 'and I want the place sparkling clean for him.'

'Of course,' she agreed. She had already scrubbed and hoovered the mews building a few weeks ago after that crowd of nurses had left the place in a state. Irina had been appalled at the amount of rubbish they had left behind, but was delighted when Maggie Ryan had given her extra money for all her hard work.

'It's still clean after the great job you did the last time so can you just give it a bit of a polish and make sure the kitchen and bathrooms are sparkling as first impressions are important.'

Irina liked the privacy of the small mews house and envied whoever was going to move in. She hoovered the house first, and then made sure the stainless-steel worktops and sink and tiles were pristine as she worked, before turning her attention to cleaning the main bathroom and the en-suite upstairs. The beds were made and she polished the mirrors, listening to the radio as she worked. Maggie Ryan was nice to work for and let her watch TV when she was ironing or listen to music as she cleaned. Caroline Dunne wouldn't even let her turn on her plasma TV or her stereo. She would quit working for that awful woman as soon as she could. There was plenty of work out there for a hard-working Polish girl.

It was over a year since she had moved to this country. Like so many other Polish people, she had heard about the Celtic Tiger and Ireland, the small country with the big economy where anyone who was willing to work could make lots of money. That sounded good, and the fact that it was a

Catholic country had persuaded her mother and father to let her go to Dublin.

It was more than money, however, that had driven her here – it was a broken heart. She had wasted five years of her life going out with handsome Edek Stasiak, a technician who worked with her in the small computer factory in Łódź, assembling the tiny components for the micro-processors they manufactured. They were madly in love with each other and she often imagined the day that they would get married. Then Edek had told her he was in love with someone else, a girl called Krysia who worked as a hairdresser. Utterly heart-broken, Irina had shouted and screamed and kicked him in the shins, packed her bags and fled to Dublin. The last she had heard from her mother was that Edek was planning a summer wedding to his hairdresser.

There was no point dwelling on the past, she reminded herself as she gathered up her cleaning things. It could not be undone. Satisfied that she had done a good job and that the house was perfect for the new tenant, she locked the mews door and made her way back to Maggie's kitchen.

Chapter Twelve

After her long day at work Irina was exhausted as she crossed over the road in the huge estate to the small three-bedroom house on Riverstown Avenue that she shared with five friends. Some days and nights there were nine or ten of them crowded into the small living room or trying to cook in the cramped kitchen or wash and dry clothes. They were all Polish, and under the small roof tried to pretend that they were still living in Kraków or Łódź or Gdańsk, united by a sense of camaraderie and nationalism. They all had jobs and were determined to earn as much as possible in this rich country. Some planned to work and save and return to Poland to set up their own businesses and buy property in their home country; others wanted a fresh start and to integrate with these Irish people, do well and make a living here. Irina wasn't exactly sure which category she fell into yet.

She was sure, however, she was not going to return to Poland with her tail between her legs and no money. The next time she saw her mother she would buy her nice clothes, a new television and pay for her to go on a holiday. As for Edek, when he saw her walking down Piotrkowska Street she would be stylish and well groomed and speak English perfectly and be far too busy to stop and even talk to him. Let him marry that girl Krysia if that's what he wanted!

Inside the house she slipped upstairs and changed out of her work clothes. Marta was lying stretched out on the lower bunk fast asleep, her breath soft as she snored slightly. She'd had an early start working at the big hospital and had obviously just come off a long shift. Irina moved silently, trying not to disturb her, pulling on a pair of comfy tracksuit bottoms and a snug red fleece top. The smell of cooking drifted upstairs and her stomach growled with hunger. She'd had cups of coffee and toast all day in the houses she'd cleaned but longed for a reviving meal. On the way home she'd stopped off and bought pork mince in the butcher shop near the corner of the estate. Tonight she was going to make meatballs and potatoes and red cabbage.

'Irina, you want a tea or coffee?' offered Jan Kaninski when she appeared at the kitchen door.

'No, thanks, I'm just going to make some dinner.'

Four people sat at the kitchen table eating pasta and a tomato sauce, a staple of the house. Two of them she had never seen before.

'What are you making?' he asked, curious.

'Pork meatballs and potatoes.'

'With paprika?'

'Yes, of course,' she laughed. 'You want some?'

A big grin appeared on his face. Jan and herself came from

the same district in Łódź Their parents had known each other for years. An electrician, he was married with two small boys and had been driven to Ireland in the hope of earning enough to purchase a home for his family. A year or two working on the big construction sites scattered all around Dublin, building apartments and shopping centres and offices, and then he would be able to return home, having earned enough to buy or build a fine house of their own and set up that small contracting business he had always dreamed of. He missed his wife Renata, and their two boys Kryzs and Olek, maybe next year they would join him. Every night, without fail, he phoned them. He missed his family so much and he really missed good Polish home-cooking.

'Jan, you wash that pot from the spaghetti and I'll get cooking,' she promised, taking a big white mixing bowl from the cupboard. She would save some for Marta too. Her friend might be hungry when she woke up; otherwise she could have it tomorrow.

The one thing about living in this house, she thought as she shaped the mince and flour and onions into balls, you would never be lonely or complain of silence. There was always someone talking or watching the big silver television or listening to the radio or phoning someone. It was like living in a train station with people in and out and coming and going all the time. Sometimes she longed for peace and quiet at the end of the day.

Jan had tipped her off about this problem and she had bought a packet of ten yellow ear plugs in the chemist's. With half the household rising at the crack of dawn to work

83

in hospitals and offices and building sites the chance of sleeping after five thirty a.m. was slim.

'Did I tell you Olek is going to play the part of a little monkey in his school's production of *Noah's Ark*?'

'A monkey? That's fun. You must be so proud. When is the play?'

'Four weeks' time.'

Irina could sense the pain in Jan's voice. He would miss it for he was not returning home till the end of August for a two-week holiday.

'Renata will take photos, send them to you.'

'I know. She is a good wife. I have a good family. I am a fortunate man.'

'Yes.' She smiled. 'Very fortunate.'

The meatballs were delicious and Irina fended off the greedy attention of the other householders as she served up.

'They smell delicious,' pleaded Josef, a bricklayer from Piła who shared the room with Jan. 'Just a little taste . . .'

'No!' she laughed as Jan passed him up a forkful of the spicy meat and sauce.

'Better even than my mother's,' cajoled Josef, his big eyes glistening in the hope of persuading her to ask him to sit down and join them.

Marta appeared downstairs wearing her big pink dressing gown. Ignoring Josef, Irina made her sit down. She grabbed another plate from the shelf and served her some warm food. She had worked overtime all week with no day off.

'So I work hard, I earn the big money and then I go home. Then there will be time for resting and sleeping!'

'That was so good,' beamed Jan, licking his lips. 'As good as my Renata's but don't tell her ever I said so!'

'Thank you,' added Marta, clearing all the food on her plate too.

Irina smiled. She had a little left for tomorrow when she returned home from the Spar shop where she worked late on a Thursday night. She would put the meatballs away in the fridge with her name written clearly on the container, otherwise Josef or one of the other men would just eat them. Someone had a DVD of a Polish game show and the latest two episodes of her favourite soap *M jak miłość* and once she had washed up she would join the throng in the sitting room to watch the continuing story of the Mostowiak family.

She yawned as she lowered herself on to the multicoloured couch, squeezing in between a skinny girl called Justnya and Piotr Boczkwoski and his girlfriend. Her body ached with exhaustion but she didn't want to just go straight to bed after working all day. Caroline Dunne had been even more demanding than usual and complained that she had not cleaned the shower in the main bathroom properly and made her redo it. At least she'd been paid, cash in hand, but she was in two minds whether to turn up next week or not. Watching the TV, for a short while she imagined she was back in her own place, in her own town listening to the gossip and chat around her.

Irina stared at the figures on TV. She laughed as on screen the contestants battled it out for the chance to win a thousand euros and a trip to London. Everyone wanted to win something. Be a winner. Yet life here was tougher than she had imagined: everything was so expensive – rent, food, the bus and Luas and trains – and yet every day more and more of her countrymen seemed to be coming to Ireland, living in rented accommodation in Dublin, Cork, Galway and Wexford. There were many stories of Polish people being successful; buying houses and property and shops and setting up businesses. Some day she would be successful too. Some day her broken heart would mend and she would forget the name Edek Stasiak, and fall in love again!

Chapter Thirteen

Ignoring the pelting rain Sarah grabbed an umbrella as she and Evie ran helter-skelter down the garden path to the mews. The new tenant was due and her mother had suddenly been called away to the funeral of an old family friend in Wicklow and had asked her to be there instead for the handover.

'Don't worry about money or anything like that,' she reassured her daughter, 'but just make sure you give Angus two sets of keys and show him how to work the heating and the water immersion and the alarm panel.'

'Will do,' said Sarah, who was curious to meet this Scottish guy her mother had been telling her so much about. His job designing computer games sounded great, really fun, but he was probably one of those computer nerds who never switched off.

Evie played around the living room and kitchen as Sarah pulled the curtains and did her best to make the place look cosy considering it was such a wet miserable night. She had a welcome bag of essentials with tea and coffee, milk, sugar, butter, bread and biscuits and had flicked on the heating to warm the place up. She loved this house. Her sister Grace had done an amazing job in terms of the simple design and making sure it captured light from all directions. Upstairs she checked the bedrooms quickly before racing with Evie to answer the doorbell.

'Who are you?' asked the lilting Scottish accent.

'I'm Evie,' her daughter said, introducing herself to the stranger.

There was a very wet young man at the door trying to balance a massive box in his hands in the doorway. Embarrassed, Sarah ushered him in.

'I just need to find somewhere to put my computer down,' he explained.

She directed him to the rectangular dining table. 'I'm Maggie's daughter, Sarah,' she said shaking his hand once it was free. 'Mum had to go to a funeral and asked me to let you in.'

He grinned. 'And I'm Angus Hamilton.'

Wow! He was just the kind of guy she always fancied: a little taller than her, skinny, with spiky hair and the very faintest tracing of a beard. He was wearing jeans and a leather jacket and boots. But it was his eyes that got her, big and dark and soulful.

'I'll just grab one more bag from the car; I can get the rest when the deluge is over.'

'Take the umbrella,' she advised, watching him disappear along by the hedge.

By the time he came back with a backpack and a flat screen

for his computer she had put the kettle on. She was dying to hear more of that lovely Scottish accent.

He dumped his jacket on the expensive metal coat stand beside the front door and paced around the downstairs.

'This place looks even better than I remember.'

'Glad you like it.' She smiled. 'I brought you over a few welcome things like sugar and milk and coffee.'

'That's kind of you,' he said, running his fingers through his damp hair.

'We only live across the garden in the basement, and Mum wanted to make sure that you were OK.'

'I appreciate it,' he said seriously as she walked him around the rest of the house and gave him all the necessary instructions.

'The kettle's boiled if you fancy a cup of tea or coffee,' she offered, hoping he wouldn't think her too pushy.

'Only if you two stay and join me,' he said, opening the pack of chocolate biscuits and offering one to Evie.

Sarah finished off the coffee and carried the two mugs over to the black leather couches where he was busy telling Evie all about the Loch Ness monster.

'She told me that she likes dinosaurs,' he explained.

Over the next hour Sarah found herself filling him in on the local shops and telling him about all the hot night spots and good restaurants to go to in Dublin that her sisters and friends regularly frequented.

'It's good to get recommendations,' he teased, 'but surely that can't beat trying out the places yourself!'

'I do go out sometimes,' she protested, 'but with having Evie to mind, it's not as easy.'

'So it's hard for you and Evie's dad to get out?'

'No, that's not it,' she said truthfully. 'He lives in Italy so we rarely see each other.'

'I'm sorry.'

'No need to be,' she said firmly. 'I've got Evie and that's all that matters. What about you?'

'I'm twenty-seven and from the parish of Barclay in Edinburgh. I have one sister and two brothers and studied engineering, specializing in computer systems, which I now design, along with games – which are a sort of sideline and hobby of mine,' he added mockingly, his dark eyes fixed on her face. 'And I have a lovely girlfriend Megan whom you will no doubt meet when she comes to visit me in a few weeks' time.'

'Great,' she replied, trying to hide her plunging dis-appointment. He was too good to be true. Someone like Angus was bound to have a girlfriend in his life. Her mother was right, though, he was a nice guy and she hoped that at least they could be friends.

'Hey, Angus, I'd better go,' she exclaimed. 'Time to get Evie to bed or she'll be like a bear tomorrow. She's going to a birthday party at the Puppet Theatre. I said I'd give the other mum Jess a hand as she's bringing twelve six-year-olds!'

'Sounds like fun!' he said and she could tell he actually meant it. 'I'm big into those kind of places myself!'

* * *

Sitting up at her own computer later that night typing a story she was making up for Evie about a dog and listening to the lashing rain and gusting winds outside, Sarah found herself genuinely relieved to know that Angus was only a minute or two away.

Chapter Fourteen

Grace checked the table one last time. The ultra-modern Finnish cutlery, linen napkins, her good crystal glasses, Meadows and Byrne candles, two stems of green leaves with a showy splash of red ginger stems, all set out perfectly on her dark walnut table with its classic elegant lines.

As the tantalizing smell of food wafted from the kitchen she stifled her hunger pangs, knowing she didn't want to spoil her appetite by snacking and tasting too much of the meal she was preparing. There were salmon fishcakes, Shane's favourites, which she had shaped with the cooked fish and egg and breadcrumbs and seasoning, all ready to heat and serve on a small bed of tossed leaves. To follow there was fillet of pork done in calvados with apple rings and a baked mixture of sweet potato and carrots. For dessert she had made a coffee cake. It had turned out perfectly and sat temptingly on her big blue ceramic plate. The room was bathed in low candlelight, Sinatra was playing in the background, an expensive Merlot was already open and a Chablis was chilling in the fridge. They say the way to a man's heart is a good home-cooked meal – well tonight she hoped that it was true as she really wanted to impress Shane. She enjoyed entertaining, having friends around for supper and drinks, but this meal was strictly dinner à deux.

Yesterday had been Shane's thirty-fifth birthday and she'd been annoyed when he told her that he was going for a business dinner with a client and the invitation had not been extended to include her.

'We can celebrate it another time,' he'd told her as if it wasn't that important. Well, they would just have to have a private birthday party, she'd decided, and had cooked his favourite meal, splurged out on some good wine and had left the office early to ensure she had plenty of time for preparation. She'd been delighted when he had jumped at her offer of an intimate dinner for two instead of eating out. The fact he was happy to stay in for a romantic evening was certainly a step in the right direction.

She'd known Shane for years. He'd been ahead of her in college, the golden boy, an architect who could do no wrong. On qualification she had done a three-year stint in Hunt Brown, specializing in reclaiming derelict buildings in some of the city's run-down areas, turning old mills, factories and churches into bright innovative living spaces. Approached by Thornton's, one of the city's biggest and brightest architectural practices, she had accepted a job offer from Derek Thornton to come and join the firm. Her path once more crossed with Shane O'Sullivan as they now worked for the same firm. Shane was living with a stunning-looking girl called Ruth Liddy, who was a journalist for the *Irish Times*, while Grace was happily dating an eager young barrister called Fintan Dywer.

Shane was always professional, polite and charming and when they had been paired two years later to work on a new hotel project in Barcelona for one of their big Irish clients, she was delighted. However, a few weeks into the job, after a pretty drunken night in the historic Els Quatre Gats restaurant, as they held hands and walked through Barcelona's Barri Gòtic in search of a taxi-cab, Shane had admitted that Ruth and he had broken up a few months earlier and that Ruth had taken off travelling around South America. Grace had read a few of her pieces in the *Irish Times* entitled 'Footloose and Fancy Free', envying Ruth's ability to just pack up and go travelling and exploring on her own.

'So much for being a happy couple,' he said drunkenly. 'Ruth and I just wanted different things!'

Grace had consoled him and told him that her relationship with Fintan had also bitten the dirt a few months previously and that he was now dating a sexy young junior counsel called Hilary.

'That Fintan must be a stupid bastard!' he said, ordering two more drinks back in the hotel bar. By three a.m., helping his six-foot frame into the lift and upstairs into the bed in his room, Grace had found herself utterly besotted.

The next day he had greeted her at breakfast with a red rose and an apology but once his hand had touched hers there was no going back. They had cancelled all meetings for the rest of the day and crept away to her very large double bed with its view of the marina. They revelled in each other's bodies, both equally surprised by the depths of the passion they were experiencing. In the city of Gaudí they explored the Güell Park and Montjuïc, arguing and laughing constantly over buildings and art, Shane buying her a crazy painted stone lizard to remind her of their time together.

Returning to Dublin, they had begun a relationship, enjoying romantic dinners which always ended up back at her place – her stone lizard Dalí gazing at her from the balcony as they made love. Grace was happier than she had ever been before and thought how lucky they were to have found each other at a good time in their lives. OK, so they weren't heady teenagers cracked out about each other but she did love him and want him to be a part of her life. Shane was charming and handsome and intelligent: everything she could want in a partner. When he told her that he didn't want to rush into marriage she had nodded understandingly, saying there was no hurry. She was prepared to wait. The very odd time she was free to babysit her little niece Evie she reassured herself that one day marriage and motherhood would happen. There was nothing to say that she couldn't have it all: career, love, children – a perfect life, balanced and beautiful

She was fixing her hair when the phone went; it was Shane telling her he had been a bit delayed.

'Everything's ready,' she pleaded. 'Don't be long.'

'Grace, I'll be there when I can.'

She'd waited, and waited, opening the chilled Chablis and nibbling a packet of almond nuts. The food would be ruined at this rate. All she could do was turn the oven down low and curl up on the couch to wait for him.

When he eventually arrived he had kissed her absent-mindedly. Grace fussed around as she made him sit and begin to eat. He scarcely mentioned the fishcakes and avoided her eyes as he ate the pork.

'Happy birthday, darling,' she toasted him after topping up his glass with a little more wine.

'Hey, go easy, I can't stay, I have an early morning meeting.'

She couldn't believe it. Surely he could relax for one night? But she was determined not to start an argument and instead busied herself with plates and dishes as she made coffee and carried his cake to the table.

It was her mother's recipe and delicious. Irresistible, even. Shane just pushed it around his plate. He looked flushed, ill at ease; perhaps he was coming down with something?

She had his birthday present wrapped ready and was just about to give it to him when he started speaking.

'Grace, we need to talk.'

Her heart skipped a beat. She stared at him. He seemed serious.

'It's been great the two of us – we're a perfect pair, we both like the same things, think the same way, value beautiful things. We've been good for each other, made each other happy . . .'

Grace held her breath waiting for more, for him to say how much he loved and needed her and wanted her to be a permanent part of her life.

'It's been fun. You're a great girl. Listen, this is so awkward, I don't know what to say . . .'

The conversation was certainly not going the way she expected. She had never seen him so tense and uncomfortable before.

'The thing is, Grace, and there's no getting around it . . . it's . . . Ruth and I are back together and want to give our relationship another go.'

'Back together?' she gasped, disbelieving. 'I thought Ruth was away!'

'She was, but she's home again. We bumped into each other in town after she came back from Honduras.'

'So you've been seeing her?' she asked, her heart heavy with the news. The missed dates and weird work schedule suddenly made perfect sense.

'Believe me, Grace, I never meant it to happen, but just seeing her and talking to her again made me realize that there was still something between us.'

'But it did happen,' she said, concentrating on the table and candles and flowers, the whole bloody lot of it, trying to escape his eyes.

'Ruth and I are getting back together,' he said firmly, his expression serious, his blue eyes unwavering.

'Shane, you told me that you and Ruth were totally finished, that it was over. I would never have got involved with you otherwise.'

'I know,' he said. 'I didn't expect to ever see her again, let alone make up with her. I'm sorry, Grace.'

Grace felt sick to her stomach, overwhelmed.

'I never meant to hurt you,' he said, touching her shoulder with his long fingers, 'but Ruth . . .'

'I don't want to hear one more bloody word about Ruth!' she exploded. 'Now get out of my apartment. You're seeing somebody else which means we've absolutely nothing more to say to each other!'

'I never meant it to end like this,' he said contritely as he lifted his jacket off the chair and grabbed his keys.

Turning her back on him she tried to stay in control as she gazed at the lights of the city and the dark swirl of water and sky below and above her. She was suspended in a weird sense of disbelief and frozen time as Shane left.

'You bastard,' she screamed ineffectually after him as the front door clicked shut.

She'd just been dumped. She wasn't good enough to measure up to her boyfriend's ex. Gutted, she kicked off her shoes and flung herself on to the cream leather couch and began to sob. Her life was a mess. Spotting the platinum designer cufflinks that she'd had specially designed for him she flung the expensive box across the room as she reached for the white wine, topping up her glass. What was she going to do? She couldn't imagine her life without him. How could she face Thornton's, see him in the office, work on projects with him? Perhaps everyone already knew he was back with Ruth. What an absolute fool she'd been. She tipped some more of the chilled wine into her glass. He had probably gone straight to be with Ruth in his apartment in Blackrock. She could imagine them both laughing at her. She couldn't stand it, couldn't stand the humiliation and the utter loss of face. She should have listened to her mother. All along Maggie had tut-tutted about him not being right for her. Or to Sarah, who had felt she was foolish to get involved with someone she worked so closely with; even Anna, who had declared him a smooth bastard the minute she'd met him. She wanted to curl up in a blanket and die. Never go out again, never admit what an absolute eejit she had been to believe in him and trust him.

She opened another bottle of wine from the fridge before collapsing on the couch again, overwhelmed with a sense of panic. It was so shitty getting dumped! Shane and the life she'd thought they might have together had abruptly vanished. Like a mirage – just disappeared. She had to face the truth that Shane didn't love her, probably never had.

Stumbling to her feet, she crossed the living room and went into the bedroom. There she grabbed the stupid lizard off the bedside table and carried him all the way back out to the balcony. He stared at her stony-faced with his big lizard eyes as she leant against the metal railings. Taking a breath she threw Dalí into the murky waters below. She remained on the balcony in the darkness, watching him disappear from sight.

A long while later she tried her sister Anna's number but the phone was switched off. There was no point phoning Sarah at this late hour and waking up Evie; even in her drunken state she knew it wouldn't be fair. Without thinking she found herself dialling the familiar number of home, the phone ringing for a few seconds.

'Yes?'

It was her mother's voice. She wondered how it was her mother always managed to sound so calm and reassuring at the end of the telephone line.

Chapter Fifteen

Maggie tossed and turned in the comfort of the king-sized bed which she had shared for more than twenty-seven years with Leo. She would never get used to sleeping alone, never. She still missed his bulk and warmth and warm breath and – even though it galled her to admit it – his awful snoring. She no longer had to prod him or poke him to beg him to stop but, oh, what she would have given to have Leo's body lying beside hers again. His empty side of the bed was a constant reminder of his absence.

Now at the end of the day she sought refuge in late-night TV or the pile of books on her bedside table, losing herself in the latest Joanne Harris, Maeve Binchy or Anita Shreve. Pictures on the screen and words on the page helped to chase away the loneliness that sometimes threatened to engulf her. How can a woman surrounded by children, friends and neighbours be lonely? she asked herself. Yet she was. She'd taken the happiness and comfort of her marriage so casually for granted. She envied couples like Detta and Tom who were devoted to each other and despite their age were ready to face the future in England together, and her sister Kitty and her husband Harry who despite arguments and a few rollercoaster years were a totally united couple and were now busy organizing her niece Orla's upcoming wedding. She just hated being on her own!

Since Leo's death she had learned to fit a lightbulb and rewire a plug, reboot their computer when it locked up, refit the brake lights in her car and sort out a dead battery and get the engine to start. Small but necessary things! She still cried with frustration when she found that she couldn't reach the top shelves where Leo had left things or was too scared to climb into her own attic to fetch the Christmas tree lights or a travel bag. During the day she kept going by keeping busy. Only alone at night did she give in to the fear and loneliness that at times plagued her. She often lay awake listening for the noises of mice, or burglars, or scary things she had never noticed when Leo lay beside her.

Tonight she was just starting to settle in to a nice relaxed state when she heard the phone ring. Who could be phoning her this late at night? God, something awful might have happened. Maybe Evie was sick and Sarah needed her! She reached for the phone immediately, trying to quell her anxiety.

'Yes?'

'Mum?'

'Grace!' It was so unlike her eldest daughter to phone at this hour and out of the blue. 'Are you all right? What's happened, pet?'

Her daughter sounded desperate, sniffing and holding her

breath in, trying to control herself just like when she was a little girl.

'Are you sick? Has there been an accident?' Maggie demanded, frantic, her mother's instinct kicking in.

'Mum, Shane and I have broken up. It's all over . . .' Grace gasped, then broke down, barely able to speak or breathe.

'Grace, is someone with you?'

'No, I'm on my own in the apartment. I'll always bloody well be on my own!'

'Do you want me to come over?' asked Maggie gently, already slipping out of bed.

'I want to come home, get out of this bloody place,' howled her daughter, totally losing control.

'Can you drive?' That was a stupid question, Maggie realized straight away, as Grace sounded as if she'd been drinking and was clearly overwrought. 'Listen, love, I'm only just getting ready to go to bed, I'll hop into the car and come and collect you. You just grab your things! I won't be long.'

'Thanks, Mum.' She sniffed. 'I'll be waiting for you.'

Maggie put down the phone then sat on the edge of the bed for a second, trying to collect her thoughts. It was one forty a.m. and Grace was drunk and in no fit state to be left on her own. Over the years Leo had usually been the one to answer distress calls from their offspring. He would lumber good-naturedly out of bed to collect them from a disco or late-night club or party. Now it fell to her. She ran into the en-suite bathroom and threw water on her face and then grabbed a pair of trousers and a navy fleece and pulled on a pair of socks and her driving shoes. Taking a second to pull a comb through her fair hair, she grabbed her handbag and left.

The old BMW engine burst smoothly into life as she drove down the road and headed into town. A shiny-eyed fox, out on a night's prowl, slunk out of her way.

Dublin at night was busy as always with crowds of young people milling about in the streets as they left the city's busy clubs and bars and restaurants. Taxis constantly relayed passengers across town and homewards. Maggie concentrated on the road, noticing the Garda checks on the way. She thanked God that Grace's apartment was at least close by as she crossed over the Liffey and neared the IFSC. The tall glass building where her daughter lived was only a stone's throw from the river, right in the heart of the city. Maggie scanned the street and managed to find a nice big parking space. She checked the car alarm was on before she approached the entrance lobby of River Buildings. She keyed in the code and took the lift to the sixth floor.

Grace opened the apartment door in an old T-shirt and what could have been a tracksuit bottom or pyjamas. She looked awful, red-eyed and snotty-nosed; her usual calm demeanour and poised exterior had totally vanished. She passed her mother a stuffed airport holdall and a plastic bag.

'Let's get out of here!' she pleaded.

Maggie pulled her close and took the bags as they walked to the car. She was tempted to ask about what had happened but since she still had to negotiate the dark late-night drive home she decided to keep the questions till they got to Pleasant Square.

'You poor little pet,' she consoled as Grace pulled tissues from the pack near the dashboard and sobbed like a five-year-old.

'Mum, he's such a shit! Such an unbelievable shit!'

Maggie murmured sympathetically but years of experience had taught her that agreeing that one of her daughter's best friends, teachers, boyfriends or lovers was a shit would always come back to haunt her once the squabbling pair had solved their differences and made up. Any harsh word used against the other would suddenly be dragged out and remembered. So even though Shane had always appeared completely unsuitable for her precious daughter this was not the time for her to say 'I told you so'.

'He's gone back with his old girlfriend!'

Maggie took a breath. That certainly was unexpected. A cold feeling of anger took hold in the pit of her stomach as she realized that Shane O'Sullivan had hurt her daughter deeply.

Grace leant her head against the car window, glassy-eyed, broken, as they neared the turn for Pleasant Square.

Maggie tried to conceal her dismay as she bustled around turning the key in the lock and making a big to-do of putting on the lights and the heating, treating Grace as if she was ill or an invalid who had just come home from hospital.

'I'll put on the kettle for a nice cup of tea,' she soothed, leading the way into the kitchen.

'Don't want tea!' protested her daughter heading for the fridge. 'There must be some wine or vodka here!'

'Do you think that's wise?'

'I'm fed up with being wise!' Grace said sarcastically, pulling a bottle of Chablis from the fridge. 'This should do nicely.'

Maggie said nothing as Grace wrestled with the corkscrew and then poured two glasses. She'd polished off a whole bottle of Baileys herself the night Leo had died.

'Come on, Mum! You have to have a drink with me.'

She was in no mood for a glass of wine at this stage of the night but could see Grace really wanted company. 'I'll have a small one then, but I'll still make some tea.'

Grace collapsed into a chair and sat hunched up sipping at the wine, looking utterly miserable.

'He came for dinner. It was going to be a special night – the works. The works is right,' she said bitterly. 'I was the one who got the works. He and Ruth have decided to get back together again.'

'That journalist girl? I thought she'd gone abroad.'

'Apparently she came back and they bumped into each other and have somehow kept bumping into each other; so when I thought he was working late or having dinner with clients over the past few weeks he was actually seeing her, catching up on old times, falling in love with Ruth all over bloody well again. Can you believe it?'

Maggie didn't know what to say. She could believe it. She could believe that a man would walk away from one woman into the arms of another without giving it barely a thought. Women had their hearts broken time after time by men who weren't even half good enough for them. Grace was beautiful and kind and far too good for the likes of someone like Shane who was clearly a womanizer and a cheat. Let that other girl have him! She was relieved that he was out of her daughter's life.

'I'm sorry, Grace, sorry he's hurt you so much.'

'Mum, what am I going to do without him?' her daughter asked despairingly, clutching the wine glass and slumping on the kitchen chair.

Maggie didn't know what to say. Grace would get over him. She mightn't want to hear that right now when she was caught up in the drama and upset of it but she was far better without a self-centred man like Shane O'Sullivan. But loss was always hard to get through.

'You will learn to forget him,' she urged. 'You have me and your sisters and your friends and lots of people to love you.'

'I feel such a fool,' she gulped. 'Such a stupid eejit! I should have copped on to what was going on!' She rambled on, talking all in a rush, one minute cross and angry, the next despairing. Maggie listened, made tea and toast and tried to get her daughter to drink and eat a little.

'How can I face going into work and seeing him in the office again? Everyone will know about us, about what's happened. They'll all think I'm such a loser.'

'Grace, you have done nothing wrong,' Maggie said firmly. 'You told me more than a hundred people work in Thornton's and I'm sure that most people are far too busy to even notice what's happened between you two.'

Grace made an attempt to try to finish off the wine bottle but Maggie poured herself a huge glass. She had no intention of drinking it but wanted to get her daughter to agree to go to bed instead of pacing up and down the kitchen as she was doing.

'Your old room is ready,' she hinted, taking in the red-rimmed blue eyes and the white, strained face. 'Maybe it's time you went to bed and slept a bit, pet. You look exhausted.'

'I am exhausted,' Grace said drunkenly.

'Then come on. We'll tidy here in the morning.'

She managed to cajole her daughter upstairs, thanking heaven she'd only freshened up the room a few days ago and had turned the radiator on before she left.

She was just about to get into bed herself when she realized that Grace had made a speedy exit and was in the family bathroom retching and puking. Poor thing! All she could do to help was hold her hair back and give her a cool soaked face flannel to wipe her face.

'It'll be all right, pet. You'll feel a bit better in the morning.'

The only consolation was that Grace would likely sleep for a few hours, putting the pain of the break-up on hold till she was calm and sober again. Maggie passed her a fresh pair of pyjamas and settled her into bed, leaving the door of the room ajar so that she could listen in case she was needed. She was relieved to see Grace curl up into her usual foetal position and fall asleep almost straight away, her pale, washed-out skin and fair hair pulled back into a scrunchie hairband making her look more like sixteen than nearly thirty years old.

'My poor baby,' Maggie murmured, kissing her forehead.

Maggie sat up in bed reading for the next few hours, wishing for Leo's calming presence, unable to doze till the early morning news on the radio came on, only then trusting herself to sleep a bit. A little heartbreak was nothing new when you have a family of daughters but this was different. Grace had really expected this relationship to work. Her eldest daughter wasn't used to failure, to things going wrong. She supposed there was one hell of a difference between what you hoped would happen when you're twenty than when you're thirty.

At nine a.m. she phoned Kate, Grace's secretary at Thornton's, and told her that Grace was ill and would not be in the office today. She sighed as she phoned Anna's number. If she had an early lecture she'd leave a message. Then once Evie had gone to school, she'd phone Sarah. If there was one time Grace needed her sisters it was now. Outsiders mightn't understand it but this was the one time her girls should stick together.

She checked on her a few times but Grace slept till nearly lunchtime, her face tight and tense, wrapped up in the duvet.

She'd cancelled her appointment for coffee with her old friend Sylvia claiming a headache, and busied herself tidying the kitchen and deadheading old roses in the pots at the back door.

'What's up, Mum?' asked Sarah, concern in her voice as she rounded the corner of the garden. 'You said it was something to do with Grace.'

'She's broken up with Shane.'

'Maybe it's just a fight or something,' suggested Sarah. 'You know how headstrong they both are.'

'No. It's definitely over. He's gone back to that old girl-friend of his.'

'Oh, poor Grace! How is she?'

'She's devastated. I collected her at about two o'clock this morning. She drank far too much wine and she's asleep upstairs.'

'Will I run up and talk to her?'

'No, let her sleep, she's exhausted.'

Maggie made a fresh pot of coffee as she and Sarah mulled over the vagaries of male behaviour and the havoc it wreaked on females.

'I'd kill any guy who strung Evie along like that!' Sarah threatened, her pretty face serious, her blue eyes unwavering.

Maggie suppressed a smile as it was exactly how she felt whenever anyone wounded one of her own precious off-spring. She'd thought that mother-lion instinct would have disappeared as her children grew up and needed her less, but she was amazed to discover that it was as strong as ever. She could have ripped Shane from head to toe for the pain he had caused her eldest daughter.

'He didn't deserve to have someone as lovely as Grace love him,' she said, relieved that he was out of her daughter's life.

Sarah nodded fiercely in agreement before having to rush off to get a few things from the shops before Evie got out from school.

'She's bringing a friend home and I promised to let them

make fairy cakes and decorate them. I need to get some icing sugar.'

Maggie smiled, remembering after-school baking sessions and the mess they created. 'Have fun, and tell Evie to save a bun for her granny.'

'I'll call in later to see Grace,' promised Sarah as she slipped out the kitchen door.

Maggie was reading the paper and eating some tuna and mayonnaise on toast when Grace finally appeared. She looked awful: white-faced, hair greasy, totally hungover as she filled a glass with cold water from the tap.

'Sit down, pet, and I'll make you a mug of coffee.'

Grace slid on to the kitchen chair. 'I'm sorry about last night, Mum, dragging you out and all that.'

'It's fine. That's what mothers are for.'

Grace stared blankly at the table and the wooden floor. 'I just can't believe it's over,' she repeated. 'I thought Shane was the one; the guy that I'd been waiting for, maybe my Mr Right!'

Maggie said nothing as she slipped her arms around her daughter and hugged her as if she were a small girl again. To her mind Shane O'Sullivan had never been Mr Right material.

'Grace, everyone makes mistakes and we don't always choose the right people to fall in love with,' Maggie said, trying to console her. However, she was determined that the next man in her daughter's life would be totally different. He would be reliable, trustworthy and kind, the type to sweep

110

Grace off her feet and want to marry her! A tall order, she supposed but if she had her way the next man Grace dated would be . . . the one.

Somehow she managed to coax her into eating a slice of toast and drink two cups of milky coffee.

'What am I going to do, Mum? What am I going to say to people?'

'You'll just tell them the truth, that Shane and this girl-friend are back together, that's all. And you'll get on with the rest of your life.'

Grace looked dubious, and Maggie wasn't surprised. She knew the reality and utter loneliness of finding yourself suddenly without a partner. Being alone was a nightmare. Despite having family and friends around her, Maggie knew far too much about being lonely and missing someone to pretend it wasn't going to be awful.

'What about a nice hot shower to freshen up?' she suggested. 'It'll make you feel better and then if you're up to it we could go for a little walk afterwards. A blast of sea breeze would do us both good.'

'I don't feel like a walk,' demurred Grace, sounding more and more like a disgruntled toddler.

After some persuasion, however, Grace had eventually given in and they walked Dun Laoghaire Pier together two hours later, muffled up against the sea breeze in warm fleece jackets. The wind caught their voices as seagulls whirled up above them and the yachts in the harbour marina bobbed up and down in the water, the clang of their rigging filling the air as the waves tossed them against their moorings. It was certainly bracing, a little bit more than Maggie had reckoned, but she could see Grace tilt her long face to the winds and inhale deeply, sucking in the energy and vigour of nature, her chin stuck out determinedly just as she had done when she was a little girl.

Chapter Sixteen

Retreating to bed again Grace took in the familiar scene of her old bedroom in Pleasant Square. She felt as if she was ten years old and right back where she'd started. Back to being a kid. Lying in the warmth of the small single bed with its springy old mattress and heavy quilt with the faded denim patterned cover she felt safe. She could pretend that she had never grown up and messed up her life so badly and that Shane O'Sullivan had never crossed her path. She looked at the natural pine wardrobe, chest of drawers and shelves around her. As a stroppy teenager she had argued with her dad about getting rid of the old mahogany wardrobe in the corner; she had wanted everything new and fresh so she could create her own look. Leo Ryan had given in and the room had been kitted out with pine furniture and bright paint. She had bedecked the walls with modern art prints and later with photographs of the work of architects Frank Gehry and Santiago Calatrava. This room had been her bolt hole, with her desk and bookshelves and make-up and clothes. A sign to 'Keep out' pasted on her door had proved little deterrent to her sisters who constantly invaded her private space. Yet now, heart sore and feelings numbed, she felt comforted lying here, surrounded by the familiar sounds of the house, her mother moving around below in the kitchen, the radio on, the breeze blowing through the leaves of the tall sycamore tree in the back garden. She snuggled up, wishing that she never had to leave this bed or this room, never had to brave the outside world ever again. Sometimes she longed to be a little girl instead of a grown-up. Hearing footsteps on the stairs she rolled over, pretending to be asleep, holding her breath as Evie entered the room.

'Sshh, your auntie is asleep.' It was her sister's voice.

'What's wrong with her?' quizzed Evie. 'Is she sick?'

'Sort of.'

'Did she get a tummy bug like Ashling? She puked on the floor in school today and it was yucky and Miss Roche had to clean it up.'

'No, not that sort of sick,' Sarah reassured her patiently, 'it's more that Grace feels sad about something. You'll understand it better when you are older.'

Grace kept her eyes tightly shut and held her breath as the two of them stood over the bed. Why couldn't they just feck off and leave her in peace?

'Mummy, has she got a pain in her tummy?'

'It's a different kind of pain.'

Curious, Evie bent down to examine her closely, her face hanging over hers. Grace tried to pretend she was asleep but her eyes flickered, suddenly catching those of her little niece.

'She's awake,' cried Evie, excitedly clambering on top of her in the bed.

'Sorry,' whispered Sarah, 'no peace for the wicked!'

'Come and give your poor aunty a big hug, I could sure do with one from my favourite girl.'

Evie, still in her school uniform, wrapped her arms tightly around her and squeezed.

'That makes me feel a whole lot better,' admitted Grace, realizing as she sat up that it was actually the truth.

'How are you?' asked Sarah gently, sitting on the side of the bed.

'Bashed and bruised and pretty hungover!'

Sarah sighed. 'Better to have loved and lost and all that.'

'Mum's favourite bloody saying,' Grace groaned, leaning up against the pillows. 'It drives me mad every time I hear it! She's already had me down Dun Laoghaire Pier in a gale-force wind trying to blow my troubles away – would that it was so easy!'

'Mum always walks the pier in time of family crisis,' Sarah reminded her. 'Don't you remember we were up and down it like yo-yos when I was expecting and after Maurizio and I broke up!'

'God, yes, I remember that.' Grace suddenly realized that her crisis paled into insignificance compared to Sarah's tumultuous love life.

Bored, Evie got up, playing with Grace's things that were scattered on the dressing table, discovering her measuring tape with a fancy light.

'Mummy, what's this for?' she asked, turning it over.

'It's for measuring things,' explained Sarah, 'and you should really ask Grace if you can play with it.'

'It's fine,' Grace said, wishing that she would never have to measure or make calculations or work in close proximity with Shane ever again. She watched as Evie pulled out the tape and began to measure the drawers, the chair and the desk systematically.

'Why don't you go down to Granny and get her to help you measure some things?' suggested her sister diplomatically.

'OK.' Evie grinned. She made for the bedroom door and went down the stairs.

As her footsteps receded, Grace turned to her sister. 'Sarah, what am I going to do about work? It's going to be a nightmare having to see Shane all the time.'

'You love Thornton's. Don't let seeing that so-and-so stop you working there,' her sister declared fiercely.

'I can't believe I've been such an absolute eejit. I should have guessed that there was something going on. Even the night of his birthday he couldn't go for dinner! I should have suspected he was seeing someone else but I didn't. I genuinely thought that he was obsessed with his career and working far too hard. Big fool me.'

'You trusted him, Grace. We believe the people we love; we trust them.'

Grace wondered how it was her youngest sister had become so mature and grown up and unselfish. Having Evie had changed her totally, making Sarah so protective of the small baby that she had to raise without a father that she had become wise and reflective beyond her years.

'He's been such a shit, lying to me, hiding what was going on with Ruth.'

'Well, then it's better for everyone that things are out in the open now.'

And so the conversation went on. Grace cried and cried for what seemed an age, Sarah sitting beside non-judgementally, handing her tissues and soothing her, putting her snotty hankies in the bin and passing her glasses of water.

'Grace, it's going to be OK. We're all here for you. Mum and Anna and me. Shane wasn't good enough for you. You deserve better.'

'That's what Mum keeps saying.' Grace sniffed. 'She's like a broken record about it.'

'Plenty more fish in the sea and all that!' Sarah risked a joke.

Grace smiled wearily. 'Honestly, I'll kill her if she says it one more time!' she sighed. 'Mum has no idea just how hard it is to meet a decent guy! I'm going to be thirty soon and the fact is that I might never meet someone.'

'Don't be stupid, Grace, guys always fancy you,' said Sarah loyally. 'You've your career and an apartment of your own and a car! I'll never be able to afford even a banger of a car at the rate things are going.'

'Sarah, you're the lucky one,' said Grace, suddenly feeling guilty. 'You have Evie. She's the most beautiful little girl in the world. I'll probably never even have a child, and end up a sad old maid living on my own.'

'Somehow, I doubt that.' Sarah tossed her long fair hair

117

back off her shoulder and snuggled up on the bed with her sister. They curled up together like when they were kids.

'Mum's making a stew,' Sarah warned her sister.

'Stew!'

'Beef with all the works. She was cutting up carrots and parsnip and onions down in the kitchen.'

'Oh God!'

'Got to feed a broken heart. You know Mum. She'll fuss and feed you and force you to get back on your feet. The thing is I'll probably end up doing the same with Evie when she gets dumped by some awful boy.'

Grace found herself actually laughing. 'That's scary.'

'You're going to be OK, honest,' Sarah reassured her, serious again. 'Listen, I'd better go down before Evie has Mum demented with the whole house measured.'

The smell of onions and the meaty stew wafted up the stairs. Grace had forgotten how hungry she was. Maybe she would get up and have dinner with the others. She checked her phone; all day long she'd been getting missed calls and texts from her friends. There was absolutely nothing from Shane. Deciding that he was no longer relevant in her life she deleted his number from her address book. But her hand had hovered over the number before she had firmly pressed the delete button.

Anna had called over after work armed with a giant bottle of Lucozade and a big bag of wine gums, Grace's childhood favourites, and insisted she give a blow-by-blow account of the disastrous dinner.

'Salmon cakes, pork with Calvados, cake!' Anna muttered fiercely. 'What a waste!'

When Grace got to the part where she had hurled the stone lizard off the balcony into the water, she suddenly found herself laughing out loud at the absurdity of it as her mother and sisters tried to control their own giggles.

'You should have thrown Shane in the bloody river!' teased Anna, her blue eyes blazing.

Sitting around the kitchen table later with Mum, Sarah, Evie and Anna, eating floury potatoes and plates of her mother's warming stew with its soft chunks of vegetables and rich sauce made her realize that even though one part of her life was a total screw-up her family were the best . . . the very, very best!

Chapter Seventeen

There was only so much comfort a body could take and after another two days of the Ryan family flapping around her like protective bodyguards and, eating her way through a constant round of homemade bread, scones, apple tart and sponge cake, Grace decided it was time to move back to her apartment and get back to work.

She cleared the remnants of the celebration meal into the bin, along with Shane's favourite cheese and the full-fat milk that he liked to have in his coffee as she cleaned the place. She'd return Shane's gift to the jewellers, and, doing a quick sweep of the apartment, bundled his two Quentin Tarantino DVDs, a bottle of Hugo Boss aftershave, a toothbrush, comb and a navy golf shirt into a carrier bag. She was tempted to donate them to charity but decided to hand them in at the office's reception desk instead. Niamh O'Halloran, one of her best friends, had sent her a succinct text: *F . . . him* before arriving at eight o'clock with Lisa, Claire and Roisin, some of her old school pals, to cheer her up. She knew the girls were trying to be supportive in her hour of need but she just wanted to get back to work, even if it meant meeting him.

Picking out her most expensive suit, a pair of Italian boots that she had bought in Milan and a classic white Quin and Donnelly shirt, she dressed quickly the next morning, determined to be in the office early, sitting at her drawing board long before Shane appeared.

Thornton's was housed in one of the most modern and iconic buildings in the city, built overlooking the docks, its ten-storey steel and glass corner structure catching the sunlight. Her office was on the fifth floor and she passed the giant sculpture of a bronze fish leaping from the water that stood in the atrium as she rode the glass lift to her floor.

The office was quiet, with only the hum of cleaners hoovering the top-floor offices as she sat at her desk. Grace's heart sank as she saw the backlog of emails on her computer and she began to trawl through them. Kate Connolly, her secretary, had left a pile of post on her desk with the most urgent letters on top alongside a list of phone messages. It would take her at least a day to get through this and she had the Carroll project to be getting along with. Ray Carroll was due in the office tomorrow afternoon and one thing the property magnate did not take kindly to was delays or poor presentation of work. If need be she would work all night on it. She slipped off the black jacket of her suit and began to quickly read through the emails. It was good to work like this without interruption before the rest of the staff came in. She heard Ali Delaney pass down the hall. They nodded at each other through the glass partition.

'Feeling better?' Ali called politely.

'Yes, thanks.' Grace was tempted to confide in the other woman about her predicament with Shane but she wasn't sure how much office gossip she had been privy to. Ali was the office manager. She lived down in Kildare and made a point of coming in early every day and leaving at four p.m. It was the only way she got the time to spend with her family of three boys. Instead she returned to her screen as Ali made her way to the office at the end of the corridor.

An hour later the building began to buzz. She could see the queues of traffic all over the city as her work colleagues began to arrive, phones ringing, copiers and faxes growling into action. She wondered if Shane was actually in the building. How was she to handle it? Ignore him? Pretend their love affair had never happened? She was totally at a loss as to what she should do.

Kate arrived in at eight fifty a.m., she got the Dart to work every day and was as punctual and reliable as they came.

'Morning, Grace, it's nice to have you back. I left a list of calls and letters you need to deal with on the desk.'

'I found them, thanks. Any word from Ray Carroll?' Grace asked in the vague hope he might have rescheduled their appointment.

'Suzie from his office phoned on Friday so it's still on track for tomorrow.'

'Good.'

Grace realized there would be no reprieve and she began to pull out the file for tomorrow's meeting. The preliminary drawings she'd worked on looked good but knowing him he would want far more detail.

'Kate, can you hold all calls unless they are really urgent as I have to get this done for tomorrow?' she asked.

'No problem, if you need anything let me know.'

Grace worked all morning, skipping the usual visit to the top-floor canteen for a coffee break. She kept an eye out to see if there was any sign of Shane, but was relieved that he seemed to be nowhere about. At lunchtime she was busy drafting a new design for the three-bedroomed apartments Ray Carroll was so keen on.

'There's got to be space for a family,' he always insisted, 'and toys and books and clothes. We're building for real people.'

Grace pored over the drawings again to see if there was any way she could fit in more storage space without losing the airy feel of the apartment. The corridors outside were wide and very spacious but would people prefer to have that extra space within the apartment? She touched the drawings on the computer screen wondering if she could try an alternative. Kate had got her a turkey and cranberry roll and coffee from the canteen which she munched on as she printed out the new versions. She was so engrossed she barely heard the door open.

'Grace.'

Shane. He was standing there wearing the grey pinstripe suit she'd picked out with him a few months ago in London.

'How are you?' he asked, closing the door behind him.

If he hoped she was going to collapse in a heap and beg him to come back he was mistaken. She was determined to remain composed and calm in front of him.

'I'm fine,' she lied.

It was unbearably awkward between them and she didn't know how it could possibly be resolved.

'I'm sorry, Grace.' He did have the grace to look genuinely shamefaced. 'It was never my intention to hurt you. You must know that. Ruth and I had gone our separate ways and had no plans ever to see each other again. It just happened!'

'Shane, I'm really busy,' she said firmly for she'd absolutely no intention of getting involved in a discussion about the end of their relationship here in her office with a client or staff member liable to walk in. 'I've Ray Carroll in tomorrow and I have a ton of work to do and—'

'I just wanted to check that you're OK.'

'Well, you did,' she snapped. 'And I am. I have not disappeared down a hole no matter how much you might have wished it.'

He looked pained and uncomfortable.

'Do people in the office know we've broken up?'

'A few do. I told Derek and Paul, and Ruth and I ran into Louise and Gavin when we were in Fitzers on Sunday.'

'So basically the fact that we are no longer an item is pretty much common knowledge!'

'Yes,' he said tersely. 'I'd guess most people know by now.'

The silence between them hung heavy.

'Grace, I'd like us still to be friends . . .' he began. 'We work together and—'

'I don't need two-timing fecking friends who do the dirt on people,' Grace replied angrily. 'Working together is fine but otherwise please just leave me alone!'

Shane looked relieved and simply nodded and quit her office.

'Good riddance,' she mumbled under her breath.

'Mr Smooth gone?' Kate buzzed a few seconds later.

Grace was surprised that her secretary had the nerve to call him that to her face. 'Yep.'

'Ray Carroll is on line one for you.'

'Shit,' she responded before taking the call, realizing that her hands were still shaking.

'Good afternoon, Grace, how are you?'

She took a deep breath and managed to seem poised and in control again as she assured her client that all was set for the next day. 'I won't let you down,' she promised. 'The new designs are looking exciting.'

Grace sat back in the leather chair a few minutes later. She still had to perform, do the job that she was trained for and be a professional. The adrenalin rush she got from seeing a job like this come together was what had made her become an architect, studying for six years and breaking her guts to work in a firm like this. Breaking up with Shane had nothing to do with it. She could let this situation with him reduce her to an emotional mess unable to complete her projects or she could pull herself together and lose herself in her work. The latter seemed a much better option and she decided to concentrate on the job in hand. Getting involved with Shane O'Sullivan had been a huge mistake, and was one she would definitely not repeat. She was through with men! Hell would freeze over before her mother would see her on some man's arm walking down the aisle. Forget marriage and romance. From now on Grace was focusing all her energy on her career.

Chapter Eighteen

Sarah Ryan studied the screen of her computer. She was online checking the balance in her meagre bank account, dismayed by the usual lack of funds. Clicking the mouse she went on to her emails, sending a funny few words to a few of her friends who were ensconced in offices around the city. Truth was, she was bored and, checking the clock on the wall, she saw she'd another hour before she had to collect Evie from school. They'd go to the butcher's and the local grocer's and then grab a DVD of Evie's favourite programme *Angelina Ballerina* on their way home.

Next year if she had found some magic way of improving their finances she hoped to send Evie to dancing class, where she could pirouette and hop and skip with all the other little girls who were equally mad on ballet. Her mum and Grace had both very generously offered to pay the weekly dance class fees for her daughter but she had turned them down flat.

'Evie's still a bit young,' she'd fibbed, unwilling to accept one more jot of charity from her over-generous family.

'Don't be so stubborn,' Grace had chided. 'Mum, do you

remember how mad we all were for dancing classes? Do you remember when we used to go to Miss Hickey's and she made us pretend that we were flowers and swans?'

'I'll think about it,' Sarah had fobbed them off, determined to find some way of creating extra income of her own. She wanted to be able to provide for Evie herself, give her the same standard of living that she'd enjoyed growing up.

She had her job in Evie's school, St Bridget's, where she worked three mornings a week teaching art and helping in the library, her part-time work with Cora's catering company and the odd bit of graphic design work she managed to pick up. This income combined with the single parent's allowance and the very odd bit of money she received from Maurizio helped her to provide for her child. It was a struggle and like most single parents who didn't work full-time she was almost constantly broke. If she weren't living rent-free in the basement of her family home she didn't know how she would survive.

With time to spare she opened her 'Mitten' file. Mitten had started life as a squiggly drawing of a cat that she had done on a sketch pad for Evie. Mitten was a very bold little cat, who got into all kinds of scrapes and mischief and drove her owner Miss Bee mad. A weekly evening course in computers had helped her convert the bold black cat from the page in her sketchbook to a section of his own on her computer and she enjoyed adding to his antics whenever she got the chance. It was a silly childish thing to be doing when she should be ironing or hoovering or cleaning the bedroom but she couldn't help herself whenever the tip of that little black tail and ears appeared on the screen.

'Oh God!' Now she'd forgotten the time and was late to collect her child. Hitting the *save* button she grabbed her denim jacket and bag and raced out the door. If she ran all the way she might only be a few minutes late. She ran as fast as she could in the rain, head down as mothers with children by the hand and buggies and prams walked towards her. Out of breath and panting she got to the door of the school where Florence Roche, Evie's teacher, was waiting expectantly for her.

'Hi, Mummy,' announced her angel, coming over and taking her hand.

'Everything OK?' asked the senior infants' teacher.

'Yes, yes, fine,' she explained, 'just caught up with a work thing.'

Sarah could see that Evie was about to ask what this work thing was and began to edge her towards the door.

'Sorry,' she apologized, but could see Florence had already forgotten and was picking up her large blue denim bag, which was filled with copybooks and papers.

'No rest for the wicked,' the teacher laughed.

Sarah paused, looking around the gaily decorated walls covered with paintings and a large cut-out alphabet that the kids had made with pictures from magazines and newspapers.

D was for dog, dinosaur and daddy. Evie had pored over Sarah's old *Cosmo*s and *Image* and *U* magazines to find the perfect picture of what she thought a dad should look like. Sarah had resisted the urge to influence her as she contemplated George Clooney and Brad Pitt and Homer

Simpson, saying nothing when she had cut out a tall curly-haired dark-eyed male model who was holding a dog from a cheese advertisement.

'I think he's a nice daddy,' she'd said firmly as she cut him out with her plastic pink scissors and put him into her school bag.

'Me too,' agreed Sarah, who'd had to go to the bathroom and throw water on her eyes so her daughter couldn't see the emotions that a stupid school task had conjured up.

'Sarah, Evie's alphabet picture was so sweet,' praised Florence as they walked together out into the small paved yard. 'And she did a lovely painting of a big green frog sitting on a green tree.'

'It's hiding,' insisted Evie from under her dark eyelashes and fringe.

'Well, you'll have to help me find it.' Sarah laughed.

'See you tomorrow, Evie.' The pretty young teacher nodded as she made her way to a silver car parked near the railings.

Sarah took her daughter's hand as they waited for the traffic lights to change and watched the car drive away. She'd always imagined herself as a teacher or something like that, busy, occupied, with a career and money, a car of her own, a different life. Yet she wouldn't change having Evie for the world. Her five-year-old daughter was the most precious and wonderful thing in her life but she just wished she was a better provider and could give her daughter everything all the other mammies and daddies could.

Stopping off in the butcher's she purchased some minced

beef. It was on special. Tonight she'd make hamburgers and fried onion and Bolognese tomorrow. Next week if she got paid she was going to buy one of their big plump free-range chickens and roast it with all the trimmings. Maybe she could invite someone over? Open a bottle of wine, be sociable instead of spending so much time alone?

'Mummy!' Evie tugged at her sleeve.

'Yes, pet?'

'There he is again.'

Sarah looked out of the shop door. That huge wolf of a dog was standing there again.

'He's hungry, Mummy.'

'Evie, he just likes waiting there, hoping to get a bone.'

'I think he's hungry,' Evie insisted, going over to pet him.

Sarah sighed. There wasn't a dog in creation that didn't attract Evie but for the moment a pet was definitely out of the question. It was bad enough having her mother help to support herself and Evie without adding the cost of an animal.

'What about we get a DVD to watch in Xtravision then I'll just grab what we need from Spar and head home!'

'Bye bye, Mr Bones,' Evie said, slipping her hand in hers. Sarah felt emotion squeeze her heart as she realized that one day her little girl would no longer automatically reach for her or need her.

The video shop was quiet and Sarah passed the rows of expensive new releases with their big stars and well-advertised features and headed for the discount children's section where a range of Barbie, Barney and dinosaur cartoons filled the shelves. Evie, with a determined expression, searched the shelf until she found the DVD of the little mouse ballerina surrounded by her ballerina classmates.

Sarah was rooting in her handbag for her money to pay when she recognized Angus ahead of her. He was wearing a black leather jacket, his black leather boots, and a bright red knotted scarf.

He spotted Evie and immediately bent down to chat to her.

'Hi.' Sarah smiled, glad to see him.

'How are you two pretty ladies?'

'Fine thanks,' she said as Evie showed him her DVD.

'Looks really good, but I'm more of a Bond man. I saw this on the big screen but I'm going to chill and watch it again. Guns and girls and fast cars – that is my kind of movie! Have you seen it?'

'No,' admitted Sarah. Trips to the cinema were a pretty rare occurrence and were usually confined to the latest Disney blockbuster that Evie would enjoy or a chick flick with her sisters or friends.

'Why don't you come round to my place later and we can watch it then?' he offered.

She tilted her head towards Evie. She'd have to organize a babysitter.

'OK, point taken. Then why don't I come over to your place instead? You provide the DVD machine and I'll bring the movie and the popcorn.'

'That sounds good.' Sarah found herself agreeing.

Suddenly she realized it would be good to have a bit of adult company.

Evie was fast asleep by the time Angus came over. Curling up in the chair chatting to him and watching suave James Bond tackle a series of odious villains and win the heart of every lady he came into contact with made Sarah smile.

'Total bloody escapism,' enthused Angus, 'just perfect for a Wednesday night.'

Sarah agreed and afterwards made a pot of coffee for the two of them and some toast as Angus gave her an in-depth rundown of his favourite Scottish rock bands. It was funny but with Angus she felt totally relaxed and comfortable and able to talk easily. He had opinions about everything, she discovered, and was really funny.

They got into a mock argument about the best five films they had seen and who was their favourite director.

'Hey what about we do this again next week?' he suggested as he helped her carry the mugs to the kitchen. 'Only this time you pick the film. We can take it in turns – that's if you want.'

Sarah did want. He was lovely, just the kind of guy she would normally fancy, but he'd been totally up front about his girlfriend Megan and she was no boyfriend-stealer! Still, it must be lonely for him stuck in Dublin midweek without her. Maybe they could just be friends, have a laugh together. There was no contest between sitting at home on her own watching stupid stuff on the TV and having Angus over to watch a DVD next Wednesday.

Chapter Nineteen

Anna was in love. Unlike her sisters who were utter disasters where men were concerned, she was in love with the perfect man, a man of intelligence, who was spiritual and intellectual and had a rare knowledge of a woman's psyche. With his dark curling hair and long face and full lips and wise eyes she suspected he could all but see into her soul.

She had fallen in love with him when she was sixteen years old and that love had never faltered or wavered over the succeeding years. He was constant and true, unlike other men, and had the ability to move her like no other person had. She had been overwhelmed by him when she had first read his poem about spreading the cloths of heaven under the feet of his beloved. The genius and brilliance of his poetry lifted her up in a whirlwind of words as she read and studied his poetry and plays. William Butler Yeats was the perfect man and no living, breathing human could come in any way close to match-ing the depths of emotion he stirred in her. Her passion and obsession for his work had driven her to study English first at UCD and then to undertake a Ph.D. at Trinity.

This love of W. B. Yeats possessed her and she could not help comparing the mere mortals she met at parties and dances and pubs with the poet. Her friends and sisters told her she was crazy but Anna persisted in choosing the life of an academic where she had the opportunity to immerse herself in the life and times of Ireland's most famous poet and his fellow writers.

'For God's sake, he was an old man and he loved Maud Gonne and he was on our Leaving Certificate exam papers,' her sister Sarah had teased her. 'How can you possibly compare him to the guys we meet when we go out?'

'Exactly!' Anna had shouted triumphantly.

Her sisters and friends constantly fell for the Heathcliffs and Darcys, the Rhett Butlers and Gatsbys of the world and then wondered why they were left vulnerable and heartbroken. Anyone who had studied literature could have told them that such romances were doomed. She herself had no intention of following that route and if she did ever decide to settle and marry would choose an intellectual companion like Philip Flynn who at least understood her passion for literature. She had shown him the latest drafts of her paper on 'The Role of Women in W. B. Yeats's Life' and Philip had been most encouraging and supportive. However, the quest to find an interesting man with a spark of genius was proving more difficult than she imagined.

As she walked across the cobbled square of Trinity College and made her way to the library she phoned Grace, agreeing to meet for lunch in Luigi's, one of the nicer Italian restaurants in Temple Bar. She was banning all talk of Shane O'Sullivan and their break-up during the meal and had got two tickets for the opening of a new play in the Project tomorrow night, which Grace should enjoy. At eleven o'clock she had a tutorial with a group of fresh first years who were still labouring under the impression that college life was a doddle and there was no need to make any effort to study or research until a few weeks before the end-of-year exams, a belief she was doing her best to shatter. She contemplated doing a small handout for them and then reminded herself that it was up to them to do the work and discover the gems hidden in the realms of language and literature they were studying.

'Ladies and gentlemen, you are explorers. Miners digging for treasure!' she reminded them as she glanced around the crowded lecture theatre at the faces of her eighteen- and nineteen-year-old students. She recalled crusty old Louis Redmond, one of the university's finest English professors, who had steered her through the rough and tumble of an English degree. She had almost swooned as he read from 'The Rose' from his copy of Yeats's *Collected Poems* in her first year in Belfield and had signed up for all his classes the very next day. At eighteen years old she was ready to have her mind opened and her spirit untethered from the usual pursuits of UCD's student life.

That had been almost ten years ago and she could never have imagined how vast was the realm of words and poetry that would enchant her, hold her, and to which she now dedicated her life. A Masters and a Ph.D. and nine months at

Harvard were all stepping stones on the route to the Holy Grail: a professorship.

She was not anti-men; in fact she liked most of them and had even enjoyed a few romances along the way with students and other academics, but nothing touched her heart the way Yeats did. A passionate fling with fellow student Brad Lewis while at Harvard; a disastrous few months dating Tom Kinsella, who lectured in Economics here at Trinity, which had ended badly. At times she did miss male companionship, sex and the giddy ease that the first days of a relationship brought, but she consoled herself with the fact that she was betrothed to the love of a genius who, with his words and insights and wisdom, had woken her to something much stronger and important than simple romance.

Chapter Twenty

Reluctantly Grace had given in to the persuasion of her sisters, friends and work colleagues to stop moping around and get back into the social scene. She had agreed to join the Saturday night crowd in Café en Seine, one of Dublin's busiest bars. She pushed through the throng with her friends, wearing a figure-hugging jade-green dress with a little black cropped cardigan, ignoring the numerous appreciative glances from the wall of men balancing pints all around them. The place was busier than ever, packed with noisy groups laughing and shouting and running the waitresses off their feet with orders.

Niamh and the girls were being more than supportive and were ensuring that she was kept topped up with her favourite vodka and orange, but she felt as if she was in some kind of market as guys eyed her up and down. Being single sucked. However, she made an effort to mingle and make small talk and look like she was having a good time.

'Come on, we're heading for Krystle,' shouted Niamh as

they finished off a last round of drinks and headed for Harcourt Street.

She was tempted to jump in a cab and go back home but realized that if she didn't want to be a total damp squib and let her friends down she'd have to make the best of the night and enjoy herself. Niamh and Lisa breezed past the nightclub's bouncers and the gathering crowd as all five of them headed inside and ordered a bottle of wine before making a rush for the dance floor.

Grace loved music and at last relaxed. She began to dance, letting her body take up the thumping rhythm of the music played by the club's DJ. The girls all around her were laughing and joining in as the nightclub began to fill. Shane would hate this, she thought momentarily before banishing him from her mind.

Back at the bar Niamh introduced her to two guys she worked with and before she knew it they were both back on the dance floor. She watched as Niamh in her low-cut top and figure-hugging trousers chatted away easily to Kevin while she made an attempt to keep the conversation going with her dance partner Dermot. She had forgotten how awful being 'chatted up' really was and after about half an hour excused herself and retreated to the ladies' bathroom with Claire and Lisa. She really was not sure that she wanted to do this any more; that she cared or had the enthusiasm to talk to utter strangers and pretend that she was interested in them. She checked her watch: another half-hour and she could beat a retreat and go home. Lisa had downed one two many white wines and was getting tearful about Tom Callaghan, the guy she had gone out with for about a year, who had dumped her and gone off to work for Goldman Sachs in London.

'I would have moved to London, followed him over and worked there,' she slurred, 'but he just told me he didn't want to bring any baggage from Dublin over to London and wanted to enjoy being single again.'

'He's a bastard, Lisa,' insisted Claire, brushing her long blond hair and making her down a glass of water, 'but for some bloody reason nice girls like us tend to fall for them.'

Grace stared at her own pale face and sad eyes and was determined that she was not going to waste the rest of her night nitpicking over her love life.

'Hey, I'm going back outside,' she said, slapping on some lip gloss.

She was walking back to the others when she spotted Mark McGuinness in the distance and ducked to try to avoid him. He was standing near the bar with a stunning-looking girl with cropped dark hair. He looked relaxed, head bent forward listening to her talking to him, his arm around her waist.

'Good evening, Miss Ryan,' he said as she passed.

'Hello, Mr McGuinness,' she said briefly, trying to be polite. 'I hope you're enjoying the night.'

He raised his glass. Funny, she wouldn't have thought this kind of place was his scene, she mused as she made her way back to her friends. Niamh was sitting up at the other end of the bar with Kevin and Dermot and she joined them. Dermot insisted on getting her another drink, before leading her back on the dance floor again as the slow set started. He was tall and well built but had downed too many pints to make conversation that was in any way interesting. Still, he seemed a nice enough guy. The dance floor was packed and he held her tightly to him as they found themselves in the middle of crowds of couples intent on getting to know each other a lot better.

His hands roamed down along the small of her back and across her hips. Once or twice she corrected him, before giving in to the rhythm of the music. Niamh and Kevin were snogging the faces off each other, oblivious to everyone around them. Emboldened, Dermot tried to do the same but she managed to deflect his lips to her shoulder and neck. She was definitely not ready for this and babbled away like an eejit as he tried to be passionate.

She smiled with relief when the music stopped and the floor began to clear. Dermot, firmly holding her hand, tried to persuade her to sit down for a while.

'I'm sorry but I'm going to have to go,' she apologized. 'It's been nice meeting you and thanks for the drink.'

'Go?' She could see him blink in disbelief as she moved away from him.

She ignored his hasty request for her mobile number and brushed a farewell kiss against his cheek as she chased upstairs to the others. Niamh was happily sitting on Kevin's lap and clearly had no intention of going anywhere. Roisin and Claire too wanted to stay on and have a laugh but felt Lisa might be ready to head home.

'She's pretty hammered.'

'No she's not – she's wrecked!'

'She can share a taxi with me and I'll make sure she gets in OK,' Grace offered, relieved to be leaving the nightspot.

Lisa made no protest as she led her outside past the crowds and hailed a taxi.

All the way home, Lisa rambled on about Tom and how wonderful he was. Grace refused to be drawn into a drunken conversation about ex-boyfriends. The taxi-driver waited patiently as she marched Lisa into her apartment in Milltown and made sure she went to bed and was fine.

Back in the haven of her own place she kicked off her high heels and stepped out of her dress. With a sigh of relief she pulled on her pyjamas. Why she had ever been daft enough to let herself be persuaded to go out was beyond her. Right now she didn't care if she never dated a man again! She put on the kettle and turned on a late-night movie, a vampire horror, curling up on the couch with some cheese and crackers, actually relieved to be totally on her own.

Chapter Twenty-one

Turning into the driveway of Airfield House Maggie felt herself relax. The old house in Dundrum, with its small farm and beautiful gardens, was the perfect spot for lunch with 'the girls'. It had once been the home of the renowned Overend sisters Naomi and Letitia, who had farmed the place and gifted it to future generations of Dublin citizens. The charming white building, with its bay windows overlooking the gardens, now housed a welcoming restaurant, which she always enjoyed. She was looking forward to seeing her friends, hoping it might cheer her up. She had found herself in a bit of a heap since the upset with Grace and the O'Connors moving. She wasn't one of those mothers who could pretend things that happened to her children didn't matter and she was still worried about her eldest daughter.

Spotting Fran and Rhona, who had managed to get a table out on the patio in the sunshine, she waved. Perfect! She said a quick hello, then grabbed a tray and made her way to the long food counter.

'God, I'm starving!' announced Louisa Kelly, suddenly

appearing beside her, wearing slim-fitting navy trousers and a cream wrap-over cardigan.

They both salivated over the choice of main courses: Cajun salmon, mustard-baked ham, a basil and tomato pasta concoction, quiches and a beef and pimento special, alongside a selection of soups and salads and homemade bread. Maggie opted for the salmon and a tossed salad and a glass of wine; Louisa went for the ham. Making her way to the table she felt her spirits lift. She was glad that everyone had been able to make it. Their monthly get-together was something she so enjoyed, old friends meeting up for a chat and lunch and perhaps a walk if the weather permitted. The venues changed so they got to try out a range of nice restaurants all over the place but it was the company she looked forward to most.

They'd been friends for more years than she dared to remember and had gone through all the ups and downs that life can throw at you: marriage, kids, work, school, illness, financial problems. The girls had stood by her when Leo had died, and she had helped in turn when Louisa's husband Brendan had walked out on her and when Rhona's husband had lost his job and Fran had got stomach cancer. There was an unbreakable bond between them and they all knew they had only to lift the phone and help would be at hand. Four old schoolfriends who still found plenty to talk about!

'Everyone OK?' she asked, balancing her tray as she sat down beside Rhona.

'I'm on blood-pressure tablets,' joked Rhona. 'With Mike working from home he has me driven up the wall. Is it any wonder that my blood pressure keeps shooting up?'

In only a few minutes she discovered that Louisa was doing her computer exams in a few weeks' time, Rhona and Mike were planning a trip to the Algarve and that Fran had got new caramel-toned highlights in her hair.

'They make you look younger.'

'Well, I feel like Methuselah,' Fran confided. 'Jenny just told me that I'm going to be a grandmother again next December.'

'Congratulations!'

'What lovely news!' they all agreed, raising their wine glasses.

'Honestly, this will be number three, and you can guess where they'll all be for Christmas. Liam and I had hoped to slip away to the Canaries for a bit of sunshine. Now I'll be looking after them all while Jenny's in Mount Carmel having the baby.'

A third grandchild, thought Maggie enviously, a house filled with kids and presents around the Christmas tree. Just the kind of Christmas she loved.

'I suppose I'm delighted really,' Fran eventually admitted, 'especially after that awful time at the beginning when Jenny thought she couldn't have kids.'

'Well, she's making up for it now,' Rhona commented, turning her face up to the sunshine.

'I have some good news too,' announced Louisa, her eyebrows arching with excitement. 'Donal is getting married to that lovely girl Melanie who works in that fancy PR firm up near Christchurch. They're having the wedding in Brooklodge in Wicklow in August next year.'

Maggie couldn't believe it. Tall lanky Donal, with the easy-going manner and lopsided smile who'd been crazy about Anna when he was about seventeen, was getting married. 'He'll make a wonderful husband,' she said, remembering what a kind young man he'd been.

There was a cheer around the table as there was nothing nicer than a wedding, even if it was more than a year away.

'Don't they all have a great life these days?' mused Rhona. 'Marriage and big careers, interesting jobs, no sitting around taking dictation and writing boring letters all day.'

'Sure do,' they all agreed.

'Remember those bad old days when we were stuck filing and typing letter after letter? One mistake and you had to start all over again!'

'God bless computers and printers and the Internet,' exclaimed Louisa, who since her separation had been immersed in a part-time course in computers and web design, which was useful for the small stationery business she'd set up, selling exquisite wedding and party invitations.

The salmon was delicious and Maggie noticed all the chairs and tables around them had filled up.

'Maggie, are you by any chance free on Saturday?' Rhona asked as she passed around a jug of iced water. 'It's just that Mike's cousin Eamon will be in town for the night. He's playing golf with Mike in the afternoon and I wondered if you'd be interested in joining the three of us in the golf club for dinner afterwards.'

Maggie widened her eyes. Eamon Farrell was a nice man who had separated from his wife two years ago. She'd met him at various dos at Rhona and Mike's over the years but now all he ever talked about was the ins and outs of his separation and the sale of his house in Kildare. Just because she was a widow, why did everyone assume she was available and in the market for a male companion?

'Rhona, thanks for the invite but I'm actually babysitting for Sarah on Saturday,' she fibbed. 'And I don't want to let her down.' She ignored the glances from her friends darting around the table.

'And how are your girls?' Fran asked diplomatically.

Maggie took a deep breath. These were her closest friends. 'Actually, Grace and Shane have broken up and she's taking it very badly.'

'That's the guy that works with her and used to go out with the journalist girl?' quizzed Louisa.

'Yes, but she's not an ex any more. He's back with her.'

'Oh, poor Grace,' sympathized Fran. 'Nothing worse than getting your heart dinted.'

'With them both working in the same firm it's making it all very awkward,' Maggie explained. 'Grace is used to things going smoothly so it's going to be hard for her in the office.'

'Bloody men and break-ups, that's the awful part of single life from what I remember,' sighed Rhona. 'But then just when you're about to throw in the towel and swear the oath of spinsterhood you go and meet someone when you least expect it!'

They all burst out laughing, remembering how Rhona had met her husband Mike: she had been reversing out of a car park and and crashed into his brand-new car. They all knew that meeting Mike Farrell had been a huge changing point in Rhona's life, their marriage and the birth of their two sons bringing her the happiness she had always craved.

'I don't mean that she's got to crash a car,' she protested, 'but the guy of her dreams could be right under her nose!'

Mark McGuinness was most definitely right under the Ryan family's nose, thought Maggie; he was still single and, from what she could gather, sparks had flown when Grace and he had met. He'd annoyed her eldest daughter intensely with his know-it-all attitude, but she knew many couples who had positively hated each other at first. Besides, Mark and Grace had a lot in common with their work. Maybe the next time they met up things might go a bit better?

'And how's my sweetheart Evie?' asked Fran.

'You won't believe it, but she's going to be six at the weekend!'

Maggie could still remember how supportive her friends had been when Sarah had got pregnant. The fact that she had thrown away her education and was far too young to have a baby had been glossed over. When Evie had been born Sarah had been inundated with baby gifts from Maggie's friends, all welcoming her first grandchild to the world. She'd always remember the kindness and care they'd shown to her daughter and her child.

'How's Sarah doing? Any love interest?' asked Louisa, full of curiosity.

'She says guys run a mile when they hear she has a child! It scares them off.'

'More fool them,' retorted Fran hotly.

They all nodded wisely; men could be such fools where girls were concerned.

'I'd love her to meet someone,' Maggie confided. 'My new tenant would have been perfect but unfortunately he already has a girlfriend.'

'Maggie, you are such a schemer,' teased Rhona. 'Fiddling in people's lives.'

'No, I'm not!' she protested.

'Yes, you are,' they all chorused.

Maggie had to laugh. 'Well, if it wasn't for my fiddling, Fran and Liam might never have met!'

'And I will never forget the night that you introduced us.' Fran smiled. 'Remember – we went to dinner in Captain America's and you got him to join us for a hamburger and he asked me out when we were leaving.'

'Life was a lot simpler then,' mused Maggie. 'I don't know why but my girls don't seem to have any intention of getting engaged or married, and as for Anna, no man can match up to her high standards.'

'So no wedding bells in your house then!' remarked Louisa. 'You've three dedicated singletons on your hands by the sound of it.'

'I suppose,' admitted Maggie, suddenly finding herself defending her daughters. 'You can't force people to fall in love and settle down. It isn't as simple as that!'

Afterwards, as they tucked into banoffi pie and coffee, she wondered how it had all got so complicated. Finding some-one to love and to love you should be easy. There'd been no mobile phones or texts or emails or Internet in her day to aid communication, and yet things had been far simpler than they were now.

She had met Leo when she'd least expected it, at an awful rugby club dance that her brother had dragged her along to. He'd asked her to dance and when the music ended, he had written her number down on a piece of cardboard from a beer mat and kept his promise and phoned her the next day. They'd arranged to meet in Kielys in Donnybrook, and Maggie was astonished when she realized just how attractive she found him. A year later to the day he had proposed. They were total opposites and had absolutely nothing in common except the fact that they loved each other – which is more than enough for any marriage.

'Your girls or my boys, we never get to stop worrying about them,' remarked Rhona as if reading her mind. 'No matter how old they are or how much they earn they will always be our babies and we just want the best for them.'

'Too true. It doesn't make any difference if it's school or college or work or careers or their love life,' Maggie admitted. 'I guess it's part of being an Irish mammy – we can't let go.'

'I'd let go of my two lumps,' Rhona joked, 'but no one will have them.'

Maggie burst out laughing. Rhona had two very handsome sons; Colm, the elder, had disappeared to Australia for the year and judging from rumours had half the female population of Sydney drooling over him, and her younger son, Gareth, was in his final year in college and was so busy between studying and playing rugby for Leinster that he scarcely had time to notice women.

'Give them time!' she warned.

'Honestly, Maggie, I'll be scouring the country looking for good wives for the pair of them. I don't want any brazen hussies for daughters-in-law!'

Driving home Maggie decided she had no intention of scouring the country for eligible bachelors for her girls. Things were not that desperate. However, a little old-fashioned matchmaking right on her own doorstep might not go amiss.

Chapter Twenty-two

Pulling on a clean pair of jeans and a vintage floral-print shirt Anna grabbed her green velvet jacket and the present in the hallway. Today was Evie's sixth birthday and although the thought of a gang of screaming six-year-olds chasing around her sister's cluttered garden flat didn't bear thinking about, she had offered to give Sarah a hand with the party and she wasn't about to let her down. Afterwards, if she wasn't too banjaxed, she'd chase in to the opening of Philip's new play in the Beckett Theatre.

'Auntie Anna!' shouted Evie, greeting her in a pink tutu with fairy wings.

'Aren't you a pretty birthday fairy!' she laughed, lifting Evie up into her arms. Shit. She had totally forgotten it was a fairy party and that all the kids were coming dressed up for the occasion in wings and floaty fairy costumes, with little wands and tiaras.

'I thought I told you to dress up,' reproached Sarah, who was sporting a pink net ballet skirt over a pair of black leggings, with a pair of wings pinned on her back. 'We're all meant to be fairies!'

'Sorry,' Anna apologized, suddenly feeling like a party pooper. 'What can I do to help?'

'Well, Mum's in the kitchen helping with the food but there's all the party games.'

Anna's heart sank. If there was one thing she hated more than dressing up in silly pink it was games. She'd hated them ever since she was young but it wasn't fair to expect Sarah to single-handedly deal with this onslaught from the fairy kingdom.

'The first game we're going to play is Musical Toadstools,' announced Sarah enthusiastically.

Anna looked around noticing that every stool, pouffe, foot rest and even piano stool the house possessed had been commandeered and placed in a circle. Her sister must have spent ages making the bright red-and-white-spotted cushions which covered them.

'Wow!' said the kids as they began to move around in a circle to Kylie Minogue. It was hilarious watching them as they danced and screamed with excitement when the music stopped. There was a mad rush for the stools and one poor fairy was left standing.

'Will you look after Tara?' suggested Sarah as the music started again.

Anna looked at the stricken fairy; she knew what it was like to be a loser. She began to hop up and down as the music began again. 'Come on, Tara. We'll dance too, we're the fairy cheerleaders. We'll cheer them all on!'

Tara looked momentarily puzzled and then began to follow her lead.

As the game continued more little girls joined the fairy cheerleaders dancing and jumping and consoling the losers; Evie grinned as she joined the merry bunch.

Next it was Pin the Wings, Crown, Wand on the Fairy. It was ingenious: Sarah had done a huge drawing of a fairy which she had Blu-Tacked on to the sitting-room door.

'Everyone must be blindfolded,' she insisted, producing a fuchsia-pink chiffon scarf.

'Me first,' pleaded Tara, who was determined to win at least one game. Everyone held their breath as blindfolded Tara groped madly at the picture with a pair of wings in her hand. There was mad tittering when she placed them firmly on the fairy's bum.

'Cold, cold!' hinted Sarah as Tara tried again. The fairy now had a pair of wings floating from the top of her head and a wand poking out from her nose.

Tara herself burst out laughing when she saw the result. Anna had to admire Sarah who was endlessly patient with the kids, urging everyone to try again. She slipped away to the small galley kitchen.

'How's it all going?'

Her mum was putting the finishing touches to a tray of butterfly buns, her face flushed with the heat from the oven as she placed the sponge wings carefully on the top of another bun. They were Anna's favourites when she was a kid, light melt-in-your-mouth sponge filled with whipped cream.

'Take one,' offered her mother.

There was a range of home-cooked goodies laid out for the kids. Rice Krispie buns, marshmallow top hats, chocolate brownies and a fabulous fairy cake with her mother's butter icing and decorated with a cluster of little hedgehogs, ladybirds, frogs and six pink candles.

'Mum, it's fabulous, Evie will love it.'

'It did turn out rather well,' she agreed, for if there was one thing Maggie Ryan excelled at it was making cakes for special occasions. 'I still can't believe she's six. It seems like only yesterday that Sarah told us she was pregnant.'

Anna could still remember the utter chaos that ensued when Sarah had finally worked up the courage to tell everyone she was going to have a baby. They'd been having Sunday lunch when Sarah had blurted it out before making a run to the bathroom to throw up her meal. Mum and Dad had almost collapsed and she and Grace had been stunned by the fact that their 'little sister' had jumped right ahead of them in the motherhood stakes.

It had been tough for Sarah, going it alone with no doting boyfriend or husband. Evie had arrived three weeks early in a huge drama which involved the Lynches from next door driving Sarah and herself to the hospital and breaking every traffic light to get there on time. Grace was away in Hong Kong, and Mum and Dad had arrived at Holles Street Maternity Hospital absolutely flootered from a dinner party. Sarah, composed and calm, had delivered a perfect, beautiful baby girl in thirty minutes; her crazy family had been a bundle of tears and hysterics as they greeted the tiny new member of the Ryan clan. Evie was adored by them all and had brought such life to the house and comfort to her mother, especially since Dad's death.

'Where are they going to eat?' she asked, nibbling a butterfly bun.

'Thank God it's dry and sunny because we've got the picnic all set up in the garden.'

The garden had been transformed into a fairy pink paradise, the lawn spread with pink coverlets and a collection of cushions and parasols lay enticingly around. There were twelve perfect picnic baskets, old mushroom baskets transformed and covered in a variety of pink patterns with a little girl's name written on each in coloured sparkles.

'Did Sarah do all these?'

'You know what she's like,' laughed her mother. 'She should have been on *Blue Peter*.'

Anna laughed too; her youngest sister was one of the most creative people she knew. She always had paints and glue and sticky tape on hand to make things!

'The fairies are getting restless, I think that they're ready to eat,' said Sarah, appearing from the living room.

The girls oohed and aahed over their baskets as they skipped out to the garden and sat down on the cushions.

'I've got chocolate marshmallows!'

'I've got a pink bun!'

Anna helped to pass around the cocktail sausages and jugs of orange squash. The kids tucked merrily into their baskets laden with food.

'What they don't eat, they can take home in their baskets!' Sarah said.

Grace arrived wearing pale blue jeans and a knitted white sweater, relieved to hear that she hadn't missed the birthday cake.

Sarah poured her a glass of wine. 'The rest of the grown-ups will be along soon,' she told her, pulling a few garden chairs up around the table.

'I invited Mark McGuinness too,' added their mother. 'I dropped an invitation in his letter box last week.'

'Mum!' groaned Anna and Grace in unison. 'This is hardly his kind of thing.' Their mother was utterly incorrigible; imagine inviting their new neighbour whom they barely knew to a children's party. It was so embarrassing!

'I thought I was being neighbourly, but he can't make it,' she said, clearly disappointed that whatever plan she was hatching had failed.

Relieved, the girls watched as Angus Hamilton walked up the garden pathway towards them carrying a large pink-wrapped present.

'Hey, you didn't tell me you'd invited him,' teased Anna, taking in the long floppy hair, stubble and Transformers T-shirt.

'Evie and Angus are great friends,' blazed Sarah as Angus hugged her warmly.

'Angus,' yelled Evie, throwing herself at him and spattering chocolate Rice Krispies all over his T-shirt.

'Happy birthday to the beautiful fairy princess.' He bowed

and produced a bubble-blowing machine and a set of fairy hand puppets, which caused a huge stir.

'Angus, I'll get you a glass of wine!' offered their mother.

Aunt Kitty, and Karen and her husband Mick, who were two of Sarah's best friends, suddenly appeared, greeting everyone as they grabbed seats under the parasol.

'Sarah, you've been blessed with the day,' said Aunt Kitty approvingly.

Grace went to get more wine glasses as Oscar from next door arrived. They all noticed his walking was stiffer and slower than usual but he tried to disguise the pain he was in as Angus pulled out a comfortable chair for him to sit on. Anna helped Evie use the bubble machine, and the bubbles drifted across the garden with the fairies in hot pursuit.

'I think we'll have the birthday cake now,' whispered Sarah, disappearing to the kitchen.

All eyes turned to Sarah as she reappeared carrying the cake with the six candles lit. They all sang 'Happy Birthday' to Evie. Anna squeezed her mother's hand as the two heads, one dark, one fair, bent towards each other.

Evie, utterly over-excited, blew out the candles before joining her friends for the last party game: a treasure hunt.

'There is a precious fairy ring hidden in the garden for every fairy,' Sarah promised them.

'What a great party.' Karen's husband Mick was full of praise. 'Most people would just take the kids to the cinema or McDonald's.'

Maggie reminded him that she would expect any of her

daughters to make their best effort for a birthday. It was a family tradition.

'And you have another birthday in a few weeks' time,' reminded Aunt Kitty. 'Grace's.'

Grace could kill her aunt! She was totally dreading her upcoming thirtieth birthday.

Half an hour later the parents began to arrive to collect their kids. Some stayed to join in the celebration and have a piece of cake and wine or coffee while others had to get home.

All the kids came up and thanked Sarah and Evie for the great party.

'It was the best party ever,' declared Hannah and Ashling, two of her schoolfriends.

'You've given us a hard act to follow,' joked Hannah's mother, a wealthy solicitor.

Anna was so proud of Sarah who, on a very limited budget, had with a bit of imagination created such a memorable day for Evie and her pals.

Sarah finally settled down on a garden chair with a large glass of wine, barefooted, as Evie pleaded to open the rest of her presents.

There was a new Ballet Barbie, Barbie outfits, two DVDs, a book of fairies, a painting set, a jewellery set which involved about a million tiny beads and book and CD tokens.

When Evie opened her present Anna suddenly wished she had been more adventurous.

'Books!' blurted out her niece. 'And a Barbie Fairy Princess and Wand!' she screamed excitedly, racing over to hug her.

Anna thanked heaven that her mum had tipped her off to add a Barbie to the two rare first-edition children's books that she had managed to buy for Evie.

Grace had bought her an Avoca pink skirt and a frilly wrap-over cardigan and Granny had brought her a big inflatable paddling pool and new swimming togs and a towel.

'Your mum and aunties had a paddling pool like this when they were small.'

Sarah and Grace yelped with pleasure, remembering the fun and craziness of summers in the back garden, jumping in and out of the little pool, and drowning their toys in it, and having races.

'Do you remember the water fights we used to have?'

'You used to get soaked,' Anna remembered.

Evie jumped up on her grandmother's lap. 'This was my best birthday party ever . . . *ever*, Granny!'

'I know it was, pet. That's because everyone loves you.'

Sarah's eyes welled with tears and unconsciously Anna squeezed her hand. Pulling herself together, Sarah announced, 'Now that the kids are gone, I think we should finish off all the food.' She disappeared off to the kitchen with Angus in tow.

'Any word from you know who?' whispered Grace.

'Not a beep,' replied their mother angrily.

They all held their tongues, watching as Sarah emerged with a tray of cakes and buns, laughing as Angus gingerly carried a dish of well-cooked cocktail sausages with the aid of an oven glove.

'He's nice,' whispered Grace.

'Perfect,' said their mother.

'Mum! He's got a girlfriend,' Anna reminded her, wondering what the heck her mother was up to.

'A girlfriend,' Maggie whispered, 'who seems to spend all her time in Scotland while he spends most of his here in Dublin!'

'He works in Dublin,' Anna pointed out, 'and usually goes back home at the weekends.'

'It's Saturday and he's here at Evie's party,' Maggie retorted with a smile, passing around some paper napkins and plates.

'They're friends,' she protested. Honestly, her mother was like someone out of a John B. Keane play, a country match-maker trying to find romance where there was none.

However, watching Angus sitting on the garden bench chatting easily with Oscar and Sarah, Anna did have to admit that perhaps her mother was right; how many men would give up their Saturday afternoon to go to a kids' party, let alone a fairy-themed one! Angus just fitted in and was mad about Evie.

An hour later Anna said her goodbyes, resisting the temptation to spend the rest of the evening on a garden chair basking in the sun drinking wine. She headed into town to the opening night of Philip Flynn's new play.

Chapter Twenty-three

Anna made it just in time to Trinity's Beckett Theatre and, tossing her wavy hair back off her face, grabbed a space in one of the front rows in an effort to make the place look fuller. Philip was floating around, as well as Simon Fleming who had done the lighting and a girl called Gina who was studying drama and had come to some of her English lectures. Philip nodded over at her and she tried to give him a reassuring smile. His aquiline features looked tauter than ever as he surveyed the rows of empty seats. She settled down pretending to read the programme, hoping that by some miracle a hundred people would suddenly manifest themselves and create a lively, enthusiastic audience. Philip had sweated blood and guts over this production over the past eight weeks and the least he deserved was some kind of audience. Most of the staff from the English and Drama Departments had been invited and it would be a poor show if a few more didn't happen along. Besides, there was a drinks reception after the play for invited guests which was usually enough to lure a few stalwarts. Mona Royston, a colleague from American Literature, suddenly appeared, her large frame squashing into the seat beside her, her breasts jiggling alarmingly under a jewelled turquoise top, blond hair cascading down her shoulders.

'Good to see you here, Anna. At least there are two of us to console Philip.'

'Console?'

'Well, you know what I mean. Being a playwright sucks. It's all so public – the humiliation.'

'The play is meant to be very good; Philip thinks it's his best so far.'

'Exactly what I mean,' Mona laughed, offering her a wine gum from a packet in her handbag.

Watching the trickle of people take their seats, Anna doubted that she would ever have the stomach for such an endeavour as having her words performed on stage. It took a rare kind of courage and ego, a kind which she definitely didn't possess. She continued to chat to Mona while watching Philip surreptitiously. He was checking things, going back and forth between front of house and backstage. A number of students from the Drama course were involved – acting, doing sets and so on – and they were all bound to be nervous. No doubt, behind the scenes Philip was soothing them. She heaved a sigh of relief as a group of about twenty students ambled in and filled in the rest of the front two rows. After a delay of about another ten minutes when only an elderly couple came in and plonked themselves in the back row, Philip finally gave the nod, the theatre darkened and light filled the stage.

162

Anna held her breath. This was the minute – well, first few minutes – when the audience made up their minds no matter who the playwright was. The lead actor came forward and began to speak, his face hidden behind a gold mask. Philip had explained months ago to her about the symbolism of the gold masks in his work. She racked her brain trying to remember. After ten minutes of actor after actor repeating the opening mantra in similar masks she still hadn't made any sense of it. The soul and society were somehow main themes but it was unclear what was happening on stage.

Mona opened her handbag loudly and offered her another wine gum. 'Pity it's not the real thing.'

Anna, despite her best efforts to concentrate, found herself drifting off and thinking about a pile of essays she had to mark. Twenty-five minutes in, the elderly couple at the back made a lot of noise lifting bags and jackets, muttering as they left the theatre.

The torture continued as a tall thin girl in a black mask, in the role of some kind of muse, did a tribal dance to the pounding of a bodhran drum played by one of the other actors. Anna sat up in her seat and tried to focus on the performance. There was a brief ten-minute interval and she raced to the bathroom. Hopefully things would improve in the second half. Mona had disappeared outside for a quick cigarette. There was no sign of Philip, and Anna admitted to a slight sense of relief that she hadn't had to give her view of the performance so far.

The second half of the play saw the stage bathed in light and the lead actor appear again, only this time there was no mask and his handsome young face displayed all his emotions. Within minutes all the other actors reappeared and repeated their initial words and actions but this time full face to the audience. Everyone was leaning forward now to see what they were saying, far more engaged than previously. The play still rambled on for far too long but at least there was something more interesting to look at on stage and the final scene with the distraught muse dancing to the drumming resonated around the theatre.

The audience clapped loyally, the actors deserved that, and clapped again politely when Philip came out and took a stiff little bow holding Ashling, the actress's, hand.

'Dear Lord, thank heaven that's over!' remarked Mona. 'I don't think Philip need worry about giving up the day job, do you?'

Anna held her tongue. She hadn't realized that Mona had such a sarcastic streak in her.

'Come on and we'll get ourselves a glass of wine. God knows we deserve it.'

A small crowd milled around the waitress serving wine and Anna had to admit she was glad of the reviving Sauvignon Blanc.

'Phew,' remarked Gina, coming over to join them. 'What a performance. Such emotion! Utterly draining, don't you think?'

'Where's Philip?'

'Backstage. He'll be out in a moment.'

Anna sipped at her wine wondering what she could possibly say that would be positive and construed as helpful. She knew from lecturing and correcting work how badly students took criticism of their writing, often taking it as a personal affront. Despite his massive ego Philip was a sensitive soul and this was his work they were talking about.

'Here he comes.' Gina grinned and gave him a hug.

'Well done!' said Mona obliquely, tipping her glass to him, much as you would congratulate a marathon runner for finally crossing the line, in recognition of his endurance. Philip looked rather shell-shocked but his eyes found Anna's as she kissed him lightly.

'Do you think it needs more rehearsal?'

'Definitely.'

'That's what I thought.' He sighed. 'Perhaps in our eagerness we rushed the production.'

Anna felt a qualm of pity for him. 'I preferred the second half.'

'Sans masques?'

'Definitely. It was much better to let Terence and that girl Ashling express themselves totally and for us the audience to appreciate the contrast.'

Philip smiled tremulously, his tall frame leaning down towards her, concentrating on every word.

Anna thanked heaven for her experience in dealing with students and the art of the careful let-down.

'We bare our souls continually; that's what I endeavoured to interpret: the condition of man.'

'Exactly.'

'Art must constantly strive to reflect this.'

Mona cast her eyes up to heaven and grabbed another wine glass from a passing waitress.

Anna, determined not to say another word, hugged Philip, relishing the smell of his expensive aftershave.

Three final-year drama students were loitering a yard away from them and Anna could see Philip's eyes light up as they congratulated him and chatted to him in a tight huddle.

'Always lick up to your professor,' remarked Mona. 'Makes exams a whole lot easier.'

'Mona!'

A small cheer broke out as the actors made their appearance, blinking in the harsh lights of the auditorium, like creatures that have suddenly appeared from the underworld.

'Well done,' said Anna, smiling as she recognized a boy who was one of her final-year English students.

'Hey, we're all going to go for a curry at the Madras House,' interrupted Gina.

'Sounds like a good idea,' agreed Philip, who had definitely rallied.

Anna disguised her disappointment. She had hoped that they could have sloped off for a quiet dinner for two instead of indulging in a post-mortem, which would no doubt reflect its rather dismal reception. Mona joined the hungry throng as they headed over towards Dame Street.

'God, I'm starving,' added the American.

'Everyone is.' Anna was suddenly aware of her own stomach growling as she dodged the traffic and crossed over to the Indian restaurant. The main evening rush was over and they managed to get a table for sixteen near the front of the restaurant. Philip sat between his two lead actors whilst Anna found herself between Simon and her English student, making small talk about the state of Irish theatre, post-grad student bursary schemes and the music of U2. Across the table she could see Philip was in his element talking animatedly. Gina and Mona were having some kind of argument which Anna decided to ignore, as she most definitely caught a whiff of the words 'unfair marking' . . .

The chat around the table was good-humoured with most avoiding talking about the play. With any luck it wouldn't get any reviews and would disappear; in time Philip might just mark it down as one of his unremarkable works. Anna washed down her spicy chicken cooked in the stone oven with some chilled Tiger beer.

'Film is the way to go,' insisted Simon, who had worked on some short experimental film that his flatmate was making. 'Lighting is such an important element and the DOP has such an influence on the production.'

Give me patience, thought Anna.

At midnight half the party departed and she found herself sitting beside Philip who was boasting loudly about the next play he was going to try and produce, which combined elements of Synge's *Playboy of the Western World*.

'Maybe we should go,' she hinted discreetly. 'You must be tired.' She didn't want the students to see him making an ass of himself at this hour of the night.

'Another glass of wine, then I'll go.'

Anna sighed. He was gifted and talented and intelligent and handsome but when he got drunk he was an absolute shit.

'Philip, I have an early-morning lecture, and a paper to

have ready for *Hibernian Magazine*. I really can't stay out any later.'

He just ignored her, his arm snaking around her shoulder. She had two options, she could flounce out of here and let him find his own way home or she could stay put and get a taxi whenever he decided to call it a night. She decided to stay, finding herself involved in a conversation about acting and the lack of theatre work in the city.

An hour later she felt she could neither eat nor drink nor converse any more and realized that Philip Flynn, now busy quoting Synge, was drunk. She *had* to go home and get some sleep as she had a huge workload and an outline of her project to finish over the next few days.

'Philip.'

He just ignored her. Well, she'd had enough. Picking up her bag, she got up from her seat, saying goodbye to the remaining few.

'I'm leaving, Philip.'

Outside on the street, she hailed a taxi, wondering why he always had to be so bloody difficult. Glancing back through the restaurant window, it was clear that Philip hadn't even noticed that she had left.

Gina had taken her seat, and his arm now rested heavily on her shoulder.

Chapter Twenty-four

Five cups of coffee, a bowl of cornflakes, a packet of jelly teddy bears and hunks of cheese fuelled Anna as she worked all through the night putting together her proposal for Stanford's exchange programme. The opportunity to get out of Dublin for two semesters and work in one of America's most prestigious colleges, living in San Francisco, was certainly very appealing. After Philip's shabby treatment of her the other night and the whispered rumour that he had ended up at Gina's place, it was abundantly clear that there was nothing or no one to hold her here. With any luck she would find someone to rent her cottage on Dodder Row for a few months. 'California, here I come,' she sang under her breath as she hammered away at her laptop.

Martin Johnston, the visiting American professor, had given her the low-down on what his college were looking for each semester, and she had broken down a proposed lecture schedule accordingly. Synge, Joyce, Behan, O'Casey, Beckett, Keane, Friel, McGahern, O'Brien and Heaney: she covered them all, the great and the good of Irish writing with Yeats as her core. William Butler Yeats would not let her down. In Stanford she would be able to carry on with her research and might even have access to college funding or a research grant for her work on the great influence of women on W. B. Yeats's poetry.

The printer was acting up and she almost attacked it when a page got stuck and she had to take the back off to release it. Anna fed it like a baby watching the pages appear. Everything had to look perfect: Martin had warned her sloppiness would mean automatic rejection. She had a meeting with him first thing in the morning where she had to give a fifteen-minute verbal presentation of her academic proposal. She was exhausted and her shoulders and back ached but she was determined to finish the task at hand. There'd be plenty of time for sleep later. She worked till five a.m. and had fallen asleep at her computer, her head touching the keyboard. Thank heavens she hadn't deleted anything.

At eight a.m. Anna Ryan was woken by the sound of the city traffic moving in the street outside her door, and in a panic showered and dressed, grabbing a simple black skirt and T-shirt and a pair of sexy black high heels, pulling her contrary hair back neatly as she slipped her arms into her velvet jacket and downed a glass of orange juice before racing to the meeting.

Passing Philip on the corridor she barely had time to say hello to him as she ran into the Dean's office and began her pitch.

Phew! She had pulled it together. She could see Brendan,

the head of the English Department, and Martin were both reacting positively during her presentation.

'We are very keen this year to have an Irish person lecture on Irish Literature, bring their own cadence and style to it,' Martin said smiling.

'How long before I know?' she blurted out, sounding madly over-enthusiastic.

'The Stanford College authorities and the heads of the English Department will make their decision quickly.'

Finishing the interview she was conscious of the fact that Martin had quite a few envelopes of résumés and proposals already under his arm as he said his goodbyes. She watched his short fat legs and stocky body propelling him across the hallowed cobblestones towards the waiting car.

'Safe journey,' she whispered.

Consulting the day's timetable, she saw she had a lecture at three and a tutorial mid-morning. Anna felt incoherent with exhaustion. She'd cancel the tutorial; no doubt her twenty students would be relieved to discover they had a free period. But the lecture in the afternoon she would give, there was no point upsetting her own head of department when she might be looking for a sabbatical next year. Anna yawned; she'd go home and sleep for a few hours, then she'd be right as rain.

Ten days later it was Mona who told her the news.

'Can you believe that schmuck Philip getting to go to Stanford for the year?' she exclaimed as they queued together in the canteen for lunch.

Anna felt her stomach lurch and almost dropped her tray. Philip Flynn had made no mention to her of applying for the year-long lecturing post that she had told him about. He hadn't said a word to her when she had been prattling on excitedly about her application and what the Americans were looking for.

'I was sure you'd get it, Anna, but what the hell do my fellow countrymen know of lecturers like you who have the ability to pack their classes and interest their students compared to egotists like Philip who try to promote their own work?'

She must have looked dismayed because Mona stroked her shoulder.

'I know he's a friend of yours, Anna honey, but I just can't take to the man. The only good thing about it is that he'll be off campus for at least six months.'

Anna winced. She had told Philip all about her intended application and he had made absolutely no mention of putting himself forward. Maybe Mona had got it wrong?

Brendan was in his office when she marched in like a virago and demanded an explanation.

'Anna, a number of my staff put forward proposals for the year's sabbatical at Stanford,' he soothed. 'Everyone here was competing with people from UCD and Galway and Cork. It was a broad field and Philip won it fair and square. The Americans liked what he was offering and he was selected. I'm sorry but it was not my decision.'

'What was his proposal?' she demanded.

'Well, obviously you are all covering a lot of similar ground, especially for an audience outside of Ireland. Philip was focusing on the dramatists, but I suppose the paper he's working on, "The Female Influence on Ireland's Great Dramatists", did have an appeal.'

'Brendan, that is my idea,' she screamed. 'You *know* that! Yeats was a complex man but the essence of Philip's study is the same as mine. He's taken my idea!'

'His proposal might have some similarities to yours,' he admitted, 'but it had a broader scope and hence a broader appeal.' Brendan Delaney sighed. God preserve him from competing academics. Philip Flynn was an arrogant prick and he himself had been surprised by his sudden candidacy and detour into academic writing as opposed to those godawful plays of his. 'I'm sorry, Anna, there's nothing I can do. Philip spoke with the people in Stanford last night and has agreed to take the position with them.'

Fuming with indignation, she left the office and strode across the quadrangle. When she found Philip she would give him a piece of her mind. He was the lowest of the low – a plagiarist! He had listened to her outline over the past few months, what she was working on, and had simply rehashed it and submitted it. She'd murder him!

Chapter Twenty-five

In a fury Anna, her hair wild and tumbling around her shoulders, her long black-and-red-striped cardigan blowing about her, searched the whole of Trinity. She searched the staffroom, the library, the corner of the restaurant where he usually sat, only to be told that Philip Flynn had gone home. Grabbing her keys she jumped into her trusty red Polo and driven to Glasnevin where he lived.

The small red-brick terrace house he shared with his mammy was close to the Botanic Gardens. Last summer and spring he had regularly taken her there for picnics and walks. Anna squeezed into a tiny parking spot outside it and ran up to the front door, ringing the bell.

Dympna Flynn answered it. She was wearing a salmon-coloured cardigan, a tartan skirt and her regulation nylon stockings and high heels. Her fair hair was immaculately blow-dried as if she had just come back from the hairdresser's.

'Is he in?' demanded Anna.

'Philip's not here but he's due any minute. He went to the

butcher's to get us a nice bit of fillet steak for the dinner.' Philip's mammy was not used to Anna using that tone of voice and looked slightly insulted.

'Then if you don't mind, Dympna, I'll wait.'

It was uncomfortable sitting in the front room with its hard sofa and display cabinet of ornaments and china. Dympna sat across from her, her hands fidgeting on her lap.

'Have you heard the good news about him going to America?'

'That's why I'm here,' Anna said tersely.

'I'm going to miss him terribly,' said Dympna, reaching for a hankie stuck up her cardigan sleeve. 'But I can't stand in his way. Philip is so excited about it. He's trying to persuade me to come out and visit him. As visiting lecturer he will have accommodation provided.'

Anna gritted her teeth. Her mother had always said never trust a man beyond twenty-five still living with his mother – she should have listened to her. 'That would be nice.'

'Would you like a cup of tea or coffee while you're waiting?'

'Coffee with milk and no sugar would be great, thanks.'

She studied the patterned carpet and the porcelain thimbles and glass animals that Philip's mother collected, the lace protectors on the chairs and the print of a stag in the Scottish highlands. Was it any wonder he wrote such shite plays! A grown man living in this place with poor Dympna waiting on him hand and foot!

Dympna was just carrying in a tray with two china mugs of coffee when Philip appeared, carrying their dinner in a plastic bag.

'Oh, hello, Anna,' he said, looking awkwardly at her, his gaze shifting around the familiar room. She had surprised him.

'I just heard about America,' she said, trying to keep her voice even.

'It was a last-minute thing,' he stammered. 'I just decided on the spur of the moment to throw my hat in the ring too.'

'Along with my proposal,' she said sarcastically. 'The study I've been working on for the past year.'

Dympna, picking up the tension, grabbed the bag from McCarthy's butcher's. 'If you two will excuse me I'll just put this meat in the fridge.'

Philip ran his fingers through his thick black hair, his expression wary. 'There is a difference,' he argued.

'And when did you come up with this brilliant idea of the influence of women on some Irish dramatists? Would it have been when I asked you to read over my paper on Lady Gregory's influence on Yeats? Or confided in you about my research on Maud Gonne?'

He moved his lips, his dark eyes searching for some kind of response.

'You are such a total shit, Philip. A schemer! A big nothing!'

'Hold on, Anna, I am as entitled to apply for Stanford as you or anyone else. A year out of this place is just what I need. OK, OK, there is some similarity between our proposals, I do admit, but mine is at a very early stage.'

'You lying little creep.'

'I am actually hoping to develop a script, write a play even while I'm away in California.'

Anna studied his handsome, smug, self-satisfied face. How in her right mind had she ever imagined that he was an interesting, intelligent guy, one she could perhaps have a relationship with!

'I could lodge a formal complaint, produce my early drafts, my original studies and notes, and send them to Martin Johnston tonight,' she threatened, 'and you can send him yours.'

'Mine is just an early proposal – barely at first draft stage,' he said, backtracking madly.

'Really!'

She knew she had him. The full extent of his cheating and lies was obvious, though she suspected he was not going to climb down and admit his culpability. 'You are pathetic!' she hissed softly, grabbing her handbag.

She could see bewilderment written all over his face. Philip hadn't even the sensitivity or emotional depth to recognize what he had done to her. How had she ever imagined he was anything special?

Dympna was standing in the hallway with a plate of biscuits in her hand. Anna guessed that she had overheard the full gist of their conversation.

'I'm sorry he upset you . . .' she began to say, fussing around offering more coffee and biscuits, as Anna, not trusting herself to say another word, headed for the hall door.

Chapter Twenty-six

Anna resigned herself to the fact that she wasn't going to Stanford, but what irked her most was the fact that Philip had muscled in on her academic territory. He might be a mammy's boy but he was still a scheming bastard! Hell would freeze over before she would ever attend one of his awful plays again.

Over Sunday lunch at her mother's Grace and Sarah had loyally taken her side as good sisters do in such circumstances, and hadn't a good word to say about him.

'Honestly, Anna, he was so rude and full of himself,' insisted Grace. 'The man thinks he's a genius!'

'He's a snake in the grass, as Granny would say,' Sarah added emphatically. 'The few times I met him, he acted as if I wasn't there!'

Anna blazed. She obviously hadn't a clue about men. Her instincts about men were so off centre that she had liked a guy both her sisters had taken such a *dis*like to.

'Anna, love, it's better you saw Philip in a true light before the two of you got more involved,' consoled her mum. 'Far better to find out now what a schemer he was before any more harm was done. Anyway a man like him is not good enough for one of my daughters!'

Anna stared at her bowl of rice pudding, stirring in a heaped spoon of sugar. It was so stupid; she had let her guard down with Philip Flynn, made allowances for his vanity and egotism by convincing herself that they were intelligent, artistic, like-minded people. How wrong could she get!

'You know that your father would never have taken to him,' added Maggie Ryan firmly.

Afterwards, as they were tidying up in the kitchen, her mother had given her a big old-fashioned hug.

'Anna, love, I know that you're disappointed about not going to America,' she began, 'and you must be hurt by what Philip has done. I know the two of you were close and had a lot in common, which is a good thing in one way, but some of these college fellows you've got involved with – I don't know what to make of them. Maybe you should give other men a chance. A man doesn't have to have a whole rake of degrees and doctorates to be kind and loving, believe me!' Maggie added earnestly.

Anna knew there was a truth to what her mother was saying but after Philip's behaviour she didn't know if she had any interest in trusting any man again!

'To be honest, I'm so annoyed about the whole stupid Philip thing that I can hardly think!' she confided. 'I feel like my brain is scrambled.'

'Maybe you should take some time off and go away and leave all that college work for a while,' Maggie suggested

'Mum, I have to try and push ahead with the Yeats study. I'm not going to have Philip turn around and say he wrote his one first. There's no chance I could go away for a few weeks to the States or anything like that.'

'Then maybe you could take a short break, go away just for a few days.'

'I just don't have time for a holiday,' Anna argued, thinking of all the first- and second-year papers she had to mark.

'I don't mean that kind of holiday, I mean peace and quiet, a chance to relax. What about a day or two in Gran's cottage? No one's been up there since last summer, and one of us should probably take a look over the place and see what needs doing before the holidays. Besides, a change of scene might do you good.'

Anna had to admit it did sound appealing, especially after the stresses of the past few days. She could do with a little tranquillity. She needed to be alone, have time to think. A few days in the peace and quiet of Granny's cottage in the West, away from everything and everyone, was exactly what she needed. How was it her mum always seemed to know what was best?

Maggie Ryan smiled to herself. A few days in Roundstone was indeed the best medicine for any tortured soul. The cottage might be a bit damp but things like that never usually bothered Anna, and she could check out if any repairs to the place were needed.

Anna set off on the road to Galway after her last lecture on Thursday.

The traffic was light as she drove through town after town: Moate, Athlone and Ballinasloe, bypassing Loughrea; at this rate she'd be in Galway before she knew it. She'd been up for a few days last summer with Sarah and Evie, and before that it had been a family celebration for her grandmother's birthday two years ago. The Ryan family had enjoyed a perfect weekend in Roundstone, with a barbecue and chilly swims on the beach and chatting long into the night wrapped in rugs around the fireplace. At eighty-two, her grandmother Annabel had been strong and well then, beating them all at poker and insisting on cooking huge meals and playing Joan Baez songs on her guitar and telling their fortunes.

Her decline and failing memory had all happened so suddenly. One minute capable and kind, organizing them all, and the next becoming a frail bedridden woman in a Dublin nursing home who could hardly remember their names. Poor Gran! How she must have hated it! Her death had brought an awkward sense of relief that the sparkling spirit of her grandmother was no longer tied to the decrepit frame and mind of an old woman.

'Thank God, she's finally free.' Her mother's words had echoed all their sentiments.

The road leading to the cottage was dark; her headlights picked up a rat running across the road. She turned off the engine and fumbled in her bag for the house keys as she grabbed her bag and locked the car.

The grass was overgrown and she trod carefully on the driveway that led to Gull Cottage, a dark shape that was perched near the sea. The sound of the waves and the smell of the sea cast their usual spell on her in the dim moonlight as she grasped the reassuring stone bird 'Gully' who perched beside the blue-painted front door, jiggling the keys as she opened it.

Inside, the air was musty and damp. She flicked on the light and looked around her. Dead bluebottles littered the windowsill; spider webs looped across the glass, which was salt-stained. The kitchen had been left neat and tidy ready for visitors with tea bags and coffee and sugar ready in their polished tins. She checked the fridge and switched it on, then plugged in her grandmother's radio and tape player. The sound of fiddle music filled the air. Gull Cottage always made every visitor feel welcome.

She got down a mug and filled the kettle after letting the water run for a minute. From the small bag of groceries she'd brought along, she opened a packet of wheaten crackers, adding two slices of cheese to them. She wrapped herself in a wool blanket as the heating got going and walked around inspecting the place. There was a leak from the roof in the bathroom, the window pane in the spare bedroom rattled ominously and in the living room there was a large patch of damp on the wall behind the blue couch. She smiled when she spotted that Evie's red bucket and spade had been left in the little bedroom ready for her next visit, along with a rubber ring and a broken sandal. She used to do the very same thing when she was small – leaving something behind in the hope of ensuring her return.

Once the cottage was warm and aired, she'd make up her bed. She looked in on her grandmother's room with its

182

old-fashioned double bed and dressing table and opted instead for the familiarity of the room she'd shared with her sisters. This time she had no rivals for the sole possession of the cosy double bed rather than the bunk beds that crowded one half of the room. She opened the window slightly to air it before making her way back to the kitchen.

The kettle was boiled and she cut herself more cheese, adding three baby tomatoes and a spoon of pickle to the plate of crackers. She hadn't realized how hungry she was as she poured milk into her tea and sat down to eat, perusing a copy of her grandmother's favourite cookbook as she did so. Monica Sheridan had been the doyenne of Irish cooking and Gran used make big jugs of homemade lemonade based on one of her recipes. Gran had scribbled notes and measurements in pencil on some of the pages along with a recipe for brown bread. She touched the perfect looped writing, emotion welling up inside her as she remembered Annabel Ryan. Her grandmother had been a bright interesting woman, filled with a zest for life and curiosity about everything – botany and plant life, nature, politics, literature and history, music and cookery – and was a great one for collecting recipes, though she never got round to using the half of them.

Once she'd eaten, Anna made herself comfortable in the sitting room, snuggling up on the couch and putting on one of her favourites tapes: Simon and Garfunkel. The tension eased from her as she listened to the words of the '59th Street Bridge Song' telling her to slow down. She flicked through two old magazines and yawned.

Bedtime beckoned and, after putting crisp white sheets on the mattress and a pale blue floral quiltcover on the bed, she soon found herself drifting off to sleep, listening to the sound of the sea and shifting shingle and sand from the beach below.

She slept in and it was late morning when she woke to perfect silence in the cottage except for the distant sound of the waves. She stretched in the comfortable bed, trying to make decisions. A walk then breakfast? Breakfast and a shower? Or should she pull on a towelling robe and go down the beach for a swim? Although it was bright and sunny outside there was a strong breeze blowing so she soon rejected the latter. Getting out of bed, she flicked on the immersion switch in the hot press before padding into the kitchen in her bare feet and putting on the kettle. First, a mug of coffee and a slice of toast and marmalade, then a shower, then get dressed. She needed some supplies: bread, milk, butter, meat, juice, plus a few odds and ends to clean the place. She'd drive into town to pick up a few things and a newspaper, then concentrate on work for the rest of the day. She jumped when she realized she had wasted almost an hour sitting at the windowsill watching honeysuckle blow against the cottage wall and wild roses dance in the wind. Her gaze was drawn to the patch of blue and the hardy souls playing and running on the beach. How was it that children and Labradors never felt the cold?

Braving the ancient bathroom Anna hopped under the useless contraption her family considered a shower. It limped into action as she turned the mixer tap frantically trying to achieve some balance of water that wasn't roasting hot or freezing. Scrubbing herself dry she flung on a pair of jeans, a washed-out pale blue T-shirt and her navy sweater as she grabbed her car keys.

Foley's shop was busy and Anna found herself smiling in recognition as she bumped into some of the locals.

'Are you down for the holidays?' asked Peggy Smith, an octogenarian who used to play bridge with her grandmother.

'It's just a flying visit till Sunday,' she admitted, grabbing some beautiful goat's cheese and slices of honey-baked ham and deliberating between a white soda bread or a brown, eventually popping the two of them into her basket.

'Well, it's good to see someone using the old place.'

Her shopping basket was full by the time she reached the checkout and she was relieved to have brought the car with her, throwing the bags on to the back seat.

Back in Gull Cottage she ate the simple lunch with bread still warm from the oven as she contemplated the rather dated interior of the cottage. As children and teenagers it had always seemed to her and her sisters the most perfect place in the world. They had relished every hour and day and week they spent in the place. Strange, but now with her grandmother gone it suddenly looked shabby and run down and in sore need of some attention.

Finishing her coffee, she pulled out her old brown brief-case, spewing across the table a pile of essays comparing Molly Keane's heroines with Edna O'Brien's. Some of the comments made her laugh. Two hours later, lured outside by the sunshine, she sat on one of the old wooden sun-chairs.

Long stripped of its original blue colour, it squatted between Granny's pots and beds and flower baskets. All were in dire need of attention and the grass was begging to be cut. Anna found herself fetching the shears from the wooden shed and checking the ancient lawnmower.

She abandoned the lawnmower after twenty minutes, realizing it needed to be either repaired or serviced and she couldn't tell which. Instead she began clipping with gusto at the weeds and thorny briars that were taking over the bed. She pulled up grass and dug up dandelions and thistles and cleared chickweed. After almost two hours she took a break with a glass of iced water and a piece of dark chocolate.

The sun was sinking before she finally stopped, her hands and nails filthy, muscles aching. She realized as she slipped off her mud-encrusted shoes and glimpsed herself in a mirror, her glowing face above the dirty sweater, that the lure of the garden and the house was in some bizarre way working its magic on her. Dinner was her priority next, then perhaps a quick walk or the pleasure of curling up with a book or listening to the radio. It was a very appealing programme.

Pasta in a pesto sauce with a crisp green salad proved delicious and she snuggled up on the couch with an ancient copy of *Heidi* that still had her name inscribed on it as she listened to the daily farmers' journal and the shipping news. By ten o'clock exhaustion had overtaken her and she was in bed, ready for sleep.

Chapter Twenty-seven

Maggie was embroiled in her household bills, trying to balance all the payments on her bank statements when Anna phoned next morning. It was a tiresome job which Leo had uncomplainingly done for years and now fell to her. Pushing aside the calculator and papers she was glad of the distraction.

'Mum, I'm going to stay on in the cottage for another few days, if that's OK? It's so peaceful here I'm actually getting some work done and I've had three swims in the freezing water and this morning I saw a pair of seals in the cove.'

'Of course you can stay. Stay as long as you need.' Maggie was relieved to hear Anna sounding more like her old self.

'I've rescheduled a few lectures and that new Ph.D. student from Belfast will take the two tutorials for me. I should be back by Wednesday night.'

'Well, enjoy the break and take care of yourself.' Maggie was delighted that Anna had organized it properly and was able to stay on. Of late, she always seemed to be rushing and had no time for anything or anyone. 'Is everything all right? You're sleeping and eating OK?'

'Mum, honestly,' Anna protested. 'I'm going for long walks and all the exercise and swimming is giving me an appetite and I'm getting plenty of sleep.'

'Any of the summer visitors around? Or the Murphys or the Kennys?'

'Not a sinner. The place is deserted. I've got the beach totally to myself. It's perfect.'

'Are you sure it's not too quiet or lonesome there for you, Anna?' she worried.

'Mum, peace and quiet is what I want.'

'Is the house OK?' Maggie continued.

'Well, I think there might be a bit of leak in the roof as there's a big damp patch on the wall in the sitting room, and another in the bathroom. Maybe a few roof tiles are missing. The garden's like a jungle and one of the bathroom taps is broken, but otherwise the cottage is the same as ever.'

Maggie smiled to herself. Annabel Ryan, her mother-in-law, had never been too good on the tidiness and neatness side of things, always seeming to live in a clutter of books and paints and garden things, with great plans to fix and do things tomorrow which were never fulfilled.

'Well, maybe I'll see if I can get someone to run out and have a look at the roof while you're there, Anna. We don't want it collapsing with rain when we go up in August. I have a list of people Annabel used for odd jobs; I'll try and get one of them to call out to the cottage and check it for us.'

'That's fine, Mum.'

'Take care of yourself, love,' urged Maggie as they ended

the phone call, glad that Anna was actually winding down and enjoying the West.

She was due to have afternoon tea with Regina Reynolds, the elderly grande dame of the square, who lived on the far corner and still enjoyed keeping up to date with the latest news of her neighbours and their families. But, as she was rooting around, she came across her mother-in-law's old Liberty-print address book in the kitchen drawer. Putting on her reading glasses, Maggie searched through the names, running her finger down the list of useful numbers. There was Tommy Leary, that rather grumpy sixty-year-old handyman who had painted the place four years ago and replaced a broken pane of glass in the kitchen that a bird or a stone must have cracked last summer. He lived about twenty miles away and she was about to call him when she remembered Robert O'Neill, the nice young man Annabel was always telling her about who could be relied on in times of emergencies and had worked as a building contractor. He'd probably know about fixing the roof – he'd once done a great job replacing the ancient back kitchen door for Annabel.

Maggie had met him only briefly once or twice on visits to Roundstone but she still remembered his kind words and expression of sympathy at her mother-in-law's funeral. He was a nice guy and lived much closer. Perhaps he wouldn't mind calling over to check the roof and also keep an eye on Anna for her while she was staying there. As she dialled Rob's number, she smiled to herself; he was unattached and rather good-looking if she recalled and had returned to the area he'd grown up in after a few years in England with the hope of settling down . . .

Chapter Twenty-eight

Anna had been digging and weeding all morning, watching with satisfaction as the pile of nettles and dandelions, leaves, dead wood and old flower heads grew. Standing beside the vegetable patch she remembered how her grandmother used to grow her own potatoes and lettuces, cabbage and carrots, and how she and her sisters fought to gather the juicy plump strawberries that Annabel Ryan produced summer after summer.

She had never realized how much satisfaction Gran must have got from growing some of her own vegetables and fruit and living in such a simple fashion; the appeal of it was only now becoming evident as she worked. Turning the soil and crumbling the earth in her hand with the sound of the sea in the distance and the tang of salt in the air, Anna found herself strangely at one with nature, all thoughts of lectures and notes and exam papers banished from her mind.

She was aware of the sound of a car in the lane but didn't react, even when she heard the rusty gate open. Maybe it was the postman.

'Hey!'

She stopped what she was doing and looked up. A stranger was approaching in a pair of faded jeans and a thick navy sweater.

'Mrs Ryan asked if I could come and check the place, said you think that there might be a problem with the roof,' he said, coming to a halt in front of her, tall and muscular, his hair tightly cut into his head, wearing a pair of wire-rimmed glasses.

Anna flushed, blinking in the sunlight. She must look a right state.

'I'm Rob, Rob O'Neill. I live about a half-mile down the road from here. I was a friend of Annabel's, the owner. I used to do some jobs for her. I noticed the other night there was someone staying in the cottage.'

'I'm Anna, Anna Ryan, her granddaughter,' she introduced herself, realizing her hand was muddy and she must look anything but attractive in the old trousers and T-shirt she was wearing. 'I'm just staying here for a few days.'

'It's good to see someone in the cottage. These places go to rack and ruin if they're left empty too long. It's much better to rent them out or sell them.'

Anna held her tongue. She wasn't going to have this guy who appeared from nowhere telling her what to do.

Without further ado she led him up to the cottage. Rob walked around checking doors and windows and taps and tiles, confirming that a few tiles were indeed missing from the roof and needed replacing.

'We had a fierce storm here in February; I should have

come and looked at the place myself. Most people lost a few tiles with it. Unfortunately that damp patch is going to need replastering to get it to look right.'

'Can you do it?'

'I'll try and match the tiles but won't be able to do it till next week, along with the window and changing the tap.'

'I have a spare key and I can leave it with you,' she offered.

'That'd be grand. You're making a good go of the garden,' he added, noticing her work.

'The grass is gone wild,' she admitted, 'but the mower's broken.'

'Will you let me take a look at that for you too? I used to cut the grass sometimes for Annabel. It was getting too much for her at the end.'

Anna wasn't sure if this was a deliberate rebuke aimed at her family for letting her grandmother live here so far from everyone on her own.

'She loved it here,' she explained, daring him to disagree with her.

'Can you blame her?' he agreed, his expression softening. 'I moved out here about four years ago myself – decided to get away from the rat race. Best thing I ever did.'

Anna suddenly found herself curious about this rather good-looking guy who was kicking at a weed that was embedded in the ground near his foot. Maybe he was a local farmer or one of those Jack-of-all-trades types who somehow manage to make a living in a place like this.

She led him towards the shed although it was clear Rob

already knew where to go. He pushed the ancient lawnmower out on to the gravel path.

'Is it totally kaput?'

He didn't answer immediately; he was bent down, totally concentrating. He tried to start it about three times and then upended the thing, lifting off various parts and examining them.

'I'll just check it over, and have a look at the motor.'

She watched him for a few minutes; he was engrossed in the problem.

'Would you have a screwdriver?' he asked eventually, lifting his glasses slightly.

She must have looked baffled. She had no idea where her grandmother would keep stuff like that. Was it in a tin in the shed or in the drawers in the kitchen?

'Don't worry. I have one in the car,' he offered, standing up and wiping his hand on his jeans. She watched his lean figure amble towards the ancient green jeep. She guessed he was somewhere around her own age, maybe a bit older, and found herself wondering if he was married or had a girlfriend.

A few minutes later he returned, ignoring her as he spread various parts of the lawnmower over the grass.

'Would you like a cup of coffee while you're working?' she offered, suddenly remembering her manners.

The kettle boiled quickly and Anna was relieved to see she still had enough milk in the fridge and that she hadn't demolished all the chocolate marshmallows. She'd put them on a plate and carry it out to him and let him get on with it.

'So you've been doing a bit of tidying inside too?'

She spun round to catch Rob standing at the kitchen doorway surveying the stacks of old tins and crockery and pots and pans which she had started to sort out and tidy up.

'Yeah. It's all got a bit disorganized.'

'Annabel was always a bit of a hoarder,' he said fondly as, uninvited, he came in and sat down on one of the kitchen chairs. 'This is the problem.' He showed her a small rusted piece of metal. 'It's the rotary pin. It needs replacing.'

'Can you fix it?'

'Well, hopefully I'm going over Clifden later this afternoon. I'll see if I can get a new one there. If not I'm in Galway next week and I'll try and get the part then. Beats having to get a new mower.' He smiled, taking the mug of coffee and adding two large spoonfuls of sugar, stirring them as he looked around. 'Always loved this kitchen. Gets the sun all day and you can glimpse the sea from the window.'

He seemed at home in the place and she tried to imagine her grandmother entertaining this man, chatting about the garden and her vegetables and the local news, proof of how well her gran got on with people and how well loved she was.

'Would you like a mallow?'

'Hey, my favourites,' he declared, unwrapping the silver foil and biting into one.

Anna could feel his gaze settle on her and was conscious of her curly hair tumbling from the haphazard ponytail she'd tied this morning with a piece of old green ribbon and the fact that she hadn't bothered with any make-up. Her fair eyelashes probably looked pretty non-existent, and the

T-shirt she was wearing could certainly do with a wash.

'How long are you staying for?'

'A few days only, I have to be back in work in Dublin for Thursday.'

'Poor you,' he said ruefully, glancing out the window at the magnificent landscape tumbling out before them.

'I'm working on an important college project,' she explained, wondering why she was trying to impress him with her workload, 'and I really can't stay away any longer.'

'I used to work in Dublin' – he grimaced – 'then London, Manchester . . .' He helped himself to another biscuit. '. . . before I found out that I'm just not the big city type of guy. I'm a country boy so I came back to my roots. Probably one of the better decisions in my life and needless to say the mammy and daddy are delighted to have the prodigal back in the family fold.'

She was curious and was just about to ask him what he did when his phone rang.

'Listen, I'd better be going,' he excused himself, glancing at his mobile and putting his mug over by the Belfast sink. 'I'll order the tiles and try and get that mower part for you, OK?'

'Thanks,' she said, giving him the spare key to Gull Cottage, knowing instinctively that she could trust him.

She walked down to the car with him and watched him drive off down along the coast road.

Anna worked for another two hours then went for a quick swim in the cove. The sea water was bracing and icy as usual; a curious seal watched her from the distance. Anna dried herself off and pulled on her sweatpants and then jogged slowly along the strand to warm up. As the evening drew in she made herself a big vegetarian stew and found herself picking up one her grandmother's old sketchbooks with its drawing of the view from the kitchen window, the heavy fuchsia, the dogwood roses and the low stone wall that gave way to the field and hedgerow and the blue line of glimmering water in the distance. Granny's love for this place was evident in every line. She had found a peace here and become part of the small local community. Anna almost envied her. She pulled out her folder of notes and references, raking through them with a fine felt pen before the ideas came and she turned on her laptop and began to write.

Over the next two days she worked in the morning and pottered around the garden in the afternoon, the physical exercise relaxing and calming her. There was no sign of Rob and she guessed he was probably too busy and caught up in work of his own to call over. Repairing her grandmother's ancient mower was hardly top on his list of priorities.

On Wednesday afternoon Anna packed up the car reluctantly. Gull Cottage looked lonely as she closed it up and she vowed to return in the next few weeks even if it was only for a weekend. Sitting into her little red Polo she braced herself for the return to the city and her normal life.

Chapter Twenty-nine

As the late April afternoon sun glinted in through the tall window of the drawing room, Oscar Lynch studied the view over Pleasant Square, taking in the street of red-brick houses with their granite steps and railings. He had considered this selfsame view, the park with its tall chestnut trees and cherry trees, the central square with its seasonal border, the small play area with its two swings and rather wonky see-saw and the grass tennis court at the rear for almost half a century. Embarking on the purchase of this house he and Elizabeth had given much thought to the amenity of having an almost private park as your front garden; each had decided it was the perfect place to raise a family, far from the newer sprawling estates that were being built around the city. The cost of a new roof, wiring, heating and a kitchen were outweighed by the charm of the square, its proximity to town and of course the park.

Year after year had passed and they had waited and waited, ever-hopeful for a much-longed-for son or daughter to arrive. Then Elizabeth had endured a miscarriage at sixteen weeks and never fell pregnant again. With every subsequent year the thoughts of a family of their own had somehow receded. Unfortunately Elizabeth would not countenance the thought of adoption.

'If we have a child, it will be our own,' she'd insisted, ignoring his pleas that they talk to one of the adoption societies. So he too in time had accepted that no child of his would run through the grass or play on the red-painted swings or lob a tennis ball across the net.

He'd watched heavy-hearted as the other families filled the square, shouting and laughing during the summer, scrunching through the leaves and searching for conkers in the autumn, building snowmen in the winter and flying kites as the breezy days of spring and early summer came around again. In time Elizabeth and he no longer spoke of that which had caused so much secret pain and hurt during their long years of marriage. He had adored Elizabeth Fortune from the minute he first set eyes on her, finding her both beautiful and intelligent, a rare enough combination for one's life partner. Nowadays of course, with the miracles of modern science and medicine, couples could have test-tube babies, IVF; all kinds of things had been invented to give hope to the childless, but all that was after their time and they had simply learned to accept it with dignity.

Instead they had filled their lives with other things: music, opera and travel. They'd travelled regularly to Italy: La Scala, Verona; all the great opera stages of the world. They drank wine in the vineyards of Champagne, Burgundy, Dordogne, Douro, Stellenbosch, Franschhoek, Napa Valley and Hunter Valley. They had explored the world, always seeking to discover more about this great earth and their fellow human beings. A dentist with a busy loyal practice, he'd worked till he was sixty-eight, filling teeth, crowning, polishing and removing them, adapting bites, curing grinding, remaining calm in the face of the sheer terror of the vast majority of his patients. At night Elizabeth would listen to him patiently as he told her about the lives and foibles of those who had graced the large leather dentist chair during the day.

'You are so kind to everyone, Oscar,' she would praise him as she cooked dinner and poured a perfect restorative glass of gin and tonic. 'They're lucky to have such a good dentist to look after them.'

He smiled, watching as two boys of ten or eleven raced each other on bicycles through the park. A McCarthy by the look of him, with a pal. That family had been reared in the park!

Of course Elizabeth was gone now and he was alone. She had died almost eight years ago. His beautiful wife had been paralysed by a stroke that hit suddenly when she woke up one morning. Seriously ill, she had been taken to hospital and over the following week had developed complications and pneumonia. She hadn't responded to the treatment and despite everyone's best efforts Elizabeth had died. It had been an awful time. He still remembered it as if it was only yesterday. The grief, the intense anger and of course the loneliness that followed. Without Elizabeth there were no more travels, no big trips. Five years ago old friends had inveigled him to the Wexford Opera Festival, but tears had rolled uncontrollably down his face as he'd watched *Carmen* performed. Never again. He couldn't do it without her.

Now his life was about to change again. He was plagued with arthritis and had become almost a prisoner in his own home, reliant on the goodwill and charity of friends and neighbours to assist him. His consultant, Tom Moore in the Blackrock Clinic, had called him in and told him he needed a hip replacement.

'There's still plenty of life left in you, Oscar,' he'd cajoled. 'Being bed-bound or immobile is no good for you or anyone else. Surgery will help you enormously. Within a few months I guarantee you won't know yourself.'

Oscar had found himself unusually wary of the procedure, worried about the length of time he'd have to spend in hospital and recuperating. Was there any point to it, he asked himself? What would Elizabeth have wanted? Still, it was his doctor's professional opinion and he didn't want to be a burden on anyone or for that matter a burden on the state! The only sensible thing to do was take his surgeon's advice and go ahead with the operation. The decision was made and today was the day. His neighbour Maggie Ryan had kindly volunteered to drive him to the hospital and he knew that he could depend on her to collect his post and look after the house and garden while he was in hospital.

His bag was packed and ready. He glanced around his house one more time: the expensive gold carpet, the polished mahogany bookcase and side table and chairs, the Adams fireplace and the comfortable high-backed wing armchair where he normally sat. He took a breath, steadying himself as he heard the car pull up outside his front door. He pulled himself upright and fixed his navy cravat in the mirror, considering his grey hair and lined face, admitting for the first time in a very long while that he was scared. Scared to leave this house, scared of what lay ahead, scared of being alone.

Chapter Thirty

Lying in bed in his hospital room, Oscar had to admit that underneath his seemingly dignified manner he was more than scared: he was almost paralysed with fear. Despite his own medical background and training, hospitals alarmed and unsettled him. All he could do was try to forget about his upcoming operation.

The nurses were kind and charming, fussing about him; a red-haired girl from Mayo called Mary checked his blood pressure and temperature to ensure he was fit for tomorrow's surgery.

Outside the window, the seascape of Dublin Bay beckoned; the tide was turning as the waves rushed towards the coastline between Blackrock and Booterstown; a crazy dog chased after a seagull that took flight, gliding in the currents of air as it wheeled out seawards; the crowded green Dart train travelled up and down the track in a loop between Bray and the city.

'Are you all right, Mr Lynch?' asked a different nurse, a beautiful young Filipina, coming to check on him.

'Grand.' He smiled, just wanting to be left in peace and not be a bother to any of the staff. He had ordered plaice and chips for his tea and from then on would be fasting. His affairs were in order. He'd been in touch with his brother James in Sydney and his cousin Gloria in Belfast to tell them of his hospital visit, in order that they were aware of his medical condition if the need should arise. He was as comfortable as could be expected and engrossed himself in a copy of P. G. Wodehouse, the antics of Bertie Wooster and the reliable Jeeves the perfect antidote to boredom as he awaited the arrival of Mr Moore.

In a haze of unconsciousness and morphine, he had dreamed about Elizabeth who looked radiant and beautiful and had stroked his brow, and called him darling. He had woken instead to discover Nurse Mary beside his bed, checking the monitor and fluid drip and drains and reassuring him the operation had gone well and that Mr Moore would be in to talk to him later. Relief washed over him as he gave into pain and anaesthesia and drifted back into a deep unbroken slumber.

The new titanium hip would seem to be doing the job and after two days he was back on his feet – well, crutches – trying to get mobile again. For the first time in his life Oscar felt old and weak as he negotiated bed to chair, chair to bathroom and made a short sortie supported by two nurses along the fourth-floor corridor, which seemed to his feeble body like an immense marathon. He knew he had immense willpower, but he still wondered how he would manage to negotiate simple day-to-day routines once he left the confines of the Blackrock Clinic.

'We're delighted with the outcome of your surgery,' his doctor, Tom Moore, had said reassuringly after checking him over. 'Another few days here with us in the clinic and then we've organized for you to have two weeks' convalescence.'

'Thank you,' he responded. 'I'm most grateful for all the excellent medical care and attention that I've received.'

'So everything has gone very well thus far,' continued the doctor from his bedside. 'You are on track to make a very good recovery. Most patients, with a good deal of support at home and regular physiotherapy, see a vast improvement in mobility. However, I did see in your notes that you live alone, which is a concern. For that reason I would suggest that you consider moving to a nursing home or a retirement home.'

'A nursing home!' blustered Oscar at the young man, who looked barely forty with his pink round face and honest eyes. 'I am very grateful for all you and your medical team have done for me but I have absolutely no intention of checking into one of those godawful places. The road to recovery is, I assure you, my own home in Pleasant Square.'

'But you do know that you must take things very slow and easy when you get home,' warned the surgeon. 'All healing takes time.'

'Of course,' promised Oscar, already exhausted from the effort of arguing as he contemplated his ability to cook and clean and wash and iron and manage in the rather large three-storey house he inhabited on his own.

* * *

Maggie had a small bunch of roses, cut from the garden, a jar of mint humbugs which she knew Oscar was partial to, the latest issue of the *Phoenix* magazine and a pair of new blue men's pyjamas that she had purchased from Marks & Spencer in Grafton Street, which she could return if not suitable. A discreet glance at Oscar's hot press had illustrated what she considered the need for fresh pyjamas for his hospital stay. She also had his post, a get-well card from herself and one from Evie which was done in garish pink and purple crayon and showed a purple whale and a pink fish jumping in the air. She was just in time for visiting and walked along the hospital's upper corridor and asked at the nurse's station where her friend could be.

Oscar had a private room with a magnificent view of the sea. She was glad to see he was getting some recompense after years of paying into an expensive health plan which he had never used.

'Maggie, my dear, how good to see you,' he welcomed her warmly from the high-back winged chair that he was sitting in. 'I do appreciate your coming to see an old renegade like me.'

Despite being rather pale and tired he still managed to be his usual gallant self and she gave him a quick hug as she fussed around with his post and presents, putting the new pyjamas in the locker near his bed.

She listened as he told her about his operation and the engineering precision needed to fit his new hip. 'The miracles of modern medicine and technology are astounding!'

'How much longer do you think they will keep you here in the clinic?' she asked, delighted that Oscar's operation had been such a success.

'Only a few more days,' he confided, 'then they're talking about me going to a convalescent home for a couple of weeks before I can even consider going home.'

'Well, that's probably for the best, they wouldn't recommend it otherwise.'

'Mr Moore even had the audacity to suggest that I should consider moving into a nursing home or one of those retirement places,' complained Oscar, suddenly getting upset and agitated. 'I am well able to manage on my own at home.'

'Of course you are, Oscar.' She knew what an independent man he was, always set on doing things for himself. She remembered one time he had tried to prune the big cherry tree next door and had got stuck up near the top of it. Luckily Sarah had spotted him and she'd rushed in and held the ladder for him, saving him from a nasty fall. 'But you will be on crutches for a while and I'm sure that you'll need to take it easy.'

Why was it that men were such bad patients, she wondered, and hated words like 'rest' and 'taking it easy' so much!

'Will I put these roses in water for you?' she offered, trying to change the subject. 'I'm sure the nurses must have some vases outside somewhere.'

After a quick search of the corridor she found a nurse at the station who fetched her a glass vase.

'How's Oscar doing?'

206

'Fine.' The young sister smiled. She had kind eyes.

'I live beside him,' Maggie explained. 'We're neighbours as well as friends and I'm keeping an eye on his place until he comes home.'

'He doesn't have any family?'

'No. Not really. A brother lives in Australia; his wife Elizabeth died a few years ago.'

'Poor man. He talks about her all the time.'

'She was the love of his life; they were a great pair.'

'Then it must be lonely for him now.'

'Yes,' confided Maggie, who understood only too well the loneliness of being widowed.

'Mr Moore, his surgeon, has suggested Mr Lynch consider moving to a nursing home. A gentleman his age recuperating from major surgery would usually need a long period of total convalescent care before returning home. Even then the hospital would need to know that there would be the necessary home help and support provided to enable Oscar to manage at home eventually.'

Maggie didn't know what to say.

'Oscar's very independent, so you can understand him wanting to go home to his own bed and house.'

'Of course,' said the nurse. 'It's just that following his convalescence he's still going to need help over the next few months.'

Maggie thanked the nurse and returned with the vase.

Oscar was dozing. He'd been a handsome man, like one of those old Shakespearian actors. He looked older, she thought, his thin face racked with exhaustion, mouth open, snoring lightly. Silently she filled the vase with water and fixed the roses, setting them on the locker near his bed. Elizabeth and Oscar had been good neighbours to her over the years, helped out numerous times when there were calamities with the children or the car had broken down, and even one time when the washing machine had gone on fire insisted on them using theirs for five days until they could find a replacement model and a plumber to fit it. Elizabeth had been a wonderful cook and hostess and they'd enjoyed great hospitality with numerous meals and drinks under the Lynches' roof over the years. Now it seemed poor Oscar was expected to try to manage at home on his own after an operation. Well, she'd help out as much as she could, but there must be a solution to it. There had to be. Bending over she kissed Oscar lightly on his forehead as she grabbed her handbag from the chair and left.

Chapter Thirty-one

Back in Dublin, Anna immersed herself in work. She managed to avoid Philip on campus as much as possible, with the exception of an awkward night when they were both asked to the book launch of Michael O'Shea's new volume of poetry in the Arts Club. It was laughable really, both of them with glasses of wine in hand trying to keep to the side of the room furthest from the other.

She found herself missing the cottage, missing the peace of the mornings watching the cormorant diving from the rocks on the beach and the near-empty landscapes, and as the final few weeks of term approached and the students began to study for their exams she decided to take a break on the bank holiday weekend, filling the boot of the car with folders and files, her boxes of books and her precious laptop and returning to Roundstone.

Anna could feel herself relax as she turned the final bend in the road and saw the dark grey slate tiles and chimney that signalled the roof of Gull Cottage. It was almost like a mirage after the hurly burly of the city and the pace of life in

Dublin. She slowed down the car to take in the view of the sea and that first proper glimpse of the house. No wonder her grandmother had insisted on spending so much time here in her later years. Stopping the car she took a deep breath of fresh air, relishing the peculiar tang of salt water and seaweed that the breeze carried in to the shore.

Grabbing her backpack she opened the door and let herself in, almost giddy with excitement as she ran around and checked the place. She smiled, noticing immediately that the roof tiles were fixed, and that the ugly damp patch in the sitting room had been freshly plastered. The window was done, the tap in the bathroom sink for once actually worked and the grass was cut, and checking the shed she discovered the mower back in its correct place. Rob must have managed to fix it all. She must be sure to pay him for everything before she returned to Dublin.

It was windy outside and, grabbing her jacket, she decided to head down to the beach for a walk after the long drive. The strand was deserted and she ran and jumped and messed around like a little kid, chasing the waves, screaming and running back and forth, her shoes and socks in a pile as she paddled and splashed, her jeans absolutely soaked. Her hair was all over the place and she even had sand in her ears.

Reluctantly, after about an hour and a half she headed back to the house as the first cloak of rain blew in off the ocean, running towards the house as it began to fall heavily. She threw off her wet clothes, pulling on her warm pyjamas and a fleece sweatshirt as she flicked on the radio. She had no interest in traffic news or what was going on in the financial markets and quickly switched it off, slipping on Simon and Garfunkel instead. Their mellow sounds filled the pine kitchen as she made herself a vegetable stir-fry with rice, curling up on the couch to eat it as the light changed and the sun slowly sank below the horizon.

That night she sat down prepared to work, to write about the women in W. B. Yeats's life: his mother, his wife, the woman he adored, his sisters, his patron; about a man nurtured by the love of many others who were satisfied to simply be part of his genius. The blank screen with its paltry sixteen lines of text mocked her as she searched for the right words and phrases to describe the intimate relationship that existed between the poet and his muse, the beautiful Maud Gonne. She reread her notes and scribbled on a rough paper pad, but no matter how much she tried to get the rhythm of the words that filled her brain on to the page she realized she could not convey her thoughts adequately. She who berated her students for their lack of depth and understanding was now unable to recreate the world of the poet she adored and respected.

'Forget it!' she said to herself, reaching instead for a book on her grandmother's bookshelf about the lighthouses of Ireland. She read for two hours and then, after making a mug of milky coffee, went to bed. The wind howled through the night but, wrapped snug in her quilt, she slept.

The next morning the beach was scattered with streels of seaweed and flotsam washed ashore, the tide was out, the water calm once more. After breakfast she decided to drive to the shops to get a paper and some milk.

Looking around at the crowded shelves and fridges in Foley's supermarket–cum–post office she was tempted to buy more. She picked out rashers and sausages, some free-range eggs and a loaf of wheaten bread, a few slices of baked ham and tomatoes and butter. Funny, but the air up here always made her hungry; when they were kids they were always starving and Granny and her mum would spend their time cooking up fries and barbecues and picnics for them.

Rose Foley asked after her mother as she paid for her groceries. 'Tell her I said hello, and not to leave it so long before she comes back up to visit us.'

'Rose, by any chance do you know where Rob O'Neill lives?' she asked as she packed the items in her bag.

'That scallywag of a nephew of mine lives up on the coast road, about half a mile past Grogan's house,' she replied. 'You can't miss it! It's the old schoolhouse.'

The car bumped along the muddy road between the over-grown hedgerows as she searched for the house, coming to a halt outside the stone schoolhouse with its new windows and bright painted gate. His car was there but knocking on the door she got no answer. Maybe she could just shove a note in the letterbox? She wanted to pay him but had no idea how much all the work and repairs had cost. In an attempt to find him she walked around the back of the building to find Rob busy varnishing a garden table and chair set in the middle of a grassy area overlooking the beach. The front of the schoolhouse had been deceptive: the back looked nothing like a school building. It had tall almost roof-to-floor windows giving a magnificent view of the sea, with glass panels built into the slanting roof.

'Wow, it's wonderful.'

He stopped what he was doing and came over to her immediately, wiping his hands, followed by a black and white Jack Russell-type mongrel.

'I got your mower fixed and the roof done.'

'That's why I came.' She grinned. 'Thanks so much for all your work. I want to find out how much I owe you.'

'Three hundred should do it.'

'Your house looks amazing,' she said as she pulled the crisp fifty-euro notes she'd got from the pass machine in Galway from her purse.

'I was going to take a break,' he said, slipping the notes into the pocket of his jeans. 'Do you fancy a coffee and Tippy and I will give you a tour of the place.'

'Are you sure I'm not holding you up? I'd love to see what it's like on the inside.'

Rob led her in through a high bright glass and pine patio door to a huge kitchen area with simple oak units and a long oak table and chairs. The sun splashed on to the white walls, picking out the granite-covered chimney breast, and high-lighting a scatter of oil paintings and modern graphic prints hanging on the opposite wall.

'It's beautiful, Rob,' she said, walking around, standing at the island unit with its magnificent view of the coast. 'It must be fun cooking here!'

A staircase divided it from the open-plan living area with another fireplace, two huge couches and a wall with a complete sound system, flat-screen TV and DVD player.

She laughed when she spotted the old-fashioned blackboard left down the back wall.

'Well, I couldn't have a schoolhouse without having a blackboard!'

Unable to resist she got a piece of chalk and wrote her name and drew a big smiley sun on it.

A small buttercup-coloured bedroom with view of the front yard and a storage room completed the downstairs.

She followed him as he led her upstairs unable to disguise her envy when he opened the door of the main bedroom. The room held a large bed which faced the tall pointed windows with the breathtaking view of the sea and beach below. The room was cream and white with three giant Aran-patterned cushions on the bed.

'My mother knitted those for me,' he confided.

The room was neat and clean, with a walk-in wardrobe to one side where she noticed everything folded and hanging in its correct place. A simple white bathroom with a glorious power shower and another bedroom, where he was fitting wardrobes, completed the upstairs.

'It's so amazing, I can't believe it was ever a schoolhouse.'

'It's taken me three years to get this far and it's been a huge amount of work,' he admitted candidly. 'I've done most of it myself but I hope that I have managed to retain some of the character of the place.'

'Rob, it's lovely. I wish my sister Grace could see it. She's an architect,' she explained. 'She'd love it.'

As they sat and had coffee back downstairs he told her how he had managed to buy it. 'My father phoned me and told me it was going to auction. I was working in Manchester at the time, but I knew the building and the location. It had been empty for about five years, windows smashed, partly boarded up, but I went to school here with the rest of my brothers so I knew it very well. They merged the boys' and the girls' school and luckily for me this was the one put up for sale. I put in a bid, it was probably a bit higher than most so I managed to get it. I got home that summer and put in for planning permission and by the autumn I had moved back.'

'Well, you've done a wonderful job on it,' she complimented him, genuinely impressed with his work.

'Aye, it's been a bit of a long road, but it's worth it.'

She had seen no sign of a wife or girlfriend and was curious as to why he had put so much work into it.

'I told you I went to school here. Well, I sat at a desk over there against that very wall. I had Mr Horan our teacher driven demented,' he said, laughing aloud. 'I wasn't good at school, all I wanted was to kick football in the yard and play hurling with my brothers. Mr Horan told me repeatedly that I was hopeless and that he didn't expect much of me. I was ten years old and his words hit me hard. Isn't it funny how someone not believing in you can sometimes spur you on to do things you might not have imagined doing?'

Despite his smile Anna could still see the hurt in his eyes and was tempted to reach for his hand.

'I guess that sort of makes me crazy for buying this place.'

The dog whined to be let out and they watched her take off like a bolt of lightning across the lawn after a seagull, barking like crazy.

'Do you fancy a walk on the beach?' he asked, surprising her. 'Tippy likes to run around and chase the waves.'

Anna thanked heaven she was wearing her loafers as they descended the steps. The dog raced between them as they fell into step together on the almost-empty beach, the waves rushing towards the sand.

'What about you?' he asked.

'Well, I'm the opposite of you,' she said honestly, staring at a sailing boat in the distance. 'I was a swot at school. I always had my nose stuck in a book! Studying and reading and learning came easily to me. I loved poetry and drama and after studying English in college I decided I wanted to lose myself in the world of academia. Now I'm a junior lecturer teaching in the English Department in Trinity, specializing in Anglo-Irish Literature.'

'I always hated poetry,' he admitted, his blue eyes honest and direct. 'I could never understand why someone wouldn't say straight out what they thought. Poems were always like a riddle comparing something to something else, instead of loving it for itself.'

'Maybe you're right.' She was taken aback by his insight and his utter lack of literary pretension.

'Lately maybe I've begun to realize that there is more to life than words written on pages,' she confessed. 'I guess spending time up here in Gran's place has made me see that.'

'That's a good thing then,' he said firmly as he threw a piece of stick for the dog who ran demented after it and chased back and dropped it at his feet. He laughed. 'She thinks she's a retriever.'

As they walked back up the sand-covered steps fashioned from old timber railway sleepers, Rob surprised her again by asking her to stay for dinner.

'It's only chicken curry,' he warned. 'You'll be saving me from another lonely bachelor dinner.'

Anna swallowed hard. She couldn't remember the last time a man had offered to cook something for her. 'Sure,' she said lightly.

She watched as he cut up chicken breast and onions, the scent of garlic and curry powder and chilli filling the kitchen as they chatted easily. She set the table, managed to find the mango chutney he'd insisted he had at the back of his cupboard and put together a green salad.

The curry was hot and spicy and she reached for the glass of iced water on the table as he threw back his head and laughed.

'I thought you said you went easy on the chilli!'

'I did.'

Her tastebuds got used to it and after a few minutes she was able to carry on the conversation without looking too hot and flushed.

'I do a creamy smooth korma,' she teased, 'you'll have to taste that.'

'I'll hold you to it,' he said, getting up and fetching two bottles of cold beer from the fridge.

They ate and chatted until it got dark; Anna was embarrassed when she saw the time. 'I'd better get going,' she apologized, thanking him for the food.

'You could stay,' he said slowly, his eyes never leaving her face.

Anna took a breath. She was tempted to nod and say yes but something was holding her back. Call it being old-fashioned but she wasn't the type for casual relationships.

'I'm sorry, Rob, but I really have to go.'

'Let me walk you out,' he offered politely. The dog followed them out into the darkness.

The night was still, the moon wobbling above them as he reached down and kissed her, his lips warm. Anna, surprised by her own response, kissed him back. The dark shape of the hedges and field and stone walls all spun together as she clung to him.

'No changing your mind?' he teased.

'No!' She burst out giggling as she fished for her keys. She fiddled, trying to start the engine, and flicked on the lights. The car jumped to life and she turned and drove back along the country road.

Chapter Thirty-two

There wasn't sight nor sound of Rob the next day and Anna had to admit she was disappointed. Maybe she was reading the signals wrong and, as suspected, he already had a girl-friend or wife stashed away somewhere. Annoyed, she returned to her papers, spending the day immersing herself in the work of Augusta, Lady Gregory, Yeats's patron and supporter.

If Rob O'Neill wasn't interested in her that was fine; he was a nice guy but certainly not the type she normally fancied. The truth was that though they got on well and were easy with each other, he was totally different from any man she had ever gone out with before. They had nothing in common. Her mother maintained opposites attract, but sheer logic dictated that there was no point getting involved with someone who was your polar opposite!

She had worked till two a.m., delighted with her progress, her mobile switched off. Tomorrow, if there were no distractions, she should probably have the rest of the chapter done.

She set to work on the laptop after breakfast and took a break for a bowl of soup and some brown bread at lunchtime. Needing to clear her head she pulled on a light fleece and headed across the lane and down towards the strand. The beach was once again empty and she walked near the water's edge where the waves slapped against the sand. There were dark clouds in the distance and the forecast had mentioned rain. She was standing daydreaming when she noticed the small yappy dog approach her.

'Tippy?' she said hesitantly. The dog jumped enthusiastically on her legs.

'Heel! Heel!' called Rob uselessly as the dog did a lap around Anna's feet. 'Sorry, but she won't do a thing I tell her!'

Anna laughed aloud as the dog cocked one ear at her.

'I called by the house and saw the car was there and the windows were open so I guessed you'd gone for a walk.'

'I needed a bit of fresh air,' she admitted. 'I was going screwy-eyed from the computer.'

'Take a break then,' he suggested. 'I'm going down to Corry's old lighthouse. I just wondered if you might be interested in coming along for the ride?'

She studied him for a minute. He was wearing old jeans, a shirt and a knitted navy sweater, his skin tanned, his eyes behind the gold-rimmed glasses honest and steadfast. He seemed completely unaware of how attractive he was.

'We could see its light from here when I was a kid,' she remembered. 'I used to pretend when I was lying in the dark that someone was sending me a secret message in code.'

'Anna, come on, leave the work,' he urged, his face serious.

She had to admit she was tempted, as it was years since she'd been down near the lighthouse. Besides, there was no comparison between spending an afternoon in his company or in that of Lady Gregory.

'OK! OK!' she agreed.

Corry's lighthouse was perched on a rocky promontory overlooking the Atlantic. For a hundred years it had warned sailors of the rocks and treacherous conditions that lay hidden beneath the waves.

'It was sold four months ago,' he explained as they drew up as near as they could, parking his Land Rover on the muddy path. 'There's three acres of land with it.'

Anna studied the shabby tower of the lighthouse. It looked so decrepit now its beacon of light was gone. It saddened her to think of its yellow beam no longer illuminating this wild part of the coastline.

'What will happen to it?' she asked.

'I'm not sure,' he shrugged. 'I haven't quite decided yet.'

'*You* haven't decided!'

'I bought it from the fisheries department,' he admitted, pulling a set of keys from his pocket, looking like a kid who has just won a big prize. 'I couldn't bear to see it falling down. Maybe it's a bit of a mad project but restoring a lighthouse, that's got to be something!'

Anna could see the enthusiasm written all over his face.

'Do you want to see inside it?'

Anna nodded, holding her breath as the heavy wooden door opened. There was a musty smell inside and the ground-floor windows were covered in grime and dirt and spiders' webs. They raced around the building like two kids, Tippy following them as they climbed the big spiral stair-case. Up and up, a sitting room and small kitchen, two bedrooms, a storage room; the views were magnificent and Anna gasped when she stumbled into the lamp room. The huge central lamp stood like a giant eye in the middle of the room.

'Does it work?' she enquired.

'Unfortunately no,' he admitted. 'It went out of service about ten years ago; the last lighthouse keeper left here in 1989.'

'Can you get it working again?'

'I'm not sure but I intend giving it a good try. I heard there's a man living over near Spiddal who knows how to repair these things.'

'Rob, it's beautiful,' she said, standing at the windows over-looking the shore and the rugged Connemara countryside.

'Thanks.'

They explored the lighthouse and Rob told her his plans: a curving window on each floor that hugged the tower yet gave a view. He intended to put in new lighting, bathroom, kitchen, and a wooden balcony deck that ringed the top view-ing area.

'It sounds amazing Rob,' she enthused as they wandered around together.

'I know it sounds grand but I just want it to be comfort-able and to make sure that the accommodation lives up to the fantastic setting.'

'How did you get into this?' she asked, curious, leaning against the window sill.

'I told you I was crap at school. In the end I chucked it in when I was sixteen and began working for Johnny Foley the builder, did my apprenticeship with him. He's Rose's husband and a cousin of my mother's.' He laughed. 'There wasn't the building boom there is now and most of the work was local attic conversions and kitchen extensions, along with a few houses. I moved to Dublin for a while, then London. I worked in Ealing and Ipswich on big building sites, then one of my brothers, Gary, moved to Manchester and I followed him. It was construction work, but mostly restoration. Old buildings! It's easy to knock them and start over but it was bringing them back and adding something fresh to them that got me hooked: barns, factories, warehouses, a station, a firehouse, an old mill. You learn a lot from old buildings. I'm not afraid of hard work and getting stuck in. I signed up for some fancy night course in the local college. It was my first time sitting behind a desk for years. Project Management's what they call it and I guess it means that when I start something I stick to it right through until it gets finished. I'm not like a contractor who comes on site, does his bit and goes off site. I get to see it from start to finish.'

Anna found herself suddenly filled with admiration. Rob was a country guy, down to earth and honest. He didn't care about poetry and language and words, his world was timber, stone, earth and water, and buildings that came from another generation. Imagine, he actually owned a lighthouse! It was mad!

'Dan Regan was the last lighthouse keeper to live here,' explained Rob, looking through a pile of old charts and newspapers. 'His grandfather Tim Corry had kept it for years and after that his uncle Liam. The Corrys were raised here, which must have been hard for them as it was actually against the regulations to have a family here. An old cottage up the field was provided for Tim's wife and children. The place didn't survive the winter gales and storms so his family moved in here.'

'I'd imagine it must have been fun for the kids living in a lighthouse!'

'Lighthouse-keeping is a fierce lonely job,' he said slowly. 'Men go mad without women and company. Dan never married. I suppose it's hard to find a bride to live out in the wilds in a place like this.'

'It has its attractions,' she said, staring out across the rugged bare landscape and ocean. She could feel his eyes on her and turned towards him.

'Loneliness is an awful thing,' he said fiercely. 'You can be lonely in the middle of a city, in a small town, surrounded by people you know even. Some people don't need lighthouses!'

She caught his eye, struck by his intensity and drawn by his honesty. Without thinking she reached up and kissed his cheek, smiling as he ran his fingers over the curve of her cheekbones and face and kissed her lightly on the lips.

They drew apart, both surprised by the mutual sense of attraction between them.

'Anna,' he whispered softly, his breath on her hair as he took her hand. They kissed long and slow, again and again, as the seabirds wheeled around the old lighthouse and the sea breeze clipped the ocean.

'We should go,' he said a long while later.

She followed him out, watching as he locked the heavy door, Tippy racing ahead of them towards his Land Rover.

'There's a great little pub about five miles down the road if you fancy something to eat,' he suggested. 'Best seafood and steak outside Roundstone.'

She laughed. 'That sounds good.'

O'Flaherty's was quiet, with only two families and about five other people eating, and a few locals sitting up on barstools chatting. They found a table near the fireplace; a log and turf fire smouldered in the grate.

Anna suddenly realized how hungry she was when she read the menu: prawns, crab, lobster, scallops, served with baked or gratin potato. She opted for the prawns tossed in lemon butter and baked potato and salad, while Rob ordered a plate of fish cakes. She had a glass of wine while he ordered a pint.

'The lighthouse is amazing, Rob, thanks for letting me see inside it.'

'When the place is done up it will be pretty special,' he admitted. 'I'm hoping to rent it out to holidaymakers, the kind of people who just want to come to the West and get away from it all, be close to nature. I've also applied for permission to build two or three small coastguard cottages on the other side of the field.'

'That's great.'

'It's funny,' he mused. 'When I was younger I couldn't wait to get away from Connemara, away from the place and the parish and all the neighbours who know me and my cousins and relations. I didn't think the place had anything to offer.'

'The back of beyond.'

'But since I've come back I've put down roots here and I couldn't imagine myself living anywhere else. I can see how it has a hold on people.'

'My granny said "the West" put a spell on her,' remembered Anna.

The food was good, O'Flaherty's deserved its fine reputation. Rob ordered a brown-bread ice cream for dessert and Anna managed to steal a spoonful of it.

They sat and chatted for an hour or two, deciding to move when the bar got crowded and people were standing waiting for tables.

The road was dark as they drove through winding country lanes, Anna stealing a glance at Rob's expression, Tippy half-asleep on her lap. As they came near the town he slowed down.

'The schoolhouse or the cottage?' he asked softly.

Anna looked across at him. He was kind and old-fashioned and good and every ounce of instinct in her soul was saying 'Follow him'. It made no sense but she knew in her heart that she didn't want to waste any more time, not one more day of being apart, not one more night of not being with him.

'Your place,' she said, reaching for his hand.

* * *

From that night on Anna spent the vast part of her time with Rob, both of them equally surprised by the intensity of their feelings. Anna had never known anything like this before and had nothing to compare it with. Rob was so different from any other guy she had been with before and made her feel like she belonged here with him. How could she go back to Dublin, leave this place, the sea, the beach, the dog (who followed her like a shadow) and Rob?

'You know I have to get back to work,' she said, curled up beside Rob on the couch. 'My students have exams and I have to set papers – I can do marking and corrections up here later but I've got to be in Dublin for a while.'

'It's OK, Anna,' he teased, ruffling her hair which had gone beyond curly. 'I'm not going anywhere. I'll still be here, OK?'

She took a breath. It was almost like a dream, a mirage, to have Rob waiting for her. She felt taut and nervous inside that something would go wrong, something would happen to ruin it but Rob reassured her, pulling her across on to his lap and holding her close, kissing the fear away.

Chapter Thirty-three

Sarah's feet were killing her. She'd been working since eleven o'clock this morning helping Cora cater for a large funeral lunch party in a private home in Blackrock. Cooked wild salmon, baked ham and creamy chicken in white wine sauce had been served to the guests and the family had been very kind and had tipped her generously as she helped tidy up afterwards and pack things away. Standing at the bus stop on Mount Merrion Avenue waiting for the number 5 she immediately recognized the large black Range Rover pulling over to offer her a lift.

'Sarah, can I drop you somewhere?' Mark McGuiness asked, rolling down the windows.

'Oh, thanks, Mark,' she sighed as he opened the car door. 'I'm on my way home from work. This bus here isn't the best, so thanks a lot.'

'How did your party go?' he asked turning towards her.

'Party?'

'Your daughter's,' he reminded her. 'Sorry I couldn't make it but I was away in Germany that weekend.'

'It's OK, I got your message. The party was great. They all dressed up as fairies and had a picnic in the garden.'

'Sounds like a lot of fun; kids' birthday parties are the days you always remember,' he said. 'And Evie's a nice kid. She's a credit to you,' he added.

'Thanks,' said Sarah, watching his profile as he drove. She slipped off her shoes.

'That's a relief,' she sighed. 'I've been on my feet for hours at the lunch I was working at.'

'I thought you said you had a job at Evie's school?'

'I do three mornings a week but today I was working at a funeral lunch; my friend Cora was catering. We just served lunch to over a hundred people. I work there sometimes at the weekends and when they have extra functions on.'

'You sure keep yourself busy, Sarah,' he said admiringly, glancing in her direction.

He is definitely rather dishy, Sarah thought to herself, in that mature smooth kind of way.

'How's your sister?' he enquired as they stopped at the traffic lights.

'I've two,' she reminded him. 'Anna's off working on some poetry thing in Connemara and Grace is an architect.'

'I think that somehow that did come up in our rather heated conversation.' He laughed.

'Poor Grace. She just broke up with this awful creep she worked with. We are all mightily relieved as none of us liked him. Of course now she is burying herself in work.'

'Hard work never killed anyone,' he said as they turned in the direction of Pleasant Square.

They chatted easily about the neighbourhood as they drove. Mark McGuinness mightn't be her type of guy, Sarah thought, but he was sound and despite Grace's opinion of him, she liked him and was glad he was moving in opposite them.

'Mark, thanks for the lift,' she said, slipping her shoes back on as she got out of the car.

'Was that Mark McGuinness I saw dropping you off?' her mother asked as she relieved her from babysitting Evie. Honestly, her mum was such a curiosity box.

'Yes, it was Mark and I'd probably be still standing waiting at the bus stop in Blackrock otherwise.'

'Do you like him, Sarah?'

'Mum, you're obsessed. Will you stop it! He's just our new neighbour and he gave me a lift and it's no big deal.'

After tea when she had bathed Evie and changed her into her pyjamas, Sarah went into her bedroom to have a root around her wardrobe, which consisted mostly of denim jeans in various hues, lengths, widths and styles. Her best friend Karen had invited her to a dinner party on Saturday and she wanted to make a good impression. Karen would kill her if she turned up in jeans. She lifted out the multicoloured Zara skirt she usually wore with a black string top; it suddenly looked too old and worn for a stylish dinner party. The same went for her wrap-around blue dress and the silk print dress she'd bought in the sales.

'What are you doing, Mummy?' asked Evie, standing in the doorway watching her.

'I'm trying to find something nice to wear for Saturday night when I go to dinner at Karen and Mick's house. It's going to be kind of fancy there.'

Evie stayed ominously silent. Then: 'Auntie Grace has nice clothes, fancy ones.'

Out of the mouth of babes and innocents, thought Sarah, getting the message.

'Take what you want!' offered Grace, throwing open the doors of her massive walk-in wardrobe with its huge amount of hanging space, and racks and pullout drawers of tops and knits and belts and wraps. She sat on the bed to watch. 'There's a few Karen Millens that might fit and that lovely corset thing I got in Rococo that goes with that flouncy skirt.'

Sarah slowly went through the rack of expensive designer clothes hanging in her sister's wardrobe: Chanel, Stella McCartney, Chloé. Grace must have spent a fortune on them.

Some of the things swamped her as she wasn't as tall as Grace, even though her figure was curvier and far less toned.

'What about this?' suggested Grace pulling a chiffon wrap-around top and matching skirt from a padded hanger. 'I bought it in Paris.'

Sarah held it up. The grey-blue colour certainly suited her, even with her blond hair, and she quickly pulled it on. The V neckline showed off the curves of her breasts and made her neck appear longer.

'Wow,' said Grace. 'It never looked that good on me.'

'Are you sure it's OK?' Sarah was hesitant. Dressing up

and looking sexy and attractive was something she hadn't done for a very long time.

'Nice strappy shoes with a high heel and tanned legs and you can't go wrong.'

Sarah twirled around studying herself in the mirror. She looked and felt good, something that didn't happen very often these days.

'You look lovely, Sarah, honest,' said Grace sincerely.

Sarah couldn't believe that Grace was actually going to lend her something. When they were younger she used to scream at Anna and herself if they so much as took a pair of socks or a T-shirt from her room. There had been battles over make-up and cotton-wool puffs and mascara and nail varnish. She was sure the Lynches next door must have thought that they were a crazy family with all the shouting and screaming and banging of doors that went on. She supposed this meant they were finally grown up and that Grace was being the big sister helping her get ready for the special occasion.

'How are you getting to Karen's house tomorrow?'

'I'll get a bus or take a taxi.'

'No you won't. I'll drop you,' insisted her bossy big sister. 'I said I'd call into Roisin tomorrow night and I can drop you en route.'

'Thanks,' said Sarah, overwhelmed with gratitude.

Evie had studied her getting dressed and blow-drying her hair and putting on her make-up, her face serious as she took in the rituals of preparation for a *big night out*.

Sarah added a last coat of mascara to her eyelashes. Combined with the silver-grey powder and the slightly mauve-tinted eye-shadow she'd found at the bottom of her make-up box she had managed to make her eyes look huge. She grabbed a spray of perfume, realizing as she stood up that she felt just right.

'You look beautiful, Mummy,' affirmed her daughter, hugging her tight.

'Oh, Sarah, you are such a stunner,' declared her mother loyally. 'You look amazing.'

Despite their obvious bias Sarah was delighted with the results of her efforts.

Evie was going to sleep at her mum's for the night and there'd be treats and drinks and a big bedtime story. Was it any wonder Evie loved staying with Granny so much!

Sarah took a deep breath as she sat in Grace's car. It was stupid but she felt nervous. Karen was one of her oldest friends. They'd been to school together and when Karen had got married two years ago, she'd insisted on Sarah being one of her bridesmaids. Her husband Mick was a great guy and they were one of the nicest couples you could ever meet. Going to their dinner party was going to be fun and she was an absolute nerd to be anxious about it.

'You look fabulous!' coaxed Grace as they turned into Sycamore Road and she dropped her outside the white house. 'Have a lovely time!'

'Sarah, it's so great to see you,' Karen welcomed her, her

wavy dark hair pinned up, wearing a clingy black dress with showed off her narrow waist and tiny bump.

'I got you some wine and choccies,' said Sarah, giving her a hug.

'My favourites! Chocolate-covered walnuts and almonds; I'll be the size of an elephant before this baby's born at the rate I'm going.'

'You'd hardly know you were pregnant!'

'Tell Mick that! I chucked up all over his car last Saturday on the way home from a party and I hadn't had even a sniff of alcohol.'

'Poor you!' Sarah consoled her. 'When I was expecting Evie I was fine except for whenever I got the smell of frying. I couldn't walk past a chipper.'

'But they're worth it!'

'Definitely.'

'Come on into the living room. I want to introduce you to a few people. Rachel and her boyfriend Don are here and Mick's cousin Ronan Dempsey is home from London for a few days.'

Sarah braced herself as Karen ensured she got to meet everyone and Mick offered her a glass of sparkling cava to start the night.

Rachel Donovan was another schoolfriend and they greeted each other enthusiastically.

'I haven't seen you since Karen's wedding!' She smiled, introducing her boyfriend. 'How is everything going?'

'Well, Evie started school and I'm still working at a few things. I've got a part-time job teaching art and helping

234

in the school library three days a week which is handy.'

'That's great,' said Rachel kindly.

'What about you?'

'I'm still breaking my butt in Goodbody's.'

'That's where we met,' interrupted Don. 'Rachel's been promoted to senior specialist in aircraft and rail leasing and I handle shipping and satellites.'

'It sounds fancy,' admitted her friend, 'but it just means much bigger contracts!'

Sarah felt a pang of guilt that she wasn't doing something more interesting but being a mother was as much as she could handle.

There was another couple, the husband Brian worked with Mick and his wife. Chloe was a tiny dark-haired girl who wasn't particularly friendly. She worked as a media buyer in one of the big advertising agencies.

After two more drinks they all sat down at a large oak table with dark brown leather chairs. Karen served a salmon mousse for starters. Sarah was sitting beside Mick's cousin and a friend of Karen's called Susan; next to her was a guy called Sean who was about six foot tall and had red hair. She sipped at another glass of wine as the conversation ebbed and flowed around her. Chloe who was sitting across from her literally ignored her. There was a delicious beef encrusted with mustard and herbs, gratin potatoes and baby carrots for the main course and Sarah congratulated Karen on her prowess in cooking.

'It's one of my mum's recipes,' she confessed, 'a family favourite.'

The talk turned to politics and Sarah wished desperately that she had made time to read the political section of the *Irish Times* more closely and had kept abreast of current affairs: American foreign policy; Democrats versus Republicans; was Ireland closer in tune to Washington or Brussels . . .

'Sarah, what do you think?' asked Ronan, good-naturedly trying to draw her into the conversation.

She could feel the skin on her neck redden and she wished she could think of something to say. 'Obviously, when you have a child, it colours everything,' she admitted, looking around the table. 'Concern for the environment and health-care and support for single parents seems better in the EU; also the fact that we have good free education and great support for kids to go to college here means Ireland is very different from America.' She could see Karen nodding in agreement with her. 'I suppose I want Evie to have the best and living here in Ireland gives her better opportunities than she might have anywhere else. Being a single parent is tough enough even at the best of times but one thing all parents, married or single, want is for their children to be happy and safe.'

'Exactly.' Karen laughed. 'And I want all those lovely EU maternity and parental leave days due to me when junior appears!'

'Hear, hear!' they all agreed as Mick opened another bottle of wine and topped up everyone's glass.

'But our government must put in place policies that will protect our resources and cut back on energy usage like the rest of the EU,' insisted Sean. 'Buying credits for emissions from other countries with less productive economies than ours is hardly the way to go.'

'Exactly,' agreed Susan and Mick.

'Hopefully the future will bring new forms of energy, heat and power and light. Who can say!' argued Chloe. 'But it's important to protect the existing businesses and buoyant economy we have, not pie-in-the-sky future stuff that might never happen.'

Sean began to argue hotly with her about some politician and an energy bill that Sarah had never even heard of. She concentrated on the delicious food, promising herself that in the next few weeks she would make the effort and cook a big dinner for her family with all the proper trimmings.

There was a delicious hot treacle tart and vanilla ice-cream for pudding. Sarah had a really sweet tooth and lapped it up like a kid. It was only as she looked around the table she realized that most of the other female guests had demurred.

'You liked that!' teased Ronan. 'I could tell.'

'I guess when you are around six-year-olds as much as I am pudding and ice-cream is pretty much the main event after any meal!'

He laughed. 'Yeah, kids are great, no pretensions.'

A man who actually liked kids and wasn't put off by them – he was too good to be true. She told him a bit about Evie and they traded stories about growing up.

'My big brother shaved my hair when I was six – gave me a blade five – and my poor mother almost broke down and cried when she saw my bald head, my first communion was only three weeks away.'

'Oh no, what did you do?'

'What could I do? I had to wear a knitted bainin cap on my head in the photos taken out in the open air but inside the church — well, I had to take the hat off! I looked like something that had escaped from a Russian gulag.'

'Poor you.'

'Certainly a day to remember,' he confided. 'That's brotherly love!'

'My sister Anna broke my big toe,' she confessed.

'How?'

'We were staying in my granny's house in Connemara. I remember it was freezing and Granny had put one of those ancient stone hot-water jars in the bed to heat it. We were sharing the bed and we must have been fighting over it when she gave the jar a huge shove. The pain of it! I could hear my toe break! Then I was stuck on crutches for the rest of the holiday wearing big goofy knitted socks as I couldn't even put a shoe on.'

'Family, you could kill them!' he nodded, topping up her wine glass.

Sarah relaxed. Ronan was good company and attractive too, with his dark curly hair and blue eyes so similar to his first cousin; the family resemblance was strong.

'How long have you been in London?'

'Six years. Though some days it feels like a whole lot more!'

'So you must miss Dublin?'

'Yeah, I suppose I do, and it seems the older I get the more I want to come home for weekends, keep an eye on the folks, catch up with people. London's great and it's been good to me but I do miss the crack here!'

Sarah smiled. She was no expert on night life and the Dublin pub scene.

'Where do you hang out, or is it always fancy dinners like this?' he teased.

'No.' She reddened. 'Karen was kind to invite me. My life is usually a lot quieter.'

'That's surprising,' he said, obviously meaning it as a compliment.

Sarah responded to his gallantry and thanked heaven that he had been put down her end of the table. Over the next few hours she discovered that he worked in graphic design, loved authentic Indian curry, lived in a small mews development near Notting Hill and his passion was wildlife photography.

'I save up all my holidays or, if I can afford it, take a month out of work and go exploring with my camera. Catching a lioness with her cubs or a humpback whale breaching in the Pacific Ocean or a group of elephants gathered at a watering hole, there's nothing like it!'

'Ronan, that sounds so exciting!'

'Well, you watch all these amazing programmes like *Planet Earth* and then you realize you can just go see it! Go do it! Explore while there are still these amazing animals and creatures and places to see.'

Sarah was immensely impressed and while Chloe and Susan and Sean debated the merits of buying timeshares in

Marbella or Portugal she made a mental vow to someday take Evie to Africa.

'What about you? What gets you going?'

Sarah was taken aback. People weren't usually interested in what she enjoyed. 'Obviously my daughter is the most precious thing in my life but the other thing that I suppose I really like doing, though it's not very exciting, is drawing and writing. I enjoy making kids' books and illustrating them myself.'

'Did you study art?'

'Yes, I went to Art College.'

'Talented lady!'

No one had ever said that to her before and Sarah could see by his eyes that he wasn't slagging her but was actually interested. 'I made a funny book about a little kitten called Mitten and its owner, and now I'm working on a sequel for Evie,' she confessed, surprised to find she felt sure enough about the merit of her work to discuss it. 'It's based on a dog Evie's mad about; I call him Mr Bones. I've made him into a curious dog detective who lives over a butcher's. I have fun doing it. It relaxes me, makes me forget about bills and money and all that crap!'

As the evening wore on people began to drift away. Karen had tossed off her shoes and curled up on the couch in the living room. Sarah went and sat beside her.

'I hope you're enjoying yourself!' Karen said.

'Yes,' Sarah replied, realizing that she was being entirely truthful. She had enjoyed the adult company, the great food and lovely wines and the fact that Ronan had actually talked to her, treated her like an interesting woman.

After a nightcap of Baileys, she wondered about calling a cab.

'We're going your way,' insisted Rachel. 'You can share with us and we'll drop you en route.'

She glanced over at Ronan. He was engrossed talking to Mick and didn't volunteer to join her or see her out. She stifled a pang of regret as she grabbed her handbag and jacket.

'It was such a lovely night,' she said, thanking Karen and Mick. Ronan politely stood up and gave her a quick hug as she said her goodbyes and raced outside to join the others.

Sitting in the back of the cab in the darkness as Rachel and Don held hands, Sarah suddenly felt more alone than ever.

Chapter Thirty-four

Thirty, Grace decided, was an awful age – no, a *shitty* age that no woman with half a brain wanted to be; certainly not an age to celebrate, not even with her nearest and dearest. Staring at the wall of her bedroom, Grace considered it like a blank canvas. She had gone through it all: from babyhood via the fun of being a kid, to a lanky know-it-all teen, then enthusiastic care-free student, to qualifying and working and becoming a young professional woman. Now nothing she could say or do would change the harsh cold fact that she was a grown-up. Her life now stretched in front of her in monochrome. She could not predict what colour, if any, would invade the canvas of her life as she contemplated this first thirty years.

Today was her thirtieth birthday, and here she was alone in her expensive pristine-white waffle-print-covered bed: a situation she had never in her worst nightmare imagined. She'd always seen a husband or a partner and a baby or toddler in the picture she had painted a long time ago of herself at thirty, instead she was utterly alone! Being single as she sailed into her middle years was something she had definitely not planned. As she stretched her long limbs she tried to shrug off the feeling of gloom that threatened to overwhelm her on this of all days. Her schedule was pretty packed for the day – deliberately – and she was having lunch in Bang Café with Niamh and Claire and Roisin, who would do their best to cheer her up.

The phone rang on her bedside table: it would be her mother singing 'Happy Birthday' in time-honoured tradition, as she had since Grace was a little girl. It almost made her weep.

'Happy birthday, Grace, darling,' Maggie called. 'I can't believe it's thirty years since I first held you in my arms in Holles Street. Such a beautiful baby, your dad and I as proud as punch with ourselves.'

'Thanks, Mum,' Grace said sitting up, trying to sound positive and happy.

'I have your present but I'll give it to you when I see you later this evening.'

'Great, Mum.'

'Don't forget now; don't be late to Sarah's as dinner in Havana is booked for eight thirty p.m. And don't work too hard today,' she advised. 'I don't know why you didn't take the day off.'

'Mum, I can't just not turn up to the office because it's my birthday!'

She could hear her mother's harrumph of indignation at the end of the line. Her mother had been making all kinds of plans to organize a big family celebration for her birthday at home with loads of old college and schoolfriends and neighbours and all the relations to mark her thirtieth birthday and had been disappointed when Grace had put her foot down and insisted on a simple family dinner instead. She certainly did not want any big to-do to herald leaving her twenties behind and joining the ranks of the middle-aged! It was just too awful to contemplate. Grace had been relieved that in the end they had opted to go to one of the local restaurants in nearby Ranelagh.

'Anyway, I'll see you later, pet.'

God, she groaned to herself, how was she ever going to get through this utter hell of a day?

She showered and took time to give herself an avocado and coconut body scrub, lathering on the moisturizer afterwards to ward off dry skin. Looking at herself in the mirror as she dried her thick blond hair, she resisted the temptation to search for a grey one. Two slices of toast and honey, a glass of orange juice and a quick mug of coffee as she listened to 'Morning Ireland', relieved to see that at least the day was bright and sunny and not pouring with rain as she began to dress.

Her face glowed from the facial she'd treated herself to last Saturday and, as she pulled on her expensive John Rocha suit and slipped on a pair of high-heeled sling backs, she consoled herself that she was looking good even if she was hitting thirty. Grabbing her keys and handbag, she raced out of the apartment and walked briskly to the car park.

She was barely at her desk in the office when Anna phoned to wish her a happy birthday. 'See you later, big sis,' she called cheerily.

Sarah phoned a half an hour later, all excited about the birthday too. 'Evie's made you a card and I've made you a cake with that butter icing you like.'

'Thanks,' she replied trying to sound in good spirits.

Her secretary Kate had organized the delivery of a huge floral arrangement from Crazy Flowers on behalf of her work colleagues and the delivery boy struggled to carry the vibrant orange display of Birds of Paradise and spiky green leaves to the fifth floor. A constant round of visitors called in to wish her many happy returns; Grace recognized the sympathy in the eyes of some of her female colleagues as they asked her about plans for the evening.

'A family dinner,' she confided.

She dealt with a rake of work and cost projections on the shopping centre development in Gorey that the company was bidding for as she answered a stream of text messages and emails from her friends. There was no sign of Shane and she was relieved to hear that he was away in London for two days, which avoided the possibility of running into him on today of all days.

At lunch in Baggot Street she took two glasses of wine as she ate her asparagus risotto and a tossed green salad. The girls had clubbed together to buy her an expensive Helen Cody handbag.

'Wow, it's gorgeous,' she said appreciatively as she studied the contrasting terracotta and turquoise print on the cream bag.

'Celebrate getting through the terrible teens and the troubled twenties,' advised Roisin who was thirty-one and ran her own small PR company which looked after clients in the TV world. 'And arriving in a place with a semblance of maturity and knowing where you want to be.'

'I'm not sure where I want to be,' admitted Grace candidly. 'I love my job but I suppose I thought things might be a bit different.'

'It's no disgrace being single,' Roisin reminded her. Roisin loved to preach about independence and the power of women but had recently started dating an old college friend, an accountant, who had returned to Ireland from Chicago.

'I bawled the day I was thirty,' confided Claire, 'and nothing Lorcan could say or do could console me. Remember he'd booked a night in that expensive country house hotel in Wicklow?'

'Of course I remember,' teased Grace, 'and nine months and two days later baby Cormac came into the world.'

'That's what I'm saying. I had no idea such good things were around the corner for me when I was thirty.'

Looking at the dessert menu, Grace considered the fact that since no loving partner was about to appear and whisk her away for a night of romance she would have to rely instead on a serving of the chocolate fudge tart to sate her carnal desires. Her friends made her laugh and she realized that long years of friendship with such witty women was certainly something to value.

'Dinner in my place in two weeks' time,' said Niamh. They all made a note of it in their diaries and BlackBerries.

'Have a great birthday night,' they all chorused as they said their goodbyes.

Back in the office she tried to concentrate on work. If she was going to end up a career woman she'd better focus herself on the projects on hand.

At home later, getting changed, she softly applied mushroom-coloured eye-shadow and cream highlighter, then added a layer of black mascara which opened up her blue eyes. She resisted the temptation to crawl into bed and stay there as she slipped into a new figure-hugging wrap dress she'd bought in London last month. She would drive to Pleasant Square and leave the car there as she'd promised Sarah she'd call into her place first for a glass of wine and at least let her little niece help blow out the birthday candles on the cake.

'You look amazing,' her younger sister complimented her, hugging her close as she welcomed her.

'Auntie Grace, I got you a present and made you a card,' boasted Evie, running out to greet her.

Her mother and Anna, who were both sitting on the navy couch, jumped up and kissed her warmly.

'The birthday girl is here!' cheered Maggie as Sarah produced a bottle of chilled white wine and glasses.

'We thought we'd do the presents here before we went to the restaurant,' said Sarah.

Grace's mood immediately lifted and she knew that celebrating another year surrounded by her family was what it was all about and her age didn't actually matter. She turned her attention to Evie, noting her little niece's giddy excitement, even when it wasn't her own birthday.

'This is my card, Auntie Grace,' Evie said, solemnly

producing a huge cardboard square which opened up. On the outside there was a blobby painting of a woman with a round smiley face, yellow hair and blue eyes wearing a pink and blue polka-dot dress and big square clunky red shoes with giant daisies all growing around her. 'That's you,' she proclaimed, 'on your birthday.'

'I can see that, Evie,' Grace said admiringly, 'and I'm all happy and smiley.'

'Now you have to open my present,' she insisted. 'It's something you are really going to like!'

Grace unwrapped the first present and was surprised by the big red kite with its multicoloured tail and string. 'Oh my God,' she laughed. 'It's perfect, thank you, pet.'

'See, Mummy, I told you Auntie Grace needed a kite. Now you have to open your other presents,' she said bossily, hunkering down in front of her.

Anna started the proceedings by passing her a big parcel wrapped in pink tissue and ribbon. Feeling like a little kid she unwrapped it. It was an exquisite low-cut Kenzo silk shirt in baby pink and ivory with a classic Japanese retro design.

'Oh Anna, I love it! It must have cost a fortune.'

'Yes,' agreed her sister, 'but I guess that you're worth it.'

'This one is from me.' Sarah smiled, handing her a heavy square gift wrapped in multicoloured paper.

Curious, Grace tore off the paper to reveal one of her sister's simple coloured illustrations framed. It was stunning. It showed a small girl, her fair hair in plaits, holding a bright red kite that was blowing in the breeze. The detail of the

248

leaves and the kite tail, the clouds and the small robin standing near her feet almost jumped off the page. 'Sarah, it's beautiful.'

'She reminds me of you when you were a kid,' said her sister honestly. 'It was fun doing it.'

'It's such a special present, Sarah, thank you so much,' said Grace, realizing that it was the first of her talented sister's works that she possessed.

'Now Granny's present,' insisted Evie.

Her mother handed her a small box wrapped in gold paper. Grace held her breath as she unwrapped it. It was a gold ring of her mother's with three small blue sapphires and three diamonds.

'Your dad gave me this ring when I was thirty years old,' Maggie said slowly. 'Now I'd like you to have it.'

'Mum, I can't take it,' she said recognizing the family heirloom that had originally come from South Africa.

'Of course you can,' she insisted. 'As you are our eldest daughter Leo would have liked you to have this. It belonged to his grandmother Grace, the one whom you are named after. In time you can pass it down to your own children.'

Grace swallowed hard. At present this seemed a very unlikely prospect and she secretly resolved to give it to Evie when the time came. She slipped the ring on her finger: it was a perfect fit. 'Thank you, Mum,' she said, almost overwhelmed.

'You still have the cake,' reminded Evie.

The cake was enormous and had at least twenty candles on top. Sarah dimmed the lights as the candles flickered and the family sang her 'Happy Birthday' as Evie with much huffing and puffing helped her to blow them all out. They all took a small slice; they would save the rest for the weekend.

'Come on, we'd better get a move on to the restaurant,' chivvied Sarah, when Sinead, a student who lived on the far side of the square, arrived to babysit. 'You know how busy they get on Friday evenings and we don't want to lose our table.'

Chapter Thirty-five

Havana's was packed and Grace was glad her sisters had had the foresight to book something special for her birthday night.

'This way, ladies,' called Jake the head waiter as he led them to a great table slap in the middle of the room. A bottle of Sauvignon Blanc was ordered and, realizing how hungry she was, Grace perused the menu. Her mother as usual enquired about all the specials and the fish dishes, the three girls casting their eyes to heaven as the young waitress patiently explained each dish.

'I'll try those salsa prawns, they sound delicious,' said their mother, finally making a decision.

Grace opted for a red pepper and mushroom starter and lime-baked sea bass for her main course.

Lifting their wine glasses her mother and sisters toasted her. 'Have a wonderful birthday, Grace!'

She suddenly felt such an eejit about tonight: here she was, surrounded by the people she loved, about to enjoy a great meal and she had the audacity to moan about her birthday. 'And here's to the best family ever,' she responded, 'and to another thirty years of fun together!'

'It has been fun,' agreed her mother, her blue eyes filled with emotion, 'having you three in my life. Grace, I remember your dad and I got such a shock when we heard you were on the way. We were married barely two years when you arrived and we hadn't a clue. It seems like only yesterday since you were born. God knows how we all survived.'

For the rest of the night Maggie regaled them with childhood stories of mayhem and mischief and Grace laughed so hard she had a fit of coughing. The food was great. Sarah tucked into a massive fillet steak while Anna had a delicious chicken and pasta mix.

'I wish your dad were here to celebrate with us,' said her mother softly. 'It's funny how birthdays and Christmas are still so hard without him.'

Grace thought of her father who probably would have insisted on a table in one of Dublin's fanciest restaurants and ordered champagne and the works for his eldest daughter's birthday. She'd always been mad about him and thought that there were very few men who could hold a candle to him. Leo Ryan had been a very special man.

Her mother disappeared to the bathroom.

'Should one of us follow her?' asked Sarah. 'She's upset about Daddy.'

'She'll be back in a few minutes,' Grace said confidently, who knew her mother occasionally still needed to have time alone. 'Just let her be.'

The desserts had arrived and there still was no sign of her.

Anna, worried, got up to find her and retreated when she saw her standing talking to some people on a table at the back of the restaurant.

'She's fine,' she reassured the others, sitting back down at the table.

'You OK, Mum?' they asked when she finally appeared.

'You'll never guess whom I met,' she exclaimed. 'It's that McGuinness man who's bought the house on the square. He's here with a few friends.'

'Mark's here!' Sarah smiled.

'I told him we were out celebrating your birthday,' beamed her mother.

Oh no, thought Grace. Knowing her mother, she would have dropped her age right into the conversation. Maggie Ryan was never known for her discretion.

A few minutes later the waitress came to the table and said the gentleman in the corner was insisting on sending them over a bottle of champagne.

'Heavens no, we can't take it!' argued Grace, wanting to send it back.

'Of course we can,' retorted her mother. 'He's just being neighbourly.'

'Champagne would be lovely,' coaxed Sarah. 'That's so kind of Mark.'

From her little acquaintance with him, Grace thought kind was certainly not a word that she would apply to her mother's new neighbour.

They waved over their thanks as the waitress brought glasses and poured it for them. A half-hour later they were all giggling furiously about one Halloween when their mother had made them dress up as the three little pigs.

'I had to carry a bale of straw,' protested Sarah, now almost hysterical.

'Excuse me, ladies, I hope that you are enjoying the night?'

They all jumped as their new neighbour suddenly appeared in front of their table with another man who was smaller and more muscular, with fair hair that was already starting to recede.

'Thank you so much for the champagne,' gushed Maggie. 'There's still a little left if you and your friend would care to join us.'

Grace felt like strangling her mother there and then as the two men, dressed in expensive business suits, hesitated for a minute before sitting down. What was her mother playing at? she wondered as Mark McGuinness pulled his chair in beside hers. The waitress brought more glasses. He introduced John, a college friend who was home from America for ten days.

'I believe this is a very special birthday?' Mark said looking at her. 'Thirty?'

Honestly, she would definitely kill her mother for telling her age and making her look such a saddo who had no wonderful date or fancy outing to celebrate her thirtieth.

'Yes.' She smiled as if it was the most wonderful thing to be celebrating.

'I went to New York for mine,' he confided. 'John and I and a few friends went on a bar crawl. To be honest I don't remember much of it, only it was a good night. Funny how you suddenly feel all grown-up even if you don't want to.'

She nodded, not sure what to say. He was describing exactly how she felt.

The talk around the table continued and Mark's friend John Maloney regaled them with stories of the bar he ran in New York and the Irish and Irish-American political dignitaries who frequented it.

'I'm really sorry but I've got to go,' Anna excused herself an hour later. She was genuinely reluctant, having thoroughly enjoyed John's witty take on American politics. 'I'm giving a lecture to a hundred and twenty American academics on Irish literature early tomorrow morning.'

'Oh Anna, I don't believe it,' protested Grace, who despite her qualms was really enjoying herself.

'Teaching Joyce and Beckett and Synge is difficult enough but believe me you don't want to be doing it with a hangover.'

'I suppose I should be going too,' said Sarah reluctantly. 'I promised the babysitter that I wouldn't be out too late.'

'Sarah, you stay, love,' offered Maggie, standing up. 'You and Grace finish your drinks and enjoy yourselves with Mark and John. I'll go home with Anna and take over babysitting from Sinead.'

Grace was instantly embarrassed by her mother's unbelievable manoeuvring. The guys must think that they were mad!

'Are you sure, Mum?' Sarah grinned. She was keen to stay on.

'Of course,' Maggie insisted. 'At my age I'll leave it to you young ones to enjoy yourselves.'

Grace cringed, noticing that Mark had ordered a second bottle of champagne for the table.

'I've settled the bill. Have a good time!' Her mother waved as she and Anna disappeared into a taxi outside the door.

'Your family are rather fun!' said Mark, looking at her over the rim of his glass. His eyes were a strange almost hazel colour and he had thick dark eyelashes, which for some reason had a disturbing effect on her as she tried to work out if he was being sarcastic or genuine. She managed to keep up some type of conversation with him about his house.

'I've great plans for it,' he confided. 'Great plans.'

Alarmed, she tried to hazard a guess about those plans. 'The O'Connors were elderly and I suppose had let the house go,' she admitted, remembering the floral carpets and awful storage heaters and the gas cooker in their kitchen.

'A slight understatement.' He laughed as he refilled her glass from the fresh bottle of champagne that had arrived at the table, his eyes roving over her dress, her neck, travelling upwards to meet her gaze.

'But they are great family houses,' she insisted. 'Well, that's what they were intended for and, although there isn't an official conservation order in place on the area, most owners would agree to be respectful of the original features and design.'

'Good for most owners!' he teased.

She suddenly realized that putting him in the same bracket as a couple buying the house to raise their family or a sympathetic fan of Georgian architecture was foolish.

Mark McGuinness was out on his own! She doubted he had ever followed anyone else's lead or gave a toss about what neighbours thought of him.

'Tell me, Grace, what you would do if the house was yours?' he asked, totally turning the tables on her.

Grace found herself mentally standing at the front door and moving room by room through the house, opening the back up to light and knocking the warren of small pokey rooms off the kitchen and basement into better living spaces. Before she realized it she had been talking for more than twenty minutes, Mark's leg against hers, the two of them rapt in their conversation, his eyes locked on hers.

'I do agree with you, it is a house with great design possibility but it still needs to stand alongside its neighbours the way it was first designed,' he said knowledgeably.

'Hey, you two, where are we off to from here?' demanded John who had his arm around her sister. 'You girls probably know the latest nightclubs!'

Oh, Mother of God, thought Grace, they want us to join them. She tried to signal to Sarah about going home, but Sarah's eyes were sparkling. She was certainly up for continuing the night.

'Come on, Grace, it's your birthday,' wheedled John. 'Surely you're not going to call it a night yet!'

'Please, Grace, Mum's babysitting and it'll be fun having a night out together,' pleaded her youngest sister.

Grace looked at Mark. She was enjoying the night; he was good company and if Sarah was up for a late night so was she!

'What about The Club?' suggested Mark as they all left the Cuban restaurant.

There was a small queue outside the door of the exclusive late-night club situated on the corner of St Stephen's Green, but the doorman waved them in, obviously recognizing Mark. The upstairs lounge was crowded as John and Mark led their way to the bar.

'More champagne, ladies?' offered John.

'No, a glass of white wine's fine for both of us,' smiled Grace, signalling to Sarah to agree.

The patrons of The Club ranged from mid-twenties to thirties and for the most part were stylishly dressed; a group of guys in black tie had obviously come on from a formal dinner and were a little drunk but determined to enjoy themselves. Grace tried to avoid them and was relieved when Mark guided them to another part of the room. An appealing combination of swing and soul came from the dance floor below. They chatted easily for a while before John took Sarah's hand and led her off to dance, leaving Grace standing there feeling awkward as Mark made absolutely no move to ask her to dance. Embarrassed, she was about to make an excuse to find her sister when he introduced her to a stunning redhead in a skimpy pink cocktail dress. The girl was pretty and young and all over him. What in heaven's name was she doing in this place on what should be a very important night in her life with a virtual stranger who had little or no interest in her? Grace thought impatiently. She must be mad. If this is what the future held she wanted no part of it.

The other girl was flirting with Mark outrageously and Grace stepped away from them, not wanting to intrude. She took herself off to the ladies' room, where she brushed her hair and chilled out, listening to the chat of all the other females who were packed into the cramped bathroom and toilets. She emerged to find herself the target of two of the guys in tuxedos, who were even drunker and more obnoxious than before. One of them blocked her way and began to whisper some comment about the size of her chest.

'Hey, Grace, I'm here.' She suddenly felt Mark's arms around her. 'Let's dance.'

Relieved, she held on to him as they walked downstairs, his six-foot frame like a buoy she could cling to.

'Why did you go off like that?' he asked, looking down at her as other couples shoved and pushed against them, forcing them close together.

'You were busy and I didn't want to intrude,' she said lightly.

'Sharon's only nineteen,' he said measuredly. 'I know her father – he's my bank manager. She's a nice girl and I've probably known her since she was ten years old, but she's had a bit too much to drink so I walked her to the door and made sure she had a friend go home with her in a taxi.'

'Point taken,' she said softly. His arms enfolded her as they danced slowly to Nina Simone. He had a good sense of rhythm and made an excellent dance partner even if he said very little. Grace just enjoyed the music and the feel of his body beside hers, imagining what it would be like to be in even closer proximity to him if they were alone. She could feel his hand warm on her waist and his breath on her neck, his mouth pressing against her skin as the music continued, neither of them saying a word. Maybe she had drunk too much or was giddy with the emotions of hitting thirty or was simply easily seduced by an attractive stranger, but whatever it was Grace realized that she wanted it to continue, this powerful feeling of sensuality that had suddenly sprung up between them.

She blinked, jolted back to reality by Sarah and John dancing close by them. Both looked animated, still talking ninety to the dozen.

'Hey, Mark!' said John. 'What about letting me have a dance with the birthday girl?'

Reluctantly Grace and Mark stopped dancing, the rhythm between them broken. But for an instant Mark kept a hold of her wrist, his fingers pressing against her pulse point. Grace looked up, but the enchantment was gone as they swapped dance partners. John took her arm while Sarah gave a twirl and took hold of Mark's hand.

'Sarah's a great girl, told me all about her kid Evie and your family,' John said as the music changed to a Justin Timberlake number. Grace did her best to relax and enjoy the rest of the night as they talked about their favourite New York buildings and the changed face of Dublin. 'It's a developer's paradise,' he joked, 'so no wonder investment guys like Mark are making big bucks.'

As time went on the floor thinned out and Grace found her eyes drawn to Mark and her sister. They had stopped dancing and were talking and laughing together over at a table on the left. Sarah, unlike her, was totally relaxed and at ease with him. As the DJ finished up for the night John and she joined them.

'What about a nightcap back at my place?' asked Mark, glancing over at her.

Grace was relieved when Sarah refused the offer.

'Thanks, guys, but no,' she said. 'Grace and I had better get going home.'

'We'll get a taxi and drop you off first at the square,' offered Mark. 'John's staying in Donnybrook with me.'

Sitting in the back of the taxi-cab Grace realized that she'd enjoyed the night far more than she had expected. The spectre of her thirtieth birthday had been vanquished by the dinner, the champagne, the nightclub and the company of two rather handsome guys.

'What a great night!' giggled Sarah as the cab stopped on Pleasant Square and she hugged and kissed Mark and John in turn. 'Thanks guys, I really enjoyed myself!'

'Yes, thanks for helping to make it a great birthday,' added Grace, saying goodbye to John. He was flying home in two days' time and had spent half an hour while they were dancing telling her about his wife Cindy who was pregnant again and not allowed to fly, and his two-year-old son Sam. He really was a nice guy and she kissed him on the cheek and then found herself hugging and thanking Mark also.

'Grace, I'm glad that you enjoyed the night,' he said, his fingers keeping hold of her hand, forcing her to make eye contact with him in the dark. 'I'm going to be away on business for a week,' he explained, 'but I'll be in touch when I get back . . .'

His eyes were serious and she could feel the pressure of his thumb in the palm of her hand as her fingers closed around his.

'Sure,' she said, suddenly flustered. Guys were always promising to get in touch, it was a line; it didn't mean a thing.

'Happy birthday, Grace!' He bent down and, to her surprise, touched his lips tenderly to hers before taking off in the cab.

Chapter Thirty-six

Maggie Ryan rose early and after a quick shower and a glass of fresh orange juice took the Luas tram into town. She was meeting her sister Kitty for breakfast so that they could get an early start on 'Wedding Outfit Shopping'.

Poor Kitty, they had trawled the boutiques on the Southside, the Northside, in Wicklow and in Gorey to no avail. The right mother-of-the-bride outfit was proving elusive and even a lovely day's shopping down in McElhinneys' famous wedding store where Kitty had tried on at least twenty outfits, none of which she liked, had failed.

'I'm the mother of the bride,' she complained. 'I have to look right on Orla's big day.' Maggie had been more fortunate and had bought a sleeveless terracotta silk dress with a scoop neckline and a matching wrap that would be perfect for Orla's wedding in September.

Over a pot of tea and toast and rashers and sausages she had to be firm with Kitty. 'We are not racing all over the place today and no detouring to handbags or shoes, Kitty. Today the focus is on the outfit. Once you get that the rest will follow. We'll try Brown Thomas first, then Richard Alan's again and Arnotts and Clerys!'

'Orla told me the designer floor in Arnotts is great,' said Kitty, 'and that her friend Jennifer's mother got her outfit in Pamela Scott's.'

Thanks be to heaven town was quiet early in the morning, thought Maggie as they went from dressing room to dressing room in all the big stores. Her duty was to pass her sister outfit after outfit and help with zips and buttons and then give a candid comment on each outfit.

'Makes your hips look big!'

'Wrong colour. It drains you.'

'Shows your tummy . . .'

Kitty was smaller and slightly slimmer than her but had a pear-shaped figure. Along the way Kitty updated her on the invitations that were being printed, the choir that Orla had engaged, the outrageous cost of bridal and church flowers. Maggie listened intently, conscious that some day she would with any luck be organizing a wedding for one of her own girls.

Crossing over the Halfpenny Bridge they found the outfit – at last – on the designer floor in Arnotts: a jade-green dress with an exquisite little matching jacket in the same colour but with a fine band of cream piped around the hem and front and collar. It fitted perfectly.

'It's gorgeous!' said Kitty, turning in every direction as they studied it from every angle.

'Is this it?' asked Maggie excitedly. She truly didn't think her sister would find anything that suited her better or made her look so good anywhere else.

'I think it is,' said Kitty, her brown eyes shining, 'but I'd like Orla to see it too.'

The grey-haired shop assistant was kindness itself and put the outfit away for Orla to come and see it with her mother tomorrow.

'Maggie, thank you so much for all your help and patience. Come on, I'll buy you a celebration lunch,' promised Kitty. They found a table in the window in Fallon and Byrne.

Maggie told Kitty all about Grace's birthday dinner and how wonderful it would be if something happened between Grace and their new neighbour.

'They're just made for each other,' she said, delighted with herself, 'but a mother as you know can only do so much!'

'Tell me about it!' Kitty said, recalling all the ups and downs with Orla and Liam's relationship before they had finally got engaged. 'What about coming into town again next week to have a look at some shoes?' coaxed her sister as they ate salmon and spinach quiche and a green tossed salad.

As they said goodbye after lunch Maggie found herself agreeing to join forces with Kitty on another shopping expedition but hoped that accessory shopping would be a bit easier all round.

On Grafton Street there was a young rock guitarist with an amp and electric guitar entertaining the crowds. Believing talent should be encouraged, she dropped a euro in his box, before running into Clarendon Street Church to say her usual prayers for Leo and the family and to light a candle for poor old Oscar Lynch.

The last time she'd gone to see her elderly neighbour he

had just moved from the hospital to Oak Park, an expensive nursing home in Blackrock. He'd been tetchy and unsettled, anxious to come home but far too frail to manage living on his own. Browsing in the bookshop on St Stephen's Green she'd bought him one of those big Sudoku number puzzle books before getting back on the tram and leaving town.

She almost fell in the door of number 23, so relieved was she to be home. She kicked off the torture of her shoes and shoved on her cosy slippers as she left the clutter of bags at the bottom of the stairs and made straight for the kitchen for a cup of reviving coffee and a biscuit.

She was just about to switch on the kettle when she realized that Irina had fallen asleep on the comfy two-seater couch near the patio door. The Polish girl's face was pale and she looked exhausted. God knows what time she had got up for work this morning. She killed herself working, thought Maggie, and seemed to go from job to job. She'd let her sleep undisturbed and silently made her own mug of coffee and went off and put her own feet up in the sitting room with a copy of the *Irish Times*.

An hour later she returned to the kitchen. 'Are you all right, Irina?' she asked softly, not wanting to frighten the young woman.

'Oh, Mrs Ryan, I am so sorry. I must have sat down for a minute after I finished doing the vacuum cleaning and gone to sleep.'

'It's all right, Irina, we all get tired,' Maggie reassured her, 'Maybe you had a late night last night?'

'No, but I woke up early this morning. It is noisy in the

266

house, and I have to get up by six a.m. if I want to get the bus at six thirty.'

'Did you have a proper breakfast?'

'A coffee and a doughnut in the newsagent's after we open up and do all the newspapers and serve the early morning customers. It gets very busy and I restock the shelves before I get the bus and come here.'

'Irina! Is it any wonder you're exhausted!'

'I was going to make a hot drink when I must have fallen asleep. You are angry with me?'

'No, not at all,' soothed Maggie, 'I'm just concerned. You get up so early and work so hard and don't seem to have proper time to eat and rest.'

'I have to work to make money to pay my rent and to save,' exclaimed Irina tearfully. 'I work as hard as I can but things in Ireland are expensive.'

'I know,' said Maggie gently, sitting down beside her. 'But you must remember to take care of yourself. Have you eaten?'

'A slice of toast and coffee would be fine, thank you, Mrs Ryan.'

'No,' insisted Maggie, 'I'll cook you something.'

Taking some eggs from the fridge and onions and tomatoes and a little bit of ham she cooked up a filling fluffy omelette as Irina set the table, telling her how in Poland they often added a dash of paprika and potato to the omelette.

'Would you think of moving nearer your work?' suggested Maggie.

'I would if I could afford to,' said Irina seriously. 'But the

267

rents are so high we must share with a lot of people to pay the landlord. It is difficult. At home in Poland it is so much cheaper to rent than here.'

'What if it was possible . . . ?' said Maggie, an idea fermenting in her mind as she thought of poor old Oscar and his predicament. Perhaps with a little matching she might be able to help solve two people's problems and they could help each other . . . 'What if there was a job coming up where there was accommodation in return for doing some house-work, a bit of cleaning and cooking, and just keeping somebody company. Do you think you might be interested?'

'I don't understand,' said Irina, looking at her dubiously.

'I have a friend who at present and probably for the fore-seeable future is in need of extra help in his home. He's elderly and lives on his own in a large house, which is per-haps too much for him to manage,' confided Maggie. 'I'm not sure he would be interested in such an arrangement but I promise I will talk to him about it, see what he thinks.'

'Where does your friend live?' she questioned.

'Close by,' said Maggie, hoping that Oscar Lynch might be open to her idea.

'Oh, I would definitely be interested, Mrs Ryan,' repeated Irina again and again as they sat down to eat.

Maggie was glad to see that despite her slim frame Irina had a healthy appetite.

Oscar was in his blazer and pressed grey trousers when she called to Oak Park convalescent home two days later. He looked exhausted, his grey hair neatly combed, his face thin and pale. It was only three weeks since he'd moved to the home after his surgery and he'd point blank refused the offer of a long-term bed there.

'I'm not a geriatric,' he'd complained indignantly. 'Not yet.'

'Of course you're not,' she soothed, fussing over him.

'It's just that I'm finding it hard to walk and impossible to bend down,' he complained. 'It's a bit of a setback as the doctor and the physiotherapist said I need at least an extra month here. The blasted hip is healing up but it's just taking longer than I planned.'

Maggie tried to hide her smile at seeing him so grumpy and gave him the lovely fresh fruit and little cakes she'd brought plus the big book of Sudoku puzzles she'd got for him. 'It'll help pass the time,' she said, girding herself to broach the subject of how he was going to manage when he finally came home.

'Oscar, you really are going to need to get someone in to help you when you move back to Pleasant Square,' she said firmly.

'I have thought about it,' he admitted as he lowered himself haltingly on to the chair beside his bed, Maggie automatically reaching to help him. 'I've always been independent, looked after myself and Elizabeth, but now with this hip it is going to be a bit trickier than I had imagined.'

'Perhaps you should have someone to live in?' she suggested.

'A carer!' he argued tetchily. 'I'm not one of those demented old men that needs a minder.'

'I didn't mean that, I just meant maybe someone could stay in the house while you're recuperating and help out with cleaning and cooking and doing messages and just keeping an eye on things,' she said slowly, watching his reaction from out of the corner of her eye.

'I don't know where you would find someone like that! How would you trust them not to rob you or take advantage of you?'

'Well, Oscar you'd have to trust them,' insisted Maggie, 'and I think I might know exactly the right person. She's looking for somewhere to rent that is reasonable and is willing to work and help out in return.' She could see she had sparked his interest. 'Irina is a charming, hard-working young woman,' she said. 'She came to Ireland from Poland over a year ago and has been working for me since then. She is totally reliable and trustworthy and the two of you would be helping each other out.'

'Where would this person stay?'

'Well, you have three spare bedrooms.'

'I don't want anyone else living on top of me,' he protested. 'Besides, Elizabeth would never approve of a strange woman sharing the house with me.'

'What about the basement?' suggested Maggie.

'The surgery! All my dental equipment is still there.'

'Well, I'm sure it could be moved,' she persisted. 'Now that you're retired, you'll hardly have need of it again.'

'I suppose you're right, Maggie. It's like an old museum down there.'

'Sarah and Evie love living in our basement,' she said

encouragingly. 'We all have a bit of privacy and yet company and support and help are only a few steps away.'

'I can see how it might work,' he ventured. 'It's just trying to organize it and move the chair and the equipment and all my stuff and then having to clean it up and paint it.'

'Listen, Oscar, Grace is bound to know a few people in her line of business who would do it. I'll ask her.'

'Then we will see,' agreed Oscar, running his long fingers over his forehead.

'Would you like me to arrange for you to meet Irina? I could bring her to visit you.'

'As long as she knows this is only a temporary arrangement. Once I'm on my feet properly again and back to full strength I might not need her.'

'Don't worry, Irina will understand,' she reassured him.

Chapter Thirty-seven

Maggie was busy putting out her summer bedding plants when she spotted Angus walking along the garden path with a pretty dark-haired girl.

He smiled and stopped on the lawn. 'Maggie, let me introduce you to my girlfriend, Megan.'

The Scottish girl! She was curious to meet the girl her young tenant was so devoted to. For once his girlfriend had made the effort to come and visit him in Dublin. She could see straight away that Megan had that stylish model look with her short dark hair, porcelain white face, big dark eyes and long skinny legs. She looked as if she hadn't eaten for months and that a bit of garden work would make her keel over as she was so fragile. Men seemed to go for that anorexic type these days!

'How long are you over in Ireland for?' Maggie asked, trying to be mannerly and hiding her clay-covered hands.

'Just a few days,' she said. 'Angus is giving me a quick tour of Dublin and then we're going off to Kilkenny for two nights.'

Maggie had heard that Megan had point blank refused to move to Dublin with Angus and complained bitterly the weekends he did not return home to Scotland.

'That'll be nice,' she remarked, 'it's always interesting to visit new places. I remember the time Leo and I went to Edinburgh, Ireland was playing Scotland and Leo had managed to get two tickets for the rugby match and . . .' She was just about to describe their trip when she saw Megan tug at Angus's arm. 'Sorry, I'm holding the two of you up, away off and enjoy yourselves. I'm trying to get this done before I have to head out. I'm going to see poor old Oscar.'

'Give him my best,' said Angus. 'And tell him I'll call on him when he gets home.'

Maggie had to admit that Megan was a lot prettier than she had expected. Was it any wonder Angus was smitten? Because now that she had actually materialized Angus couldn't be considered a prospective partner for anyone.

Maggie continued her garden work as she wanted to get the whole tray of begonias in before Irina arrived. She'd promised to take her over to Oak Park today to meet Oscar properly and have a chat with him. She laughed when she saw poor Sarah, lugging an enormous basket of washing, bumping into Angus and Megan. Sarah was looking rather bedraggled in cut-off denim jeans, a U2 T-shirt and a pair of a sandals, her fair hair dragged up in a ponytail while Megan was in an immaculate cream short jacket over a tightly fitting black skirt and high heels which made her legs look impossibly long. Evie raced around them all with her football. Sarah and Megan were introduced and she thanked heaven that Sarah was at least chatty and friendly though Evie was pestering Angus to play football for a minute with her.

'OK, OK.' Angus gave in and spent a few minutes showing Evie how to dribble the ball up and down the lawn as the two girls looked on.

'Angus,' said Megan peevishly, 'I thought that we were going shopping.'

'All right.' He grinned good-naturedly, passing the ball back to Evie as he followed Megan to the lane where his car was parked.

Dropping the basket, Sarah came over to Maggie.

'Well, what did you think of her?' Maggie asked, putting aside her trowel.

'She's really beautiful,' sighed Sarah. 'Why do guys always fall for girls who look like that?'

'Not always,' said Maggie gently, seeing the deflated look in her daughter's eyes.

'Well, Angus is mad about her,' she said vehemently as she turned to go back inside.

Maggie sighed seeing the spark of envy that Megan had ignited in her normally calm, easy-going daughter. She wondered what had possessed the young Scotsman to get himself embroiled with someone like Megan.

She was just finishing up, watering her plants with the watering can, when Irina appeared. She was taken aback to see Irina had made such an effort: instead of her usual jeans, jumper and boots she was wearing a pale pink dress, a little cardigan and neat flat shoes. Her hair was washed and gleaming to meet her elderly neighbour.

'You look lovely, my dear,' Maggie complimented her.

'I want Mr Oscar to like me,' she said simply.

Mr Oscar did like her, and Maggie left the two of them talking like two old friends about Warsaw and some Polish opera company that she had never heard of as she took a stroll around the grounds of the convalescent home. On her return Oscar announced his agreement to Irina coming to live with him temporarily.

'Thank you, Maggie dear, for introducing us, and I'm sure that Irina and I will get along fine. You're right, it will be good to have someone staying with me till I am back on my feet and able to manage again.'

Irina's eyes were shining and Maggie felt enormous relief that one of her plans had worked out and that Oscar would have someone to take care of him over the next few months.

Chapter Thirty-eight

Sarah was engrossed trying to draw Mr Bones, the story of the dog detective with his big nose and ears always searching for clues inspired by the mutt they met every week at the butcher's. She giggled as she drew a leaf floating down towards his nose. Her phone rang and she grabbed it, still laughing.

'Well, you sound in good form.' She recognized the voice immediately. It was Mick's cousin Ronan calling from London. It was a few weeks since they'd met. He was returning to Dublin next weekend and wondered if she would be interested in joining him and a group of friends for supper. 'We're going to that nice place in Sandymount village: Mario's. The table's booked for eight thirty.'

'That sounds great!'

'What about meeting there?'

'Perfect,' she agreed.

'I enjoyed our chat in Karen and Mick's,' he admitted. 'I was on an early flight to Heathrow the next morning so I slept at their place. I've invited them along on Saturday too.'

Great, thought Sarah, at least I'll definitely know someone else. Putting down the phone a few minutes later she couldn't believe that he had got in touch with her and asked her to dinner. OK, so it wasn't a proper romantic dinner date, but he had phoned and asked her out. She had tried blind dates and speed dating before – with zero success, seeming to attract only oddballs and weirdos – and lately had even toyed with the idea of internet dating, but was rather nervous about it. Having Ronan ask her out definitely sounded like much more fun. All she had to do was to organize a babysitter!

Sarah couldn't believe it, her mother was busy, going to the Abbey Theatre with her friends Fran and Rhona on Saturday night.

'I could cancel if you're stuck,' she offered. 'Who is it you are going out to dinner with anyway? Is it a man?'

'No, Mum, it's just a thing with Karen and Mick and a few others. Don't worry, I'll get someone else.' Her mum enjoyed her trips to the theatre with her friends and it wasn't fair to ask her to forgo something she had probably organized weeks ago. But she was disconcerted to discover her two sisters were by freak coincidence both away the coming weekend. Anna was taking a student group to a seminar on Paddy Kavanagh's poetry in Monaghan and Grace was in Manchester and had organized to stay overnight.

'Maybe you could change your dinner date,' suggested Grace. 'Then I could babysit for you.'

Well, she couldn't do that, so Sarah trawled through the small list of local teenagers and students she normally used.

Sinead had college exams, Lucy Conway was sick with tonsillitis and Aoife Mulligan had recently got a job as a barmaid in one of the local pubs and had given up baby-sitting. Disaster: she had absolutely no one to mind Evie.

Later that evening she was in the middle of putting her to bed when Angus called at the kitchen door.

'Let me settle her, Angus. Then we can have a cup of coffee.'

Evie wanted to show Angus the new books she'd got from the library.

'If I read you one, will you promise to be good and go to sleep straight afterwards? Deal?' he offered

'Deal,' agreed Evie. Sarah wondered how on earth it was that Evie would behave for him when sometimes it took her ages to get her to quiet down. She put on the kettle and rooted around for the malted milk chocolate biscuits that Angus liked. She listened at the bedroom door as Angus read the story of *The Princess and the Pea* in his soft Scottish accent, Evie quiet and enthralled, the two of them chatting easily when he was finished. Angus rounded off the story-telling with a Scottish lullaby. Afterwards he sat at the bedside saying nothing for a while until Evie turned over and, snuggling up to her big white teddy, fell asleep.

'Angus, you're a wonder-worker!' she praised him. 'I wish that I could get her off to bed so easily every night.'

'I seem to have a way with getting kids to go to bed,' he joked. 'Not so sure about the grown-up females of the species though!'

Sarah reddened at his teasing. Angus ignored her

278

discomfort as he grabbed his mug of coffee and ladled two heaped spoons of sugar into it. She passed him the biscuits hoping they hadn't gone soft. They sat companionably down in front of the fireplace, Sarah tucking her bare feet up under her.

'You said you wanted to ask me something,' she prompted.

'I was just wondering if you were around tomorrow.'

For one crazy moment she thought that she was going to be asked out twice in the same day, but realized a few seconds later that Angus had no intentions in that direction and saw her only as a neighbour and his landlady's daughter.

'It's just that I'm getting a new computer delivered and I wondered if you could let them in.'

'Of course,' she offered. 'I'm not working tomorrow.'

'I've a meeting with some of the Google guys tomorrow which I don't really want to cancel.'

'Sure.' She smiled, knowing that Angus worshipped at the gods of the internet.

Fumbling in his pocket he gave her the spare key. 'You don't have to do anything but make sure they put the box down carefully.'

Sitting chatting with him, Sarah realized that perhaps she had also found the solution to her own problem.

'Angus, are you by any chance free on Saturday night?' He was bound to be doing something interesting or flying back home to Edinburgh to see Megan. She held her breath.

'Actually, I've nothing on this Saturday, Sarah, so I'm all yours,' he said, grinning at her in anticipation.

'Well actually, all Evie's!' she fumbled, suddenly feeling

279

awkward. 'I've been invited out to dinner with friends and I'm really stuck for someone to mind her. Mum and my sisters, my normal babysitters – everyone's tied up. I wouldn't ask you, Angus, except that it is a sort of an emergency.'

She could see the change of expression in his face. 'It's all right if you say no, Angus, honestly.'

'No,' he said, suddenly serious. 'I'm in Dublin this week-end and if it's important for you, Saturday night is great for me. I'd be delighted to babysit for one of my favourite young ladies. What time do you want me for?'

'Seven thirty, if that's OK. Evie will be thrilled.'

'I'm glad one of the Ryan young ladies appreciates my company,' he said thoughtfully, putting down his mug.

'Angus, stay!' she found herself saying. 'I'll make more coffee.'

'Sorry, I've got to see a man about a banner,' he joked, getting up to leave.

After he was gone, Sarah reflected how much she really liked Angus; they always felt relaxed and comfortable around each other and the fact that he lived so close by and that they could help each other out was a wonderful bonus. He was great with kids and old people like Oscar, and made her smile even when she was sad. In her opinion he was the perfect man: funny and witty and able to beat her hands down on any computer game known to mankind. That Megan girl was lucky to have such a great boyfriend!

Chapter Thirty-nine

All Sarah's plans for dinner with Ronan and his friends went out the window when Evie started running a high temperature on Friday night.

She looked at the expensive conditioning treatment and decided tonight was perhaps not the night for trying to put it in her hair as Evie was demanding her full attention.

She sat with her daughter on her lap on the couch. Evie's face was hot and red, her eyes heavy and she was tetchy and complaining, wanting cold water and for some bizarre reason a bowl of red jelly.

The next morning she was unable to eat even a morsel of breakfast. Evie normally bounced around the place with energy, especially on a Saturday, but today she was listless and quiet. All she wanted to do was lie in on the couch wrapped in her pink blanket and watch TV. She had no signs of a cold or runny nose and her throat looked fine and Sarah was unsure about trying to get an appointment for the doctor on Saturday morning which was usually reserved for utter emergencies.

'Can I get you anything, pet?' she offered, trying to coax her to sit up and eat.

'Ribena, please, Mummy.'

All Evie wanted was glasses of her favourite blackcurrant drink. Sarah was tempted to phone and cancel her dinner date. What kind of awful mother was she who would contemplate leaving her child when she was sick!

Evie slept on and off all afternoon, and seemed a little better when she woke up. She nibbled a small toasted cheese sandwich for tea.

Sarah had phoned Karen, wondering what she should do. 'Do you think I should cancel?'

'Sarah, it's just dinner and it's not like you're going to be miles away,' she reassured, 'I'm not drinking so I can drive you home if Evie needs you.'

Realizing the time, Sarah, in a mad panic, hopped in the shower to wash her hair and began to get ready. Maybe fate wanted her to skip dinner and stay home.

She was still undecided and in her dressing gown when Angus arrived. 'Evie's sick,' she explained, feeling guilty. 'I can't leave her when she's like this. It's not fair, maybe I should just stay in.'

Angus said nothing and went into the sitting room and studied the patient who was watching TV. 'I think she'll live,' he said solemnly, 'but give me your mobile number in case I need it.'

'Oh, thanks Angus, are you sure?' she asked, relieved. When he assured her he was she raced off to get ready.

In her bedroom she pulled on a pair of tight-fitting jeans

and a low-neck pink shirt. Maybe it was just a bit too casual? She stared at herself in the mirror, and then raced out to him.

'What do you think of this?'

Angus was sitting near Evie, reading the sports section of the *Irish Times*, and looked up, a grin on his face crinkling up his eyes as he studied her. 'You look great.'

Sarah valued his opinion not just because he was a man, but because he was usually dead honest about everything.

'Now, just wait a minute.' She chased back into her bedroom and pulled on her slim-fitting pink-print coloured skirt, jade-green top and a low-slung leather belt.

'Angus!' she announced, twirling around. 'Is this better?'

She wasn't rooting for compliments, just a bit of help about the momentous decision of what to wear. Unlike Grace and Anna she was a disaster about making her mind up about things. They both instantly knew what to wear and what clothes suited them whereas she could never decide!

'You look lovely in both,' he said diplomatically, 'but the skirt . . .' He was staring at her in a way that made her feel he was giving her one hundred per cent attention. 'Wear the skirt.'

Back in the bedroom, she put on her make-up quickly and brushed her hair, grabbing her jacket when she heard the doorbell ring. The taxi must be outside.

She gave Evie a quick hug and a kiss and passed Angus the piece of paper with her number and the name of the restaurant. 'Promise you'll phone me if you need me?'

'I promise,' he swore, 'but Evie will be fine, don't worry.'

* * *

Mario's was packed, and any misgivings Sarah had were put aside when Ronan greeted her with a welcome hug and insisted she sit by him. He'd wisely booked the big round table near the front of the restaurant and Karen and Mick were already there. He introduced her to two friends of his, James and Chris, who had both been at college with him. They were all perusing the menu when his sister Mary, a pretty dark-haired girl, and her boyfriend Brendan appeared. They were a friendly group and Sarah relaxed immediately as everyone tried to make up their mind what to order. She ordered the prawns to start and then after a bit of secret deliberation the stuffed cannelloni and salad. The service was quick and smooth and everyone opted for the Italian Barolo, but Sarah decided to take it easy on the alcohol in case she had to go home quickly to Evie.

The food was great, the conversation fun and Ronan kept everything light.

'How's your book going?' he enquired as he tackled a massive pizza.

'Sssh, Ronan, it's not really a book,' she exclaimed. 'It's just, something I'm having fun doing.'

'I'd love to see it,' he said, manoeuvring a large slice of tomato and pepperoni pizza to his mouth.

She really couldn't make out if he was teasing her or just found her so naive it was amusing.

'Honestly, I mean it,' he said, putting the pizza down. 'I'm redesigning the logo and publishing catalogue for one of the biggest children's publishers in London. The stuff they publish is just fabulous. Kids' books are huge at the moment – well, that's what my friend Jilly tells me, and she's one of their top editors. If you want I could get her to take a look at yours, even a few pages. All she can do is say no!'

'Do you mean it, Ronan? You're just not stringing me along?'

'No. Jilly and I are great buddies.' He grinned, spearing some salad from the plate between them. 'I used to go out with her brother.'

Managing to keep a smile on her face, Sarah remained composed as she wondered had she heard correctly what he'd said. Maybe she was imagining it. 'That would be great, Ronan, really great.'

Her thoughts were in turmoil as the conversation around the table turned to the property market. Since she hadn't a bean to buy a home of her own and was dependent on the benevolence of her mother for her accommodation, it was a discussion to which she could contribute little, except to state that people were mad to be paying out half a million euros or more for what was nothing more that a concrete box of an apartment in some high-rise development in the middle of nowhere with no parks or playgrounds or even a place to go for a walk. What would happen to the children and toddlers living in these places in the future!

Karen got up to go on one of her frequent trips to the Ladies' and Sarah excused herself and joined her.

'God, I shouldn't have had all that pasta,' joked her friend. 'I feel like I'm going to explode and all the Ballygowan is swishing around me like a fishbowl.'

Sarah giggled as Karen gave a discreet belch. 'Better!'

'A bit. God, this baby is playing havoc with my digestive system. First I couldn't look at food and now I'm starving all the time.'

'Do you remember my salami cravings?'

'Irish whiskey salami!' She giggled. 'You ate bags of the stuff. Are you glad you came out tonight?'

'Yes, I'm having a great time,' she admitted. 'Ronan's so nice and everyone's such fun . . .'

Karen stared at her in the mirror. 'Yeah, it's such a shame that some of the nicest guys are gay.'

Her eyes must have given her away.

'You did know, Sarah!'

'Of course,' she fibbed. 'It's no big deal.'

'Remember I told you about him at my wedding? That he was away travelling around Fiji with some friends and couldn't make it home? He's such a character!'

A character was right. She sure had her wires crossed. Was she that long out of the dating scene? Composing herself, she put on a slick of lipstick and made her way back to the table.

It made no difference: Ronan was the best company ever and told her she was looking gorgeous when she returned to sit down beside him. He entertained them all with the trials and tribulations of designing the album cover for a new rock band. 'They had an awful name, looked awful and to be honest the music was dire.'

'What did you do?' asked Karen and Sarah.

'We rechristened them "Ice House" and put an animated version of them on the cover. Rumour is the record company

286

got the backing singer to sing lead vocals on their first single to be released.'

'And what happened?' asked James.

'The album sold well, the single got lots of plays and last I heard they'd been offered a tour in America. What's going to happen after that when people see and hear them live, God only knows!'

As the others began to order coffees and nightcaps she finished the end of her glass of wine and reached for her purse.

'Don't say you're going already!' protested Ronan.

'Sorry, but with Evie sick, I have to get back home.'

'When am I going to see these lovely pictures and stories of yours?' he asked.

'I could post them to you or try and scan and email them.'

'Listen, I'm around all tomorrow afternoon, maybe I could call into your place to see them?'

'Are you sure?'

'My flight's not till about nine. That way you can maybe give me a few pages to show Jilly.'

Sarah couldn't believe his kind offer and gave him a big hug as she got up to leave.

'I'm sorry about having to go home,' she apologized to everyone.

'Well, I'm worn out, so I can drop you off,' offered Karen. 'All I want is my bed at this stage of the night.'

She accepted the lift as she could tell Karen really wanted to get home and put her feet up while Mick was ready to go on with Ronan and James and the others and have another few drinks. They were all up for a late night and were heading for Leeson Street.

Sarah had really enjoyed the night out with a crowd, having a laugh and talking about grown-up things. When they reached Pleasant Square, she asked Karen if she wanted to come in for coffee.

'No, thanks, I'm just too tired, Sarah, I'd only fall asleep on your couch.'

'OK. Safe home,' Sarah called, hopping out of the car.

The living room was quiet, the TV on but muted, playing an old Alfred Hitchcock movie; Angus's skinny frame was sprawled across her sofa. He was dozing, his hair standing on end, his laptop abandoned on the carpet.

Evie was to her amazement fast asleep in her bedroom, her blanket gripped tight.

'Hey,' she called softly, resisting the bizarre urge to curl up on the sofa beside him.

Angus roused himself, running his fingers through his black hair, making the tufts of it stand up even more. 'Hey, I thought you wouldn't be home for hours,' he said sleepily.

'I didn't really want to leave her too long,' she explained.

'All's been quiet on the western front, promise,' he whispered. 'She had a drink of Ribena and a few spoons of yogurt. I think she's feeling a bit better now that the spots have started to come out.'

'Spots!'

'Probably chicken pox or one of those kinds of things.'

'Oh, God, Angus, I'm so sorry for landing you with something like that! I didn't realize she was that sick.'

'She'll be fine, Sarah. I had them when I was a kid and I'm sure the invasion of chicken pox is probably spreading as we speak!'

Sarah thanked heaven for Angus being so calm and relaxed about something that would freak most guys out.

'Anyway, how did the hot date go?' he asked, sitting up and stretching.

'Not so hot!' she laughed. 'It wasn't really a date, as I found out, just dinner with friends – which was fine and a bit of fun.'

'So no dancing and romancing the night away,' he said slowly, staring at her.

'No chance.' She gulped. 'I got it so wrong. Ronan's a great guy but I am definitely not his type.'

'I find that hard to believe.'

'Yeah, well, it just shows how crap I am,' she admitted, 'thinking because some guy talks to me and is nice that he likes me. No, what I meant is Ronan *did* like me, we're friends but not in a physical way – he's really great but he's gay. And I'm such a klutz I didn't cop on!'

Suddenly she felt miserable. She was so stupid and pathetic. Why she was telling Angus was totally beyond her.

He laughed, standing up and pulling her into his arms and down on to the couch. 'Any guy who didn't fancy you would have to be gay,' he assured her hugging her close.

'Thanks, Angus.'

'I mean it,' he said. 'You are very fanciable. When I saw you in that skirt tonight I . . .'

She couldn't believe what she was hearing.

'You're lovely, Sarah,' he blurted out.

Was she so drunk that she was imagining what Angus was saying to her? Or had she so many wires crossed from lack of sleep and worry about Evie that she had lost her marbles?

Suddenly she felt his lips on hers, warm and tender, and she was kissing him back, enjoying the experience, kissing and kissing . . . mmm, it was lovely. She had forgotten what it was like to snog someone you really liked. He was holding her chin in his hands, his fingers on her neck, the kiss getting deeper and deeper, Sarah responding. She kissed his cheeks and his eyes and his neck and then his mouth all over again. He smelled lovely; his skin tasted salty and sexy. She wrapped her arms around him as he pulled her closer. A long long time later, they pulled apart.

'Sarah.'

'Angus.' She giggled, it was crazy. He was her babysitter, her friend, he lived next door and he was Scottish and betrothed to the bonny Megan.

'Don't say anything,' he said huskily, tracing her lips with his finger. 'The situation will be sorted, I promise.'

She watched, still in a state of shock, as he got up from the couch, tucking his shirt in and reaching for his phone.

'I'd better be going,' he said, gathering his laptop from the floor. 'I hope the patient will be a bit better tomorrow.'

Barefoot she walked him to the door, thanking him again for babysitting Evie.

'Remember to lock up when I'm gone,' he reminded her.

She resisted the mad impulse to ask him to stay with her as she watched him walk across the garden path and back to the mews.

Chapter Forty

Ronan Dempsey had been more than true to his word and had called at the flat on Sunday afternoon with a tub of honeycomb ice cream, a packet of chocolate flapjacks and a bunch of freesias. She put them in a glass jug of water, her brain still reeling, thinking about Angus and trying to cope with Evie's horrendous outbreak of itchy spots.

Evie, normally friendly, was embarrassed, and was literally covered in top to toe glorious chicken pox spots. They were everywhere. Her eyelids, her lips, her head and face and all over her poor itchy body, and after saying a very shy hello to Ronan she had hidden in her bedroom, eating a bowl of the cool ice-cream.

'Poor thing,' he commiserated. 'I remember when my brother and sister and I got them we were off school for a week and drove my mother mad trying to vie with each other as to who was sicker and had the most spots.'

Over coffee he'd insisted she show him her work and she could see he loved Mitten the Kitten and her antics almost as much as she did. He pored over the words for Mr Bones and her first few sketches for it.

'They're great, Sarah,' he said, genuinely impressed. 'They're simple and fun and I'd guess kids of all ages would like them.'

'Do you think so?'

'Can I take copies of *Mitten the Kitten* for Jilly? And if you have copies of *Mr Bones*, even a bit of the story and one or two drawings, I'll let her have a look at them too.'

'Ronan, I can't believe you are being so kind,' gushed Sarah, chasing around the flat for a big envelope and sheets of paper and hunting for the stapler.

'Jilly tells me they get thousands of submissions every year but most of the stuff is utter rubbish. You don't want *Mitten* getting lost in the slush pile so I'll give it to her directly. That way at least you know she's read and looked at it herself.'

'I can't believe it, my little book actually going to London to a publisher.'

'Sarah, don't get your hopes too high!' he warned. 'I think it's great but I'm not a publisher.'

'I know, I know,' she accepted. 'Everyone turned down Harry Potter so I can't expect anyone else to like *Mitten*. But I've had great fun doing it and Evie and I love her!'

Ronan was the best of company and he entertained her with the antics of Mick and himself and the rest of the guys after she'd left them the previous night. They'd all headed into town to a nightclub and when they left at four a.m. taxis were scarce and those that did appear had refused to take them.

'Mick and I had to walk home,' he confessed. 'I swear I had to almost carry him and then had him snoring in the spare room with me as he didn't want to disturb Karen.'

'A wise decision,' confirmed Sarah.

When the time came for him to leave to go to the airport, Sarah wished that he didn't live so far away.

'You take care,' he said giving her a last hug. They promised to keep in touch.

During the week Angus had studiously avoided her and simply sent a text to cancel their regular DVD night. Disappointed, Sarah rented out a copy of *Bridget Jones's Diary* to console herself.

Ten days later Jilly Greene phoned Sarah from her London office. Sarah almost dropped the phone in shock as the children's books editor told her how much she liked *Mitten the Kitten* and her art style and invited her over to meet her in her offices in London the following week.

Sarah screamed and yelled and jumped up and down like a five-year-old with the good news as Evie, sitting colouring on the kitchen table, looked perplexed.

'What is it, Mummy?'

'Something lovely has happened, Evie,' she explained. 'A lady in London likes my story about Mitten and wants me to go to London to see her and the art director. They might make it into a book, I just can't believe it!'

'But it is a book,' Evie pointed out.

'I know,' Sarah agreed, it was already a very special book to the two of them, 'but they might make it into a book that sells in the shops or you borrow from the library so that other kids will get to know Mitten too.'

Evie flung her arms around her and hugged her tight, caught up in the excitement. It was only about ten minutes later that it hit her: how could she go to London and leave Evie? What about the costs of the flights and a hotel? It was impossible, there was no way she could go. The negative voice inside her was battling against the excitement of something good and positive happening to her, a door of opportunity opening to her which was beyond her wildest dreams. Maybe her mum could take Evie for the day or even two days. And there were cheap flights advertised all the time on the internet, maybe she could get one of them.

'Come on, Evie, let's go up and tell Granny the good news.'

Maggie Ryan had been almost overcome with emotion when she heard about the trip to London and the possibility of Sarah's book being published.

'Sarah, I always knew you had talent. You've been drawing and painting since you were Evie's age. Just wait till the others hear, they'll be thrilled!'

'Mum, I'm excited but I don't want to say too much till I go to London and meet the publishers,' she confided.

'Of course,' said Maggie proudly, delighted for her youngest daughter.

'Mummy's book is going to be in the shops and kids can read it, Granny,' announced Evie, her blue eyes huge and sparkling, 'and she has to go to London.'

'Isn't it wonderful news, Evie?' Her grandmother smiled. 'And maybe you will come and stay for the day with me while Mummy is away.'

'Yes,' beamed Evie, 'and Mummy says that if I am good she will bring me a present.'

'Well, that would be lovely, darling,' said Maggie, watching as Evie disappeared over to the couch to watch children's TV.

'You did hear that poor old Angus has the chicken pox now,' Maggie told Sarah as she put the kettle on for a celebratory coffee. 'Apparently he's covered from top to toe with spots.'

'But he told me he'd already had chicken pox before,' Sarah blurted out. 'Honest, he did!'

'Well, obviously not,' Maggie continued, buttering some freshly made scones. 'It must have been some other childhood illness.'

'He must have caught it from Evie,' she admitted, instantly blaming herself.

'He's had the doctor and has been very sick for the last few days,' her mother confided, pouring two cups of the filtered coffee. 'Apparently he'll be off work for a while, it's more serious in adulthood and you know what bad patients men make!'

'The worst,' agreed Sarah, remembering how her dad would act if he had a cold or a cough. They'd all know about it: he had them running up and down like Florence Nightingales tendering to his every whim.

'Maybe you should call in and see if he's OK,' suggested

her mother. 'After all, Evie did give it to him. I phoned him and left him a pasta bake with cheese, but to be honest I didn't go into the mews as I might get some kind of virus myself. Remember how sick poor Ita Brennan was with the shingles.'

'Mum, you've got it all mixed up; you couldn't get shingles from Angus.'

'Well, I'm not taking any risks, much better you keep an eye on him, Sarah.'

Honestly, was her mother trying to meddle again? Sarah took a sip of coffee. Still, poor Angus! She was annoyed with him for ignoring her since the night he babysat and had wondered why he'd suddenly started avoiding her when all the time there was a perfectly good reason for his not being around.

'Well, I'll phone Angus later and try to see if I can help,' she offered.

Angus Hamilton was stretched out in bed upstairs in the mews when she called bearing newspapers, a DVD of a Hitchcock film and fifteen freshly made fairy cakes with pastel icing and a bottle of pink Caladryl lotion.

'You look awful,' she said, staring at the spotted face and arms and the trail of huge red weals on his chest and hands as he clutched desperately at the quilt.

'Go away,' he said hoarsely. 'Let me die in peace.'

'You are definitely not going to die,' Sarah chided, 'but if you sit up I'll make you a coffee.'

She chased back down to the kitchen, emptying his smelly

bin and throwing some dirty clothes in the washing machine. By the time she got back upstairs with two mugs of coffee she noticed he had brushed his hair, smoothed out his sheets and was eating a pink-topped bun.

'Aren't they yummy?' She smiled. 'I knew you'd like them much better than chicken broth and all those disgusting invalid foods.'

'I'm not an invalid,' he protested as Sarah, trying not to look at the big scabby blisters near his lip and on his chin, passed him the coffee.

'Sorry about the chicken pox, but I thought you said you'd had it already.'

'Apparently not, my mother tells me now that I've had every other blasted childhood illness under the sun but not this one.'

'Poor you,' she said, sitting on the edge of the bed, wondering how was it that men mostly looked so bad in pyjamas, chicken pox or not!

'I feel like shit,' he admitted.

'You'll be a bit better in a few days once all the blisters have scabbed over,' she reassured him. 'Evie was flying around then.'

'I was meant to go to Edinburgh tomorrow,' he said, propping himself up with the pillows, 'but I'm not well enough. Megan's going mad because we had tickets for a charity ball which is held in Edinburgh Castle. It's one of the biggest bashes of the year.'

'Sorry,' she mumbled again as she looked around the bed-room, noticing two photos of the beautiful Megan with her bobbed straight black hair and pale face. In one she was with Angus in formal evening wear, a sculpted black silk dress; in another she was sitting on a pier with the sea and an island behind her. She was a classic beauty with a svelte figure and a great sense of style; no wonder Angus was mad about her.

'She's beautiful,' she said, realizing he had caught her staring at the photographs.

He said nothing and Sarah felt a strange awkwardness between them.

'Will Megan come over to soothe your poor spotty brow?'

'Doubtful.' He sighed. 'She's not particularly gone on Dublin and when I told her that I was covered in spots you'd think that I had leprosy – she almost jumped away from the phone. No doubt she'll find a willing replacement partner for the ball.'

Sarah suddenly thought of her mother's old adage to look close at a lover and see how they behave when illness comes knocking on the door. Perhaps the beautiful Megan wasn't as perfect as she seemed.

'I brought you over a container with some of my lasagne and I've put it in the freezer. It'll save you cooking.'

'Thanks,' he said weakly, scratching at his arm.

'You know you should really rub some of that pink stuff all over you,' she advised. 'It really helped Evie stop scratching.'

'Maybe you could rub it on me,' he teased.

Sarah laughed, glad to see Angus was getting his sense of humour back. 'I'm making meatballs in a tomato sauce and rice for tea tonight, I'll pop over with some later if you fancy it.'

'Thanks,' he said, reaching for her hand and clasping it in his. 'You're an angel.'

He looked so lost and lonely and miserable that she was tempted to stay and keep him company for a while. If she were Megan and had a nice boyfriend like him she wouldn't leave him reliant on the goodwill of neighbours and friends when he was sick. She'd fly to his side at once. But he wasn't her boyfriend, she reminded herself, he was just a friend whom she'd come to care about.

'Angus, I'd better get going,' she said, passing him up the newspaper. 'I've a few things to do before I collect Evie. I'm trying to get organized to go to London next week, to see a publisher who likes my book.'

'What?' he exclaimed, almost jumping out of the bed. 'That's *great* news, Sarah. I'm so pleased for you.'

'Ronan gave it to her and she read the story and liked it. I'm trying not to get my hopes too high,' she explained, 'but it is exciting!'

'You'll knock them dead when they meet you,' he said simply, 'and the book is great!'

Standing outside the mews she tried to gather her thoughts. Even though she was young and single, she was a parent, and she didn't need the complication of falling for someone like Angus, no matter how charming and fun he was, for the harsh truth of it was that he was already taken.

Chapter Forty-one

As Sarah Ryan walked through the busy Terminal 1 in Heathrow, her precious manuscript and photocopies of her story safe along with a change of clothes in the roomy black leather shoulder bag Grace had lent her, she couldn't help smiling. She was going to London to talk to a real pubisher about a story and character that she had created – it was just too incredible. Thousands of people passed by, caught up in their own lives and problems and work as they rushed and brushed alongside her in the huge airport. Keep calm, she reminded herself as she ignored the panicky feeling in her stomach and tried to suss out which way to go. She was to take the Heathrow Express Train that would bring her into central London and then it was just a short cab ride to the offices of Little Bear Books. She was naturally nervous about meeting a big publisher and discussing her work on a professional level, but was also excited at the prospect.

What was meant to be a simple day in London had turned into a weekend visit! Ronan, when he'd heard about her appointment with Jilly, had insisted she stay on the Friday and Saturday night in his place.

'Fingers crossed we'll be celebrating,' he insisted, 'and we'll go out for a lovely dinner.'

Her mum and sisters had been equally supportive. Her mother was minding Evie today, and tomorrow Grace would take over as Maggie was going to Knock on a pilgrimage with Aunt Kitty.

'Evie will be spoiled rotten while you are away,' they'd all insisted. 'It's only for a few days!'

Her flight had cost half nothing and she'd blinked away the tears when her sisters and mother had insisted on giving her some extra shopping money. Karen had told her she was proud of her and Angus had hugged her and wished her luck.

She hated leaving Evie but knew in her heart that with her granny and aunties she was in safe hands. The prospect of a few days in London was very tempting. She'd only been to London twice previously. Her first time had been with her class of eighty convent girls, and they had spent most of the trip sightseeing for boys their own age and drinking secretly in the rooms of the student hostel that they were staying in. Then she had come over for a twenty-first birthday treat with Grace and Anna when Evie was just over a year old. They'd had tickets for *Les Misérables*, and all she remembered was missing Evie, who had developed a sore ear, and wishing she was home.

This time was different. She had total faith in her family's ability to babysit and was here on business.

* * *

Sarah took a deep breath as she paid the cab driver and stepped through the door of Little Bear Books. There were poster displays everywhere for their latest books and she recognized some of the titles.

A security guard pointed the way to the lift to the fifth floor where editor Jilly Greene had an office. Jilly was tall and dark-haired and very slim, her big eyes and brilliant bone structure emphasized by the amazing silver earrings that dangled from her ears. They were of a spider's web. Sarah, unable to help herself, stared.

'They're cool, aren't they!' She smiled, pointing to the seat opposite her desk. 'Jess, one of my friends, made them for me. They go with a book I've just done about a spider who can foretell the future. Who knows, maybe next time I'll be getting kitten ones!'

Sarah blushed, relieved that Jilly was so taken with her story.

Jilly professed her fondness for Ronan and then asked her to spread her story out on the desk and talk her through it.

'It's so simple and cute but I defy anyone from three to ninety-three not to like it,' she said, fixing Sarah with her intense gaze. 'You've done a lovely job with the character of the cat and of course of her owner. We are keen to publish it, and sign you up for a second book: that's why I asked you to come over to meet us.'

Sarah stared at the table strewn with her story and drawings, not really believing what she was hearing. It was every art student's dream, every writer's hope to get a book

302

published, and here it was happening to her. She dared not say a word in case like an absolute eejit she broke down and cried.

'We would hope to publish for next Christmas. We're too late for this year, obviously, and would want it for the UK, Ireland, Australia, Canada and New Zealand. Your agent will obviously sell the rights for the rest of the world.'

'I don't have an agent,' she admitted.

'Don't worry, that will change, and if not, we will sell the rights.'

Sarah felt like jumping across the table and hugging Jilly.

'We'll pay you twenty thousand pounds for two books which will be spread out and paid not just on signing the contract but on delivery and publication of each book.'

Sarah concentrated on her drawing of Miss Bee trying to coax Mitten down out of an apple tree. This was too good to be true. Money to go into a bank account for herself and Evie, money for ballet classes, for new shoes, for a trip to the hairdresser's to get proper highlights instead of her usual do-it-yourself job.

'Is that OK with you?' asked Jilly grinning.

Sarah nodded. 'I can't believe it.'

'Well, do believe it,' added Jilly, serious now, 'because we really do like the stories and your style. I would like to see another one or two Mitten stories with Miss Bee. I also think that your dog detective Mr Bones has great potential and it is something else we might be interested in optioning.'

Sarah sat dumbfounded across from her, thinking how lucky she was. If she hadn't gone to Karen and Mick's for dinner and got talking to Ronan none of this would have happened.

'Would you like a tea or coffee?' asked Jilly. 'Jeremy our art director wants to come in and say hello as he will be the one working with you on the art and design.'

'Coffee please,' she said, trying to relax and enjoy the moment.

Jeremy Howard wore dark black-rimmed glasses, a black jacket and bright red shirt. He was the same height as her and she guessed was about forty years old. He introduced himself and reeled off a few of the children's books he had worked on previously. Sarah was delighted to hear one or two that were favourites of Evie's. She listened attentively as he talked through the artwork and some suggested layouts.

'We have to decide on page length, size, endpaper design, and which illustration should be the cover.'

Sarah's stomach flipped over with excitement as she took in all that he was saying. Mitten the little marmalade kitten was actually going to be in a proper book, not just a bedtime story for Evie or a distraction on her computer.

Two cups of coffee and a chocolate chip cookie later Jilly gave her three copies of the contract for *Mitten the Kitten* to take back to Dublin to read and sign.

'What are you doing for lunch?' asked Jilly as she got ready to leave.

'Nothing.' She shrugged. 'I'm going to Ronan's later when he finishes work, but I thought I'd just have a look around the shops for a while.'

'Come on then, I'll treat you to lunch,' offered her editor.

'There's a nice Italian down the street that does a great mushroom tagliatelle and seafood cannelloni.'

Sarah glanced around Jilly's office before they left, taking in book covers and posters and publicity material, pink and purple pigs, a dancing duck, swans doing ballet and a rabbit magician. Mitten and her author were already beginning to feel at home!

Chapter Forty-two

Grace had volunteered to mind Evie while Sarah went to London for the weekend. 'Are you sure you'll be able to manage a six-year-old for all that time?' Sarah had asked as if she doubted her capabilities.

'Evie will be fine,' she'd promised. 'I'll collect her from Mum's on Friday evening after work and guard her with my life. You just go to London and concentrate on selling your book. Evie is in good hands with Auntie Grace.'

Sarah was so grateful to her for minding Evie so she could have just two nights away that Grace felt horribly guilty about having been such a self-centred cow and not having been a better aunt and sister. To compensate she had loaned Sarah her expensive travel bag and a new fitted honey-coloured jacket that she had only worn twice.

To tell the truth she was actually looking forward to having Evie as company in the apartment. The weekends since breaking up with Shane had become an abyss of gloom. She just hung around watching DVDs, shopping, sleeping in and recovering from nights out late clubbing and drinking with her friends. The promised phone call from Mark McGuinness had, as she suspected, failed to materialize; obviously the fact that he had half the single female population of Dublin after him meant that she had barely figured on his radar. Her mother had quizzed her about seeing him again but Grace had put her off by saying that she was far too busy at work to get involved with anyone at the moment. At least this weekend with a six-year-old around was going to be different: fresh air and walks, a trip to a playground, cooking something nutritious and staying home at night. If Sarah could do it, she certainly could!

Evie was jumping up and down with excitement about coming to sleep in her apartment when she collected her after work. It made more sense for her to take her this evening as her mother and Aunt Kitty planned to get up at the crack of dawn and get an early start joining the parish group on the bus for their annual pilgrimage to Knock.

'I'll say prayers for all your intentions,' she promised, 'and ask Our Lady to be good to you all and answer your special requests.'

Maggie Ryan and her sister Kitty had undertaken the annual pilgrimage to the Holy Shrine in Mayo to thank the Lord for his blessings ever since Aunt Kitty's awful diagnosis with breast cancer. Her mother's handbag was already stuffed full of letters and petitions from neighbours and friends, every one of them looking for favours and requests.

'Grace, there must be something you'd like a bit of divine intervention on,' she coaxed. 'Anna and Sarah have already given me their letters.'

Grace grabbed a piece of notepaper from the pad in the kitchen and scribbled something, hunting in the drawer for an envelope, and then sealed it shut.

'There,' she said, passing it over.

Her mum looked relieved. She loved to have things to pray for: exams, health, decisions, careers. She'd always been the religious type, a real Irish Catholic mammy who loved going to mass and talking to the saints. She was spiritual in her own way but ever since Leo's death she'd derived great comfort from prayer and helping out in the parish. Grace would bet her mother was doing this pilgrimage in the hope of the Good Lord finding her daughters husbands. She smiled to herself. Maggie Ryan was looking for a miracle if she thought any decent men were suddenly going to appear on the scene, prayers or not!

'Auntie Grace, I'm sleeping over in your house tonight!' squealed Evie, her red and black ladybird backpack at the ready. Grace smiled, remembering the excitement of going to stay with Aunt Kitty or Granny when she was younger, half nervous about missing your mother but anticipating something different: a new bed, strange food, a break from the humdrum routine of childhood.

'Remember, if there are any problems, phone me!' urged her mum as she walked them out to the car. 'And no fizzy drinks before bed or she'll be awake half the night.'

'Mum, she's going to be fine. Evie and I are going to have a great time together.'

'I'll say a prayer for the two of you,' smiled her mother, waving as they set off.

* * *

Evie ran around the apartment three times like a small puppy checking everything out while Grace made a start on fixing them dinner: chicken strips tossed in a golden coating of flour and herbs then roasted and served with potato wedges. Her niece had been to visit a few times before, but without Sarah, it was now all new territory. Curious, she pulled open the kitchen presses and the larder cupboard and the fridge before checking out the small spare bedroom where she was to sleep. Grace had bought three pink pillows in Dunnes and a ballerina-patterned lampshade for the bedside light. She'd been tempted to go to town and change the whole room and make it more child-friendly but had settled on a girly touch.

Evie carefully unzipped her backpack and Grace helped her to put away her clothes neatly in the drawer, taking out a photo of Evie and Sarah at the zoo and putting it beside her bed. Evie ran in and checked Grace's bedroom before going back and racing out on to the balcony where she was fascinated by the boats and water beneath her.

'We're so high up,' she giggled, tossing a geranium leaf in the air and watching it float downwards.

Grace supposed it was a bit different from the basement flat that she was used to.

'Evie, why don't you get into your pyjamas after dinner and we can watch the DVDs I got?'

'Auntie Grace, aren't you getting into your pyjamas too?'

'Of course I will.' She smiled as she served the plates of food, glad that Evie was a kid with a good appetite and not one of those faddy eaters.

309

* * *

It was just gone eight o'clock on a Friday evening and she was getting into her pyjamas.

'Everyone wears their PJs at sleepovers,' giggled Evie, following her into the bedroom and watching her undress while jumping up and down on her big double bed. Grace joined in the fun a few minutes later!

She had bought dolly mixtures, midget gems, marsh-mallows and a bag of toffee popcorn along with apple juice and chocolate milk. She had managed to get a copy of *Mary Poppins* and a cute-looking DVD about a dog called Merlin who could do magic. Evie was big into dogs by all accounts.

They snuggled up on the cream couch using a throw from her bed to wrap themselves in as Evie, entranced, followed the story, her small face serious, her dark hair falling over her smooth cheeks. Her eyes almost popped out of her head as Mary Poppins worked her magic and her fingers reached for Grace's hand. Grace watched the film but spent half the time watching Evie. Sarah was so lucky to have such a lovely kid!

Evie got up and danced to one or two of the songs totally unselfconsciously, making Grace join in, and laughed like a trooper when Merlin the dog turned his owner into a rabbit and began to chase him.

When she saw Evie's eyes begin to get heavy and ready for sleep, Grace announced that it was time for bed and Evie without any protests had washed her face and hands and brushed her teeth and clambered in between the crisp white sheets.

'I'll read you a story,' Grace offered, sitting beside her. She took up the illustrated copy of *Cinderella and the Glass Slipper*, one of her niece's favourites.

Evie's dark eyelashes gradually closed and Grace sat in utter silence for half an hour, entranced, simply watching her breathe.

Later Grace curled up in a chair outside on the balcony. The city was in darkness; the Friday after-work crowds were making their way to bars and restaurants; the river was slipping by below her. Life, like the dark water of the Liffey beneath, was passing her by. Where was the time going to? She had the best family in the world, had enjoyed an almost perfect childhood and was fortunate to work in the area she had always wanted. Yet she still wasn't satisfied. She wanted more. Her life was as empty and shallow as a life could be. She was thirty and single and facing a lifetime of being on her own, of being an aunt and maybe never a mother. She didn't know if she could bear it! They'd all thought Sarah was crazy when she'd jumped in and followed her heart when she was nineteen and never thought of the consequences. With her perfect child, at least she had something to show for it! And Anna might say she didn't give a toss about love and men but it was clear to everyone that she had fallen for this guy in Connemara. A tear ran down her face. She had read somewhere in a survey that fifty per cent of American women were living on their own and would go through life like that. At the rate things were going she was likely to find herself in the same position and she'd better get used to it.

All the nice men she knew were already either married or engaged and the ones that were left wanted to date twenty-year-olds with short skirts and hair extensions. She watched the moon above smile down on the city and heard the sound of music coming from one of the moored boats. She resisted the urge to get a glass of wine and went to the kitchen and poured herself a comforting tumbler of chocolate milk instead before deciding to call it a night and go to bed herself.

She was half asleep when she became aware of the small figure standing in the bedroom doorway in pink and white cotton pyjamas. Evie stumbled into the room and clambered up beside her.

'Where's Mummy?' she whispered sadly. 'I can't find her.'

'She's away in London tonight, pet,' Grace reminded her. 'Remember you're staying with me and I'm minding you.'

'But I want my mummy, I miss her.' Evie began to sob.

'I know I'm not your mummy,' Grace said calmly, 'but I do love you and you're safe here with me. We'll phone your mum first thing in the morning and tell her about our sleep-over, will we?'

Evie nodded silently, her body cuddling up beside her. Grace took her in her arms and stroked her hair, singing to her softly until eventually she relaxed and they both fell asleep.

Chapter Forty-three

Forsaking her normal healthy muesli and yogurt, Grace had made pancakes with maple syrup for breakfast. The kitchen looked like a bomb had hit it after Evie helped her to mix the batter. There was a sticky layer all over her granite worktops and she gave the place a quick wipe as Evie told her that they tasted almost as good as the pancakes Granny made.

They phoned Sarah, who told them the great news about *Mitten the Kitten* going to be a proper book, and Evie gave her a blow-by-blow account of their sleepover.

Grace had quite an itinerary mapped out for the day ahead and thanked heaven for the bright blue sky and sunny day.

'First we're going into town shopping,' she told Evie, 'and then we'll go and look at the baby ducks and swans in the park and have a picnic there.'

'I love picnics,' declared Evie solemnly.

She had worked out a route that went round a few toy shops and knick-knack places that would appeal to any child. Evie, oohing and aahing, played with the wooden painted puppets and the pieces of furniture from a big dolls' house that was on display in a shop near the Westbury. Grace bought her a baby bed and chest-of-drawer set along with a princess puppet. In the Avoca shop she found a perfect pair of ruby slippers and a magic fairy book which came with a cut-out fairy doll; downstairs she bought some food for the picnic along with two bottles of freshly squeezed orange juice.

St Stephen's Green, the city centre park, was busy with families strolling in the sunshine and heading for the playground. Evie squealed with delight when she spotted the swans and their cygnets and a load of baby ducklings following their mother. They ate sitting on a bench near the big water fountain and as the afternoon was getting warmer decided to have a quick few goes on the slide and swings before heading back to the apartment.

Evie discovered her red birthday kite during a game of hide and seek. It was still in its birthday wrapping, unused.

'Auntie Grace, why don't you fly your kite?' asked Evie, her blue eyes serious. 'Don't you like your present?'

'I do like it,' Grace explained, 'but I've been very busy lately, so I haven't had the time to fly it yet.'

'Then can we fly it today?' pleaded Evie. 'Please, please please?'

'I'm not sure today is a good day,' she said, trying to distract her, but Evie, like most six-year-olds, wouldn't give up. Half an hour later they were down on Sandymount Strand, ready to give the new kite a try.

It was still sunny but the sea breeze was strong along the seashore where walkers and joggers paraded along the strand.

Evie helped her unroll the long tail of the kite and unwrap the string holder.

'Evie, I want you to run along with the kite for a few minutes,' Grace explained, 'and I'll run behind you, and when I tell you to you must just let it go, OK?'

Evie nodded as if she understood but after twenty minutes of trying to get the kite to lift and catch the winds neither of them had succeeded. It was harder than it looked and most people just ignored them and passed them by. Even Evie was beginning to lose interest and was bending down, talking to an elderly lady with two golden Labradors.

'Come on, Evie, a few more goes and we'll get it to fly!' Grace promised as Evie took off running again.

'Let go, let go,' she screamed as the wind began to catch the string but her little niece wasn't fast enough and the red kite plummeted straight to earth again.

'Hey! Do you want a hand?' called a jogger who had stopped to watch them. She looked up gratefully only to see Mark McGuinness coming towards them. He was wearing a pair of tracksuit bottoms and a T-shirt but still managed to look stylish. Horribly conscious how windblown and dishevelled she was in her pale blue jeans, she would seem churlish if she refused his offer. Besides Evie, having recognized him, was already waving madly.

'Hi Grace. Look I'm sorry that I didn't get in touch, it's just that I've been away and caught up with things: I honestly did intend to call you.'

Grace said nothing. She didn't believe him, but smiled up

at him as if it didn't matter at all because Evie stood between them, holding the kite.

'Hey, how about Evie and I hold the string and you take the kite and run with it,' he suggested.

'Great,' she called, starting to run across the sand.

Holding the kite up high Grace ran as fast as she could letting her fingers ease off the string near the frame as the wind began to catch it and lift it up above her head.

Suddenly it caught. The wind lifted it; it gave a swirl, tugging away from her and zooming skywards, caught in a wind pocket. Mark gauged the tautness of the string and helped Evie to ease it up and up; then he quickly unwound it and let the kite fly high in the air, its long multicoloured tail dancing below it. The red kite soared across the blue sky above the sand and the sea. It looked truly fabulous and Evie was so excited as, Mark standing right beside her, she proudly manoeuvred the kite above her. Everyone walking along the strand was looking up at it, all clearly as entranced as Evie. It *was* beautiful, Grace thought, so simple yet so exhilarating. The scene reminded her of when they were young and her dad used to take Anna and Sarah and herself up to Deerpark, near the woods in Mount Merrion. It was the best park in Dublin for kite-flying, with its great views over the bay and the strong air currents from the sea mingling with those from the city. Maybe she'd take Evie there another day to try it out.

'Keep the string tight and let it out very slowly, make sure the wind is catching it before you unroll it,' said Mark, bending down and showing Evie.

The red kite seemed miles above them dancing up towards the heavens; it seemed extraordinary that it could be controlled by such a small girl down below. Yet Evie was holding firmly on to the string.

'She's doing fine.' Mark was full of praise. 'She's a natural.'

Evie's eyes were shining, her face rapt in concentration as she stared upwards.

'Thanks. Thanks for helping,' Grace said, acknowledging that Mark had gone out of his way to do so. He could have simply jogged by and ignored their predicament. 'We'd never have managed to get it flying only that you came along!'

'It's usually a two- to three-man job getting started,' he replied, 'until you get lift-off and begin to feel the air currents. When did she get it?'

'Actually, it's mine,' she confessed. 'Evie gave it to me for my birthday and she just found it and insisted we try it out.'

'So you're just a big kid!' he teased.

'Actually I'd forgotten how great it is! That's the good thing about minding Evie – I get to do those things again.'

They stood watching the kite in companionable silence, each taking a turn flying it. Evie told them what to do as she ran between them. As the kite flew above them, Grace was acutely aware of Mark's dark hair and handsome face concentrating on passing the string-holder back to Evie and making sure that she had a proper grip on it.

'I'd better get going,' he said after a while, 'continue my run.'

Grace thanked him again and watched his tall frame pick up pace and jog off across the sand.

Evie was in her element and moved slowly up and down along the beach. Grace watched the red kite soar and dip and catch the air pockets, dancing free above them, wishing somehow her heart could be like that!

Then, suddenly, out of the corner of her eye, Grace spotted two boys on bicycles racing across the sand, a flash of red and black metal paint and silver, pedalling furiously, racing each other. She shouted, trying to warn them. Evie was engrossed looking upwards, and didn't see them. She stepped into their path and the wheels and speed of the bikes knocked her over on to the ground in a tangle of wheels and grazed skin and blood. Evie lay in a heap, sobbing, screaming, her voice piercing.

Grace, panic making her hands tremble, pulled the bikes off her.

The twelve-year-olds looked shaken, and apologized.

'We didn't see her!'

'Sorry! I couldn't stop.'

'You were going too fast, not watching!' she shouted angrily at them, bending over Evie.

The small girl's bare legs were shaking, her knees gashed and bleeding and covered in sand. Evie had let go of the kite; in shock, she was unaware that it was floating away. One of the boys grabbed the string.

The lady with the dogs came back, the Labradors sniffing around the ground and the bikes. This time Evie ignored them.

'Just see if you can stand,' urged Grace, trying to lift her up.

Evie wailed the minute she touched her arm. 'It hurts!' she moaned.

'Maybe it's broken?' said the older woman kindly. 'It's best to get it checked. She's probably going to need a tetanus injection too.'

Evie wailed even louder and Grace stood there frozen. She didn't know what to do. If Evie needed an X-ray she would have to take her to the children's hospital in town. She somehow had to get her off the beach and then into a car. It was a nightmare. How was she going to manage?

'I'd bring you,' said the lady, 'but my car is about two miles away.'

'It's fine, my car is up in the car park,' Grace thanked her as she tried to manoeuvre Evie up into her arms without hurting her sore arm. She failed, and Evie began to cry harder.

'Here, let me.'

She turned to find Mark was back standing beside her, taking Evie from her as if she were a feather.

The two boys looked miserable, thinking that they were in big trouble.

'You two learn a lesson from this!' he warned. 'Watch where you're going. You've no business cycling like maniacs on a public beach where little kids are playing!'

Grace took the kite and the rewound string one of the boys passed her before he sloped off guiltily with his friend, the two of them slowly wheeling their bikes away.

'My car is just there, you can see it,' he said firmly. 'I'll drive you. Temple Street is probably the nearest children's hospital.'

'Don't want to go to hospital,' protested Evie.

'Temple Street is where all the good children go when they're hurt,' he said kindly. 'The doctors and nurses there make them better.'

Grace was overwhelmed with relief at his appearance and surprised by how at ease he was with Evie, calming her down and yet firmly telling her what was going to happen. What would she have done without him?

Taking his keys, she managed to open his black Range Rover and sat in the back seat. He passed her Evie, who stretched out lengthways on top of her, her knees too sore too bend.

'It's all right, pet. Everything is going to be all right,' Grace reassured her, trying to keep the fear out of her own tone as the car headed across the East Link Toll Bridge. The whole way to the hospital she prayed that Evie's injuries were minor.

The Accident and Emergency Department was busy and Mark kept hold of Evie and sat down in the queue while she went to the desk and filled in the name and address and information forms. Sitting there trying to give them vital medical information about her niece's inoculation history, she felt absolutely useless.

'My sister's in London,' she explained, 'and I'm just babysitting for the weekend.'

What a disaster! Some babysitter I am, she rebuked herself. What was she going to say to Sarah? The minute she had some information she'd phone her to let her know what was going on. She went back to the waiting room and joined

Mark. Evie was dozing in his arms, her face pressed against his shirt.

'I'll take her off you if you want, Mark, then you can go,' she offered, sliding into the empty seat beside him. 'We'll be fine, honest.'

'Let her sleep,' he whispered. 'She's had a shock.' He showed no inclination to leave despite it being a Saturday evening.

All around them in the busy department were kids and parents with every conceivable injury that could befall any-one on a Saturday evening: football disasters; a teenage skateboarder with a broken finger; a scared little boy with five bee stings whose hand was swollen up; a little girl with a big white plastic bowl throwing up non-stop; a kid with a piece of stick stuck in his leg; and red-faced kids running temperatures and wailing. There were two small babies with petrified young mothers and a ten-year-old boy with his father who had injured his leg playing football in the back garden, the two of them kitted out in matching Manchester United shirts.

It's hell, thought Grace, feeling sick herself every time the little girl across from her puked.

'Go and get some air,' urged Mark.

Outside on the street, she gulped in the fresh air and wondered how in heaven's name did people cope with being parents? She'd had her tonsils out here in this hospital when she was eight years old, but her only memory was of getting a new doll called Colleen and eating big bowls of strawberry ice-cream after her operation. Her mum and dad must have been up the walls. She tried Sarah's phone but it was switched off.

Trying to compose herself, she headed back inside to find Mark, unperturbed, chatting away to the United fan's father.

'Evie Ryan,' called the nurse, looking around the busy waiting room. Grace stood up, Mark following with Evie in his arms, carrying her into the large treatment area. The smiling Filipina nurse led them to an open cubicle. Evie grimaced and cried out in pain as she was lowered on to the narrow trolley bed. April, the nurse, gently examined both knees and asked Evie about her arm. A few minutes later the doctor appeared. He looked really young, his greasy mouse-brown hair standing on end, the lapels of his white coat covered in Star Wars badges, worn open over a Rolling Stones T-shirt.

'Hey, Evie!' he called, trying to get her to smile. 'I'm Dr Delaney.'

Evie looked up at him but closed her lips stubbornly.

'What happened?' he asked.

Grace began to tell him the story about being on the beach and the bicycles—

'If you don't mind,' he interrupted, 'I'd prefer it if Evie could tell me in her own words.'

A sudden thought occurred to Grace. Did this doctor think that she was responsible for what had happened to Evie?

'I was flying a big red kite,' Evie said slowly. 'It went high and Grace and Mark were helping me and there were two goldy dogs called Honey and Bailey and bold boys came on their big bikes and they hit me.'

'They hit you?'

'With the bikes,' she said, her voice wavering.

'And are you hurt?'

She nodded. 'My arm and my legs.'

Dr Delaney examined her quickly, checking her chest and her ribs and stomach, then tried to get her to lift her arm and move it. Evie winced with pain.

'Can you squeeze my hand?' he asked. She couldn't.

A few minutes later he gave her a tetanus injection and sent her for an X-ray with Nurse April.

'Mum and Dad, you can stay here, it won't take long,' he said, rushing off to another young patient. Grace was embarrassed by his assumption that Mark and she were Evie's parents and a couple. She could tell Mark had heard it too.

'It's a clean break,' the doctor explained on Evie's return. 'She'll need a cast but will be fine in a few weeks. The legs and knees are OK but badly grazed, we need to clean and sterilize them before we let you go home. Get that sand out of the tissue. I'll give her some local pain relief first.'

Grace was overwhelmed with relief. Evie was going to be able to come home tonight. 'You are such a brave girl,' she said, kissing the top of her head.

Evie was very quiet as Nurse April, once her knee area was numb, began to clean it and irrigate it with water from a syringe before putting a special film of antiseptic ointment and a dressing on both knees.

'I know it feels bad tonight but by tomorrow it will be a

whole lot better,' explained the nurse, her dark eyes serious. 'It's good she walks around but just gentle exercise for a few days, not too much playing and jumping, to let the skin heal up. Any sign of infection you can bring her back to us or to your GP. Now let's get this cast on her arm.'

Evie was very wary when the nurse got a metal tube and inserted her arm into it, covering it with a layer of bandage, then pulling the tube away and leaving a perfect layer of bandage on her lower arm which she then began to add plaster to. In what seemed only a few minutes the cast was done. Evie had opted for an almost neon-pink one. Finally the nurse cut a sling to fit comfortably around Evie's neck.

'Thank you so much,' said Grace appreciatively as they got ready to go. Evie definitely looked as if she'd been in the wars. Grace had phoned Sarah's number in London a few more times but her phone was still turned off. She'd try her again later. Mark made a great fuss admiring Evie's cast and telling her about the one he'd got when he broke his leg when he was ten. 'I was trying to climb an apple tree in the garden. I managed to get up into the tree, the problem was coming down!'

Evie giggled as he scooped her up and carried her out to the car.

It was dark outside, the streets quiet, disturbed only by the flickering blue flash of an ambulance pulling up outside the hospital doors.

'Mark, I'm so sorry,' she apologized, realizing how many hours they had spent in the hospital. 'We've totally ruined your Saturday night.'

'Come on and I'll get you two home,' he said, starting the engine. 'Anyone fancy something to eat? Chips or whatever?' Grace suddenly remembered how long it was since they'd eaten; she was starving. He stopped off at Burdock's, the city centre chipper; Grace persuaded Evie to eat a few chips and to take a few sips of orange in the back of the car. She looked exhausted, her face pale and strained, too tired to eat any more. It had got chilly and Mark made her take his grey cotton hooded top and put it on to keep warm.

Evie was out cold, fast asleep, by the time they got to the apartment. Grace ran ahead of Mark to open the main door and the lift, and her apartment door, showing him to the main bedroom.

'Put her here in my bed,' she whispered as Mark lowered Evie on to the cushions. Evie barely stirred as she eased off her sandals and socks and pulled the quilt over her. She stood watching her for a few minutes, the sense of panic that had been bubbling away in her finally easing as she saw Evie sleep.

'She's going to be OK,' Mark reminded her, as she went back out to the living room. 'You heard what the doctor said.' He was walking around studying the view, the bookshelves and her stack of CDs and DVDs, paying attention to the prints and artwork on her walls. 'Nice place, very nice.'

Grace was for some strange reason relieved that he approved of her taste.

'Would you like a drink or something?' she asked, belatedly remembering her manners.

'A coffee would be great.' He smiled, following her as she

went into the kitchen. His T-shirt was covered in blood and dirt. She hadn't even noticed it earlier. He leant against the polished wood and steel units watching her as she filled the kettle, got milk from the fridge and produced some fudge brownies she'd bought for Evie.

'I can't say how grateful I am for today,' she began. 'I don't know what I would have done if you hadn't been there. There're not many people who would stop and help like you did and come to the hospital. You've been so good, Mark—'

'Ssh,' he said, reaching for her hand. 'I told you it's OK. It's no big deal.'

'It *is* a big deal,' she said softly, touching his face and cheek, something she'd been wanting to do for the past few hours. She could see the smile on his lips as he pulled her close.

'Then it is a big deal,' he said, looking her straight in the eye, moving a strand of hair off her face before claiming her mouth and lips with his.

His kiss was warm and tender and loving. Grace, opening her eyes, surprised, saw a look in his eyes that left her in no doubt that the attraction and feeling between them was mutual.

'Interesting,' he said, raising his head.

Grace blushed; the situation certainly was interesting. Mark McGuinness was not at all what she had expected. She had got him totally wrong, made stupid assumptions about him, but the past few hours had shown her a very different side of him. He was one of those good old-fashioned men her mother was always talking about.

'Very interesting,' he teased, kissing her again.

Grace definitely liked having him hold and kiss her this way. She pulled him closer, running her lips over the skin of his neck and throat and almost collapsing with desire when he in return began to kiss the nape of her neck and up under her ears.

Grabbing their coffees, the two of them made it to her living room. Mark pulled her on to the couch, his hand straying up under her T-shirt caressing her skin; she pushed herself closer to him, moulding her body to his. The emotion between them was heightened, the desire obvious, yet Grace was unsure what to say or do. He was utterly gorgeous: she was torn between having wild rampant sex with him or curling up on the couch on his lap and just watching the way he breathed or how his hair curled at the back of his head. She was scared; whatever there was between them she didn't want to spoil it by simply having slam-bam sex. She wanted more from it, she realized, holding his hand in hers and studying the way small dark hairs patterned beneath his knuckles as he raised her fingertips and kissed them one by one. She wanted to be much more than just a one-night stand. She wanted a relationship with him.

She moaned as his head went down, his lips pushing the cotton from across her shoulders and chest, reaching for her breast.

'Mark!' she said, trying to regain some control of the situation. Then her mobile rang, just at the moment she was about to throw all caution to the wind. She wondered who it could possibly be at this time of night, then saw Sarah's number flash on the screen.

'I have to answer it,' she told him, picking it up. 'It's Sarah.'

Mark groaned, throwing his arms and head back against the couch, gazing at her flushed face and tumbled hair, unnerving her.

Her sister had just come back from supper and a gig in a nearby club where some of Ronan's friends who were in a band had performed. She was all excited and a bit tipsy.

'Is everything OK?' she asked. 'It's just I had voicemails from you.'

Grace took a deep breath, dreading what she had to say, unwilling to burst her sister's bubble of happiness. 'Evie had a bit of an accident,' she began. 'She's fine but she's broken her arm and cut her knees.'

'Broken her arm! How?' asked Sarah, sobering up in an instant.

Grace explained the situation.

'I'll get a flight home immediately,' screamed her sister. Panic had set in.

'You've missed all the late flights,' Grace explained. Being a regular business visitor to London she knew the airline schedules from Heathrow and Stansted pretty well. 'You may not be able to get a flight any earlier tomorrow; they usually get pretty booked out at the weekends.'

'I should never have left her,' Sarah blurted out. 'Never.'

'She's going to be fine,' Grace said firmly. 'She's fast

asleep now and I don't want to wake her but she'll phone you first thing in the morning, promise.'

'Grace, thanks so much for taking care of her. I can never thank you enough,' said Sarah, eventually putting the phone down.

Grace's eyes welled with tears. Even after the accident, Sarah was still grateful to her.

Mark caught her hand and squeezed it, wrapping her in his arms. 'You're tired,' he said gently. 'You need to go to bed and sleep too.'

She nodded.

'Alone,' he added, standing up to go. 'I'm not an absolute heel, and I want things to be right between us, with no stupid regrets. Evie's the one who needs you tonight!' Then he kissed her again, leaving her in no doubt that the feeling between them was mutual.

'Auntie Grace,' came Evie's voice, calling sleepily from the bedroom.

'I'd better go,' Mark said, kissing her forehead just before she ran in to take care of Evie.

Grace got Evie a drink from the kitchen and gave her a spoon of Calpol to ease the pain. Then, watching as Evie began to doze again, she wondered if she had somehow imagined the last hour in Mark's arms, kissing him, feeling the amazing chemistry and physical pull between them. Suddenly exhausted, she threw off her clothes and crawled into the bed and lay down near Evie. But she couldn't get Mark McGuinness out of her head.

Chapter Forty-four

Grace had slept badly, trying to stay on the alert in case Evie woke in pain and needed her. She had finally drifted off about four a.m., her mind in a whirling vortex of kites and bikes and dogs and Mark somewhere in the middle of it all, making it all right.

Evie to her relief had slept in and it was late morning before they both woke up, Evie telling her that she was starving and that her arm felt much better. She put her niece on the phone to Sarah in London straight away as she made them breakfast.

In the afternoon she'd taken Evie back to Pleasant Square where her mother had made a great fuss of her. By this time Grace herself was near to tears at what a mess she'd made of babysitting.

'Kids fall and break bones as quick as you can say Humpty Dumpty,' her mother told her, reminding her of the litany of falls and scrapes and casualty visits that she and her sisters had endured over the years.

* * *

Sarah's eyes welled with emotion when she saw Evie, her arm in a cast and sling.

'My mummy's back from London!' Evie chanted, jumping up and down with excitement as they all watched.

'Hey, slow down, baby, I've got some presents for you,' Sarah tipped three packages out of a bag on the table. Evie squealed with delight.

'Can I open them?' she begged.

'Of course. They're for being such a good girl for Auntie Grace while I was away.'

In five minutes flat the pink ballet tutu, the fairy princess doll and a musical magic wand Sarah had bought in Harrods had been unwrapped. Evie, despite their worries about her arm, had insisted on changing out of her pyjamas and, with a little help, trying on her new ballet tutu, dancing around the sitting room and touching things with her wand as Grace gave Sarah a blow-by-blow account of the accident and their hospital visit.

'The doctor says Evie has to go back next week to check that her arm is healing up,' she said, relieved that Sarah was back home and in charge again.

'I can never thank you enough for taking care of Evie so well and looking after her in the hospital.' Sarah hugged her, much to her embarrassment. 'I'm glad that Mark happened to be there too and I'll go and say thanks to him as soon as I can. I told you he was one of the good guys!'

Grace's eyes were shining as she talked about Mark McGuinness and she was unable to disguise her change of feelings towards him.

'Evie's a great kid,' she admitted enviously, 'and despite the broken arm we've had a wonderful time. But tell us about London. I can't believe I have a sister who's going to be a published writer. I'm so happy for you, Sarah, honestly I am.'

'A book on the shelves by my daughter, I'll be so proud,' added their mother, popping a creamy fish pie she had made earlier into the oven and opening a bottle of wine to celebrate.

Anna arrived and after a breathless retelling of the broken-arm tale they sat down to supper as Sarah told them about meeting with Jilly Greene, lunch, Ronan's amazing apartment in Notting Hill and the fancy Japanese restaurant he had taken her to. Her busy itinerary had continued with a visit to the National Gallery, a spin on the London Eye and an amazing shopping trip followed by supper with Ronan and some of his friends. Sunday had been brunch in his local pub, a stroll in the park and then a mad rush to get the Express back to Heathrow.

'The whole thing was like a dream,' she confessed. 'I know that you and Anna often travel, but for me it was just so different to be away without Evie or the family and to do things by myself. I feel as if I've been away for a week or two.'

Evie couldn't stop yawning and as soon as they finished eating, Sarah put her to bed, snuggling up under the duvet with her for a few minutes until she was fast asleep.

'She's out cold,' Sarah reported as she came back upstairs and sat at the kitchen table.

'She's a bundle of energy,' admitted Grace, 'I can't believe that she got me to fly a kite down on Sandymount Strand.'

Taking a sip of her wine Sarah told them all about the plans for her first book and how excited she was.

'I can't believe it,' Anna admitted, leaning across the table. 'There's me trying to write a book for years and you go and come up with a story for Evie about a little cat and end up going to London to sign up with a big publisher.'

'But yours is an important book,' Sarah said seriously, 'while mine is just a little book for kids about an old lady and a funny little cat!' She really didn't want her sister to be jealous.

'Thousands of kids around the world will read your book about Mitten while I'll be lucky if a few dusty old professors eventually pick mine up!' said Anna honestly.

Sarah nodded. She hoped that would be true. She might not have been the brightest or the best at school and at exam times, unlike her sisters, she had struggled, but here was something she was good at!

'Ever since you were a little girl you've been drawing and writing,' her mum reminded her. 'So it's lovely that someone has recognized your talent. Your father would be so proud of you, you know that.'

Mum and Dad had always encouraged all of them to paint and draw and write. Christmas after Christmas, birthday after birthday, there had been gifts of colouring pencils and paint sets and pads and canvas and pastels and oils. Sarah remembered her artwork being displayed all over the house. Maggie and Leo had nurtured each of their children's talents, something she was trying to do with Evie.

'Sarah, I'm so thrilled for you,' said Grace. 'As Mum says, nice things happen to nice people! And you deserve to have something really good happen for you and Evie. One thing this weekend made me realize is just how hard you work minding Evie and what a good mother you are. If I'm half as good as you when the time comes I'll be lucky!'

Sarah couldn't believe it, her family paying her so many compliments and being so supportive.

'Now, tell us about this guy in Roundstone,' quizzed Sarah, turning the tables on Anna.

'Roundstone?'

'Yes, that lovely guy you've met there,' they teased. 'It's no use denying it!'

Anna's blue eyes widened. There was indeed no denying it – Rob O'Neill was a lovely guy, just the one for her, and she began to tell them all about him.

Maggie Ryan sat back on the kitchen chair sipping her cup of tea, listening as Anna talked about Rob and thinking what a change he'd made to Anna's life already. Then there was Mark McGuinness who had been so kind and caring helping Grace with Evie. She'd always thought of him as a good catch but it seemed he was more than that, he was a good man: the sort Leo would have approved of. He was, she suspected, very taken with her eldest daughter and Maggie said a silent prayer that he wasn't the sort of man who would let Grace down.

Chapter Forty-five

Irina Romanowska couldn't believe her immense good fortune as she surveyed her new home. It was a dream come true: a place of her own in Pleasant Square. The basement flat had a large sitting room which got the afternoon sun and looked out over the back garden and paved terrace; a small kitchen to the front with cream-painted cupboards; a big bedroom; a small boxroom where Mr Lynch stored the remainder of his dental equipment and supplies; a bathroom with a bath and a shower; and a staircase that led up to the hallway of the main part of the house. It was a beautiful house, built so long ago, a house filled with history and love. How lucky she was to be living in such a place and able to afford the rent.

At first she had been very nervous when it was proposed she live in a house only three doors away from where she worked, but meeting Oscar Lynch had immediately re-assured her. This proud, elderly Irish gentleman, recovering from surgery, was certainly in need of a watchful eye and willing spirit ready to help out and make his life a little easier. He reminded her of her grandfather Tomasz who had died when she was sixteen.

'I am so grateful, Mrs Ryan, for the opportunity you give me.'

'And I am grateful to you, Irina, for agreeing to help out my very old friend.'

'I will do my best,' she promised.

She had resigned from her job in the newsagent's; Pat Delaney the owner gave her a big box of chocolates and a bottle of wine to say thank you. Now in the mornings she did not get up until eight o'clock, when she checked on Oscar and organized his breakfast.

He ate a small bowl of milky porridge and took either scrambled eggs or a poached egg on toast with a mug of coffee. Then he read the paper and did the crossword before he took a shower and got dressed. Once he was settled Irina set off for the group of regular households that she cleaned. Some days she arrived back in time to make him soup or a toasted sandwich for lunch, otherwise he managed himself, but in the evening she made a point of cooking him a good nourishing dinner. Her mother Hanna had ensured she knew how to cook the best meals using good vegetables that were in season and she could tell Oscar appreciated the home cooking as he literally licked his dinner plate clean every night.

'It will be a lucky man who gets you, Irina,' he praised her. 'You will make some fellow a wonderful wife.'

Irina had smiled ruefully, as that wasn't what Edek had thought when he tossed her aside for that cheeky brunette with high heels who worked in a hairdresser's and she doubted she even knew how to boil an egg.

She had signed on for English classes and two evenings a week went to Harcourt Street, to study seriously in a room packed with people of all nationalities struggling to make sense of this new tongue. Once she had good English she could maybe work in an office or for one of the technology firms.

Her friends had been a little envious when she told them of her new position and the benefits it entailed. Marta's mouth had opened when she saw the big blue couch and chair in the sitting room and the peaceful white bedroom with the old medical file cupboard now turned into a wardrobe for her clothes.

'It is lovely, Irina,' she said, hugging her. 'I am so pleased for you.'

'Some nights you stay,' Irina offered generously.

She had laid her few possessions out around the flat to make it seem more homely. Her photographs of her family and the pretty pink wrap she'd bought in the marketplace in Łódź now served as a throw on her bed; her good-luck statue of a silver swan now sat on the circular table near the window alongside the polished piece of crystal she had found down near the river when she was seven years old. With her wages she would save and buy a few things, mugs and cups and bowls and a coffee pot. She hated the instant coffee that Irish people seemed to consider reviving and refreshing and longed for the familiar scent of coffee brewing, filling her senses with anticipation.

With her mobile phone she had taken photographs both inside and outside the house and sent them to her mother, knowing how impressed she would be. Hanna Romanowska would be boasting to her neighbours and family how well her daughter was doing now that she had gone abroad.

Irina sighed, work was different now and Oscar was such a kind man. He was lonely and constantly talked about his wife whose photos dominated the large sitting room and the dining room. Elizabeth Lynch had been a beautiful woman and he must have loved her very much. The wardrobe in one of the bedrooms upstairs still held some of her clothes and shoes and handbags; her perfume and face powder and red lipstick still stood on the dressing table. It was sad that death had separated them, she thought, as she dusted and cleaned the silver frames, and polished the old mahogany sideboard and tables with beeswax. She wondered if any man would ever love her in such a way, or had her mother been right that Edek had been the closest she would ever come to finding love and marriage? She pushed the unwelcome thought away philosophically. In moving to Ireland and to Pleasant Square it seemed as if she had been granted a second chance and being an optimist she had high hopes that things were definitely going to improve.

Chapter Forty-six

Anna had finally got around to inviting her sisters for dinner. Entertaining was never high on her list of priorities but simple fairness had finally dictated it was her turn to cook for them. It was a pretty rare event and was partly fuelled by the need to meet up to decide what to get their mother for her birthday. Maggie Ryan had been dropping massive hints about coming along too but the fact that she was babysitting Evie had at last given them the chance to get together on their own.

'Mum's so happy about sorting out the arrangement with Oscar and Irina,' said Grace as she settled herself into Anna's living room. 'She just loves meddling in people's lives.'

'Irina had Oscar out for a stroll on his crutches in the park yesterday,' said Sarah. 'Evie and I met them and he's so happy to be home again.'

'Mum's intentions are good' – Grace laughed – 'but she told me last week that I shouldn't be tempted to use fake tan and that men prefer women with a natural complexion.'

'Ouch!'

'Honestly, my natural complexion is ghostly pale; people would think I was a corpse if I didn't slap a bit of colour or bronzer on.'

'She said I was letting myself go,' added Anna, 'and gave me an article she'd cut out of a magazine about makeovers!'

'She dropped a hint to me that I needed to get a haircut or everyone would think that Evie's mum was a hippy.'

'She didn't!'

'She did! But she gave me the money to go to Joseph's for a cut,' admitted Sarah. 'I'd put off going for ages because I wanted to get Evie a new pair of shoes and a skirt I saw in town, but Mum said that my looking good was as important as Evie looking nice.'

'That's true,' each sister agreed, wondering how on earth it was that mothers always seemed to know best.

Glancing around her small sitting room Anna was glad that she had made the effort for this sisterly meal. She'd cleared everything away and covered the bed in the small spare room with all the bundles of papers and books she wanted to hide. Candles and tea-lights burned on the table and on the mantelpiece over the fireplace and on one of her bookshelves. A bunch of tall delphiniums made a splash in that lovely glass vase Grace had given her, and she had finally got around to hanging the painting of a smudgy bunch of weird daisies that her artist friend Tanya had done, along with the black and white graphic of a boy on a bicycle that she'd bought at the opening of an exhibition by Lars Linney, a Swedish artist who'd moved to Ireland. The smell of the lemon chicken and rice pilaf she'd made filled the air and she topped up the glasses with more wine as she finished laying the small circular table, which usually served as her desk, where they were going to eat.

'Everything looks and smells so lovely,' said Grace approvingly.

Anna smiled gratefully, glad that her humble abode and entertaining skills had satisfied her sister's extremely high standards.

'Mum is set on finding a match for us all, you know,' Grace went on, sipping her Sauvignon. 'She believes that somewhere out there is the perfect man for each of us.'

'She's such a Mrs Bennet trying to scheme and find a husband for her poor spinster daughters.'

'Mrs Bennet?'

'*Pride and Prejudice*,' Anna reminded Sarah.

'Oh I loved that book, we did it in school. The whole class wanted to meet Mr Darcy, Sister Veronica included.'

'God, you lot used to give that poor nun such a hard time,' teased Anna.

'She was such a romantic,' Sarah protested. 'She used to read Mills and Boons!'

'Well, there are no Darcys in this neck of the woods, and having an interfering mother ready to fling you at the first stranger that comes along at our age is—'

'Embarrassing.'

'Cringe-making.'

'To say the least,' agreed Grace. 'She doesn't understand you just don't go and meet someone out of the blue like that and fall in love.'

'Definitely.'

'That's how she met Dad,' Sarah reminded them.

'Things were different then!'

'Guys were different then.'

'That was a century ago,' giggled Grace.

'Pity,' said Sarah, her expression softening as she remembered how her father would go and kiss her mother in the kitchen, stand behind her when she was cooking and sneak his arms around her, ignoring her protests about hot pans and pots, and kiss her and nibble the nape of her neck.

'But it *is* different nowadays, everyone is busier, there's such pressure on our time with work and socializing and networking with people, most of us are too wrecked to bother getting to know some random stranger,' insisted Grace, dunking a tortilla chip in the creamy garlic dip, trying not to sound bitter. She was secretly hurt by the fact that she hadn't heard a word from Mark, not even a text message. It was as if the Saturday night in her apartment had never happened.

'I read in a report somewhere that men have no intention of settling down till careers and travel and finance and houses have all been sorted,' snorted Anna, 'and that women are pretty far down their to-do list except for sex.'

'Mmmm,' they agreed. 'Mum just hasn't a clue!'

'Though it would be nice to meet someone,' Sarah said wistfully, cradling her glass. 'Not just for Evie's sake but for mine. You kind of get fed up being on your own.'

'You're not on your own,' protested her sisters loyally. 'You've got us.'

'I know.' She smiled, not wanting to admit that it wasn't

the same thing at all as having a nice man to love her and to love.

The chicken had turned out perfectly and Anna served it with a tossed salad and rice, all of them starving as they tucked in.

'Delish,' Sarah congratulated her, taking second helpings. 'That chicken is melt in your mouth.'

'Thanks,' said Anna, grateful that she had for once had the patience to follow the recipe and taken care instead of cooking in her usual slapstick fashion, which only led to culinary disasters. Next time she saw Rob she intended cooking this dish for him, to show him that she had some domestic skills.

'So what are we going to do for Mum's birthday and what will we give her?' Anna asked as she opened another bottle of wine.

They tossed around a variety of ideas, before finally settling on a pampering treat.

'Mum loves facials and massages and all those kind of treats,' Sarah mused.

'Then what about a fancy spa pampering weekend in one of those new places?' suggested Grace. 'That one, Anua, in Wicklow, looks pretty amazing!'

'Would she go?'

'Of course she would. We could give her a voucher for two people and maybe she could bring Kitty or one of her friends.'

'She'd love that.' Anna was positive. 'Anua overlooks a lake and there are lovely walks and amazing pools. I saw it on a TV programme last month and the whole place looked fabulous.'

'That's sorted then, I'll phone and organize it tomorrow,' said Grace. 'We'll combine and give it to her between us. We can each put in a bit. What about booking Roly's for her birthday lunch? She always loves it there and it means Evie can come along too.'

'OK, time for dessert.' Anna smiled nervously as she collected the empty plates and disappeared to the galley kitchen to take the sticky toffee pudding she'd made out of the oven. She'd never made it before and wasn't sure how it would turn out, but it looked great. She sighed with relief, grabbed the vanilla ice-cream from the freezer and brought them to the table.

Her sisters greeted the pudding with raptures, leaving Anna totally bowled over by the satisfaction of creating a perfect meal as she watched her sisters lick their bowls in utter silence.

For their part Sarah and Grace were surprised by Anna's sudden conversion to the delights of cookery, which she had resisted for so long.

'Well done!' they congratulated her, both now definitely convinced that Rob O'Neill was working some kind of transformation on Anna.

Chapter Forty-seven

Sarah had been basking in happiness ever since she came back from London. She was feeling better about herself than she had in a long, long time; instead of feeling a failure she had begun to realize that writing and illustrating books for children was something she was good at and if she was prepared to work hard at it it could possibly become her career.

She had called at the mews all excited to tell Angus her good news about the book and the drama about Evie's arm, and was disappointed to find he wasn't there. She had left a message on his phone and sent him a text, only to be disappointed by a simple *congratulations* reply. He was in Scotland for a few weeks, he told her, and wasn't quite sure when he'd be back. She was hurt. She liked Angus and she thought that he liked her too. Well, if he wanted to play it cool after the night he babysat and act like nothing had happened between them, then that was fine with her! Let him have his life in Edinburgh with Megan, their perfect couple life. She was used to guys thinking she was fair game because she was a single parent, used to constantly being on her own! She didn't need a boyfriend or a man in her life to make her feel good. She had Evie and at long last things were looking up for her.

Mrs Boland, the school principal, and the rest of the school staff were delighted for her and she sensed a new respect from them since her trip to the UK.

Evie was due to start her school holidays soon and Sarah was looking forward to her annual trip to the cottage in Connemara with her mum and Evie. She loved the summer and maybe if some of her publishing money came through she could afford to take Evie away to Eurodisney for a weekend, give her a real treat.

She had stayed up late watching a weepy love story, and was just wondering why she put herself through emotional turmoil when she already had enough of it in her own life, when she heard a commotion out in the back yard. Maybe it was a cat or a fox – or a prowler! She jumped up anxiously from the couch, checking the back door to make sure that it was locked.

She switched on the outside light and peeped out of the window, prepared to catch the burglar or intruder in the act, only to see Angus Hamilton blinking at her instead, looking much the worse for wear. He had stumbled over a pair of pink roller skates that Evie had abandoned on the path and was slumped on the ground near the washing line.

'Oh Angus, I'm sorry,' she apologized, unbolting the door and rushing out to him. 'I told Evie to put her skates away. Are you hurt?'

'Don't think so,' he said slowly, patting his thighs and

side. 'Nothing broken anyway,' he added, trying to stand up.

She could smell beer on his breath as she went to help him and he looked shattered. He'd dropped his bag and laptop case on the grass. He must have just got back from Scotland and gone drinking somewhere en route home. He looked stressed as well as tired, and his jet-black hair fell over his face as he got up and tried to brush himself off.

'Everything OK?' she asked.

'I've had better weeks.' He grimaced. 'A fortnight in head office is a bit of a head-wrecker and I had something important to sort out with Megan.'

'Come on, let's get you home,' she said, lifting his bag and computer case and getting him to follow her along the path to the mews. She watched as he turned the key, opened the door and dealt with the alarm, noticing how long his fingers were.

'God, I'm beat,' he said, flopping down on the leather chair.

'Maybe you should just go to bed, Angus?'

He ignored her and picked up the remote. He flicked on the TV, punching through the channels aimlessly.

She retreated into the small neat kitchen and switched on the kettle. She'd make him a quick coffee and then get back to Evie. She opened his fridge only to find a disgusting half-finished litre of milk which had gone sour. She binned it and made him a black coffee instead. Into it she ladled two heaped spoons of sugar.

'Take this,' she said, sitting down near him. 'You've had a fall and a shock.' She watched as he sipped it wordlessly.

'Now come on, Angus, go to bed,' she ordered, as if he were a little kid.

'I'm fine here,' he protested, stretching out, kicking his shoes off and yawning.

'No, you're not. You are going to bed,' she insisted.

Disgruntled, he followed her as she led him up the narrow wooden stairs to the bedroom. It was tidy and clean, the bed orderly with a white quiltcover and pillows and a tartan throw on top, the shelves filled with his stacks of CDs.

'Bathroom, then bed,' she said.

'Yes, Mam.'

She sat on the edge of the bed waiting till he reappeared, watching as he flung his black leather jacket on the chair and dived for the bed in his shirt and trousers.

'Angus, take them off!' she prompted.

He made a half-hearted attempt and failed. Leaning over, she helped him. He'd got a grass stain on his trousers and the makings of a big bruise on his side.

'Get in beside me,' he said drunkenly. 'Come on!'

'Not tonight, Josephine,' she laughed, fixing the quilt over him and hanging up his jacket and trousers. Almost at once his breathing got heavier and his snores filled the room.

A good night's sleep would work wonders. She left the lights on the landing on and one downstairs in the mews before heading back down the path to her own door. Angus would have a hell of a hangover tomorrow, that was for sure, she thought, locking up and going to her own bed.

He'd phoned while she was at work, leaving a message, and

surprised her a few hours later by calling at the door when she was putting Evie to bed.

'How's the head?'

He squirmed. 'Bad.'

'You tripped over Evie's skates, do you remember that?'

'I'll live. Anyway, I just called to say thanks.'

'I was just being neighbourly,' she said softly.

Taking in his forlorn features and hangdog expression, she momentarily considered inviting him in but her better judgement decided against it.

'I'm just putting Evie to bed,' she explained.

'Look, I won't hold you up then, but I just wanted to know if you would like to have dinner this weekend.'

'Dinner?' she said, surprised.

'You know, two people sitting across the table, with good food on plates, a bottle of wine, some music and maybe a candle?' he said coaxingly. 'I thought it might be a fitting tribute to the newly contracted author illustrator.'

She smiled. 'That sounds nice.'

'I'll cook us dinner in my place or we can go out, whatever you want. What about Friday?'

Dinner alone with him in the confines of the mews might not be the best idea given he had a girlfriend, she reminded herself. A restaurant would be a lot safer.

'Out would be nice,' she found herself saying.

Sarah had taken a bit of care with her appearance, opting for the floaty pink and turquoise Avoca patterned skirt that her sisters had bought for her birthday last year and a little white string top with the new pink wrap cardigan and a gorgeous pair of rose-coloured high heels she'd treated herself to in London. Evie was already fast asleep, her mother ensconced with the remote control watching the television. She had jumped at the chance of babysitting.

'I'm glad to see that Angus has finally had the good sense to ask you out for a celebration meal,' she said with a twinkle in her eye.

'Mum, for heaven's sake, will you stop matchmaking? Angus and I are just friends, you know that. It's lonely for him stuck here in Dublin with his girlfriend back in Scotland. We just keep each other company sometimes.'

'Is that what they call it?'

'Mum, honestly, your generation are obsessed with love and romance. Nowadays men and women can just be friends.'

Maggie Ryan held her tongue, for once not stating the obvious.

Angus took her to Chapter One, the award-winning restaurant situated beside the Writers Museum on Parnell Square.

'I thought it might be an apt place for a literary celebration,' he teased as they were led to their table.

The menu was fantastic and Sarah was in a dither about what to order, opting for the seafood pancake followed by monkfish in a champagne sauce as Angus ordered a bottle of Pouilly Fumé.

'Here's to Mitten – that wonderful Kitten!' he toasted. 'I promise I shall be first in line in my local bookshop to buy it.'

'Don't be silly, you don't have kids.'

'I have a godson, Jack,' he protested. 'At his last birthday he was three. And I have a niece and a nephew. Anyway, I can keep it for when I have children.'

'I'm sure you'll have loads.' She smiled. 'I mean you and Megan.'

He didn't answer and she presumed he wanted her to mind her own business in terms of his relationship plans with Megan. Point taken. She speedily attempted to divert the conversation.

She regaled him with the tale of her trip to the publishers and Jilly's book offer and how good Evie had been in her absence, until she realized how quiet he was being.

'Is your meal OK?' she asked, concerned.

'It's about Megan,' he said, putting down his knife and fork and looking directly at her.

'Listen, Angus,' she apologized, 'I'm sorry. I've over-stepped the mark totally, making comments about the size of your family. Your and Megan's plans have absolutely nothing to do with me. Maybe she doesn't want kids, or wants just one, or you'll have a football team. I don't know . . . I know from what you've told me that she's a lovely girl.' She was prattling on in embarrassment.

His fingers caught her wrist, forcing her to stop talking. 'Megan and I have broken up,' he said slowly, his expression serious. 'It's over.'

'What! I don't believe you.'

'She's a great girl; she's done nothing wrong. It's just that I've discovered the life that I had planned out is now heading in a totally different direction and that Megan is not the person I want to share it with.'

'Angus, I'm so sorry,' Sarah said, stunned, taking his hand. 'I know how much you loved her. You two were made for each other.'

'That's just it, I'm not sure that we were,' he explained, his face serious. 'I had to go to Scotland because James and I are signing off on a big media project. Megan and I got a chance to talk, spend time together.'

Sarah suddenly felt sorry for the Scottish girl; Angus had probably broken her heart.

'Normally when I go home at weekends it's always the same thing; Megan and I go out to parties and dinners and clubs and see friends. We never seem to have enough time to be on our own or just to sit down and talk. Megan knew it too. We had both got so caught up with things, stupid commitments to family, work; there was always some sort of excuse.'

Sarah sighed. If she loved someone all she'd just want to be around them, talk to them, go for walks, hold their hand, lie on the couch watching TV and telling each other stories and jokes.

'Funny thing is Megan was feeling the same, the very same,' he said, his gaze unwavering. 'That's why she wouldn't move over here to Dublin with me. It's weird, we've known each other since we were thirteen and yet maybe we didn't know each other at all. We started going out when I was seventeen; our families have known each other for years, my dad plays golf with her dad. Then we went to Edinburgh

University together. We just became a couple without really thinking about it. Everyone assumed we were going to get married and live happily ever after!'

Sarah didn't know what to say.

'That was part of the reason I came here to Dublin, I guess, just to do something different. The physical distance between us made us both realize that the relationship wasn't as strong as we had imagined. I didn't miss her the way I first did,' he admitted slowly. 'I didn't feel the need to go to Edinburgh to see her every weekend, and the three weekends she came over here to me we were in a crowd, for the rugby, St Patrick's, apart from those few days we went to Galway. Then I began to think of someone else . . .' he added, 'and I wanted to be with her all the time instead of being with Megan.'

Sarah could feel her breath catch in her throat.

'Sarah, I couldn't get you out of my head. I wanted to be here in Dublin with you all the time. I didn't want to leave you.'

What was that crazy Scotsman saying? That he fancied her, wanted her? She couldn't believe it.

'I wanted to kill that guy Ronan when he asked you out! I'm not the jealous type – well, I didn't think I was. I felt a right fool after that night babysitting in your place. I wanted more – you know that. You deserve better. I didn't want to pretend any more, I knew I had to tell Megan.'

Sarah stared into his eyes; he was telling the truth. She could see it, clear as the wine glass she was holding.

'Megan said she'd already guessed,' he explained. 'She

said she could tell. It was bloody awful but we'd both felt it coming. She's kind of got a thing for one of the guys in her office. He's older, always asking her out, but she was nervous too, couldn't let it go any further because of us.'

Utter silence fell between them, taken up with the clatter of the restaurant and the people at the tables around them talking and eating.

'Are you sure?' asked Sarah. She had no intention of coming between them if there was something left of the relationship.

'It's over with Megan, I promise. I wouldn't say it otherwise. Megan and I, we're friends, old friends, and she will always be special to me but there is nothing more to it.'

She stared down at the pattern on the plate, at the vegetables and the baby new potatoes tossed in herbs. Angus didn't have a girlfriend, she told herself. He didn't have a girlfriend any more.

'If you just want to stay friends, the way we were, I'll understand,' Angus said slowly, his eyes darting around nervously. 'But I'm mad about you. From the first day when I came to see the mews and your mother made you show me around the place I fancied you. I watch you going in and out to put the washing on the line in the mornings.'

'Angus, I'm in my pyjamas!' she protested.

'You look cute,' he said firmly. 'To me you always look cute.'

She grinned, the smile spreading all over her face. Angus Hamilton really fancied her. He fancied her big time. She could tell by the way he was looking at her and holding her hand.

'We're already friends,' he said, his thin face serious, 'but I want more.'

Sarah could feel her eyes well with tears. She was such a stupid eejit. Angus was kind and funny and made her laugh and Evie and he got on really well. He wasn't like any of the other guys she'd met. Evie's existence had never bothered him, not in the slightest, and when he was around he made her feel safe and relaxed. He was fun and attractive and now, the best thing of all, he was available.

'Me too,' Sarah replied, deliberately, her gaze meeting his.

Chapter Forty-eight

Ever since Leo had died Maggie had found it hard to manage the constant repairs and upkeep an old house like this needed. Painting the woodwork, staining the back fence, coating the railings with rust-proof paint, pruning the conifers and large trees, oiling the locks and bolts about the place. Leo had looked after a hundred million manly things without complaining or saying a word and now she was landed with it all. The bathroom tap had been dripping for weeks and the last few days she could hardly sleep with it. On top of that the fitting for the shower head needed to be replaced and the sink in her utility room was blocked. She had tried to get a plumber only to be told he was booked for the next few months. Enquiring round she was told that getting a plumber to come and do a few small jobs was nigh on impossible.

From her sitting-room window Maggie watched daily the constant flow of workmen – carpenters, plumbers, electricians, plasterers and painters – renovating the O'Connors' old house. Mark McGuinness himself had been absent for the past few weeks and, seeing his big black Range Rover parked outside in his usual spot again, she decided to take matters into her own hands.

He had looked surprised when she had knocked on his door explaining the problem she was having with regards to a plumber, and amused when she invited him to lunch in her house.

'I'll see what I can do about the plumber,' he said, 'and I usually take a break about twelve thirty, if that suits you for lunch.'

'Ideal,' said Maggie.

Two hours later he had appeared just as he promised and before they sat down to eat Maggie showed him around the house, highlighting her plumbing issues. Mark admired all the work Leo had done: the coving in the hall, the restored staircase, the plasterwork on the ceilings and the hand-painted kitchen that Leo had insisted suited the old house.

She had prepared a simple lunch of salad, slices of oak-smoked salmon and her own homemade brown bread. She told him about speaking to Tom and Detta recently on the phone.

'Detta's joined the church choir and all seems to be going well for them. Thank heaven it was a good move.'

'A good move on my part too.' He smiled. 'I like the square. It seems a good place to live.'

'So you will be living here?' she prompted, trying to get a bit of information out of him.

He laughed. 'Of course, that was always my intention.'

'I also wanted to say thank you properly for helping with my granddaughter and for bringing her to the hospital. We are all extremely grateful to you,' she said, passing him the mayonnaise.

'It was the least I could do,' he said politely.

'Grace says she wouldn't have managed without you.'

He flushed slightly at the mention of her eldest daughter's name. What on earth was going on between the two of them? she wondered.

'Have you seen her?' she asked, deciding to throw caution to the wind, not caring whether he thought her an interfering busybody.

'No, I've been away in America, tied up with a family problem,' he said. 'You know how it is.'

'Not really,' she said. 'Grace is my eldest, my first child. She may appear one of those cool sophisticated career women, eldest children often do – you'd understand if you had children – but underneath she's soft and has the kindest, biggest heart of anyone I know.'

Mark nodded, taking in what she was saying.

'I wouldn't want anyone to hurt her or damage that heart of hers,' she said firmly.

'I understand,' he said slowly, spearing a last piece of fish on his fork, 'and believe me, Maggie, my intentions towards Grace are only good!'

'Well, that's nice to hear.' She nodded for she did believe him.

As they finished eating, they talked about the neighbourhood and Maggie filled him in on the residents' association.

She found, to her surprise, that he was rather good company as they chatted and had coffee.

'I have a very reliable young plumber called Adam Czibi, he does a lot of work for me. I'll send him over to you first thing tomorrow morning,' promised Mark as he was leaving.

He's a *gentleman*, Maggie decided, someone Leo would have approved of. He would make a lovely son-in-law if only he would make his feelings towards Grace clear.

Early the next morning she had tidied the bathroom, scrubbing at the shower tray and polishing the big glass mirror that hid away her old mascaras and perfumes in the bathroom cabinet. The plumber was punctual and she was impressed with the tall serious young man from Poland who without any further ado began to sort out the problems. She made him a cup of tea and produced a packet of chocolate Club Milks which he devoured, sitting across from her at the kitchen table.

Adam told her about moving to Ireland three years ago with his brother Josef and setting up their own business.

'The first year and a half in Dublin we work on big building sites of apartments on the docks. Then we get sense and we work for ourselves. Now we have plenty of work, big jobs and little jobs.'

'Your family must be very proud of you,' she said.

'They are at home in Poland, but my brother's wife Sylvie she came to Dublin in January. We share a house together.'

'And do you have a wife too?' she quizzed, her curiosity sparked.

'No, no girlfriend. Nobody! I work too hard. Sometime I will meet a nice Irish girl or a Polish girl. My mother she prays for that.'

Maggie smiled. He had a sense of humour. She only knew one Polish girl but she was a nice girl. The type his mother would definitely approve of . . .

'Adam, can you excuse me a minute?'

There was no time like the present and she phoned Oscar quickly. He was just about to leave to play bridge with some friends.

'Oscar, are you still having problems with your hot-water heater?' she asked, instantly getting her older neighbour's attention. 'It's just that I have a plumber here with me.'

'Yes, it's worse than ever. Do you think he'd come in here to take a look at the immersion?' he begged. 'The blasted thing is driving me cracked. The water is either boiling hot so that you think you're going to be scalded alive or stone cold freezing. I'm terrified to have a shower and poor Irina nearly had the hands burned off her the other evening when she went to wash up.'

'I'll ask if he's interested, but who will let him in?'

'Irina's here,' he explained. 'She can show him the hot press and explain the problem to him and naturally I will pay whatever the cost.'

'Perfect.' Maggie laughed. It couldn't be better. It was sheer happenstance. There would be no need for introductions, he was a workman coming to do a job; the fact that he was tall and blond and very handsome and spoke Polish was a very definite advantage; but it was up to the girl next door to recognize that. Her matchmaking skills did not extend that far, it was up to nature and mutual attraction to do their work. Fate, she sometimes suspected, just needed a little shove in the right direction!

Irina had hoovered the house from top to bottom and changed the sheets, pillowcases and quiltcover on Oscar's bed. Then she had to do some homework for English class tonight. Write a letter to an employer and another to a friend to apologize for forgetting her birthday. She sucked at the top of her Biro searching for the correct words and how to lay the sentence out. Oscar on his way out had gabbled something about Maggie's plumber coming to fix the immersion. She shrugged; it was about time that stupid boiler was mended.

She answered the hall door an hour later and showed the plumber upstairs to the hot press. It only took her a few minutes to ascertain that Adam Czibi was not only Polish but from the tiny town of Tuszyn. His cousin, a teacher and her family, lived in Łódź only three streets away from her family.

'You can't go anywhere but you meet a fellow Pole,' he shrugged looking at her with those immense blue eyes.

She made him coffee, the proper type, and a sandwich with beetroot and that baked ham Oscar liked, watching him as he ate.

'You live in this big house?' he asked looking around him.

She explained her role and about the kindly old man who was her boss. She told him about her English classes and her plans for the future.

As he packed up his tool bag she held her breath.

'You know the Polish group Zido?' Adam asked, standing in front of her.

She nodded. Every day she listened to Polish radio and followed what was happening back at home.

'They are playing in Dublin on Saturday night and if you want we could get tickets and go to hear them together?'

Irina took a breath. He was tall and very handsome and had just asked her out on a date and she had said *tak*, *tak*, *tak* . . . yes, yes, yes . . .

Chapter Forty-nine

Anna Ryan looked down at the group of eager enthusiastic faces sitting in front of her. American, Canadian, Australian, German, Japanese, Italian and French, a truly culturally mixed bag of literature-obsessed fanatics keen to learn even more about one of their heroes. Yeats and his work was the discussion topic of the day. Why she had signed on for the two-weeks-long summer school held in college was beyond her!

She had photocopied the poems and texts she was using and put them up on the internet too. The lecture room was stuffy and hot but they had to put up with it. She began to read from Yeats, 'He wishes for the Cloths of Heaven', a poem she knew so well. The small Japanese man seated in the front row with his pretty younger wife kept asking question after question. He was, she guessed, a fellow academic who would purloin half of what she said for his own lecture series back in Tokyo or Osaka or Kyoto next term. No matter, he would spread the word, which was the important thing, words and language and the poet's imagery appealing to generation after generation, among all nationalities. Yeats had long since passed the boundary of his Irishness and reached a massive global audience.

As she read the words of love and obsession, the poet offering to spread his dreams under the feet of his beloved, she thought of Rob walking along the beach with the dog, the water running across the sand, the spray of the water lashing against the rocks. She stopped for a minute, lost, looking at these strangers, becalmed in words. The truth was she missed him. What was she doing on a fair summer's day talking to strangers about love and dreams and the hopes of another when the one she loved and hoped for was so far away!

Over the next few days there was a tour of the National Library and a look at the Yeats collection, a visit to Trinity College and a lecture on the history of the Abbey Theatre. Next week there was a visit to Lissadell House and Gardens in Sligo after which she could perhaps bow out and escape to Connemara. Her department head Brendan had suggested she take on two or more similar groups in mid-August but she had been very clear that she had no intention of doing so. She was heading for Gull Cottage for the rest of the summer. Sarah and Evie and her mother were going up there after the weekend and Grace would probably join them for a few days.

Anna planned to spend as much time as she could there combining work on her papers with being with Rob. She didn't even want to think of next term and the distance between them.

She was tidying up and switching off the PowerPoint and large screen when Brendan appeared. Her group had gone off to sample the delights of lunch in the college dining hall.

'A few bigwigs in the group,' he said, casting his eye over her notes and group list.

'I noticed,' she said packing up her laptop and notes.

'Anna, you're great at this,' he praised her. 'Both academics and students love you and the evaluations are always top notch.'

'Thanks.' She smiled. 'But I'll be glad to have the rest of the summer off to work on my own papers and relax.'

'I can't get you to change your mind, then?' her department head asked as she got ready to leave.

'Brendan, I told you already, I'm off to Connemara for the rest of the summer.' She grinned, tossing her hair back over her shoulders, thinking of Roundstone and Gull Cottage and endless days being with Rob. 'Enjoy the holidays!'

Chapter Fifty

Grace couldn't get Mark McGuinness out of her mind. She kept replaying in her head the feel of his mouth and lips against hers. She had finally lost it, she admitted to herself. She had given up trying to banish him from her thoughts. Yet again she found herself waiting for his call. She was pathetic! Falling for someone like Mark was a disaster. Ever since he'd come to her apartment with Evie, she had been waiting and hoping he would reappear at her front door. He had sent her a text to say he was thinking of her but otherwise had made no other effort to contact her. Sarah had said she thought he might be away but her mother had let slip she'd seen his car back outside number 29.

Gutted, she buried herself in work. She had even volunteered to check all the financial projections for a new health centre in Cork which a colleague, John O'Leary, was working on. His wife had just had a new baby and he wanted to take a few days off to give her a hand and bond with his child.

'It's fine, John. If there're any problems on it I'll phone

you at home. I'll fly down to Cork on Thursday morning to meet the surveyors and the contractors and go through the figures with them.'

'Thanks, Grace.' He beamed as he cleared his laptop and the silver-framed photo of his wife Lizzie and his new baby son Killian off the desk. 'I owe you big time.'

'No, you don't, John. Lizzie and Killian are far more important.'

Sitting at her desk she suddenly realized how her priorities were shifting; lines and drawings on paper and stone and glass and concrete and steel could never compete with the tiny infant with the fuzz of hair in his wife's arms.

She sat at her desk, overwhelmed.

At the weekend she had invited Niamh and the girls for dinner on Saturday night. Lisa surprised them with the announcement that she was moving to work in London with AIB bank. She would really miss her but Lisa had promised a bed for the night for anyone wanting to visit.

'But what will you do about Tom Callaghan?' Roisin asked the question on all their minds as they considered how he'd dumped Lisa when he'd moved to London.

'It's a big city, but I'll see plenty of him, and I'll pester him till the big oaf realizes that he loves me too,' she said firmly.

Grace had made paella with shellfish and chicken and served it with a red pepper salad. Roisin, the baker of the group, had excelled herself with a massive chocolate torte for dessert. There were two big jugs of sangria and she found a really nice Rioja to serve with their food.

They stayed chatting at the table for hours and Grace thanked heaven for her girlfriends. Niamh with a huge smile on her face told them she was dating Kevin, and already Grace got the sense that it was serious between them. She stifled a pang of envy and hugged her as she knew how hard Niamh had found breaking up with her previous boyfriend Dave after living together for two years.

It was almost three a.m. when they finally said goodbye and fell into two taxis.

On Sunday there was a family lunch in Roly's to celebrate her mother's birthday. It was one of Maggie Ryan's favourite restaurants and held so many memories of birthdays and exam results and special occasions shared by their family over the years. The waiter made a great fuss over them as he led them to their table upstairs near the window. Their mum was delighted with their present and was thrilled at the thought of sampling the delights of the fancy new Wicklow spa.

'I'll take Kitty along with me; she could do with a bit of calming down and relaxing before the wedding. Harry has her driven mad doing costings for every item they need and Orla's wedding dress is too big and needs to be taken in since she did two weeks on the Atkins diet!'

'Mum, you deserve a bit of pampering yourself,' they all insisted.

On Monday Grace had just finished a meeting with Derek when Kate told her that she'd missed a call from Mark McGuinness. He'd left his number on her voicemail and as she played and replayed the message she resolved not to return the call. She had no intention of chasing him!

'So the lady doesn't do callbacks,' he teased about an hour later. Grace, touching her flaming cheeks, was so relieved that they weren't on videophone.

'How are you?' he asked slowly.

'I'm fine,' she said, trying to appear relaxed and calm.

'Grace, will you come for lunch today? I'm flying to London and on to New York tomorrow but I really want to see you before I go.'

'Lunch would be great, Mark,' she said, agreeing to meet him in Dobbins just off Baggot Street around one o'clock.

Looking at herself in the bathroom mirror in the ladies' cloakroom in Thornton's, Grace wished that she had worn the new pale cream suit she'd bought in Paris instead of her standard lightweight beige one and that she had taken the time to blow dry her hair properly before she went to work this morning. She thanked God for the GHD she kept in the drawer in her office, which was for when she came back windblown from building sites.

Her heart was pounding as she walked to meet him. She spotted him immediately in a booth near the back of the restaurant. He was wearing an expensive charcoal suit. He kissed her the minute they met and the electricity between them jolted her as his skin touched hers. She held on to the table for a minute before sitting down beside him.

They ordered quickly, fish for her and steak for him, the waiter bringing them a half-bottle of nice Bordeaux.

She had no idea what to say to him and waited to see if he would say why he hadn't bothered to call her.

'I'm sorry about not getting in touch,' he said. 'I've been away in America for the past few weeks. A bit of a crisis has blown up there and I have to attend to it. In fact I'm flying over again in the morning and I may not be back for almost a month.'

Grace stared at the starched linen tablecloth.

'I missed you,' he said, reaching for her fingers, entwining them in his.

'I didn't know what to think.' She hesitated. 'I thought that night at my place something pretty special was happening between us and then – nothing! Not a word from you, Mark, it's so weird!'

'Grace, in a few weeks all this will be sorted. I promise. Then there will be time for you and me, I swear.'

She nodded. She understood that she was way down the bottom of his list of priorities while he was someplace at the top of hers. They were definitely at odds with each other and she didn't know if all the chemistry and attraction in the world could bridge that gap.

'Is it some kind of building or property problem?' she demanded.

'Trust me, Grace, it's nothing like that. It's personal. Family business, I guess.'

She took a breath. A wife, a girlfriend, a messy divorce: she didn't really want to get embroiled in whatever situation Mark McGuinness had got himself into and he obviously wasn't prepared to share it with her.

They made polite small talk; he asked about Evie's arm and chatted about the progress on his house.

'Listen, Mark, I'd better get back to work. I've a meeting with a client in half an hour.'

'I'll walk back with you,' he said, which surprised her.

Outside it was sunny and bright. Couples strolling through Dublin's city streets in shorts and T-shirts and summer skirts surrounded them as Mark took her hand.

On the steps in front of Thornton's they stopped and looked at each other awkwardly. Grace found herself trying to banish the thought of skipping work for the rest of the afternoon and spending it with Mark.

Mark broke the silence. 'I'll see you when I get back,' he promised, kissing her slowly. Almost despite herself, Grace responded, stroking his cheek with the palm of her hand and wishing he didn't have to go.

Back at her desk in the office she sat staring at her new screensaver – a big red kite flying in a clear blue sky – trying desperately not to cry.

Chapter Fifty-one

Maggie lay sideways on the rug on the sand, dipping in and out of her paperback as she watched Sarah and Evie and Anna play at the water's edge. Looking at them she suddenly felt old and tired. Ten years ago she would have been messing around with them; now, like a cat, she was happy to bask in the August sunshine, feel its warmth on her skin and bones as a new generation hollered and chased and splashed. It was good to see the girls running around the beach and having fun just like when they were kids; Sarah in her shorts, tanned and fit and happy, and Anna, her hair all curly from the salt water, giggling like a twelve-year-old as they both tried to catch Evie. Yes, coming back to Gull Cottage year after year did them all good.

Some friends had holiday homes and apartments in Marbella and Alcudia and the Algarve, but they were blessed with having Annabel's cottage to come to, Leo's childhood haunt. Unspoilt and easy and relaxed, overlooking the beach and rocks, it was the perfect getaway. Leo had adored the place and summer after summer and on school breaks and holidays they had packed up the car and fled west. Sometimes Annabel was here, other times she would let them have the place to themselves as she visited friends and relations in England and far-flung places. The children had grown up with Gull Cottage, learned to swim here, and play tennis and sail and surf. It was a place for firsts. Lying here on the rug brought back a flood of memories of other summer days: Sarah learning to walk across the sand; Anna jumping off the rocks and breaking her leg; Grace spending hours making intricate castles and houses of sand. Her memory was of summers of ice-creams and warm bottles of lemonade, Tayto potato crisps, buckets and spades, sandals and towels, wet hair and togs, long walks on stormy days with anoraks and caps, watching the constantly changing colours of the water season after season and the roll of the sea as year after year passed. They had always planned when Leo retired to spend more and more time here, pottering around. The locals were lovely and Annabel Ryan had been a much-loved member of the community, involved in the village and devoting herself to reading and painting and gardening. Inheriting the house from her mother-in-law had been such a lovely gift and, despite Leo's death, his brother David, who lived in Seattle, had been glad to see the old summer house stay in the family.

'Are you getting in for a swim, Granny?' coaxed Evie, standing over her. She'd been swimming for ages, and it never failed to amaze Maggie how small kids never felt the cold.

'I'm just in a good place in my book.'

'You weren't reading: I was watching you! Come on, please. I want to show you my backstroke.'

Maggie smiled. Evie was like a little fish and now that her cast was off was making the most of being able to swim.

'OK! OK!' she relented, standing up, taking off her sunglasses and sunhat and leaving her book with the page marked as she took Evie's hand.

Evie was such a good kid and an absolute joy in her life. She made being a grandmother easy with her sweet disposition and funny ways.

The water was cold and her toes curled with fright at the chill of the waves lapping around her feet.

'Come on!' urged Evie rushing in.

'Give Granny a chance,' warned Sarah who had waded in ahead of her. 'It's better to dip down quickly and get it over with,' she advised, diving in and disappearing under a wave.

Maggie walked a little further out, the water lapping against her knees and thighs and hips, freezing the blood in her veins. Taking a deep breath she dipped right in and began to swim.

Evie popped up beside her like a porpoise. 'Granny, watch, watch!'

She trod water chatting to the girls as Evie turned around and began to do a very good backstroke, arms and legs kicking in perfect time. They all clapped and she beamed with pride, her dark hair sleek and clinging to her head.

'Good girl,' said Sarah, proudly hugging her.

Anna ventured out deeper, then turned and swam parallel to the shore, her strokes even and strong, back and forward.

Maggie swam along with her for a few minutes, before turning back for the beach as the cold water began to chill her.

'I'm getting out before I freeze,' she called as they swam on. She wrapped herself in the towel, scrubbing at her skin, drying herself off a bit, and then took off for a brisk fifteen-minute walk along the strand so the sun could warm her up.

The others were drying off, huddled on the rug sharing some chocolate she'd left hidden in her beach bag, when she got back. She took a square. Evie was sitting on Sarah's knee regaling them with silly jokes she had heard in school.

'Rob's coming over for dinner tonight if that's OK,' said Anna. 'I'll cook.'

Maggie smiled, catching the knowing glint in Sarah's eye. 'That's great, love. He's a nice guy. Your grandmother always relied on Rob and had a lot of time for him.'

It surprised her to see the sudden affinity Anna had developed with the place. She was relaxed and at ease with herself here; the landscape and its simplicity had a hold on her and falling for Rob O'Neill had certainly had a great deal to do with it. Whenever he was around Anna it was clear to see that they meant a huge amount to each other. She didn't want to interfere but if Anna was serious about him she was going to have to make some decisions.

'Grace will be here on Friday; she's coming straight from work,' Anna reminded them. 'Rob said he might hold a barbecue on Saturday in his place if everyone is free.'

'That would be lovely.' Maggie smiled, thinking how well things were working out for Anna and Sarah. The only one she had to worry about was Grace. Whatever was going on between her eldest daughter and Mark was a mystery!

'Angus is going to come up on Saturday; do you think Rob would mind him joining us?'

'The more the merrier,' Anna said as she lashed on some sun block. Her skin was the fairest in the family and she didn't want to look like a boiled lobster.

'Angus has never been to the west of Ireland, he thinks it might be like the highlands! He wants Evie and me to go to Scotland with him for a long weekend at the end of the month before Evie goes back to school.'

'So you'll get to meet the Hamilton clan,' exclaimed Anna, tightening the lid on the bottle of sun lotion.

'Yes. It's a bit scary, I suppose.'

'And we might see the Loch Ness monster,' added Evie, kicking the sand with her feet and burrowing with a small piece of driftwood.

'We're only going for three days,' Sarah reminded her, 'so I'm not sure we'll be anywhere near there!'

'If his family are even half as nice as Angus you'll be fine,' Maggie reassured her. She could see Sarah was nervous of Angus presenting a girlfriend with a child but any time she had heard him chat about his parents they seemed kind, good-hearted people.

'Things must be getting serious!' teased Anna.

Sarah flung a flip flop at her. 'You're a fine one to talk!'

Maggie picked up her book. She was saying nothing; she had interfered enough. At this stage it was up to them!

Chapter Fifty-two

Anna stood in the centre of Rob's kitchen chopping tomatoes and slicing peppers and cucumbers for the salad while he checked the marinated chicken pieces and rubbed a little crushed garlic on the steaks. His parents, Pat and Sheila, and his sister Dee and her family had all arrived about half an hour ago. Sheila, in a denim skirt and linen blouse, was outside wandering around looking at the plants in the garden. She'd brought Rob a pot of rosemary which he'd placed out on the kitchen step.

'A few sprigs are great when you're roasting a bit of lamb or a chicken,' she encouraged him.

'Great match in Thurles today,' ruminated Pat, pouring himself a glass of red wine. 'Galway should get through to the quarter-finals now.'

'Tony Fahey was on fire,' agreed Rob, and the two of them began a deep discussion on the merits of the GAA football game.

Watching him she could see the two of them had an easy relaxed relationship and a similar outlook on life. Dee was small and plump with mischievous dark eyes and a great sense of humour. She worked part-time as a nurse in the local hospital and her husband Luke and two boys were sitting in the garden. The salads done, Anna carried them outside in three big ceramic bowls and, grabbing a glass of wine, joined the others. Dee was on sparkling water as she was expecting again in December.

'The boys are so wild, I don't know how we'll cope if we have another,' she joked as seven-year-old Tim and younger brother Ferdia wrestled fiercely and tumbled on the grass.

'Hey, you two, behave!' warned their grandmother, plumping on to a sun-chair beside her.

From the road outside Anna heard the sound of a car stopping and ran to welcome her own mother and sisters and Angus, leading them inside to meet everyone.

'Wow!' said Grace admiringly the minute she saw the house, taking in the tall windows and magnificent sea views.

After fixing a drink for everyone Rob proudly gave them a quick tour of the place while Anna made the salad dressing and checked the potatoes they'd tossed in oil and herbs that were roasting in the oven.

Angus was very impressed and made Rob give him a blow-by-blow account of the conversion from country schoolhouse to such a stunning home.

'You've done an amazing job!' Grace was full of praise. 'It's spectacular and Anna tells me that you're doing a similar job on the old Corry Lighthouse.'

'It's a totally different project, but it's great to be involved in restoring rather than bulldozing a place!'

Sheila and Maggie, the two mothers, were getting on like a house on fire, gossiping about the neighbours and poor Angela Reynolds who lived on her own in the village with a little Yorkshire terrier and was ill and refusing to go into a nursing home.

At first Evie had hung back and clung to the grown-ups but once she got talking to Tim and Ferdia she forgot about her shyness and was soon racing like a lunatic after the football that Ferdia had discovered under a bush, the dog barking and racing alongside them.

'She's having great fun!' Sarah was delighted, her eyes shining.

Rob had heated up the barbecue and in no time the smell of beef and chicken and sausages cooking filled the air.

Anna had already set the table and soon Rob was handing out the meat and tasty big fat sausages. The kids immediately smothered them in ketchup. Anna passed round the bowl of piping hot potatoes.

'Compliments to the chef!' teased Luke as he tucked in.

Anna grabbed a seat beside Grace who she could tell was feeling rather out of it.

'This place is perfect,' Grace said softly, 'and so is he.'

'Sssh.'

'Anna, I mean it,' said Grace seriously, gazing into her eyes. 'Rob is perfect for you!'

'I know,' she admitted, glancing up the table to where he was sitting laughing with Angus and his mother and telling some crazy fishing story. 'Sometimes I just can't believe it, we're complete opposites but somehow it seems to work.'

'You're lucky.' Grace smiled a little enviously.

'What about you?' she coaxed. 'Any word from Mark?'

'He's still away,' confided Grace, 'but last week he sent me a text to say he's thinking of me. I'm not exactly sure what it means but it's something. He doesn't phone or call or email me, just this silly three-word text!'

'At least he got in touch with you,' Anna said consolingly as she took a sip of her wine. She glanced around the garden and terrace; everyone seemed to be enjoying themselves. She'd been dreading having both families for a meal and if Rob hadn't insisted she wouldn't have agreed to it. Now she was glad that they had made the effort. Sitting here looking out over the waters of the Atlantic sharing food and wine on a summer's day with those they both loved made her feel somehow complete.

Later, after everyone had gone home and they'd washed the dishes and tidied up they lay in bed watching the moonlight shimmer on the water, her body a little on top of his, replete, passion spent, wrapped in each other's arms.

'I want you to stay,' he said.

'I am staying.' She laughed, pressing her knee against his thighbone.

'No, I mean I want you to stay always. Not just some week-ends and holidays and nights here and there. I want you to stay here with me, live with me, move in with me and . . . the dog.' He had sat up a bit, leaning forward, watching her reaction.

She could see his eyes and the way his stubby dark

380

eyelashes made them seem bigger, and the scars from when he was a teenager and had acne, and the small dark freckle on his neck.

By rights they had nothing absolutely nothing in common. Rob was a builder who had left school at sixteen, she was an acknowledged expert in Anglo-Irish literature; he hated poetry and namby-pamby books, while she lived for language and words; he was a country guy and she a city girl. Yet she knew that she couldn't live without him and that every separation was a little like dying, killing her. She had hated the real world, wanted only the type of romance and love written about in literature; now all she wanted was this warm, loving, ordinary man. Before Rob she had wanted to close her eyes to the world, enjoy her silence and solitude, but he, like a knight of olden times, had rescued her from the high walls she had built around herself. Now when she woke there was coffee and laughter and talk about the day and the future and everything that life held . . .

'Yes,' she said softly for she wanted it as much as he did. She had wasted enough years. She had no idea how they would make it work. Her career, work, finances, her house back in Dublin, the possibility of applying to Galway University to get some lecturing work . . . It was all up in the air but the logistics didn't matter, the important thing was that she was going to move in with Rob and spend her life with him. She reached up and kissed him, wrapping her arms around his neck as slowly they took turns showing how much they loved each other.

Chapter Fifty-three

Maggie took a deep breath as she took in the sweeping drive-way and magnificent view of Anua, the low building of wood and glass and stone that was perched overlooking the tranquil waters of Kilcara's lake. A lazy heron spread its wings and took off in flight across the water.

The luxury spa in its Wicklow setting was beautiful. It deserved the accolades heaped on it, she thought as she drove along the wooded avenue and came to a halt in the discreetly planted hidden car park.

She could curse her sister Kitty for coming down with a strep throat in the middle of the night and backing out of their planned two-day break. She had sounded dreadful when they'd spoken earlier and Harry, worried by her high temperature, had got a doctor to call to the house. She was on high-dose antibiotics and prostrate in bed. Poor thing! No doubt the stresses and strains of organizing Orla's upcoming wedding were taking their toll.

Maggie had been in two minds as to what to do about their booking. Her first instinct had been to cancel it. However, a quick call to the spa had confirmed that a no-show would result in almost the full cost of the voucher being gobbled up in a cancellation charge. Urgent calls around to the girls and a few women friends had been to no avail. Grace was away in Amsterdam on business and Anna was in Connemara. Sarah would love to come but who would mind Evie at such short notice? Fran and Louisa were both busy and Rhona had her dragon of a mother-in-law Lily coming to stay for the week.

'I could do with a bloody spa weekend,' she moaned, 'but Lily is already en route from Cork.'

So she was faced with a choice: cancel the break and forfeit the money, or go along on her own. Mustering her spirits she had opted for the latter course.

'Mrs Ryan, as your guest cannot join you we can offer you a third night here instead,' said the pretty receptionist as she checked in.

'That would be lovely.' She smiled, trying to mask the fact that with the exception of stays in hospital to have her children and the removal of her appendix she had actually never spent a night away from home totally on her own. It would be a new experience and, in this awesome setting amongst the trees and woods, she hoped a pleasant one!

Maggie had come prepared with books and magazines, determined that a solitary weekend in the countryside dedicated to body and soul was just what she needed to recharge her batteries and give her the impetus to sort out some new routines focused on the fact that she was now single. Her daughters had their own lives to lead and it was high time she laid down some kind of track of her own.

As she walked through the glass lobby and down the corridor towards her room she passed two couples in thick white towelling robes obviously off to the pool and jacuzzi area. She had already spotted the inviting open-air hot tub with its view of the lake and was dying to try it out herself. The spa was beautifully designed with a feature wall of glass, polished oak wood floors and plain white walls, which displayed a fabulous collection of abstract art. Rich-coloured woven rugs that depicted the elements of sky, earth, air and water warmed the austere simplicity of the decor.

Her bedroom was magnificent. Its ceiling-to-floor window overlooked a square of ornamental lavender and the wooden jetty that dipped into the lake. There was a massive king-size bed and oversized mauve and purple cushions provided a splash of colour against the pristine white cotton sheets and quiltcover. A rounded couch fitted snugly into the curve of the window with a matching footstool and simple oak table. The bathroom was like something out of a fancy magazine with two curving black basins and polished stone floors and walls. She discovered a small fridge, which held a selection of juices and waters and a few small bottles of organic wine. Leo would have loved this place, she thought as she perused the timetable of activities on offer over the next few days. Swimming, hydrotherapy, yoga, Pilates, dance, massage of every body part, wraps, exfoliation, hair removal, lymphatic massage and drainage, colonic irrigation, facial peels, along with mud and algae baths and a range of exotic-sounding treatments which she was tempted to try. Since Kitty couldn't make it she had twice the amount of vouchers to use for pampering sessions and she had every intention of spoiling herself. She slid open the heavy glass and wooden door and stepped out on to her private deck, which contained two curving wooden chairs bedecked with plush sand-coloured cushions and two pots of scented lavender. She studied the list of other activities: forest-walking, pony-trekking, archery, sailing, kayaking, cycling, painting and clay-modelling. She would definitely try some of these and just wished that Kitty was along so that there were at least two of them making eejits of themselves.

She unpacked her bag and then, after studying the spa menu again, opted for a quick swim and a turn in the hot tub, and then she'd go for a walk to get her bearings and maybe book in tomorrow for a head massage and facial and an eyelash-tint.

She pulled her swimsuit from the case wishing that she had managed to stay on the Atkins Diet for a month instead of a measly six days, which had resulted in only a three-kilo loss. Tucking in her tummy she wrapped herself in the plush folds of the Anua wrap and slipped her feet into the matching cosy towelling slippers and made her way to the pool. Four other guests were already there and Maggie nodded to them as she slipped into the water and began to swim. The pool was amazing, giving the impression of being out in the open but protected from the elements by glass. One section of the glass concealed a door which opened to the open-air part of the pool and the magnificent hot tub and sundeck. She swam a few lengths up and down before stepping outside and into the hot tub. A couple in their thirties and an elderly woman in her seventies already seated there were chatting easily about the glory of the place and the dinner menu for the night.

'The food here is divine,' the older lady, who was a regular, assured them. 'Better than most fancy restaurants and it's all organic and natural.'

'I heard that they grow most of the vegetables themselves,' Maggie ventured.

'If you go for a walk down past the rose bushes and follow the path you'll come to the kitchen garden, the vegetable fields and the glasshouse. It's full of tomatoes and I saw strawberries there. It makes a change to know where your food is coming from.'

The couple, Renata and Karl, were German and recommended the reviving mud bath. 'Your skin will be glowing after it,' promised Renata.

'I'll give it a go,' Maggie said as she watched them walk off hand in hand. Yes, Leo would definitely have loved this place. OK, so she might have had to drag him kicking and screaming but once he'd arrived he'd have relaxed totally and gone with the flow. He'd have tried everything. She sincerely hoped the place wasn't full of couples as it would only emphasize her own loneliness.

Strolling around the grounds she spotted three girls Grace's age, a pre-wedding treat she imagined as she heard one of them mention guest lists and tables. She had ordered a herbal tea and a brown scone in the lounge, which she enjoyed before changing and heading off for her mud wrap. The Hungarian therapist patiently explained the benefits of the mineral-enriched treatments as Maggie tried to stop herself getting a fit of the giggles when she caught a glimpse of herself in the mirror. She looked like a big fat mud-baby and she thanked God there was no one around to witness the state she was in. The separate cubicles beside her were occupied and she heard a masculine guffaw of laughter from the one beside hers.

'You ain't seen nothing yet,' said the hidden voice and Maggie laughed so hard that she thought that she was going to crack all her drying-out mud. After an hour the therapist cleaned her off with a strong spray of water and then massaged her with a sweet-smelling almond oil. Her skin felt like a new baby's and she discovered that she was absolutely starving.

Back in her room she ignored the temptation just to crawl into bed and order room service and put on a turquoise linen dress that Leo used to like, clipped on the silver designer earrings that Grace had given her two Christmases ago and slipped on a pair of summer slingbacks. Her skin was glowing and she already felt as if she had been away for a few days. She grabbed an Anita Shreve paperback along with her handbag and made her way to the fabulous lakeside dining room. Candles flickered on every table and many of the tables were already full. She was shown to a small side table where, while perusing the dinner menu, she took a good look at her fellow spa guests. Couples; a group of girls away from their office giggling and chatting at the big table in the centre; the wedding girl and her two friends; and a small group of mature people who were arguing in the corner over wines. She'd order, read, eat quickly and slip away to bed early, she decided, but for the moment she'd enjoy the view as the sun set slowly over the water, the sky tinged with crimson.

Leila her waitress was chatty and friendly and was pleased to tell her about the various dishes. She had no intention of dieting strictly here and opted for the healthy eating options which included salmon served on a bed of summer salad, followed by roast lamb and sweet potato and vegetables. She wouldn't drink a bottle of wine on her own and ordered a glass of chilled Chablis to start. She hated picking wines and had always relied on Leo's knowledge to guide her and was relieved to find the wine she'd chosen was perfect. Two very pregnant friends sitting at a table close by her ordered a fruit punch as they tucked into two big steaks and a gigantic salad.

She relaxed, sipping her wine and, trying not to eavesdrop on their conversation, picked up her book so she didn't look quite so forlorn.

'Excuse me,' said a voice and she looked up over the rim of her reading glasses. 'I was sitting over the far side of the room and I noticed that you are on your own. I was wondering if you would like to share a table over dinner, enjoy a bit of conversation and companionship as we eat.'

Tight-cut silver hair, a broad face, attractive in an ageing rugby player kind of way, a wedding ring firmly on his finger, she noticed.

'Only if you want to,' he added, about to move away.

'That would be lovely,' she found herself saying, slipping

her book off the table and back into her bag. 'Please sit down and join me,' she offered.

'Are you sure?'

'Of course,' she reassured him as the waitress carried over his drink from the other table and placed the bottle of red wine in front of them.

'I'm Myles, Myles Sweeney,' he said, introducing himself as he sat down.

'And I'm Maggie Ryan.'

'I often find that there is nothing harder than sitting at a table in a restaurant on your own,' he said.

Maggie had to agree with him. It was a situation she hated and avoided as much as she could. Often she went hungry rather than face the embarrassment of eating alone in a restaurant or hotel. A little company for an hour was certainly not going to kill her and might actually be fun!

Over dinner she discovered that he had been widowed two years ago: his wife Patricia had died of breast cancer. He had two grown-up sons, two daughters-in-law and five grandchildren.

'Patricia was there for the weddings and three of the christenings and got a few years longer than her doctors and everyone expected,' he confided. 'She was a great mother.'

Maggie told him about Leo and her own loss, and could see the understanding and sympathy in his eyes. The two of them laughed out loud when they discovered that each had been sent to the spa by their respective families.

'The girls were determined to send me, get me out of their

hair. My youngest is throwing a party tomorrow night and doesn't want her elderly mother there cramping her style!'

'Less of the elderly,' he retorted. 'Besides I can't imagine you would cramp anyone's style!'

'Well, I try not to,' she admitted.

'My boys are going on about me losing weight,' he confessed, offering her a glass of red wine. 'It's hard. Ever since Patricia's death, I tend to eat a lot of takeaways or have big business lunches. It's no fun cooking for one or just using those microwave meals. The boys worry about me and thought I should take a bit of time out for myself. Fresh air and a healthy regime! I had that mud wrap thing earlier and it's like being trussed up like an oven-ready chicken; you should have seen the state I was in!'

Maggie burst out laughing. 'I heard you,' she admitted.

He was a nice man and rather funny and to her surprise Maggie found herself relaxing and enjoying uncomplicated male companionship. He insisted on her sharing his wine and Maggie, looking around, felt the two of them were the same as everyone else here as they chatted and relaxed. They both went for fresh raspberries and cream for dessert; over coffee Myles told her about his business. She noticed people moving across to the comfort of the lounge with its plush couches and footstools, and was surprised when Myles excused himself and said goodnight, thanking her for the good company.

'Goodnight,' she said watching his tall figure lumber past the waitress, who had started to clear the tables.

She yawned. Perhaps it was time she went to bed herself,

the goosedown quilt and crisp clean sheets beckoned. She would read for a bit.

Standing out on the wooden deck in the moonlight before slipping between those sheets, she thought of Leo, so far away, in another world, another dimension. 'Goodnight, my love,' she whispered as she closed the door and pulled the curtains.

Chapter Fifty-four

Sarah's heart was in her mouth when she heard that Aunt Kitty was sick and it looked as if her mum's trip to the spa in Kilcara was about to be cancelled. Her mother had encouraged her to invite a few friends over on Saturday evening and already she had invited fifty people to a 'small party' in the house and she had visions of a nightmare day trying to scale it back.

'What are you going to do?' Grace asked on the phone from Amsterdam where she was assessing a property for a client.

'Fingers crossed Mum will still go. She was on to the manageress of the spa and she said they can't refund the cost at this late stage. She was even trying to get me to go with her but I said I couldn't because of Evie, and anyway I'm looking forward to the party.'

'The party will be great, Sarah. I'll phone her and encourage her to go on her own,' promised Grace. 'And I'll see you tomorrow night. My flight is the last one out of Schiphol to Dublin so I'll probably come straight on, OK?'

Maggie Ryan, despite her qualms, had indeed gone on her own, and had insisted on donating half a dozen bottles of white wine to the party and told Sarah to use her candles around the house and garden.

'Candlelight always adds to the atmosphere, no matter what the time of year,' she said, hugging Sarah goodbye. 'Have a great time, pet, and say hello to everyone from me.'

Sarah spent the whole of Saturday cleaning and tidying the place and setting up tables in the garden. She had made a big dish of spicy chicken and another of minced beef in a light chilli sauce; she would serve them with tacos and fajitas and all the trimmings and two huge bowls of salad. Everyone could help themselves. She believed in keeping it simple. She would lay them out on the big table in the kitchen and if the weather was good people could go outside and find a seat. There were fresh towels and clean soap in the bathroom, and her mother's clutter of newspapers, magazines, letters and papers that strewed the kitchen and the living room were banished to her dad's old study. A quick run of the Hoover and a few flowers from the garden flung into her mother's collection of glass vases and the place looked·great.

Angus had surprised her with some crates of beer which he put to chill in the fridge and in Evie's old baby bath in the back garden. He'd also bought giant bags of tortilla chips and crisps.

'I'll give you a hand to set up,' he offered, helping to position one of the speakers out in the garden.

She had spent the past few days sorting out her CD collection and had downloaded some great stuff on to her iPod to play.

Evie was completely over-excited, running around the place stealing crisps from the bowls and asking who was coming.

'Angus and all my friends,' Sarah told her. 'Auntie Grace and Orla and Liam and Karen and Mick and lots of people.'

'Can I stay up for the party?' she pleaded, her face eager.

'You can stay up for a little while,' she promised, 'but you have to swear to go to bed when I say so.'

Evie hesitated, her lower lip signalling stubbornness.

'Otherwise you'll have to go to bed before the party starts,' Sarah threatened.

Evie had agreed and after a quick tea they both had got dressed up in their party frocks. Sarah wore a pale green dress with a cross strap that she'd bought in Coast and a pair of gold sandals, while Evie as usual opted for her fairy dress.

The place looked amazing and Sarah couldn't believe her good luck with the weather, which was holding fine as the first guests arrived. She went out of her way to introduce Angus to everyone and was glad that Karen and Mick had gone to the trouble to bring a bag of jelly dinosaurs and a Barbie colouring book for Evie along with some wine.

'Thanks for being so thoughtful.' She hugged her best friend and led them through to the kitchen and garden.

'I'm bagging a chair as I've no intention of standing all night,' Karen insisted, throwing her handbag and wrap across one. 'Only five weeks to go to D-Day, thank God!'

Orla and her fiancé were next and Evie was thrilled to hear everything about their upcoming wedding and the fitting for her dress.

'How's my favourite flower girl?'

Evie did a twirl in her dress and showed how she would walk solemnly up the aisle.

'Perfect,' enthused Orla, giving her a big hug and a kiss.

As more and more people arrived they spilled out into the garden.

'Ronan!' screamed Sarah as Ronan Dempsey, looking dashing in a cream linen jacket and sand-coloured chinos, arrived. She had invited him but hadn't really expected him to come all the way from London.

'Another weekend in Dublin, honest is it any wonder I'm torn between the two places? Thank heaven for Ryanair.'

She grabbed his arm and introduced him to as many people as possible. She couldn't believe the huge crowd. She'd give it another while and then start serving the food. Angus was a great help and had taken over the awful job of opening wine bottles. Ronan and he were getting on famously with Ronan regaling him with tales of a Hogmanay trip he'd taken to Edinburgh four years ago.

Irina had come along with a tall good-looking guy. He was Polish too, and seemed very keen on her, judging by the possessive way he kept his arm around her for the night.

Mark McGuiness to her surprise had also turned up brandishing a huge bunch of flowers and two bottles of red wine. She had invited him as a way of saying thanks for helping with Evie's broken arm.

'It's not my birthday!' she giggled, giving him a big hug.

'A lady should always receive flowers,' he teased, 'no matter the occasion.'

She dragged her new neighbour along and introduced him to a few of her schoolfriends and to Karen and Mick, only to discover he already knew Mick through some kind of business connection.

'He always knows people no matter where we go,' remarked Karen, glancing proudly at her husband.

Sarah was having such a good time that she almost forgot the food and had to turn on the cooker and oven in a hurry and give everything a quick blast. Irina gave her a hand to set it all out on the massive table which was bathed in candlelight.

Everyone took a plate and began to line up to help themselves. Grace arrived at last and immediately grabbed their mother's blue-and-white-striped apron to help her serve the food.

'Thanks,' Sarah gasped, relieved to have an extra pair of hands.

'Wow, you've got a great crowd,' said Grace admiringly, looking around the room.

'Just friends.'

But they were good friends. They had stuck up for her and stood by her during bad times when she was low and lonely and now that good things were beginning to happen she wanted them to be able to celebrate them too.

'You never told me that he was coming!' whispered Grace, pushing her fair hair back off her face.

'Ronan? I didn't know myself that he was.' Sarah laughed, glancing out towards the garden where Ronan was sitting at the table stuffing himself with a fajita packed with cheese and mince and peppers.

'No, I mean Mark.'

'For God's sake, Grace, of course I'd invite him. He's our neighbour and a friend!'

Sarah couldn't believe the way Grace's face flamed and decided to say nothing else as Clodagh Flannery, who lived on the far side of the square, was already busy chatting Mark up. Clodagh usually had men falling at her feet, with her jet-black hair and perfect model figure, and had broken up only eight weeks ago with a member of the Irish rugby team. From the kitchen window Sarah could see Evie was beginning to wilt and excusing herself went to check on her.

'Come on, fairy girl, time for bed!'

'Mummy, I'm not tired yet,' she protested, her eyes heavy with sleep. But once reminded of her promise Evie said a reluctant goodnight to everyone.

Grace stepped in and offered to put her to bed. 'It's your party, Sarah. Besides, how often do I get the chance to be with my fairy goddaughter?'

She was so lucky that Grace as well as being a great auntie was the perfect godmother and took the role pretty seriously. Sarah kissed Evie and then went to check that everyone had drinks. Everyone had eaten now and the food had been cleared away, she put out a few nibbles for anyone who was still hungry. The party atmosphere was really relaxed now, and one group were dancing outside on the patio.

Grabbing a glass of wine, Sarah went outside to join Ronan, Karen and Mick, Mark and Clodagh and a few pals from Art College whom she hadn't seen for years. Ronan was deep in a discussion with them about the vibrant art market in the city and which were the best galleries to show in.

'Hey, party lady, what about a dance,' interrupted Angus, coming up behind her.

Taking her hand he led her to the makeshift dance floor and pulled her into his arms. He was a great dancer and really into the music; laughing, she followed his lead.

'Great party,' he enthused, 'and you've got a wonderful bunch of friends. I really like them.'

'I wanted everyone to meet you tonight,' she said. 'My friends from school and college, my cousins and neighbours and everyone . . .'

Angus was being so attentive and she loved having him around; he just seemed to fit in.

'You look divine, Sarah,' he whispered, touching her neck and placing his lips on her bare skin. 'I've been dying to do this all night.'

'Angus!' she teased.

He looked serious and pulled her closer, leaving her in no doubt about his feelings. Sarah responded by wrapping her arms around his neck and kissing him back.

The party went on for hours, wine bottles littered the kitchen, the stone steps and the patio wall and the baby bath had only empty beer cans left bobbing in it. Grace reappeared and Sarah saw Mark make straight for her, take her arm and lead her down to the wonky wooden bench at the bottom of the garden, a bottle of wine and two glasses in his hand. Grace was wearing her beige work skirt and a little short-sleeved white blouse, but still looked stunning.

Now it was very late and Sarah said goodbye to her guests, glowing with the fact that she had repaid all the dinners and parties she had been invited to and had managed to pull off a seemingly perfect night. Evie was fast asleep, curled up with her teddy bear Gideon, undisturbed by the music and noise.

As the crowd disappeared Sarah kicked off her shoes and began to tidy up, putting a few more plates and glasses in the dishwasher.

'Leave it,' urged Angus dragging her back outside, Karen was dancing barefooted with Mick, her belly huge, her skin tanned and glowing. In a few weeks her best friend would be a mother too, and would discover how much her life was going to change. Ronan was still deep in discussion with a friend of Sarah's from Art College, the two of them arguing good-naturedly, but it was seeing the way Grace and Mark were dancing together that really surprised her. They weren't saying a word, just gazing at each other, her sister's fingers clasped in his.

One last bottle of wine was opened and they all danced easily together to her mum and dad's old Burt Bacharach CDs, Sarah resting her head on Angus's shoulder as they smooched to the music.

'This guy is in love . . .' he whispered.

Chapter Fifty-five

Maggie yawned, stretching; she couldn't believe that she had slept so well.

Her body for once felt rested and relaxed and this massive bed was probably one of the most comfortable that she had ever slept in.

From the strip of sunshine flickering in through her curtains she could guess that the day was fine and the thought of a walk around Anua's acres of land and the nearby woods was certainly appealing. She padded across the room and opened the curtains, her breath taken away by the view outside and the clear blue sky. This was utter bliss. Opening the door to the deck, she gulped in the fresh air coming off the lake, and watched a family of ducks meander across the water. Glancing at her watch she realized that she'd slept late and if she intended getting any breakfast she'd better get a move on.

She showered quickly in the glitzy bathroom and dressed in soft grey cotton pull-ups, a white T-shirt and her trainers. Surveying herself in the long mirror she added a flick of mascara, a touch of lip gloss and a quick run of the brush through her hair before grabbing her key and making her way to the restaurant.

Only a few lazy sleepyheads were still eating breakfast, the rest of her fellow guests were probably already exercising or partaking of various treatments. Looking around she saw no sign of Myles. The breakfast buffet was incredible and she filled a large Stephen Pearce bowl with fresh fruit and a delicious, creamy homemade yoghurt. She had cherries and apple and strawberries and peach and a sprinkle of grated hazelnuts and a large glass of freshly squeezed orange juice. Afterwards she tucked into a few slices of warm wholemeal bread and a smooth fig spread and a pot of tea at a table overlooking the grounds. What a perfect start to the day. A walk first, then she planned on joining the Pilates class before heading to the pool for the aqua-aerobics class, something that she had been dying to try out for ages. She had a list of treatments organized in the afternoon: an Indian head massage, a facial and an eyelash tint and a French manicure. Grace and Sarah and Anna were right, there was nothing like a bit of pampering.

Grabbing a light jacket she walked right down to the water's edge. The lake water was clean and she suspected it was probably teeming with fish, judging by the fishermen spread out along the far shore. She would follow it for a bit and then take the path that led up through the woods.

Her breath echoed in her ears as she walked, but the only other noise around was the sound of birdsong and the odd scuffle of a squirrel or cooing of wood pigeons. The trees were ancient and she had to take care not to trip over the gnarled roots that pushed their way through the mossy path. She took her time absorbing the beauty of the woodland around her as the path climbed higher and higher. She met two other residents of the spa, a mother and daughter who were rushing back for an appointment with the hairdresser and told her of the great view up ahead. Maggie kept on walking, noticing that the shady cover of the trees was beginning to give way to a warm dappled stretch of sunshine. At last she found herself bursting into a clearing which gave way to a tumbling view of the lake and countryside below. She felt giddy with the sheer beauty of Kilcara's wood and lake. She stopped for twenty minutes to take it in, feeling utterly solitary yet at one with the rich landscape spread out below her.

Gathering her thoughts she began the trek back, taking care not to stumble where the path sloped downwards and pitched her forward. She promised herself to do this walk again tomorrow.

Back at Anua, she joined the small class of ten doing Pilates in the bright and airy games room. Leanne, the pretty young instructor, showed them ways of stretching and moving their bodies that Maggie would not have believed possible. Flopping down on the mat afterwards, she was certainly ready for a nice cool swim.

The pool was fairly busy and she blushed, noticing Myles up the deep end. He waved to her and rather than be rude she swam towards him.

'Nice morning?' he asked.

'Perfect,' she replied, telling him about her walk.

'Ladies and gentlemen,' called the aqua-aerobics instructor Rudy, 'please gather over by this side of the pool so we can begin class.'

'I'm getting out of here,' protested Myles. 'I'm booked in for a session in the steam room.'

Maggie smiled, relieved that he wasn't going to witness her huffing and puffing through a fitness workout.

'See you later,' he called, getting out of the pool.

She watched his tanned, rather chunky body disappear in the direction of the steam room as she joined the wedding girls and the large office group who were on hilarious form as Rudy put them through their paces.

'Kick those right legs, twenty times,' he ordered. 'Now twenty times for the left leg.'

A workout in the pool certainly relieved the impact on bones and muscles but it was at a faster and more furious pace than she expected. The young girls around her were giggling and chatting and seemed well able to keep up. At times she struggled but with Rudy's encouragement and Nikki, the girl who was getting married, urging her to keep going she managed to enjoy the aerobics, relieved to have a bit of a relaxed swim afterwards.

After quickly towelling off and changing she opted for a simple lunch of carrot and ginger soup and a leafy green salad with crispy bacon croutons. Nikki and her two friends insisted she sit with them and through the meal she listened to the plans for next Saturday's wedding.

'Pray for good weather,' pleaded Nikki. 'I don't know what we'll do if it rains!'

'Of course,' laughed Maggie, remembering the massive rain shower on her own wedding day.

The afternoon passed in a haze of oils and lotions and her body being massaged, her skin cleaned, peeled and renewed and every bit of her feeling absolutely pampered. It was years since her body had received even half of this attention and she was so tired after it all she crawled into bed at five o'clock and fallen fast asleep.

The phone ringing beside her bed woke her, and for an instant she panicked wondering if she had slept the night through.

'Hello,' she answered sleepily, surprised to discover that it was Myles wondering if she would join him for dinner again.

She hesitated. She barely knew the man but the thought of facing the dining room and sitting at the table alone convinced her. Besides, he was good company and she had no intention of cramping Nikki and her friends' pre-wedding girly talk this evening.

'That would be lovely,' she said, accepting Myles's suggestion of a pre-dinner drink in the lounge.

She surveyed her minuscule wardrobe and opted for the cream dress with the scoop neckline and a beige wrap Sarah had insisted she brought along. Her skin was glowing and all she needed was a little lipstick. The dyed eyelashes made her eyes look huge and as if she had lined them already. She looked the picture of good health and her face had lost that careworn appearance it usually carried. The miracle of products and treatments was hard to beat, she acknowledged as she took a last twirl at the mirror.

Myles was sitting out in the open air on the large wooden deck that opened from the lounge, nursing a glass of chilled white wine, complaining about the lack of Guinness and beer available.

'It's not really a bar,' she teased him. 'Remember it's a health spa we're visiting.'

She opted for wine also and sat beside him, watching the evening sun's reflection on the lake.

'This place is great,' he enthused. 'There's nowhere else like it. I've actually switched my mobile phone off.'

'Me too!' she admitted. She hadn't given home or family a thought since breakfast.

'Don't know how I'll manage when I get back,' he said ruefully, 'but it's been well worth every euro!'

'You're leaving tomorrow?'

'I've postponed it,' Myles confessed. 'I'm taking an extra day.'

Maggie could feel herself colour. The majority of guests were checking out around midday and heading back to normality. What if she and Myles were the only two left in the place? It would be so embarrassing!

'There's a group of Americans checking in tomorrow afternoon but I managed to keep my room for another night,' he explained.

'That's great.' She smiled. 'So we'll both be here.'

'You don't mind, Maggie, do you?' he asked, totally straight up.

She considered for a second. He was entitled to the extra day's break just as much as she was. He was a nice man, a little lonely like herself, and the few days here away from work and home would do him good.

'Not at all.' She smiled again. 'In fact I'm delighted for you.'

The dining room was busy on Saturday night; obviously locals opted to eat here too. Maggie and Myles were shown to a small table on the far side of the restaurant. Maggie was starving after all the day's physical exertions.

'I think I'll go for the prawns to start and the roasted salmon and vegetables,' she said, reading over the wide-ranging menu.

'Crab cakes and a steak,' ordered Myles as the waitress opened a bottle of wine for them.

Maggie suppressed a smile. Why was it that men of a certain vintage always ordered the same thing on the menu? It didn't matter what exotic foods or dishes Leo was offered, he would nine times out of ten order a steak. She had spent a lifetime cooking steak.

This time over dinner they talked about their backgrounds and childhoods and Maggie was surprised to discover that they had so much in common. He had gone to the same boarding school as Fran's husband and was a mad GAA player in his day. 'Hurling and football, I played them both,' he boasted. 'Represented Limerick for a year or two playing football. Now I have to content myself with a seat in Croke Park.'

She smiled.

'Your husband wasn't a GAA man, he played rugby!' he joked. 'So you must have gone to a lot of matches in your own time.'

'I wasn't the biggest sports fan,' she confessed. 'I was never sure what I was shouting for on the sidelines.'

Myles laughed and told her about the small solicitors' firm he owned with offices on Lower Mount Street. 'We mostly handle conveyancing and bit of contract advice and some family law,' he explained. 'We've a good loyal clientele who expect you to always be at the end of the phone in case of disaster. Alex, my youngest son, joined the firm after he qualified and had built up a bit of experience working in Goodbody's, so it's good to have him on board. My other lad is a paediatrician in the children's hospital in Crumlin.'

She told him about her three daughters and grand-daughter, discovering that his mother Dorothy was still alive and lived on her own in an apartment in Ranelagh, only a stone's throw from Evie's school.

'She's very independent,' he confided, 'and at eighty-eight can run rings around the rest of us.'

They liked similar restaurants, and had two or three friends in common, and both had visited Kelly's Hotel in Rosslare regularly, except in different months of the year.

Leo would like him, she found herself thinking. They were the kind of men who would have enjoyed a pint together, watched a match, shared a meal. Almost overcome, she made a dash to the bathroom.

Nikki and her friend Suzie were standing in front of the mirror chatting about this day week.

'Imagine, I'll be married!' Nikki grinned with delight.

'All the best for next Saturday,' said Maggie, 'in case I don't see you tomorrow before you leave.'

'It'll be brill,' laughed Suzie. 'The wedding of the year!'

'Thanks.' Nikki smiled again. 'Your husband seems very nice. Maybe Joe and I will be like you two and come here for a break in a few years' time.'

Maggie was about to try and explain that Myles was not her husband, and in fact was someone that she had just met, but she could see the girls had already lost interest and wanted to get back to their table.

'Everything OK?' asked Myles, standing up as she returned to the table, his eyes full of concern.

'Fine,' she smiled.

The waitress brought dessert and Maggie took a small spoon of the perfect crème brûlée as Myles tucked into a huge plate of homemade ice cream topped off with a caramel sauce.

'Have a taste if you want,' he tempted her. Maggie was aware of the sudden intimacy between them as she scooped some ice-cream into her mouth.

He grinned. 'Told you you'd like it.'

Over coffee they talked politics, and about the changing face of Dublin, both getting riled up and then bursting into fits of laughter at their reaction to the mention of the Government.

'Nothing like a good argument, that's what Patricia used to say,' he admitted, 'though it's funny how you miss them!'

'Me too,' she said softly, understanding exactly what he meant.

Looking around, Maggie suddenly realized that the dining

room was virtually empty and the staff were throwing them impatient glances.

Laughing, they picked up their wine glasses and retreated to the lounge to continue their conversation. An hour later they finally called it a night and Maggie realized that it reminded her of when she was a teenager and didn't want to say goodnight.

Myles smiled. 'I'll see you tomorrow,' he said, giving her an awkward hug.

Back in the bedroom Maggie stared at the bright-eyed woman in the mirror, telling herself to wise up and not be such a fool about the first decent man to have crossed her path since Leo.

Chapter Fifty-six

The sun was high in the sky as Maggie made her way to breakfast. She had already done a few laps of the pool and had enjoyed it so much that she vowed to take up swimming in her local pool when she got back home. The dining room was quiet and she grabbed a copy of the *Sunday Times* and retreated to a small table with her fruit and yoghurt. She refused the offer of eggs and bacon and stuck to toast and tea.

There was an open-air kick-boxing session at eleven and she decided to give it a go before another good walk. After lunch there were only a few therapists on duty and she was fortunate to have managed to book in for a seaweed wrap followed by a full body massage.

Quite a large group gathered on the front lawn and it was hard not to laugh as they kicked and punched and aimed at unseen assassins. Myles was over at the back kicking hard, his tall frame towering over everyone else as their instructor demonstrated one move after another.

'That was fun,' he admitted afterwards as they downed a sparkling water.

'I'm going to go for a walk,' she said, putting her trainers back on and grabbing a spare bottle and her zip-up jacket.

'Would you mind if I joined you?'

She hesitated. She had enjoyed the peace and tranquillity of yesterday. Maybe having Myles along would spoil it?

'A long walk is exactly what I'm in the mood for, and that ridge near the woods you told me about last night sounds great. Otherwise I can set out a bit after you!'

There was no point following each other, she thought, almost reluctantly agreeing to his company.

Down by the lakeshore they stopped to drink in the view as a pair of swans dabbled in the water, before following the uphill path through the woods. Maggie was relieved that Myles was not set on talking the whole time but happy to fall into step with her without saying too much. When a rat scurried from the bushes, she jumped and grabbed his arm, relieved that he was with her.

'You OK?'

'Yes,' she nodded, continuing. 'Sorry, but I can't bear rats!'

It was even warmer than yesterday and she slipped off her jacket and tied it around her waist as they began to climb through, the sunlight splattering the woodland floor.

'What a beautiful spot!' agreed Myles as he stood at the top taking in the view of the woods and fields and lake below them. The sky was clear and it seemed that they could see for miles over the surrounding countryside.

'I told you that it was worth it,' she said, conscious of his broad shoulders and sturdy legs standing in front of her.

'Thanks, Maggie,' he said slowly.

She grinned. 'No problem.'

'I don't just mean for bringing me up here,' he said, 'but for the past two days. I was dreading coming to this place but having a bit of company, a bit of female company . . . I guess has made the difference!'

'I was going to cancel too,' she admitted, 'but now I'm glad that I didn't. Sometimes it's just so awful doing things on your own when you're not used to it.'

For some strange reason she suddenly felt shy with him and she gazed in the distance trying to compose herself and hoping that he didn't notice.

'Come on, we'd better get back,' he said, taking her hand.

They slipped and slid and laughed the whole way back down through the woods, giggling like a pair of kids, Maggie in a rush for her seaweed wrap while Myles was heading off to a foot treatment.

Maggie joined him again for dinner, letting him order the wine as they perused the menu. The noisy group of Americans sat at the other end of the room quizzing the dining-room manageress about every item on the menu and how it was cooked.

He toasted her. 'You look great.'

'So I should.' She laughed. 'Mind you, if you'd seen the state of me this afternoon covered in layers of a seaweed jelly kind of thing . . . I looked like the monster from the lagoon. Then that lovely girl from Cork, Hannah, gave me the most wonderful massage ever. Every knot of tension or stress in my body has been unravelled. I feel great.'

They opted to share a platter of sushi to start and both went for the tender Wicklow lamb.

'Back to the grindstone tomorrow,' said Myles, filling her glass.

'I phoned home and thank heaven the house survived the party! Sarah and her pals had a great time and nothing was broken or destroyed, thank the Lord!'

'That's the difference having daughters; my lads would have trashed the place. One time Patricia and I came back from a weekend in Prague to find Alex had burned every pan in the place frying sausages and blocked the toilet bowl. It wasn't pretty! We had to get that Dyno-Rod drain-cleaning crowd out!'

'Yuck,' she grimaced. 'Though you have to let them have them! I'm dying to hear about Sarah's party when I get back.'

'Lads never tell you a thing,' he complained. 'I guess that's why I find it so hard without Patricia. Miss the chat. She was a great talker!'

'You had a good marriage . . .' she ventured.

'We suited each other,' he said simply.

She thought about that for a second, realizing that in a few words he had said a lot about his wife. They had balanced each other out, shared routines, cared for each other over many years. Leo had suited her. He had come along when she was young and flighty and insecure and rescued her. Over the years she supposed they had taken it in turns to rescue each other; like a sturdy boat tossed on the ocean their marriage had weathered quite a few storms and also enjoyed many calm balmy days.

'Leo suited me too,' she said, playing with the stem of her glass. 'That's why it's so hard without him.' She sighed, thinking of her return to the house on Pleasant Square and the loneliness of it.

'I hope that you won't think me too forward,' Myles said slowly, his gaze concentrated on her, 'but would it be all right if we kept in touch? Perhaps went to a play or a film together or even a walk?'

She considered. It was not as if she was being disloyal to Leo, nothing on earth could change her love for her husband, but it would be nice to see Myles again: two friends enjoying a meal out or a walk together.

'I could phone you.'

'Myles, to meet up as friends again back in Dublin would be lovely,' she assured him, 'absolutely lovely.'

The lamb was perfect, delicious and moist served with a sweet mint jelly. For dessert she had been tempted to try a pear and almond tart, promising Myles a piece of it. The food here, though simple, was better than most of Dublin's finest restaurants and she could understand how it attracted those living in the locality.

'Have you a photo of Patricia?' she found herself asking as their waitress brought them coffee.

Myles passed her a photo from his wallet. 'It was taken in Tuscany, outside a little villa we used to rent. Patricia loved the place.'

She stared at the tanned face of his wife with her cropped dark hair and merry eyes and flamboyant scarf. A row of tall cedars stood behind her.

'She looks lovely,' she said, returning it to him and reaching for her photo of Leo taken when they had hired a boat on the Shannon, six months before he died. Leo and herself were trying to steer the stupid boat and not ram the prow into the riverbank.

'A man after my own heart,' said Myles, studying it carefully. 'They're awful things to get the hang of but once you master it you're away.'

'It was a crazy week,' Maggie remembered. 'We were hopeless sailors! My sister Kitty and her husband Harry talked us into hiring the boat between us.'

He returned the photo to her and, putting it back safely in the compartment in her wallet, she sighed, relieved that it was out in the open. They were both totally aware of each other's past and partners.

It being their last night they decided on a nightcap. Maggie opted for her favourite, a glass of Baileys on ice, while Myles went for a port. They took their drinks out on the deck, and sat overlooking the garden. The weather was still warm and the place was quiet; the Americans had already retreated to bed.

'They're early risers by all accounts,' Myles said, pulling his chair close to hers as they began to reminisce about favourite holiday destinations.

'What time are you leaving at tomorrow?' she asked.

'I've a meeting at ten o'clock in town, so I plan to get up and be on the road by seven thirty.'

'I'm in no hurry so I'll try and get a last swim in before breakfast.'

'Actually I'd better call it a night,' he admitted, yawning. 'Let me walk you to your room.'

Maggie could feel her cheeks turn crimson. She hoped that he had no notions of joining her there.

As if reading her mind, he burst out laughing. 'Maggie, my intentions are totally honourable.'

She giggled as he walked her across the huge lobby and down the glass-sided corridor to her room. His room was over on the other side of the complex.

'It's been great meeting you,' he said sincerely, taking her hand, 'and I'll be in touch.'

'I'll look forward to it,' she found herself saying as he kissed her cheek. 'Goodnight, Myles,' she whispered. She watched him walk slowly back down the corridor. Smiling, she turned her key and stepped inside, closing the door softly behind her.

Chapter Fifty-seven

Grace hadn't expected Mark to turn up at Sarah's party and though she had tried to avoid him, the minute he had taken her hand in his all her resolve had disappeared. She was like a moth drawn to a flame and they had ended up talking and dancing and smooching for hours. At the end of the night Mark had been annoyed when she refused to go back to his apartment and stayed with Sarah in number 23. That hadn't been because she didn't want to be with him, rather it was because she didn't trust herself to survive his taking whatever it was between them so casually. He was the one who had disappeared for weeks with barely a word and expected her to be standing there waiting for him when he came back!

She was redraughting the air-conditioning system for Ray Carroll's project when Kate arrived in her office with a massive bouquet of creamy white roses.

'The florists just delivered these two dozen roses for you, Grace!' she said, passing her the message card.

Grace touched the perfect fresh blooms as she opened the card. *Thinking of you, Mark.*

Fifteen minutes later, as she finished a call with a client, Mark phoned her.

'Grace, will you come to dinner tonight?'

'That would be lovely,' she agreed as she thanked him for the roses.

'I'll pick you up at your place at about eight,' he said firmly.

It was only when the call had ended that she realized she had no idea where they were going.

All day long she was filled with anticipation and found it hard to concentrate. What had she let herself in for going on a date with Mark McGuinness? Yet despite her reservations she couldn't wipe the smile off her face.

She was like a teenager as she searched through her well-organized wardrobe, pulling on five or six of her favourite outfits trying to decide what he would like, and in the end opting for a simple black dress with a fine pink satin trim and a pair of black pumps. She stared at herself in the mirror, taking in the straight shoulder-length blond hair and blue eyes with her defined brows and full lips, dabbing a bit of her favourite Armani scent on her pulse points as he rang the bell. She ran downstairs to meet him as the danger was if he came upstairs they might never actually make it to dinner.

She could see his eyes widen appreciatively as he took in the dress and they greeted each other rather formally, Mark holding open the car door as she slipped into the passenger seat.

'I thought we might skip town and eat in Caravaggio's in Sandycove,' he suggested.

'That's lovely, Mark; I've never been there before.'

'One of my friends owns it,' he said, glancing over at her.

She suddenly felt herself tongue-tied and awkward with him, and was worried he must think she was a ninny not able to think of anything to say. Fortunately he asked her about Sarah and Evie and her family so she could rabbit on about her sisters.

The restaurant was upstairs in a house overlooking the sea and they were shown to a table right near the window.

'Max always looks after me,' he grinned as he ditched his jacket and sat beside her. He was wearing a pale blue shirt and a pair of chinos and smelled so nice she was tempted to touch him. Grabbing the menu she discreetly took the chance to study him, admitting to herself as she ordered that he was most definitely her type. She went for a mozzarella and tomato starter and a seafood tagliatelle, while Mark went for prawns and a creamy spinach and beef tortellini.

'How's the house going?' she asked, interested as he explained the plans for it.

'I'm thinking of putting a second tank in the attic and a booster . . .'

Fifteen minutes later he stopped, embarrassed. 'You're on a night out, Grace,' he apologized, 'the last thing you want to hear is more building specs.'

'It's all right.' She smiled. 'Honestly.'

'No, it's not fair,' he said, topping up her wine glass. 'Tell me about yourself.'

Grace swallowed hard. She hated talking about herself because although she had accomplished much on the professional scale her personal life was a shambles. 'Well, thanks to my mother you know what age I am,' she said softly, 'and you know what I work at and some of the partners in the firm I work for, and let's face it you know exactly the house I grew up in, have met half my family and you've even been in my apartment.' When she thought about it, she was aghast at how much he actually knew about her already. 'I'm single and into art and architecture and like to cook and dance and am a bit of a workaholic. My indulgences are well-made clothes, organic muesli and Evie.'

She smiled brightly at him, relieved the personal inquisition was over. 'What about you?' she asked, realizing that apart from the fact he was going to be her mother's new neighbour and was good at flying kites she knew literally nothing about him.

'I'm thirty-seven years old. I grew up in Rathmines and have one sister and one brother, both happily married, and two nieces and three wild nephews. My dad died when I was eighteen and my mum died last year of colon cancer.'

'Oh Mark, I'm sorry,' she said, reaching for his hand.

'You would have liked her,' he said, 'everyone did. She was such an important part of my life; the other important person is my son Josh. He's fourteen and lives in New York with his mum Belinda. She's American. I normally get to see him three or four times a year. These past few weeks have been an exception.'

Grace took a soft breath. She hadn't imagined Mark having a child – a teenager!

Without saying any more he pulled out his wallet and

passed her a photograph of a tall curly-haired boy laughing as he tried to wield a baseball bat.

'He looks a lot like you,' she said gently.

'He's a good kid normally but this past year I don't know what's going on in his head. He got in with some weird kids in his school and started messing with dope. He got caught smoking a joint and drinking tequila with them, which got him expelled. The doctors recommended a rehab programme that's set up for kids his age.' He paused. 'Belinda has done a great job raising him,' he went on. 'We met when I was on the J1. It was a Long Island summer romance but she got pregnant and like Sarah decided to keep the baby. I offered to make it legal but she wouldn't have it. She got married to an engineer called Denis about ten years ago. He's a nice guy, gets on well with Josh. Josh has a stepsister Katy who's nine and a little brother Billy who's five. They all get on great. But this past few months Belinda's had her hands full with him and he's my son . . . I had to be there for him.'

She watched as he refolded the wallet and put it securely back in his pocket, strangely glad that he had been upfront and told her.

'He's moving school in September and hopefully that will work out. If not Josh will come over here to me for a while, give Belinda and Denis a break.'

'So that's what's been going on,' she whispered, watching his face, seeing the emotion well up in his eyes.

'For God's sakes, Grace, he's only fourteen; when I think of how things could have turned out . . .'

'Josh will be fine,' she said. 'He's got a dad who loves him very much and that's the important thing – and he knows it!'

Mark reached for her hand. 'When I think how different things were when I was a kid. I used to help my dad cleaning and tidying and painting up old wrecks of places. After college I worked in investment banking for a while and then realized I was making money for other people not myself so I jumped ship and bought another wreck, a Georgian red-brick on the Northside, renovated it and sold it on.'

'Is that what you will do with Pleasant Square?' she asked.

'No,' he admitted, looking at her directly. 'That might have been my intention but now I want the place to be a home. I've my apartment in Donnybrook but a house would be great for when Josh comes to stay. Teenagers need a bit of space!'

The food was good and the conversation flowed easily. Mark regaled her with stories of a rival developer and his misfortunes with the revenue commissioners. She was surprised how many mutual interests they had, both declaring Roddy Doyle's *The Commitments* one of their favourite films and Jack Yeats their favourite artist.

There were only a few couples at tables around them and gradually they realized that they were the only couple left as the waitress discreetly cleared plates and wine bottles. Mark paid the bill and they strolled outside. 'If you want we can go on to a nightclub or a late-night bar?' he offered.

'I'm not really into nightclubs,' she admitted as he took her hand in his, his fingers lacing through hers, both of them keenly aware that parting and saying goodnight was not something they wanted to contemplate.

In the car he kissed her and they found themselves necking hotly like two teenagers frantic to touch and grope each other.

'I'm not sure this is a good idea,' he said, studying her face and tumbled hair, 'I think we might both end up being arrested.'

She burst out laughing, he joined in and the two of them got almost hysterical as they pulled apart.

'My place then,' Grace said softly, sitting back into the leather of the seat as Mark drove, his hand caressing her bare knee.

In the lift up to her apartment they kissed like crazy and her heart was pounding as they went up floor after floor. Mark pulled her into his arms the minute she managed to open the door, the physical rush between them so strong they fell straight on to her bed, casting clothes and all caution aside. The first time was quick and frantic and urgent, the next slow and generous, Mark holding her in his arms until he fell asleep.

Afterwards she lay watching the rise and fall of his chest and ribs, his black eyelashes fanned closed, his dark hair standing on end, and knew that he was the one.

The realization took her breath away and she felt overwhelmed. Mark had been more than a passionate and caring lover, he'd been the balance she had been missing, the perfect match her mother was always talking about. Scared, she turned on her side as emotion got the better of her, but Mark reached out in his sleep and pulled her close beside him, winding his arm around her. She pressed her cheek and lips

423

against his skin, never wanting to be apart from him as she finally slept.

Grace woke at eight a.m. to find him fully showered and dressed but unshaven, standing at the end of the bed.

'The alarm went off forty minutes ago,' he said, smiling, 'but I turned it off.'

'Mmmm,' she said drowsily.

'I've a breakfast meeting in the Four Seasons but I'll talk to you later.'

'I'll be dead late for work!' Grace protested, suddenly coming to and struggling to sit up as he passed her a mug of coffee. 'You should have woken me.'

'Thornton's will just have to survive,' Mark said firmly as he bent to kiss her. She stroked his stubble with her fingertips.

'I'll shave in the car,' he promised, 'and I'll see you tonight.'

She was about to protest again at his assuming she was free but seeing the candid expression of desire in his eyes knew that there was nothing that she would let interfere with seeing him again in a few hours' time.

'Till tonight then.'

She smiled to herself, wondering how she would get through work, willing the hours to pass and the day to end so she could be with Mark.

Chapter Fifty-eight

Oscar Lynch went through the gentle exercises the hospital's physiotherapist had shown him. Little by little his strength and mobility was returning. The pain of arthritis in his hip no longer gripped him and he could sleep comfortably in his own bed. Coming home was the best thing ever and having Irina to help had been a godsend. It felt good to have a woman in the house again and he knew Elizabeth would approve of the sparkling china and glass on the sideboards and in the cabinets and the freshly laundered cushion covers, bedspreads and household linens that Irina provided.

She was a wonderful girl and he enjoyed helping her with her English, encouraging her to attend classes and improve her ability to speak her new language. She in turn was teaching him a few words in her complicated native tongue so that when he was back on his feet and out and about in Dublin's restaurants and shops and bars he could exchange a few words with her countrymen in their own tongue.

The house was filled with music as Irina listened to the

radio and sang as she worked in the kitchen baking fresh bread and cakes and concocting nourishing soups and casseroles to feed him up as if he were a child. Already he had put on three kilos! Every day she made him dress up and go out for a little walk, helping him negotiate the steps and stairs and getting him to the street corner and then the park and then right around the park. Having Irina was better than having nurses and carers as with her bright smile and blue eyes she encouraged him constantly to get better.

The neighbours had been more than attentive, Maggie dropping in regularly and Gerry Byrne bringing him down to the pub for a drink. The young Scot Angus called in and had played chess with him, kindly letting him win and promising a rematch next week. He had his newspapers, the TV, the radio but now with Irina living in the cosy flat in the basement he had something more. He no longer felt lonely.

He enjoyed her company and often they would watch soap operas together or those complicated medical murders that were solved by genius forensic examiners. Whenever her friends called, Irina always introduced him and chatting to them he found it interesting to see how this new community was making its way in Ireland. One young caller was more persistent than the rest and it was clear that the Polish plumber Adam who had come to fix their immersion heater was falling for Irina – and who could blame him? Night after night the young man sat in his kitchen talking to the girl or they played music and laughed down in the basement flat.

It was good to hear the music and young people laughing

and in love in the old house. Perhaps someday Irina and this young man would marry; property prices in Dublin were outrageous, far too expensive for young couples to find a home, and yet here below him there was a perfect home for a couple, for children too. He found himself thinking of children playing on the landing, on the stairs, in the garden. Elizabeth would have liked that. Perhaps a simple visit to the solicitor with regard to his will and everything would be in order. He smiled thinking about the future, this house and the correct thing to do.

Chapter Fifty-nine

Myles had phoned Maggie to invite her to a jazz night in the Pavilion Theatre. Leo had hated jazz but she had always had a fondness for it and, taking a deep breath, Maggie had accepted. His voice had sounded hesitant on the phone and she knew it had taken courage for him to ask her out.

She had phoned Kitty, like a basket case, demanding her sister come over immediately to discuss if she was doing the right thing, and if she did go ahead and meet Myles Sweeney what she should wear!

Kitty was dieting for the wedding and had drunk three mugs of black coffee as they had talked the situation through.

'You're not agreeing to marry the man or have sex with him!' her sister argued, putting everything in context. 'You're just friends who happen to be different sexes going along to a night in the theatre.'

Then Kitty had sat on the bed and watched as Maggie pulled on tops and skirts, suits and trousers, trying to decide what would suit for the occasion.

'The black trousers, the cream shirt and your little cream jacket!' her sister decided.

The day before the outing, racked with guilt, Maggie had almost cancelled, imagining the spectre of Leo haunting her as she sat down with Myles and tried to listen to the music, but after a night's sleep she had decided that Leo would not have wanted her to be lonely and would certainly not have begrudged her a bit of male companionship.

Since Myles was collecting her at home she decided to tell Sarah so it wouldn't be too much of a shock if she bumped into him on the doorstep.

'Is that the lovely man you met at the spa?'

'Yes,' she gulped, feeling like a sixteen-year-old as Sarah took in her guilty expression. 'Don't say anything,' she begged her daughter. 'It's simply two friends having a night out.'

The small theatre was packed but they had wonderful seats up near the front where they were able to see and hear perfectly as the musicians played their hearts out. They went through all the jazz classics with the sound of the bass and rhythm guitar getting everyone going and itching to dance or move in their seats. Myles's large frame and feet were tapping to the music too.

They bumped into Fran and Liam during the break and Fran could barely disguise her surprise when Maggie introduced Myles. The four of them arranged to go for a drink in the pub across the street afterwards. Driving her home at midnight Myles revealed how much he had enjoyed the night and she had to agree with him. It felt good to be a sort of couple! They had sat chatting in the front of his Jaguar and she had simply held his hand when they said goodnight, arranging to meet up again the following week to try out a restaurant that they had both heard was great.

Chapter Sixty

The Pleasant Square Residents' Association had organized their annual End-of-Summer Barbecue on the last Saturday in August. Maggie Ryan insisted that Mark McGuinness should be included, even though he was technically not a resident yet because he did own a house on the square, and of course her tenant Angus Hamilton.

The committee, which included Gerry Byrne and Maggie's long-time neighbours Jim and Sheila Flannery and Hugh and Liz Grogan, had organized the loan of barbecues and parasols, tables and chairs from the residents. Hugh's son Dylan, who was in a band, had been hijacked with a few of his mates into helping set up the music and speakers and lights with the promise of unlimited burgers later on. Garden lamps were placed around the park and a red and yellow bouncy castle loomed temptingly through the trees.

The Saturday was clear and warm and one hundred potatoes wrapped in tin foil were baking in Maggie Ryan's oven. Sarah had made four trays of chicken wings and a huge tomato and onion salad. Evie picked up on the excitement as she watched neighbours start to make their way to the park.

'Will Granny come on the bouncing castle too?' she asked.

'No,' giggled Sarah, 'but I'm sure Grace and Anna and Angus will.'

Grace pulled on a pair of cut-off cream cotton trousers and a pale green T-shirt, grabbing sunglasses and a cardigan just in case it got chilly later in the evening. She couldn't miss the square's barbeque! She'd been going ever since she was a kid. Mark was coming too. He'd told her he had to take care of something first but would join her there.

Anna and Rob had come to Dublin for the weekend as Anna wanted to move the rest of her books, clothes and knick-knacks from her rented house in Dodder Row to Roundstone, so her mother had roped them into coming along and travelling back to Connemara tomorrow. Anna, to everyone's shock, was taking a year out of Trinity and had signed on for five hours a week lecturing in UCG in Galway. A few more hours' work tutoring or teaching and she should be able to survive.

Anna was wearing a pretty multicoloured skirt which clung to her hips and showed off her tall figure; with her brown hair held back with a band of green ribbon she looked amazing, relaxed and laughing as she paraded Rob around for all the neighbours to meet.

The square was starting to fill up when they arrived and the noise of laughter echoed through the summer's air. Her mother was sitting over at a table with Sheila Flannery, mother of the gorgeous Clodagh, and a few women friends; Gerry Byrne was on duty at the barbecue along with Hugh Grogan and Oliver Crowley, who had moved to the square five years ago, and the smell of chicken and burgers and sausages cooking filled the air.

'God I'm starving!' announced Grace, laughing as she placed the Greek salad she'd made on the big gingham-covered buffet table.

'Let's go and say hello to Mum and Sarah,' Anna said.

Their mother waved at them and introduced them as her 'beautiful daughters'. Sheila and all the friends said hello. Oscar was sitting holding court on a proper wooden garden chair wearing a panama hat and his striped linen blazer.

'I'm on one crutch now,' he said proudly as Helen Byrne topped up his glass.

'I brought some wine and a few beers too,' Grace said. 'Where should I put them?'

'In the red cool box near the table. There's a load of ice in it.'

She grabbed a glass of wine and Anna took a can of beer as they strolled over to join Sarah and a gang of friends. Angus was with her sister.

'God, those two are mad about each other,' hissed Anna. 'They make such a perfect couple.'

'Sshh,' warned Grace. 'He's exactly the kind of guy Sarah needs.'

'Hello to the pretty ladies,' Declan Byrne welcomed Grace, kissing her warmly on the cheek.

'You didn't call us that a few years ago when you were holding us hostage in the trees over there,' she joked.

'We were only playing pirates,' he reminded her.

Three of the Byrne boys were present, all well built and sturdy like their father.

Matthew the eldest introduced them to his wife Christine who was expecting at the end of September; Barry and his girlfriend Melinda showed off their son Daniel who was fast asleep in the buggy.

'Your dad is doing a great job cooking, I see,' commented Anna.

'It's a laugh,' Barry confided, lowering his voice, 'Dad doesn't cook a thing at home, the old dear does it all, then he comes along here and puts on his stripy apron and suddenly he's "the chef"!'

They all clapped when Vince Flannery appeared in a pair of surfer shorts and blue and white shirt, his arm around a leggy blonde in a sundress.

'Surf's up!' teased Barry.

He'd been away working in Australia for the past two years and introduced Katie, his girlfriend from Melbourne.

'We're staying here with the folks for a few weeks until the apartment we've bought in Carrickmines is ready.'

The chat was easy and they stood around listening to the music as Evie ran around with two other little girls.

'Hey, I think we'd better make a move on the food before it's all gone,' suggested Rob.

Grace scanned the park looking for Mark, then joined the queue and piled her plate with a chicken breast, a burger, one of her mother's potatoes and a load of salads. She needed a seat if she was going to eat this lot. She squeezed in at a table beside Irina and a handsome blond man, who she discovered was from Poland too.

'Did you know that your mother introduced us?' asked Irina. 'Adam and I both come from Poland and yet we had to come to Dublin to meet.'

Irina had made a delicious creamy potato salad with chives and made them try it. 'I am trying all the recipes in Oscar's cookbooks, that way we don't get bored having dinner,' she explained.

Rob and Anna had gone off to get a few more cans of beer when Evie came over and grabbed Grace by the hand.

'Please, please come on the bouncy castle with me, Auntie Grace. Mummy said you would . . .'

She glanced over. The castle was crowded with an assortment of kids bouncing like there was no tomorrow; one or two mothers were trying to hold on to smaller kids as the castle wobbled and shook.

'OK, pet,' she said, kicking off her cream leather sandals and jumping on to the castle. Bouncing up and down as Evie squealed and laughed with her she remembered her parents hiring a smaller one of these for her birthday party when she was about eleven or twelve. They'd had it up for two days in the back garden, herself and Anna and Sarah bouncing on it in their pyjamas before they went to bed and back up on it again first thing the next morning.

Dylan Grogan and two of his friends got on, the young college students bouncing so hard they made the kids fly off their feet. Grace grabbed hold of Evie's hand as they were thrown around.

She glanced down at the crowd watching their antics and saw Mark McGuiness standing with a grin on his face. Ten minutes later she was out of breath and flushed and in dire need of a cool drink. Anna hopped on and took Evie's hand so Grace could clamber off, practically falling into Mark's arms.

'Would you like a drink?' asked Mark, supporting her as she fumbled to put her shoes back on.

'Water and ice would be great, thanks,' she said and he magically produced a glass of Ballygowan from the kids' drinks table close by.

'Wow, you forget how they make it look so easy,' she laughed as she got her breath back. 'I think I'm getting a bit beyond it.'

'This is some party,' he said, looking at the crowds of neighbours sitting around the tables and on rugs on the ground under the trees, candles and lamps flickering as the park got darker.

'I've been coming every year since I was born.' She smiled. 'Everyone makes the effort to be a part of it, all the parents and kids and the older people like Oscar Lynch and of course Regina Reynolds. She lives in the house at the far end of the square with the big old glass sunroom at the side. She must be ninety and is as deaf as they come.'

'Then I am glad to have been included in such an illustrious gathering.'

'You live here,' she said softly.

For a few giddy moments as she caught his eye she felt as if she was back on the bouncy castle with the air knocked out of her. She swallowed hard as he smiled at her.

'Come on,' he said. 'Let me get you something a bit stronger.'

Sarah was off sitting on her own with Angus, their heads bent close together, engrossed in talking. Anna was still bouncing with Evie, skirt flying in the air, and Maggie was laughing her head off with Gerry and Helen and Oscar, knocking back another glass of wine.

'I've a lovely burgundy,' Mark offered, leading her over towards the park bench.

The wine was smooth and rich and reminded her of France.

'Did you eat?'

'Not yet.'

'Come on then,' she ordered, grabbing him a plate. 'Before everything is gone.'

They went back up to the barbecue line, where Dylan and his friends were asking for more burgers.

'This is your fifth!' reminded his father, Hugh, scooping a quarter-pounder on to his paper plate.

The chicken was all gone so Mark had a piece of steak and a burger and some blackened-looking sausages, topping up with potato and a spoon or two of salad. He was wearing jeans and a fitted pale blue shirt, his body long and lean, his skin tanned as he led her back towards the bench.

'Want one of these sausages?' he offered.

She dipped a piece of sausage in his ketchup, her hand brushing against his; he caught it.

Every touch of his skin ignited her need for him and, embarrassed, she took a sip of her wine. This was a neighbourhood barbecue for heaven's sake!

'Come on and I'll introduce you to some people,' she said once he'd finished eating.

He was charming and polite and fielded question after question about renovating the house as she introduced him to Gerry and Helen, Jim and Sheila Flannery, and Oscar and Regina.

'When are you moving into that old house?' asked Regina, craning her wizened face upwards, straightforward as usual, her piercing eyes running up and down as she assessed him.

'I hope to move in very soon,' he shouted, raising his voice so that the old lady could hear him. 'Very soon.'

'A bit of new blood will be good for the place.' She nodded, patting his hand. Grace glanced at him, relieved that Regina liked him.

Music began to fill the air and a few people got up to dance.

'Grace, can we dance?' he asked, 'Please?'

She loved dancing with him and gave in as he pulled her along by the hand. They joined the group of couples and fathers and mothers and kids on the makeshift dance area. Anna, who was dancing with Rob, raised her eyebrows when she saw them. They danced to the Beatles and Abba, Thin Lizzy and the Boomtown Rats, and as the music slowed, Mark pulled her into his arms as the voice of the man – Van Morrison – drifted over the park. She could feel his heart beating through his shirt, his skin warm against hers as he held her.

'Grace, can we go? I want to show you something,' he said softly, taking her by the hand. It was getting late and the neighbours were beginning to disperse, the barbecues growing cold.

They said their goodnights and slipped away on their own, Mark leading her out of the park and across the street to number 29.

A flickering trail of tea-light candles lit up the path and steps that led up to the front door.

'It's finally finished,' he whispered, as he pulled the key from his pocket. Grace hesitated on the step for a minute, nervous, not sure she wanted to see the massive changes that he had wrought on the O'Connors' old house. But then Mark put his arms around her and ushered her inside, turning on the light and closing the front door.

'Oh, Mark!' She gasped, taking in the utter transformation all around her. 'It's so beautiful.'

She walked with him through the hall and drawing room and dining room. It was exactly the way she had imagined; it was almost word for word the way she had described it to Mark months ago. She looked around the old hallway with its classic banisters and balustrade restored, the original oak floorboards polished and sealed and the walls and traditional dado rail painted in Farrow and Ball's muted buttermilk, an original Waterford glass chandelier hanging from the ceiling. He took her hand in his as they walked from room to room.

The living room bore little trace of the O'Connors except

for the polished white marble fireplace. The walls were painted a rich gold, an expensive hand-woven carpet graced the central square over the perfect revealed floorboards. A large cream-and-gold-patterned sofa stood in front of the fireplace and an antique server in the bay window.

The dining room echoed the same colours but a polished mahogany table and chairs and a simple sideboard gave the room a warm feel. The back of the house contained the massive kitchen with its bright glass and wood extension leading out to the back garden. The units were hand-painted in ivory white and it was the most perfect kitchen she had ever seen, a designer's dream! There was a huge island, expensive German appliances and, sitting prettily in the middle, a huge family table that reminded her of the one they had at home.

Upstairs he showed her the room where Josh would sleep when he visited, and the fancy bathroom with the double shower and mini Jacuzzi, and the uncluttered guest room, and the room for a small child with its line of red kites and blue clouds dancing around the edge of the walls. She could hardly breathe as he led her to the main bedroom.

'Our room,' he said. White roses and candles everywhere! It held a massive bed that was like a floating island in the room, the mushroom and cream and white colour scheme making it restful and warm as Grace caught their reflections in the mirrored glass of the dressing area with its his-and-her rails and luxurious en-suite.

'Mark, it's perfect! Absolutely perfect! Everything is just right,' she said, overawed by how much effort and energy and love he had put into this beautiful old house.

Taking her hand again, he led her back downstairs and out into the newly landscaped garden, to show her the modern lighting and more candles in white glass holders hanging from the branches and nestling between the planted beds of shrubs and lavender and herbs. Grace was glad to see the old apple trees still standing near the back wall. Detta's bird house was freshly painted and hanging from a branch.

There, standing in the moonlight, Mark had taken her hand and told her how much he loved her and never wanted to lose her.

'Grace, marry me, please?' he'd asked, his eyes filled with emotion. 'Live in this house with me, be my wife!'

She touched his face and kissed him and told him yes.

The ring he gave her was white gold with a single perfect diamond and Mark slipped it on to her finger as easily as if it had always meant to be there.

Chapter Sixty-one

Maggie Ryan gave thanks for the perfect clear September day. There wasn't a cloud in the sky for Orla and Liam's wedding. All their prayers and novenas had been answered.

A quick call to her sister Kitty had confirmed the utter bedlam in the Hennessys' household as Harry bellowed in the background looking for his gold cufflinks and bow-tie. Here all was calm as she slipped on the lovely terracotta silk dress she'd bought, until Evie ran in to show off her pale pink layered dress, her dark hair laced with baby roses, and Sarah chased in after her trying to fasten the clips to hold them steady.

'Evie, you have to be good today, no running in the church or Aunt Kitty and Orla will be mad at you.' She raised her eyebrows at Maggie. 'Honestly, Mum, she's so over-excited!'

Sarah had invested in a funky Karen Millen dress which made her look absolutely stunning and she twirled around the bedroom showing it off.

'Mum, we'd better hurry as Angus doesn't want to get

442

stuck in the heavy traffic and have us all late.' Sarah and Angus were giving her a lift to the church.

The crowds had begun to arrive at the little Blue Church in Kilternan and Maggie hugged her nephews and their families. Kitty was glowing, her hair immaculately blow-dried, wearing the lovely jade ensemble with a simple swirl of a cream silk headpiece in her hair – the perfect mother-of-the-bride outfit.

'Kitty, you look absolutely wonderful,' Maggie complimented her, passing her sister a tissue as the tears had already started.

The church pews began to fill up and Maggie said hello to cousins and relations as Myles Sweeney, looking rather dashing in his dress suit, met her near the church door. She knew that he was nervous meeting all her family and relations today but Kitty had insisted that the wedding was the perfect way to break the ice and introduce him to everyone.

Grace and Mark came in and joined them. They were a handsome couple totally devoted to each other, Grace, excited eyes shining, clasping his hand in hers. Maggie still couldn't believe that they were engaged with only eight months to their own wedding which was to be held in Donnybrook Church and then in the private club which Mark belonged to on St Stephen's Green.

A Ryan family wedding! Soon Maggie would be the one searching the shops for the perfect outfit for Grace's big day. She liked Mark, had so from the beginning, and as she had suspected he was a perfect match for Grace. He had swept her daughter off her feet and made her so happy. She'd always known Grace was the marrying type. Across from them Liam and his brothers were nervously joking on the other side of the church, his parents nodding 'hello' in her direction.

Sarah was in her element organizing Evie and the other little girl Amy, trying to ensure they didn't spill all their rose petals from the dainty baskets before the bride arrived. Angus proudly floated around with his fancy digital camera, taking photos of them.

The music was just starting as Anna and Rob pushed in beside them too. Another wedding, she smiled. Not till after their child was born. Anna's pregnancy had been such a surprise and she was so excited, planning for the baby with Rob O'Neill who was himself delighted with the news of her pregnancy and his impending fatherhood. A simple ceremony in Roundstone with close family and friends to witness their marriage was what they both wanted.

They all stood up as the singer began. Evie and Amy and the two bridesmaids, Sheena and Melanie, who'd been in school with Orla, led the procession, all dressed in their floaty pink frocks. Maggie tried to keep a straight face as Evie tossed the rose petals along the red carpet. Harry looked very handsome in his suit and was trying to contain his emotion as he escorted Orla up the aisle.

Her niece looked absolutely lovely in a classic off-the-shoulder fitted cream dress, her light brown hair framing her face with a dainty tiara of pearls, and carrying a circular bouquet of cream roses. She was a beautiful bride and when Harry passed her over to Liam, it was clear that the young man was totally smitten with the apparition before him.

The ceremony was beautiful. Kitty brought up the gifts to the altar with Liam's mother and Conor, Gavin and Sheena and a few of the friends did the readings and prayers. As the marriage ceremony ended and the priest gave the final blessing, Orla and Liam began to walk down the aisle and everyone cheered for the happy couple.

The hotel in Kildare had rolled out the red carpet for Liam, Orla and their guests and Maggie really enjoyed the family celebration. The meal was perfect; Myles enjoyed the roast beef and all the trimmings. Harry was finally able to relax when he had got through his famous father-of-the-bride speech and joined them all for a few drinks in the bar before the dancing started. Kitty was over the moon that there had been no disasters and that everything had gone so smoothly. She hugged Grace, admiring her ring and telling Mark McGuinness that he was lucky to have found himself such a good wife. Maggie blinked away a tear, thinking of having the two of them so close by, another family growing up in a big house overlooking Pleasant Square. Anna and Rob were a perfect match too, and she had never seen her middle daughter happier in her life. Pregnancy suited her and she was glowing, swimming every day in Roundstone and walking miles along the beach with the dog. She watched as Angus cradled Sarah in his arms on the dance floor, his thin face animated as they talked and laughed and planned for the future . . . perhaps the happiest of them all.

Myles coughed to gain her attention and asked her to dance. They made their way on to the crowded dance floor where he took her hand in his, leading her in time to the music. He was a good man and since they'd met there had been dinners and concerts and a wonderful dinner party at Fran's and a Sunday lunch at his son's house when she had met his crew. Hesitant, Myles had shown her the brochure for a wonderful tour of 'The Gardens of France' next spring, taking in the gardens at Versailles, Monet's garden in Giverny, a sculpture garden, the lavender fields of Provence and staying in a host of magnificent French chateaux. Leo had hated gardens and gardening, but Myles loved them. It sounded wonderful, something they would both enjoy, and throwing all caution to the winds Maggie had signed up with Myles to go on the seven-day trip. Life and the passage of time had taught her at least one thing: there are far too many lonely people in the world, and when a man who is loving, kind and good comes along and takes your hand perhaps the only thing to do is follow!

THE END

Author's Note

'Matchmaking' has always been a great Irish tradition from the 'bachelor festivals' in Lisdoonvara to the late great John B. Keane's observations on 'Matchmaking'.

But matchmaking is no longer just the preserve of love hungry farmers and parish spinsters but the love hungry twenty and thirty year olds of the cities – Dublin, Cork, Galway – looking for the perfect partner to settle down with!

Watching my own three daughters and their friends, the girls of today, who have it all, careers, money, travel and property and yet so often let romance pass them, the idea for 'The Matchmaker' came!

As girls wait for a 'Mr Darcy' to come along and sweep them off their feet, they often forget the lovely men around them! What is a good mother supposed to do?

Matchmake!!!

This is a book about love and romance definitely but is also about mothers and daughters, loneliness and friendships and the search to find the person that makes us happy.

THE HAT SHOP ON THE CORNER
by Marita Conlon-McKenna

Hats! Hats! Hats! Upbrims, sidesweeps, silks, ribbons
and trims all become part of Ellie's life when she
inherits the little hat shop on Dublin's South Anne
Street. But the city is changing and Ellie must decide if
she wants to follow the hat-making tradition of her
mother or accept a generous offer to sell the shop.

Encouraged by her friends, Ellie takes on the hat shop
and her quirky designs and tempting millinery
confections soon attract a rich assortment of customers
all in search of the perfect hat.

Creating hats for weddings, shows, fashion and fun, and
falling for the charms of Rory Doyle along the way, Ellie
is happier than she has ever been before. But as her
fingers work their magic she discovers a lot can happen
in the heart of a city like Dublin . . .

'Warm and uplifting – an absolute joy to read'
Patricia Scanlan

9780553817898

BANTAM BOOKS